D1114829

"I DON'T KNOW HOW MANY TIMES I'VE ASKED GOD TO FORGIVE ME."

For years Waneta had wrapped herself in a veil of sadness. For years she had been the object of heartfelt sympathy from her husband, her family, her friends, her neighbors. Now she was on the verge of revealing the dark secret she had kept so long—the secret about how her five little babies had really died.

But Waneta's confession and graphic description of each murder were only the start of District Attorney Bill Fitzpatrick's ordeal. He had to face down the doctor who insisted the babies had died of SIDS ... and he had to find a way to convict the woman who had committed a mother's ultimate sin. . . .

"Goodbye, My Little Ones is vitally instructive to a society in which child abuse has become epidemic."
—Jack Jones, author of
Let Me Take You Down:
Inside The Mind of Mark David Chapman

"A vivid, fascinating account."
—Cyril Wecht, M.D., J.D., Past President, American Academy of Forensic Sciences, and author of *Cause of Death*

GOODBYE, MY LITTLE ONES

THE TRUE STORY OF A MURDEROUS MOTHER AND FIVE INNOCENT VICTIMS

Charles Hickey, Todd Lighty, and John O'Brien

AN ONYX BOOK

ONYX
Published by the Penguin Group
Penguin Books USA Inc., 375 Hudson Street,
New York, New York 10014, U.S.A.
Penguin Books Ltd, 27 Wrights Lane,
London W8 5TZ, England
Penguin Books Australia Ltd, Ringwood,
Victoria, Australia
Penguin Books Canada Ltd, 10 Alcorn Avenue,
Toronto, Ontario, Canada M4V 3B2
Penguin Books (N.Z.) Ltd, 182–190 Wairau Road,
Auckland 10, New Zealand

Penguin Books Ltd, Registered Offices:
Harmondsworth, Middlesex, England

First published by Onyx, an imprint of Dutton Signet,
a division of Penguin Books USA Inc.

ACKNOWLEDGMENTS

This is a true story. No names have been changed. No anonymous sources have been used. All the conversations are based on interviews and on public and private record. In cases where no records were available, we relied on the recollection of at least one of the principals involved in the conversation. During the course of reporting this book we reviewed hundreds of documents, from one-page death certificates to medical records and court transcripts totaling thousands of pages. We also interviewed more than 150 people, some of them several times for dozens of hours. One way or another, every key source involved in the story of Waneta Hoyt spoke to us. Several of them deserve special mention.

This book, like the Hoyt case, would not have been possible without Onondaga County district attorney William Fitzpatrick Jr. His wife, Diane, and his parents, Bill and Anne Fitzpatrick, were equally generous with their time, as were members of his staff.

The Hoyt investigation grew out of the case of Stephen Van Der Sluys, which was recalled in vivid detail by Robert Chase, retired New York State Police senior investigator Harvey LaBar, Jane Bowers, and her parents, Jim and Anita Bowers.

Members of the Hoyt task force, organized by Tioga County district attorney Robert Simpson and state police senior investigators Robert Courtright, deserve special thanks, especially investigator Susan Mulvey and William Standinger and Trooper Robert Bleck.

Waneta Hoyt's defense team—Tioga County public defender Robert Miller, co-counsel Raymond Urbanski, and paralegal Annette Górski—provided invaluable assistance throughout the case, as did Tioga County judge Vincent Sgueglia and court clerk Peter Hoffmann.

We are grateful for the recollections and expertise of many doctors and nurses who helped us understand the medical complexities of this case and the enduring mystery of sudden infant death syndrome: Dr. Linda Norton, Dr. Michael Baden, Dr. Larry Consenstein, Dr. Stuart Asch, and nurses Thelma Schneider and Corrine Dower.

This story would not have been complete without the insights of scores of people who played parts big and small in the lives of Tim and Waneta Hoyt and their children. Special thanks go to the Rev. James Willard, the Rev. Phil Jordan, George Hoyt, and Chuck and Loretta Hoyt.

We thank our colleagues at the Syracuse Newspapers for their encouragement of this project, most of all Mark Murphy, who reviewed this manuscript and made many valuable suggestions.

We owe more than we can ever say to our families, who endured a two-year disruption in their lives so we could pursue this effort. Thank you Jody, Chuck, and Emily Hickey; Mitzi, Trevor, Hannah, Aidan, and Tessa Lighty; Cathy, David, and Luke O'Brien.

In the end, only one source set a condition for his cooperation. Bill Fitzpatrick asked that we dedicate this book to the victims.

Eric, James, Julie, Molly, and Noah

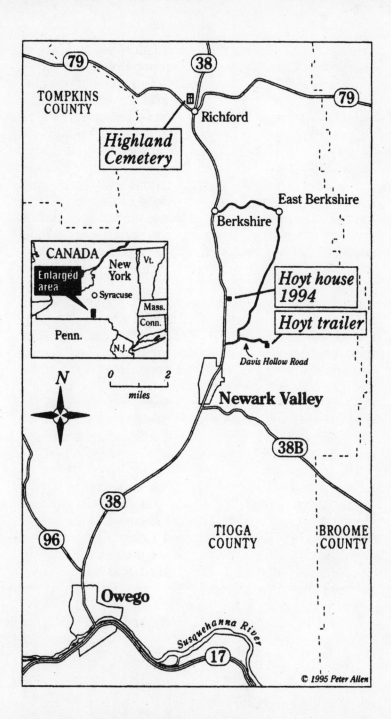

Prologue

Sometime during the night, while lying in bed watching TV, district attorney Bill Fitzpatrick put aside his doubts about the confrontation looming between the New York State Police and Waneta Hoyt. Fitzpatrick liked to say that being brought up by Irish people, he never hoped for something to happen, because then he knew it wouldn't. But this night he fell asleep believing that when the investigators approached Waneta Hoyt in the morning, she would agree to talk. She would tell them how her five children had died more than twenty years ago. She would confess. And the hunch he had pursued for the past eight years would pay off.

In the morning, the rituals of family life kept Fitzpatrick's doubts in check.

Wednesday was a workout day, so he did twenty minutes on his NordicTrack. He showered, put on the gray suit that represented one-fifth of his business wardrobe, and joined the household bustle.

His wife, Diane, left for her law office in Syracuse when the baby-sitter arrived at eight-thirty to watch the couple's two youngest children. Shortly before nine o'clock, Fitzpatrick walked his four-year-old son, Danny, to nursery school.

The daily walk was part of the special bond Fitzpatrick shared with Danny, the sensitive, round-faced boy he and Diane had wanted so badly. As they started down the gravel driveway hand in hand, the sun shone.

March 23, 1994, was starting out as the kind of brilliant early spring day that winter-weary Upstate New Yorkers cherish. Barely three hours after sunrise, the temperature had already climbed above 40 degrees. Danny still wore his red ski jacket, but Fitzpatrick didn't make him put on boots; light rain the past two evenings had washed away most of the snow.

Father and son walked up the street toward the main road. LaFayette Nursery School stood to their left, across a sloping field dotted with young evergreens. Just before hitting the road, they turned onto a footpath. A row of maples with bare branches lined the left side of the path; tall fir trees stood on the right. As they strolled along the spongy lane, Fitzpatrick launched into a familiar line of questioning: "Danny, what's Daddy do?"

"You're district attorney," the boy said.

"Well, what's that?"

"You're a, you know, a policeman."

"Well, not exactly, honey."

He and Danny had recited this dialogue so often it had become a refrain. This morning, Fitzpatrick introduced a new verse.

"But Daddy's gonna do something important today with some policemen," he said. "We're going to try to catch somebody who hurt their kids."

It all depended on Waneta Hoyt. Fitzpatrick knew the confrontation could end one of three ways: she could confess; she could agree to talk but not confess; or she could ask for a lawyer, stopping the questions cold.

"Why'd they hurt their kids?"

Fitzpatrick saw his son's puzzled look. How to explain Waneta Hoyt to a child barely old enough to parrot the words "district attorney"? How to explain a mother taking her children's lives?

"We don't know, honey. They did it a long, long time ago," he said. "And the kids never got to grow up."

When they reached the front step of the shingle-sided nursery school, father and son completed their morning ritual. Fitzpatrick knelt, wrapped Danny in his arms, and kissed him on the cheek. Danny kissed him back.

Hugging his son, Fitzpatrick realized how lucky he was to have children. And then it struck him: Waneta Hoyt had not felt that way. Her children had provoked something entirely different in her, something he didn't understand.

Doubts rushed to the surface. How would Waneta react when she faced the truth? Did she have a conscience? Could they reach it?

Fitzpatrick squeezed Danny tight. "This is a big day for Daddy. Wish me luck."

"Good luck, Dad. I hope you catch 'em."

Fitzpatrick held on to that hope as he walked home. An hour later, his chief investigator arrived to drive him to the showdown with Waneta Hoyt in Tioga County, seventy miles south of Syracuse.

Shortly before they set out, two unmarked state police cars started cruising north, up the narrow valley that held Waneta Hoyt's secret in its fold.

PART ONE

The Mother

The Mother

Chapter One

Newark Valley woke to a typical winter morning on January 26, 1965. The temperature struggled to creep above freezing as the Hoyt family stirred from the aging farmhouse in Davis Hollow, a tiny settlement tucked into the valley's eastern slope. Tim Hoyt left around seven-thirty for his job as a shipping clerk at National Cash Register in Ithaca twenty-five miles away. His mother, Ella, who owned the house, had already gone to her job at a shoe factory in Johnson City, fifteen miles in the other direction. Waneta Hoyt, Tim's wife of a year, was alone in the house with their three-month-old son, Eric. She was feeding Eric orange and apple juice when his face suddenly turned blue and he started gagging. Waneta had taken Eric to doctors when he suffered spells before, but this one was different. This time he bled from the mouth, she said.

Waneta ran barefoot across Davis Hollow Road to the home of Rodney and Betty Lane.

Betty Lane followed Waneta back to the Hoyt farmhouse. When she walked through the back door, Lane saw Eric lying on his side on the kitchen table. A thick substance resembling cereal with pink streaks hung from the baby's nostrils.

She watched Waneta pick up the child's limp body, cover his lips with her mouth, and blow. When Eric didn't move, Waneta put him down. Lane couldn't bring herself to touch the baby. She told her husband to call an ambulance and rushed home, shaken by what she had seen.

"The baby appeared to be dead to me," she said.

The sudden death of Tim and Waneta Hoyt's first child attracted no more attention in the valley than did any other fleeting tragedy. The police didn't investigate, and the coroner, Dr. Arthur Hartnagel, didn't perform an autopsy. Hartnagel apparently took Waneta's word that Eric had suffered earlier spells in which he turned blue; he listed congenital abnormalities of the heart as the cause of death.

A funeral was held at MacPherson Funeral Home in the village of Newark Valley. Eric was dressed in a light-blue plastic diaper and a blue sweater, and his parents placed a tiny sterling silver ring stamped with a chain of hearts in his wooden casket.

Eric was buried in Highland Cemetery, in a shallow grave that the caretaker dug by hand. A small gray headstone marked the baby's place among a grove of pine trees overlooking the valley. Generations earlier, Waneta Hoyt's family had farmed this land. Over the next six years, she would reclaim it one grave at a time.

In the valley, the land itself speaks—of the people, their way of life, the passage of time. No part is more remote than Richford, a town of 1,153 pinched between steep hills in the northeast corner of Tioga County. Farmers drawn from western Massachusetts settled the upper reaches of the valley in the 1790s. They coaxed enough crops from the fertile soil to feed themselves and their livestock, but the hills, thick with cherry, maple, oak, and hemlock, sustained them. They harvested hardwoods to feed local lumber mills and processed hemlock bark for tanning hides.

The wooded hills, the county's tallest, sheltered as well as isolated. Rain and melting snow drain from the hills, feeding the stream that links Richford to the outside world like a thread. The runoff flows into the east branch of Owego Creek, which ripples south, following the valley floor through the progressively larger towns of Berkshire and Newark Valley before joining with the west branch in Owego, the county seat, where it empties into the Susquehanna River. Like the creek, the life of Richford's most famous son served as a stark reminder that the road to fame and fortune led out of the valley.

John D. Rockefeller was born a pauper July 8, 1839, in a house on the east side of the valley. When he was four, his family headed south to Owego, where John D. got the education that would help him build a fortune worth nearly $1 billion. Richford's oldest residents recall July days during the 1920s when John D. came back to town in a chauffeured car. Boys and girls would line up at Bert Rawley's general store to get a newly minted dime from the oil tycoon. Otherwise, Rockefeller didn't give a plugged nickel for Richford. He called his birthplace a "Godless town" and wrote a poem in which he said, "I shudder to think what I should have been if I had stayed in Richford all my life."

Richford didn't care much for Rockefeller either. In the 1980s, local officials questioned whether he deserved a mention on the Welcome signs that motorists saw upon entering the town. Some wanted to honor a more loyal scion of the valley, perhaps a doctor or a teacher who had helped the town's children. Eventually, the signs went up: RICHFORD EST. 1882 THE BIRTHPLACE OF JOHN D. ROCKEFELLER 1839–1937.

The debate reflected the pride of generations that had stayed in Richford to scratch a living from the hills. People like Waneta Hoyt's ancestors, the Nixons. For more than a hundred years, the Nixon family had farmed the hill west of the crossroads that marks the center of Richford. In the 1880s, Bert Nixon received $800 for a small parcel that became Highland Cemetery. Generations of Nixons passed the farm along until

Waneta's parents, Albert and Dorothy Nixon, came into possession of one hundred acres and thirty-five milking cows.

Albert and Dorothy's family grew at the pace of roughly one child a year, starting with the birth of Albert Jr. in 1939. Archie, Ruth, and Dorothy Joan followed. The Nixons' fifth child, Robert, was born in 1944 and died of spinal meningitis two and a half years later. Another son, also named Robert, died at birth in 1947. The umbilical cord had gotten wrapped around his neck, and he choked to death.

Between the two Roberts, the Nixons had a baby girl. Dr. Arthur Hartnagel, the country doctor who did double duty as coroner, delivered the black-haired infant on May 13, 1946. The Nixons named her Waneta Ethel, taking her first name from Albert's sister and handing down Dorothy Nixon's middle name. With the arrival of their last child, Donna, less than two years later, the five-bedroom farmhouse was full.

Waneta grew up contented, by all accounts. Her family lived comfortably by valley standards, although Albert Nixon had to work for the state highway department to supplement the income from his small dairy herd. He sanded roads in the winter and repaired them in the summer, while his sons tended to the farm. To help feed the family, Albert and the boys hunted. Years ago, Albert said, rabbits were so plentiful that he could shoot three or four an evening. "My kids ate more rabbit and venison than beef," he said.

Although Dorothy Nixon sewed baby clothes in a factory later in life, she stayed at home until her children were grown. She believed women were put on earth to bear children and make their men happy, and that's how she raised her daughters. The girls helped her with household chores, and for a time Waneta even did housework for a neighbor. Each Sunday, Dorothy Nixon took her daughters into town for services at the First Congregational Church.

The family's emotional life seems to have been as spartan at the rest of their existence. The Nixons were considered taciturn people, not given to a lot of hugging and kissing. But the children's affection for Waneta showed in their endearing abbreviation of her name to Neta. The girlish nickname would endure long after the blush of childhood passed away.

Neta attended grammar school in Richford for three years, then finished the primary grades down the road in the slightly larger town of Berkshire. Except for a couple of childhood diseases, she enjoyed good health. A severe bout of measles at age eleven left her with poor eyesight. Thereafter, she could see only shadows without glasses.

Donna, the sister closest in age, became Neta's favorite playmate, although they developed contrasting personalities. While Neta clung to her mother, Donna tended toward independence; while Neta sought sympathy by fretting about her health, Donna's self-assurance permitted few complaints. The two sisters became fast friends, riding bicycles together or splashing in Owego Creek.

Neta, a pleasant, soft-spoken girl, seemed just as comfortable with solitary pursuits, such as reading. Childhood friends recalled seeing Neta off by herself, staring into the distance, as if in a trance. Years later, family and friends would wonder about the faraway look in Neta's eyes. But whatever secret place she had found to retreat to with her thoughts, no one disturbed it. Accustomed to having so much of their lives played out in plain view of church and school and extended families, folks in the valley seemed reluctant to intrude on an individual's zone of privacy.

Neta matured into a slender, five-foot, four-inch teenager with coal-black hair and deep green eyes. She had a fine nose and narrow chin, like her mother. She wanted to be a hairdresser when she grew up, but styling her mother's and sisters' hair was as close as she came to fulfilling that ambition.

In 1960, Neta went to high school in Newark Valley, a ten-mile bus ride from the farm. She was an average student who didn't play sports or involve herself in other school activities. She kept pretty much to herself because, she explained, "I didn't like being in crowds." She noticed boys, however, and her freshman year she picked out one she liked.

Tim Hoyt, a strapping six-foot-tall, blue-eyed farm boy from Newark Valley, was the last student to board Neta's bus in the morning. As a senior, he claimed the right to stand at the front, near the driver. A girl Neta knew on the bus boasted that she was going to date Tim. Not to be outdone, Neta told a girlfriend seated next to her, "I'm going to marry him someday." Tim Hoyt was the first boy Neta dated. Like Neta, he was quiet, wore glasses, and grew up on a struggling dairy farm.

Tim was the sixth of George and Ella Hoyt's nine children. The Hoyts lived on a farm on Davis Hollow Road, in a small settlement at the foot of the hills northeast of Newark Valley. Compared with the Nixons, they were a boisterous lot. George A. Hoyt worked for forty-three years as a laborer making minimal money at the Endicott Johnson shoe factory. An alcoholic, he drank up most of his wages, forcing his large brood to scrape along on their own. Every day was an excuse to get drunk. He stopped drinking once, when his oldest son and namesake went off to the Korean War. He went to the back of a church and made a vow: He would stop drinking if God brought young George home safely. It became one more promise George Hoyt didn't keep.

"Get him away from the booze and there wasn't a better man you wanted to be around," young George said. "You give him a few drinks and he was a mean son of a bitch."

The Hoyt children clung to their mother. Sharing the

misery of George Hoyt's destructive drinking helped shape the Hoyt children into a tightly knit band. Tangling with one meant taking them all on, especially the boys.

Tim grew up sturdy amid the rough-and-tumble play of his four brothers. The boys liked to wrestle in the dump, amid the garbage, trying to grind each other's faces into half-eaten grapefruit. Like any large family, the Hoyts also loved razzing each other. Once, while riding in the family car, Tim started musing about what he wanted to do when he grew up. He told his brother George about his grand plans for erecting a tower in the sky so he could look out across the universe. But that's not quite how it came out.

"He said he wanted to put his rectum up into the sky so he could look out," George said. "We knew what he was talking about, but he just didn't understand. And the more he talked about it, the more we laughed."

Tim's gentle nature earned him the nickname Abigail. Even as a teenager, he didn't go in much for rowdiness. He and his friends liked to cruise the valley on weekend nights, swigging muscatel from a bottle. But Tim mostly drove, while the others mostly drank. Drinking didn't hold much allure for him anyway. Like the other Hoyt children, Tim paid a price for his father's drinking: He had to forgo high school sports to help support his brothers and sisters. He never complained. He simply accepted the burden of being George Hoyt's son, even when it cost him dearly.

Tim and his brothers Don and Chuck came home from school one day and found that their father had stolen their thirty-five dairy cows. George Hoyt had sold his sons' herd to finance a drinking binge that took him all the way to Florida. Don and Chuck got angry, but Tim showed no emotion. He couldn't quite bring himself to believe that the man he loved had betrayed him. Like many children of alcoholics, Tim remained blindly loyal to the person who hurt him the most.

Neta and Tim drifted apart when Tim graduated from high school in 1961. Tim followed his brother George to New Jersey, where George had gone to make $3.69 an hour in a factory. It was better than farm work in the valley or some $1-an-hour job, George said. Tim didn't stay away long. He worked at a hospital in Connecticut before returning to the valley.

Tim rekindled his relationship with Neta, and the couple soon became inseparable. They went to drive-in movies on dates or just drove around, happy to be in each other's company. Nearly everybody commented on the way Tim and Neta clung to each other. Wherever they went, they were seen holding hands. Even around friends, they stuck together like Velcro dolls. If Tim drifted away from Neta at a social gathering, she'd call him over. If Tim wasn't touching her, she'd rub his back, place her hand on his knee, or tug at his elbow. Neta wanted all of Tim's attention, and he was glad to oblige her. And despite her shyness, Neta wanted others to notice her too. As time went on, Neta would try to grab all the attention she could get.

The prediction Neta made on the school bus finally came true: She and Tim decided to get married. The outgoing Hoyts welcomed Tim's prospective bride into their family, but Dorothy Nixon didn't approve of her daughter, a seventeen-year-old high school senior, getting married. She made Neta leave the house weeks before her wedding. Neta moved into the Hoyt farmhouse on Davis Hollow Road with Tim, his mother, and his sisters Ann and Nancy.

Tim and Neta married on January 11, 1964, a bitterly cold Saturday that never saw the temperature rise above the young bride's age. The bridegroom sported a crew cut, dark suit, and narrow tie. The bride wore a white short-sleeved wedding gown and a veil. Together, Tim and Neta made an attractive couple in the

style of the day. The Rev. Doran Edwards conducted
the small ceremony in the parsonage of the Faith Bible
Church in Richford. In keeping with tradition, the new-
lyweds posed for a picture that showed them feeding
each other pieces of wedding cake. One thing marred
the occasion: Dorothy Nixon shunned the wedding, a
harsh blow for Neta, who still hoped to please her
mother.

The teenage bride suddenly found herself in a
grown-up world. The principal of Newark Valley High
School summoned Neta to his office when she returned
for the last half of her senior year. Ann Hoyt went with
her new sister-in-law. The principal said he didn't
think Neta would be a good influence on her classmates, now that she was married. "There was a possibility she may come in and tell all about her sex life,"
Ann recalled.

Neta Hoyt left school, never to return. She continued
living with Tim and his family in the Hoyt farmhouse.
Tim helped support the household as a laborer in the
shipping and receiving department of National Cash
Register. Neta stayed at home. She made no move to
get a job, telling friends that her first interest was taking care of Tim. But the couple's roles were reversed
when Neta became pregnant a month after the wedding; for the next thirty years, Tim would take care of
Neta.

Five months after they were married, Tim and Neta
experienced their first family tragedy. Alcoholism had
plunged Tim's father deeper into despair. He sought
help at least six times at Binghamton State Hospital,
but he never escaped his demons. On May 17, 1964,
Don Hoyt went into the silo on his farm in Newark
Valley and found his father hanging by a rope. George
Hoyt had ended his tortured life at age sixty-four.

The Hoyts carried on much as before. If George
Hoyt had taught his family anything, it was how to endure in the face of adversity. His legacy was a hard-

working, self-sufficient clan that drew strength from within. Tim Hoyt picked up his life, which revolved more and more around Neta, and went on.

When Neta went into labor the morning of October 17, 1964, Tim took her to Tompkins County Hospital in Ithaca, thirty miles away. Labor for the first-time mother lasted nearly eleven hours. At 6:16 P.M., Dr. Noah Kassman helped Neta deliver a perfect seven-pound boy. Tim and Neta named their son Eric Allen. Three days later, Tim and Neta took Eric home to the Hoyt farmhouse, where Neta set up a crib for the baby in the bedroom she shared with Tim.

In the hospital records, nurses wrote that Eric was a healthy newborn with no abnormalities. The nurses let Eric go with a note destined to become a refrain: "Discharged to mother in apparent good condition." But Eric was not well, according to Neta. The baby suffered spells in which he turned blue, she said, as if he had stopped breathing.

"Then, one time, he had a real spell, and we took him in an ambulance to the hospital," she would tell others later. Doctors, unsure what was wrong, gave Eric antibiotics on the chance he had pneumonia and sent him home.

Eric suffered his last spell on January 26, 1965, two weeks after Tim and Neta's first wedding anniversary. His death at three months, ten days, didn't raise any questions at the time. But later, some family members wondered about the strange way Neta responded to Eric. She never cuddled the baby, some of the Hoyts said. She always held him away from her body. Neta needed so much attention herself that she seemed unable to give it to her child.

Neta's craving for attention struck some of the Hoyts as odd. They noticed her habit of acting up when she found herself on the periphery of a situation. Chuck Hoyt, the second oldest brother, recalled the time a group of folks visited a farm in the neighboring

town of Berkshire. When Chuck and Tim headed to the
barn to fetch some bales of hay, Neta tagged along.
She was talking to Tim, but he wasn't paying much attention.

"So, we're up at the barn and she's about twenty
yards, twenty-five yards behind," Chuck said, "and she
goes, 'Oh, I feel faint.' Plop. Tim turned around. He
stopped. Well, he said, let her lay there for a while,
she'll get over it. When she saw that nobody was going
to feel sorry for her, she got up."

There were other fainting episodes, and over time
Neta acquired a litany of health complaints, real or
imagined. Family members would ask Tim and Neta
how they were doing, Chuck said, and Tim would say,
"Oh, fine." Tim was always fine. Not Neta. She'd say,
"Oh, my back aches, and my hair is falling out, and my
ear aches, and my toenails are growing crooked,"
Chuck remembered.

Neta sought treatment for whatever ailed her, piling
up unpaid doctors' bills. Her claimed susceptibility to
every conceivable illness became a running gag in the
Hoyt family. George Hoyt and his sisters started concocting illnesses for themselves. They would come up
with a new one almost weekly and give it a fancy
name. Neta listened intently as her in-laws discussed
their symptoms—dizziness, perhaps, or shooting pains
that immobilized their arms. "Lo and behold," George
said, "three days later, she had it."

If Neta liked anything, it was being pregnant. Tim's
sister, Marion, joked about the way Neta reveled in the
attention people lavished on expectant mothers. "Well,
Neta had sex last night," Marion would tell her brother
George.

"How do you know?"

"She has a maternity dress on today."

While the Hoyts traded stories about Neta's behavior, they knew better than to mention it to Tim. Their
brother's faith in his wife was absolute.

After Eric's death, Neta got a job at Endicott Johnson, the shoe company where Ella Hoyt worked. But Neta quit after nine months because, she said, "I just couldn't stand the pressure of people around me so much."

With Tim looking after her, Neta didn't worry about the financial hardship. "We never had much money," she said, "and what little I made never made much difference." Besides, Tim and Neta wanted another baby right away. A second pregnancy had ended in a miscarriage, but that didn't deter them; she got pregnant again. Eight months after losing their first baby, the young couple seemed to have their life back on track.

Tim and Neta still went out occasionally to see a drive-in movie or to play miniature golf, but otherwise they generally stuck close to home. They watched NASCAR races on television and took long walks along Davis Hollow Road. Neta still liked to read, especially *Reader's Digest* and medical books that explained illnesses. She spent hours at home working on word-search puzzles or crocheting afghans that she gave to neighborhood children as birthday presents.

The rest of their social life consisted of visiting with family and friends. Tim and Neta loved card games, especially canasta. Sometimes as many as a dozen people would gather at one of the Hoyts' homes to play cards. Dealing started in the evening and didn't stop until early morning. They'd drink cans of beer, lemonade, and soda through the night. Players who got tired could curl up in a kitchen corner or stretch out on the living room couch and rejoin the game later.

Tim and Neta mixed easily with their neighbors on Davis Hollow Road. The men teamed up to paint fences, fix cars, and dig fence post holes. The women dropped in on each other to discuss the day's events over coffee. Families generally didn't own two cars, so the women borrowed each other's cars to go grocery shopping. If they didn't want to bring their children along, one of the women would stay behind to watch them.

A month before Eric Hoyt died, Art and Natalie Hilliard and their nine-month-old son, Dana, moved into a ranch house kitty-corner across Davis Hollow Road. The newcomers soon became Tim and Neta's best friends. Art and Tim often hunted deer together. Natalie Hilliard, a former Girl Scout, loved campfires, and the couples liked to gather around a campfire in the evening. Natalie considered Neta the sister she never had. They never missed each other's birthdays, remembering the occasion by buying each other perfume, a blouse, or perhaps a piece of jewelry.

Neta and Natalie would visit each other at least three times a week. If Neta was making an afghan, she would bring that along and work on it while they gossiped. They talked about everything: unpaid bills, their families, and their sex lives. "Anything and everything," Natalie said.

Natalie believed they kept nothing secret.

Neta went into labor a second time on May 31, 1966. Tim took her to Tompkins County Hospital, where Dr. Kassman helped her deliver another healthy boy. Tim and Neta named their second son James Avery, and everyone soon called him Jimmy. Although hospital records again said the baby was "discharged to mother in apparent good condition," Neta told family members that Jimmy had a heart problem.

In 1967 Tim and Neta moved out of Ella Hoyt's farmhouse, but they didn't go far. They bought a small trailer—twelve feet wide, but only fifty feet long—and put it on land behind the farmhouse. The young family seemed to be thriving. Tim had joined the laborers' union and was working construction jobs, Jimmy seemed healthy, and Neta was expecting another baby.

Julie Marie Hoyt was born at Tompkins County Hospital on July 19, 1968. Nurses noted that she was a normal newborn. Four days later Tim and Neta took the baby home to meet her big brother.

Jimmy had grown into a two-year-old bundle of energy. He had light brown hair and his father's pouty mouth and sad, puppy-dog eyes. The toddler liked to run across the open field to Ella Hoyt's house shouting, "Grandma, Grandma, here I come." One of Jimmy's and his grandmother's favorite pastimes was picking up rocks in search of snakes, bugs, and toads. Ella Hoyt watched Jimmy like a hawk, afraid something unexpected might happen to him, as it had to Eric. But Jimmy's liveliness spoke only of good health.

Early on the morning of September 5, 1968, Tim set out for a highway construction site. His job as a laborer relegated him to menial tasks, such as clearing stones or waving traffic by with an orange flag. At least the mild weather on this late-summer morning promised a nice day to work outdoors. Neta was alone in the trailer with Jimmy and Julie. She explained later that she was feeding Julie rice cereal at the kitchen table when the skin around the baby's mouth suddenly turned blue and she started choking. Neta told Jimmy to go sit on the couch, and she ran outside for help.

Neighbor Evelyn Bond heard Neta screaming and called the Newark Valley ambulance. Members of the volunteer service tried to revive the baby, but they were too late. Julie Marie Hoyt was dead at the age of one month and seventeen days.

Dr. Hartnagel concluded that Julie had strangled from eating the rice cereal and ruled her death an accident. Once again, Hartnagel apparently took Neta at her word, because he didn't perform an autopsy and there was no police investigation.

MacPherson Funeral Home handled the arrangements again. Julie was placed in a cement casket wearing an unbuttoned cardigan sweater over a light-colored top, a diaper, and white shoes. She took her place near Eric in Highland Cemetery, buried without a headstone.

Outsiders could only imagine how Tim and Neta felt. The couple had been married less than five years and already they had buried two babies and weathered a miscarriage. But it was at tragic moments such as this that the valley offered its comforting embrace. Family and friends grieved with them. And as they tried to help the young couple cope with the loss, the mourners took comfort from the thought that Tim and Neta still had Jimmy.

George Hoyt remembered that Tim and Neta stopped by his house with Jimmy on the Sunday two weeks after Julie's funeral. George had a son around Jimmy's age, and the two cousins ran around the house like squirrels. Jimmy, dressed for action in bib overalls and a red shirt, had the time of his life, George recalled. As he watched his nephew chase Sniffy, the family cat, he couldn't help thinking about Eric and Julie. At least Jimmy was healthy, he thought.

The following Thursday, September 26, Tim left home for a construction job in Waverly, about a half-hour drive. Neta fed Jimmy breakfast. He went outside to play, and she went into the bathroom to get dressed. "I heard this screaming for Mommy, and I stepped out into the hallway, and he collapsed coming up the hallway," Neta recounted later. Jimmy's nose and mouth were bloody. Neta picked him up and ran screaming from the trailer.

Natalie Hilliard looked out the front window of her house and saw her best friend running down the road with Jimmy in her arms. Neta carried the boy into the Hilliards' house and laid his limp body on a couch in the front room. Natalie called for an ambulance, then made another call to alert Tim in Waverly.

Henry Robson, a member of the ambulance crew, arrived and tried to revive Jimmy. Natalie noticed that Neta's blouse was open and recommended she button it before any more people arrived. Natalie shooed her son, Dana, into his bedroom, but the curious four-year-old kept coming back to see what was wrong with his little friend. "James is sick," Natalie explained. "They're trying to help him. Please go back to your room and play."

Robson tried to bring Jimmy around with mouth-to-mouth breathing and heart massage. "I continued doing so until the coroner, Dr. Hartnagel, came and told me the boy was gone, stop what I was doing." Jimmy died at the age of two years and four months; it was the longest any of Neta's children ever lived.

The question of what was killing Tim and Neta's children hung in the air after the ambulance crew took Jimmy's body away. Hartnagel didn't have the answer, and Tim asked the coroner to have Jimmy's body autopsied.

Later that morning, Dr. James Mitchell, a pathologist at Tioga General Hospital in Waverly, did the postmortem examination. Mitchell noted that Jimmy was about three feet tall, well nourished, with no obvious signs of injury. He opened Jimmy's body to examine the internal organs and found no signs of disease. Although Neta said Jimmy had bled from the nose and mouth, Mitchell saw no evidence of hemorrhaging inside the boy's head.

The doctor's four-page autopsy report suggested that acute adrenal insufficiency might have contributed to Jimmy's death. The adrenal glands sit atop the kidneys and secrete several chemicals that regulate the body's vital functions. The loss of adrenal function often proves fatal, but it remained unclear whether that had anything to do with Jimmy's death. Hartnagel wrote on the death certificate that Jimmy had an enlarged thymus. The thymus gland extends from the neck into the chest and normally shrinks with age. Although there was a precedent for attributing the sudden death of an infant to suffocation by an enlarged thymus, the theory hadn't been taken seriously since the 1920s. With only Jimmy's body and Neta's story to go on, the doctors could not determine the cause of death.

Jimmy's body took the now familiar route from MacPherson Funeral Home to Highland. Cemetery, where he was buried next to Eric. Unlike Julie, Jimmy got a headstone, a tiny gray monument with his name inscribed beneath two doves.

The jolt of Jimmy's death coming so soon after Julie's stirred some talk in the valley. Howard Horton, Newark Valley's town cop, asked Chuck Hoyt point-blank if Neta was killing her kids. The question came as a shock. Chuck didn't know what to say, and Horton didn't press the issue.

But Chuck heard the same accusation from his brother George. The two were in Ella Hoyt's house after Jimmy's funeral when George spit out what was on his mind. "Neta's killing those kids," he said. He couldn't forget how Jimmy had looked the picture of health just a few days before. "Here is a kid, rosy cheeks, like any other kid, going rippity hell through my house," George said. Now he was dead.

George Hoyt didn't give Tim any hint that he thought something was wrong. After all, the doctors had found no evidence of abuse, and Howard Horton dropped the matter. George could do nothing but harbor doubts about Neta. He had no proof, just a country boy's gut feeling.

The prospect of another tragedy befalling Tim and Neta weighed on some of the Hoyts. Tim's sister Ann talked to her brother and Neta about not having any more children. "Well, Mom said I ought to try again," Neta said.

"Goddamn it, let your mother have them then," Ann said.

Dorothy Nixon had instilled in Neta the notion that a woman must bear children. "And she was trying her damnedest to have them," George Hoyt said.

One way or another.

Chapter Two

The Old Testament tells the story of a woman in Judah who gave birth to a son. Three days later, another woman in the house also bore a son. One night, as they all slept, the second woman's baby died. She took the living baby from the side of the first woman and placed her dead child in the woman's bosom.

When the first woman rose in the morning to nurse, she knew the dead baby was not her son. Each woman claimed the surviving child as her own, and it fell to King Solomon to settle the dispute. The women argued back and forth until Solomon called for his sword. "Cut the living child in two," he said, "and give half to one woman and half to the other."

In anguish, the child's mother cried, "Please, my lord, give her the living child—please do not kill it!"

"It shall be neither mine nor yours," the other woman said, "Divide it!"

At that, Solomon declared: "Give the first one the living child! By no means kill it, for she is the mother."

While the wisdom of Solomon resolved the issue of maternity, the sudden and unexpected deaths of infants have remained an open question for nearly 3,000 years. Each age has sought an answer to the tragedy in its own way. According to 1 Kings 3:16–27, the second woman's child "died in the night because she overlaid it." For centuries, sudden infant death was commonly attributed to mothers who lay on top of their sleeping babies and accidentally smothered them. Although it made sense for infants to share the warmth of their mothers' beds in an era of primitive heating, even early authorities deemed it a dangerous custom. A German placard dating from 1291 forbade mothers from taking children under three into bed.

In time, overlaying came to be associated with negligence. Mothers in seventeenth-century Florence covered their babies with a wood-and-iron device to prevent overlaying. As recently as 1933, British law made it a crime if, under certain circumstances, a baby died in bed with his or her mother. But as sleeping habits changed and more babies died unexpectedly in cribs, people needed another way to explain sudden infant death. While never denying the darker possibility that a parent might deliberately smother a baby, Western societies seemed to recoil at the thought of infanticide. With the introduction of scientific methods into the practice of medicine, doctors began to look for a natural cause of sudden infant death.

The first attempts to systematically unravel this medical mystery foreshadowed modern research strategies. In 1834 an article titled "Sudden and Unexplained Death in Children" appeared in the British medical journal *Lancet*. Dr. S. W. Fearn reported nearly identical findings from postmortem examinations of two healthy infants who died in bed. Although one baby had been in bed with its mother, the other was sleeping alone, leading Fearn to question whether either child had been suffocated by overlaying, which was still the standard explanation. Given the similar autopsy findings, he speculated that a sudden and violent heart action had caused the children's deaths.

In 1892 a police surgeon named Templeman published a report in the *Edinburgh Medical Journal* examining 258 sudden infant deaths in Dundee, Scotland. Templeman found that more infants died at night, during the winter and in the first three months of life. Illegitimate infants and those from the poorer classes were particularly vulnerable. His effort to describe the characteristics of sudden infant death is regarded as the first organized epidemiologic study of the phenomenon. Templeman blamed the death toll in Dundee on overlaying, which he saw as an outgrowth of the victims' squalid living conditions. But a social historian who reviewed Templeman's study nearly one hundred years later argued that many of the babies probably were victims of infanticide.

Post–World War II research in Britain and the United States followed these parallel paths. Pathologists performing autopsies with more exacting diagnostic tools amassed a host of tantalizing clues to supplement Fearn's findings. At the same time, increasingly comprehensive epidemiologic studies sharpened and corrected the picture of sudden infant death drawn by Templeman. Although the presumption of overlaying faded in the light of scientific inquiry, sudden infant death remained an enigma. The uncertainty resonated in the language: Sudden infant death became known as crib death, a term that suggested neither cause nor blame.

By the early 1960s, theories abounded on what caused crib death: accidental suffocation in bedding; viral infections; allergic reaction to cows' milk; heart ailments; deficiencies in vitamins or minerals; environmental hazards. Some theories raised expectations until researchers realized they had been led down blind alleys. The notion that hypersensitivity to cows' milk caused crib death held sway in Britain until several studies proved otherwise. In the meantime, activists in the United States encouraged the false hope that breast-feeding could prevent crib death. None of the research showed what triggered crib death, much less how to prevent it. And despite the growing body of knowledge, doctors could not predict which babies were at risk.

New findings continued to crop up haphazardly, and

researchers began to refer to crib death somewhat derisively as "a disease of theories." The name reflected the frustration of a generation that had seen medical science conquer killer diseases with new antibiotics and vaccines. For parents mourning the loss of a child, the lack of progress seemed intolerable. But the same factors that made crib death so traumatic for parents also made it resistant to assault by science. At the center stood the awful paradox of sudden death striking an apparently healthy infant.

Crib death came without warning. A parent typically put a baby down to sleep, then returned minutes or hours later and found a lifeless body. Death was silent; the parent heard no cry of distress. The parent might see telltale signs of death—a pink froth spilling out the nose from the buildup of fluid in the lungs; a loss of muscle tone that left the soft tissues of the nose and cheeks looking compressed from the pressure of lying facedown in the crib—but many such babies looked perfectly normal.

Doctors were powerless to explain what had happened. Pediatricians who had pronounced children well shortly before they died had little to offer after the fact. The pathologist's postmortem examination provided small comfort to grieving parents. Autopsies of crib death victims revealed only negative findings; the cause of death could be inferred but never proven. After the pathologist had ruled out all the known causes, the parents' question remained: "How did our baby die?"

The void left by victims of crib death became a reservoir for grief and guilt. Many parents agonized over whether they could have done something to save their child's life. Or worse, whether they had done something to cause the baby's death. Pointed questions from the police sometimes added to their pain. While the chance to have more children gave some parents hope, it filled others with dread. During the 1960s an estimated ten thousand babies died of crib death each year in the United States. Who was to say it couldn't strike more than once in a family?

Although crib death took proportionately more children from parents who were poor, young, or black, it knew no class. White couples in their thirties living in wealthy suburbs lost babies too. Not content to remain isolated in their grief, some affluent parents looked to medicine and government for answers. When the response fell short of their expectations, their grief turned to outrage. They believed society was ignoring a devastating medical problem. Some even accused medical bureaucrats of conspiring to keep the public ignorant about crib death. Like many other indignant Americans of the sixties, crib death parents organized to demand redress for their grievances.

Mary and Fred Dore helped establish the Washington Association for Sudden Infant Death Studies in Seattle after they lost a child to crib death in September 1961. Two years later, Fred Dore, a Washington state senator who chaired the Appropriations Committee, persuaded his colleagues to allocate $20,000 for a crib death study. The bodies of all infants who died suddenly and unexpectedly in the Seattle area were brought to Children's Hospital, where they were autopsied by Dr. Bruce Beckwith, an early leader in crib death research.

The organizers of the study were as concerned about the feelings of crib death parents as they were about anatomical findings. After the autopsy, parents received a condolence letter intended to assuage any feelings of guilt. "Your child died of a real disease entity that is neither predictable nor preventable," the letter said, adding, "You are in no way responsible for your child's death." The emphasis on absolving parents of guilt set a pattern that eventually obscured more disturbing explanations for sudden infant death.

The handful of crib death groups that popped up independently around the country were typically the work of influential parents. In 1962, Jed and Louise Roe established the Mark Addison Roe Foundation in Greenwich, Connecticut. The foundation took its name from the six-month-old son the Roes lost to crib death in 1958, and it counted among its trustees Lowell Weicker Jr., a future U.S. senator and later governor of Connecticut. The organization, renamed the National Foundation for Sudden Infant Death, consolidated with the Washington state group in 1969. The national foundation spread its influence through local chapters organized by crib death parents. The organization's national leaders saw research as the responsibility of government and the medical establishment and turned their attention to lobbying and public education. Both efforts came to embody some of the worst aspects of special-interest politics—infighting among competing groups, pork-barrel funding, and distortion of the problem the foundation was dedicated to solving.

The foundation mounted a crusade in the early 1970s to dispel the idea that some crib deaths might be homicides. In their effort to mobilize public opinion, foundation officials played down the inconvenient fact that an autopsy could not distinguish crib death from smothering. Instead, they highlighted horror stories about parents who had been subjected to callous questioning or wrongly accused of killing their children. The foundation focused its public education program on eliminating the suspicions of those most likely to respond to the sudden death of an infant—funeral directors, clergy, police, firefighters, and reporters. Coroners and medical examiners became targets of a different campaign.

Foundation officials realized early that the authority of coroners and medical examiners to investigate unexpected infant deaths put them in a position to undermine the sympathetic treatment of parents. Foundation officials believed that crib death was caused by a disease, albeit unknown, and they wanted cases treated as natural rather than suspicious deaths. Under the guise of promoting humane handling of crib deaths, the foundation focused on coroners and medical examiners, trying to impose its heartfelt if unsubstantiated views on them. Coroners, often elected officials with no medical background, were susceptible to pressure from local foundation chapters. But medical examiners, with their training in pathology, were less pliable. Some had seen many victims of subtle child abuse and were unwilling to rubber-stamp cases as crib death. Medical examiners who didn't embrace the foundation's agenda were publicly attacked. The foundation demonstrated its clout by persecuting New York City medical examiner Dr. Milton Halpern, one of the nation's leading pathologists and a believer in ruling out foul play before signing out a case as crib death.

The foundation's campaign had a chilling effect on investigations of sudden infant death. It became routine for coroners and medical examiners alike to quickly attribute all infant deaths to crib death, often without an autopsy. Police and prosecutors were reluctant to pursue suspicious cases for fear of incurring the wrath of local crib death activists. With the authorities cowed, average citizens had nowhere to turn when they suspected something more depraved in an infant's death.

The politics of grief flourished in the gaps left by medical research. Diverse studies had generated reams of information about crib death without isolating a cause. The lack of a coordinated research program fed the frustrations of crib death parents. Researchers couldn't even agree on a name for what they were studying. That changed in 1969, at the second international conference on the cause of sudden infant deaths.

Researchers from the United States and Europe gathered in Eastsound, Washington, near Seattle, to mark the progress made in the study of crib death since the first conference in 1963 and to chart new directions for their work. The term "sudden infant death syndrome," or SIDS, was proposed to describe a malady with increasingly distinct characteristics. Dr. Bruce Beckwith, the pathologist who worked on the 1963 study in Seattle, offered a definition for SIDS: "The sudden death of any infant or young child, which is unexpected by history, and in which a thorough post-mortem examination fails to demonstrate an adequate cause of death." Except for the reference to "young child," the definition endured.

SIDS was less a diagnosis than a finding by exclusion. When doctors couldn't figure out what caused a baby's death, they attributed it to SIDS. Theories abounded about what might cause SIDS, but nobody had answers for the grieving parents. Only questions.

The conference revealed a growing consensus among researchers that SIDS involved an obstruction of the airway. Several researchers suggested a connection between SIDS and apnea, the temporary cessation of breathing that many infants experience while asleep. The discussion on sleep apnea became the inspiration for Dr. Alfred Steinschneider, a newcomer who would soon change the course of SIDS research.

Although he had never studied crib death, Steinschneider came to the conference with enough scientific training to sustain two researchers. After graduating from New York University in 1950, he earned a master's degree in experimental psychology from the University of Missouri. He received a Ph.D. in the same subject in 1955 from Cornell University, then worked a couple of years at the General Electric Advanced Electronics Center in Ithaca and published seven papers in psychology or psychiatry journals. In 1957, the twenty-eight-year-old psychologist turned to medicine.

Steinschneider enrolled in Upstate Medical Center, a teaching hospital that New York State had taken over a few years earlier from Syracuse University. He quickly became involved in research being conducted by Dr. Julius B. Richmond, the chairman of the pediatrics department, and Dr. Earle L. Lipton, an associate professor of pediatrics. Their work focused on the autonomic nervous system, which controls such vital functions as heartbeat, breathing, and blood pressure, and how it affected disease in newborns. To aid their research, Lipton helped develop one of the first monitors to record apnea spells, a common occurrence in premature babies. A tiny sensor that measured air movement was taped below one nostril. If the baby didn't breathe after a preset interval, usually five to twenty-five seconds, the sensor triggered an alarm that would alert nurses.

Steinschneider threw himself into his teachers' research and started writing scholarly articles with Richmond and Lipton while still a medical student. Their collaboration continued through Steinschneider's internship and residency, and in 1965, he was invited to join the medical center faculty as an assistant professor of pediatrics. By the end of the decade he was publishing his own papers.

Steinschneider's work revolved around the Children's Clinical Research Center, a federally funded unit within the hospital. The center looked like any other pediatrics ward, with hospital beds and nurses' station, but it had its own director and a special mission. The department of pediatrics had set up the center so faculty members could study babies in the hospital. Each child had to be admitted under a particular research protocol, and the government picked up the cost of the hospital stay.

Like many pediatric researchers during the 1960s, Steinschneider was only vaguely aware of crib death. But his familiarity with apnea in newborns came close enough to some of the questions surrounding crib death to earn the forty-year-old doctor an invitation to the second international conference.

"I certainly was aware of the fact that there were babies dying suddenly and unexpectedly," Steinschneider later explained. "I knew that as a physician. What came as a surprise to me ... was the fact that so many babies were dying."

Participants in the conference estimated that one out of every three infant deaths involved an apparently healthy baby who died suddenly of no obvious cause. The enormity of the problem and the willingness of pathologists who had pioneered modern SIDS research to admit their ignorance spoke to the scholar in Steinschneider. More important, he saw a role for himself in their work.

"Individuals presented information to suggest that there were babies who were apparently healthy who would have a sudden cardiac-respiratory arrest. They would suddenly be found by their parents not to be breathing, would turn cyanotic, pale, would be resuscitated. And the notion was that these babies might, in point of fact, be at increased risk to die of SIDS. In fact, the term that they were using at the time was the term 'near-missing' or 'near-miss SIDS.' And as a clinician, that was a very intriguing notion, because it meant that there may be babies out there in our community, who were described in just that manner, that might help us."

Steinschneider returned to Syracuse and set up a new protocol at the Children's Clinical Research Center. He put out word among his colleagues that he was looking for babies who had experienced the kind of life-threatening episodes described at the conference.

Chapter Three

To the outside world, Neta Hoyt gave every appearance of being a mother grief-stricken by the sudden deaths of her three children. A Tioga County public health nurse who made a routine visit to the Hoyts' trailer shortly after Jimmy's funeral suggested that Neta get some counseling. The nurse referred her to Dr. Waldo Burnett, a psychiatrist affiliated with the county's mental health clinic.

Neta told Burnett on her first visit that she felt depressed and insecure. She had slept only three or four hours a night since Eric's death more than two years earlier, she said, and she cried several times a day. She talked about her children's deaths, offering Burnett a curious explanation that went far beyond what any doctor had said. Eric, Julie, and Jimmy had all died of enlarged thymuses, she said. The condition might be hereditary, she added, because six other children in her family had died from the same thing.

Burnett made no note that he questioned Neta's explanation of the children's deaths. He was more concerned with consoling her; he had concluded that she didn't suffer from any mental illness. "It is true that she is unhappy; however, her unhappiness seems to me to be a normal grief reaction," he noted. The psychiatrist suggested Neta get involved with church activities to overcome her grief.

Burnett found Neta more cheerful with each visit. Tim was taking her out at least once a week, either for supper or to the movies, and she was enjoying watching TV and filling in the word-search puzzles she first fell in love with as a child. Neta still had bouts with depression, however. During a visit just before Thanksgiving 1968, Burnett noted that she was worried about mounting debts. Tim and Neta were making monthly payments on a TV set, their trailer, a car, and a truck, but medical bills for her and the children were unpaid. Money was so tight that Neta's father had to provide the two plots in Highland Cemetery to bury Jimmy and Julie.

Neta last visited Burnett in February 1969. The doctor believed her spirits had improved, and they agreed that she no longer needed to see him. Once again, Neta found comfort in the prospect of having another child.

When a pregnancy that year ended in a miscarriage, she and Tim decided to adopt a child. Neta filled out an application at the county's social services agency on May 26, 1969. The couple told the caseworker they preferred a white boy between the ages of one and two. Dr. Arthur Hartnagel and Tim's and Neta's friends and neighbors supported the application with letters of recommendation.

Natalie Hilliard told the county that her best friends had been good parents and seemed to have an excellent understanding of children. "They get along very well with the neighbor children, of which my five-year-old son is one, and he likes them very much," she wrote.

The Hoyts' minister, the Rev. Gary Kuhns of First United Methodist Church in Newark Valley, said the couple deserved a child after all their suffering. They'd lost three children through no fault of their own, he said. But Kuhns did offer a note of caution. Tim and Neta were limited intellectually and financially, he explained, and there was no guarantee that an adopted child would relieve Neta's grief. But Kuhns believed the Hoyts could overcome those problems.

The minister made one more argument for an adoption. "In my opinion, and it is only my opinion," he wrote, "Tim and Neta have not faced the fact that children born of them is now NOT a wise decision in view of the three deaths." His letter proved prophetic. That summer, Neta got pregnant, and she and Tim dropped their plans to adopt.

Doctors, concerned about Neta's two miscarriages, gave her hormones the day after Christmas 1969 to make sure her body didn't abort this baby. Less than three months later, on the night of March 18, 1970, Neta gave birth to a baby girl at Tompkins County Hospital in Ithaca. Molly Marie Hoyt arrived three weeks early. At six pounds, eleven ounces, and nineteen inches long, she was the smallest of Tim and Neta's babies, but she appeared to be healthy. Tim and Neta were parents again.

Molly's medical charts noted that three other children in the family had died of unknown reasons in their first two years of life. Doctors performed extra tests, but the lab work showed no evidence of abnormalities. Molly appeared to be a normal newborn. She was taking her formula well and gaining weight. Four days after entering the world, Molly went home with Tim and Neta to the trailer on Davis Hollow Road.

The baby did well until about the eighth day at home, when Neta said Molly suffered a cyanotic spell shortly after feeding. Neta told doctors she found Molly asleep in her crib, quiet, blue, and barely breathing. Pinkness returned to her face after Neta rushed her outside for fresh air. Neta took the baby to a doctor, who found nothing wrong and sent them back home. They didn't stay long.

On the morning of April 7, Neta called Molly's physician, Dr. Roger Perry, to tell him the baby had had another spell. This episode sounded much like the first. Neta had fed Molly breakfast and put her down for a nap. When she checked later, Molly had turned blue and wasn't breathing. This time, Neta told Perry, she revived Molly with mouth-to-mouth resuscitation. Perry told her to call the Newark Valley ambulance right away.

Ambulance crew member Vivian Balzer put an oxygen mask over the baby's blue face to help her breathe. Molly clenched her tiny fists as she gasped for air. Neta hopped in the back of the ambulance for the ride to Tompkins County Hospital. Tim, who had rushed home, followed in his car.

Molly appeared to be fine in the hospital. She breathed normally and her color was good. Tim signed forms to allow doctors to perform additional tests. Molly had more chest X-rays and blood and urine tests, but they showed nothing wrong, and she had no more apnea spells.

Perry made notes in the medical records about Molly's two spells at home. "Otherwise, baby has done well," he added. "Good weight gain . . . 3 siblings have died sudden deaths following meals. The remainder of the family history is unremarkable. Investigation by social service showed no evidence of foul play, and I would believe this to be true." Neta's version of events had become the accepted interpretation for the onset of Molly's condition.

Perry sent Molly home with the suggestion that Neta have her examined by Dr. Alfred Steinschneider at Upstate Medical Center in Syracuse, seventy miles north. He arranged an appointment for Steinschneider to see Molly a week later at the Children's Clinical Research Center. But before Molly could get to Syracuse, she was back in the emergency room at Tompkins County Hospital.

Neta told doctors she had fed Molly about one and a half ounces of formula, and the baby had become pale and cold to the touch and had vomited. The baby also lost consciousness, and Neta had to save her again with mouth-to-mouth resuscitation. Doctors at Tompkins County Hospital again found nothing wrong and

sent Molly home. The next day, April 15, 1970, Tim
and Neta drove to Upstate Medical Center, where they
met Steinschneider for the first time.

Tim Hoyt would always think of the forty-year-old
pediatrician as hairy. Steinschneider's crop of dark,
wiry hair was augmented by mod sideburns and bushy
eyebrows that arched above his glasses. The woolly
appearance seemed part of the doctor's genial personality. He spoke to the parents of his patients in gentle
tones that carried hints of his Brooklyn roots, and the
corners of his mouth had a way of turning up in a be-
mused expression that suggested he possessed some
special insight. His colleagues knew him for his sharp
wit.

Steinschneider was on the lookout for babies who
had suffered the kind of life-threatening spell that Neta
described in Molly's case. Seven months after returning from the Second International Conference on the
Causes of Sudden Infant Death, Steinschneider saw
promise in the connection between apnea and one of
the more obvious characteristics of SIDS: Its victims
apparently die in their sleep.

Apnea was a common, if poorly understood, occurrence in sleep. Babies, and some adults, often experience brief periods of apnea during sleep and then
resume breathing on their own. Steinschneider theo-
rized that an exaggeration of these spells—prolonged
apnea—might lead to the sudden death of an otherwise
healthy baby. After the SIDS conference, he developed
a research protocol using apnea monitors and other devices to study babies in a laboratory while they slept.

Steinschneider told Tim and Neta he would admit
Molly for study in the research center, where grants
from the National Institutes of Health paid the cost of
hospitalization. On average, five children a day underwent studies in the center, which was on the hospital's
fifth floor—5C—one floor above the pediatrics ward.
A central work station with glass windows allowed

nurses to keep an eye on their patients. Some babies stayed for weeks, and nurses tried to give the center a homey atmosphere. There were mobiles hanging from cribs, a baby swing in one walkway, and rocking chairs where nurses and parents could feed the children and lull them to sleep. The head nurse had even let one subordinate go because she wasn't affectionate enough with the babies.

Steinschneider admitted Molly with a diagnosis of apparent apnea. Neta told him that Molly often held her breath during bottle feeding, then resumed breathing when Neta took the nipple out of her mouth. She also gave Steinschneider medical histories of her other children.

"Eric ... had recurrent cyanotic 'passing out' spells during which he would gasp to get air 'like he couldn't get his breath,' " the doctor wrote. "These episodes tended to occur about one hour after being fed while asleep. It was intended that further studies be performed to evaluate for possible congenital heart disease. He died suddenly on 1/26/65.

"Julie ... On 9/5/68 during bottle feeding she suddenly 'seemed to choke,' turned blue and died.

"James ... On 9/26/68 appeared well. However, following breakfast he suddenly called out 'Mommy,' bled from nose and mouth and died suddenly." The medical notes contained no mention of enlarged thymuses.

Steinschneider ordered an array of tests for Molly. The results showed she was healthy, except for some diarrhea. He gave the nursing staff instructions to check Molly's vital signs every four hours, to record the room temperature, note her skin color, and weigh her periodically.

Steinschneider also had Molly wired to an apnea monitor on the ward. If she stopped breathing for fifteen seconds, the monitor's alarm would alert the nurses.

Two days after Molly was admitted, Steinschneider noted she experienced frequent apnea during sleep. "Although none of the apneic episodes were of sufficient duration to be associated with clinical difficulty," Steinschneider wrote, "I believe similar breathing could relate to the problem described by the parents."

He tested Molly in his autonomic laboratory the next week and found an increase in periodic apnea. He told Tim and Neta he wanted to keep Molly in the hospital until the spells decreased, and they agreed.

Tim's work schedule limited the couple to visiting the hospital on weekends. They couldn't afford to stay in Syracuse overnight, so they drove the seventy miles from Newark Valley and back each day. Nurses noted the parents' visits in Molly's medical records. It was part of nursing routine. They had been trained in school to record what they could see with their eyes or measure with instruments, and they dutifully logged how much Molly ate, the consistency of her stools, when they bathed her, when they sat her in the swing, or when they held her and rocked her to sleep. But as the nurses watched Neta's visits with Molly, they began to make subtler observations that didn't seem to fit in the medical records. They noticed that Neta never asked how Molly was doing and seemed to resent the attention Tim gave the baby. If Tim held Molly in a rocking chair, Neta would take the baby out of his arms and interpose herself on his lap. Neta never cuddled Molly either, preferring to prop the baby on a knee.

According to Steinschneider's notes, the apnea monitor's alarm, set to sound when Molly had stopped breathing for at least fifteen seconds, went off fifteen times. On a couple of occasions nurses tapped Molly's foot to make sure she was breathing, but they never had to administer mouth-to-mouth resuscitation as Neta said she had done at home. Other times, the monitor sounded when there was nothing wrong. Molly's color looked good, her heart was beating solidly, and she was breathing normally. Her shallow breaths apparently triggered the alarm.

The frequency of Molly's apnea spells decreased after nearly three weeks. As Steinschneider prepared to send her home, Neta raised the possibility of taking the baby home on an apnea monitor. She had watched nurses operate the machine and thought she could learn to do it. Steinschneider agreed. While nurses trained Neta in how to run the hospital's Air-Shields monitor, Steinschneider arranged to borrow a machine for the Hoyts. Although Neta said she had already resuscitated Molly at home, nurses taught her and Tim proper CPR techniques in case the baby had another spell.

On May 8, Molly Hoyt became the first baby in the United States to be sent home on an apnea monitor. Having concluded from Molly's twenty-four days in the hospital that her apnea occurred more often when she slept in a warm place, Steinschneider told Tim and Neta to keep her room at home at seventy-five degrees. The doctor also told them to call immediately if there were any problems and to bring Molly back in a week for follow-up studies.

Home for Molly was a new, larger trailer Tim and Neta had bought and set up not far from their old trailer. They purchased an air conditioner and installed it in the living room, which they had converted into a bedroom for Molly.

Tim and Neta planned to take turns sleeping with Molly, but their rest was fitful. The apnea monitor sounded frequently the first day home. After the alarm went off twenty times around suppertime on May 10, Neta called Steinschneider. Molly had been cranky with a runny nose and a mild cough, she said. Then Molly stopped breathing, and Neta had to resuscitate her. Tim was not at home. Steinschneider told Neta to bring the baby back to Upstate Medical Center. The first experiment in home apnea monitoring had lasted a little more than a day.

Steinschneider tested Molly in his lab again and re-admitted her to the research center. She was kept on an apnea monitor that was set to detect fifteen-second interruptions of breathing. But whenever the alarm sounded, Molly either resumed breathing on her own or a nurse simply tapped her on the foot. The baby never required resuscitation in the hospital.

After ten days, Steinschneider sent Molly home. He gave Tim and Neta the same instructions and told them to bring Molly back in two weeks. But she returned to the medical center in a Newark Valley ambulance twenty hours later.

This time, Neta told Steinschneider she had fed Molly in the morning and put her in the crib. About forty minutes later the monitor's alarm sounded. When she checked, she found that Molly had turned blue and stopped breathing.

Molly went back to floor 5C so Steinschneider could study her. Tim and Neta told him they had found a propane gas leak in the trailer and that the leak could be detected in Molly's room. Steinschneider asked a public health nurse in Tioga County to check the trailer to make sure it was safe. He was trying to rule out any possibility that the slow gas leak could have caused Molly's breathing problems.

The nurses had grown fond of Molly during the month she spent at the research center. They bought her toys, dresses, and sleepers, as they had done for many other long-term patients. Nurse Corrine Dower liked to come in on her evening shift and bathe Molly or put her in the swing to play. But the nurses noticed a change the third time Molly came to the hospital. The baby was listless, her cry weak.

"Child has a dull appearance. Does not relate well to nurses or surroundings," head nurse Thelma Schneider wrote in Molly's medical charts on May 29.

Molly's flat expression haunted Schneider. "Child has little or no affect," she wrote on June 2. "Looks to the left most of the time during care. Does not smile at people. Has been noted to smile at mobile, or once while sitting in the swing."

The nurses continued to note Tim and Neta's visits. Once, the apnea alarm sounded while they were playing with Molly. They got excited and started shaking the baby. But Molly was fine. A lead had fallen from her chest, triggering the alarm. A nurse reattached the wire and the alarm stopped. The monitor malfunctioned often during Molly's third hospital stay.

Dower, a nurse for thirty years, noticed that Neta seldom held Molly. Dower saw the same vacant, faraway look in Neta's eyes that people in the valley had seen. She became so concerned about Molly that she spoke to Schneider. "Thelma, something's going to happen to Molly," she said. "If you send that baby home, that woman is gonna smother it or kill it."

Schneider carried her colleague's concerns to Steinschneider, then noted the action in Molly's permanent medical records. "I discussed my concern for this baby with Dr. Steinschneider this a.m.," she wrote June 4. "At times, Molly will not respond to her surroundings at all—her head is turned to the left and she has a glassy stare. At these times, the baby totally lacks affect and appears retarded. At other times, she has been known to 'coo' and watch the mobile. She rarely smiles in response to another person."

Schneider added an observation about Neta's relationship with Molly: "The interaction between mother and baby is almost nil in my opinion."

But Steinschneider had decided to send Molly home that evening. Tim and Neta arrived at the hospital about seven, and Steinschneider gave Neta final instructions by phone: Keep Molly on the apnea monitor; let her sleep on her back; keep her room cool; bring her back in two weeks.

Joyce Thomas, a licensed practical nurse, helped Dower put a pink dress on Molly for the trip home. Molly was getting to be a big girl. She had grown three inches since birth and now weighed ten and a half pounds. Thomas put Molly in a portable crib for the elevator ride to the first floor. She carried her out to the curb and put her in Tim and Neta's car for the trip home. When Thomas returned to the ward, she cried.

Dower kept looking at her wristwatch that night. "Well, Joyce," she said, "do you think she's still alive?"

Friday, June 5, 1970, had the look of a beautiful spring day. The morning sun had already warmed Newark Valley to fifty-five degrees. The day started nicely in the Hoyt trailer on Davis Hollow Road; Molly seemed fine. After feeding her, Neta said, she put Molly in the bassinet for a nap, hooked her up to the apnea monitor, and left the room. Sometime later, Neta said, the alarm sounded, and she found that Molly had stopped breathing. "When I got to her, she was all bluish-pink color," Neta explained later. "I mean, she was just real funny looking."

Neta said she tried to revive Molly with mouth-to-mouth resuscitation, then called Ella Hoyt and Steinschneider. The Newark Valley ambulance squad also responded. As the ambulance passed a service station owned by Tim's brother Chuck, a crew member shouted they were headed to Tim and Neta's place. Chuck arrived at the trailer and saw Neta sitting on the couch with Molly in her arms. He thought he heard Molly gasp for air, so he picked her up, pinched her nose, and blew into her mouth.

An ambulance worker took Molly and thought he detected a faint heartbeat. Two crew members took turns doing CPR on Molly outside, but she never came around. Chuck believed Molly had died right there, on the lawn outside the trailer.

The emergency workers put Molly's body into the

ambulance, and Chuck headed off to tell Tim his fourth child was dead after two months and eighteen days.

Steinschneider stopped by the research center and told the nurses that Molly had died. The nurses cried. They knew Neta and Molly had always been alone when the baby stopped breathing at home. It was always Neta who heroically resuscitated Molly. The baby had never needed resuscitation in the hospital, and she had spent sixty of her seventy-nine days of life in either Tompkins County Hospital or Upstate Medical Center.

"We used to talk about it, and we just said we're sure something's going on," Thelma Schneider said. "It didn't make any sense to me because we hadn't had any problems while she was in the hospital. It just didn't add up."

But Schneider and the other nurses had nothing but suspicions to go on. An autopsy on Molly was inconclusive. There was no police investigation, and Steinschneider didn't ask any questions.

"It was the doctor's patient," Schneider said. "It was his responsibility to do something if he thought it was deemed necessary." She wondered later if Steinschneider had become too focused on his research.

Once again, MacPherson Funeral Home handled arrangements for a Hoyt baby. Molly wore a beige dress in her Styrofoam casket. Tim and Neta added a music box, a red bow and flowers, then Molly took her place with Eric, Julie, and Jimmy in Highland Cemetery. The Hoyts still struggled financially, but Tim promised to give funeral director David Cooley $5 or $10 every payday until he settled the bill for Molly's funeral. The couple could not afford a headstone for Molly.

A week after Molly's death, Neta and Tim reapplied to adopt a child, and Tioga County assigned a caseworker to the couple. After making several visits to the couple's trailer, the caseworker learned that Neta was pregnant again. Her fifth child was due in May 1971.

The Hoyts had wanted to have a natural child and to adopt another child at the same time, but social services put their application on hold.

In the meantime, Tim and Neta had also approached a private agency in Tompkins County about adopting an older child. Family and Children's Services in Ithaca called Tioga County officials in January 1971 to find out more about the Hoyts. Social services commissioner Russell Rawley and caseworker Alberta Weisz responded with a letter pointing out that the couple dropped their first application when Neta became pregnant with Molly.

"It would appear that this couple has suffered a great deal of grief. Neither have resolved their emotional need for a natural child. It almost seems like the couple considers the adoption process as a second resource, but not a complete fulfillment," they said.

"It does not seem a particularly good time to introduce an older child into a home during final months of pregnancy. A child may be subjected not only to a strange home at an inappropriate time, but may be subjected to the emotional upheaval that the Hoyts would undergo with the birth of a new child. It seems like an adopted child could be an 'insurance policy' for the family. The Hoyts need a child in their home to help them through the fifth pregnancy. They need the child in their home to buffer the grief should the fifth child not survive. The question in mind is whether a child needs them as parents."

If the adoption agencies had any concerns about how the Hoyt children died, they would have been allayed by the medical forms that Dr. Noah Kassman filled out for the couple. "Patient has had four live births. All children have died in infancy, possibly from poorly understood genetic disease. Parents and children have been under study at Upstate Med Center."

Neither agency came through with a child, but Neta seemed destined for motherhood. On May 9, 1971—

Mother's Day—she gave birth to her fifth child, a boy with slightly woolly hair. She and Tim named him Noah, after Dr. Kassman, who had delivered all their children.

Unlike the Hoyts' other children, Noah did not go home right away. Dr. Roger Perry, the pediatrician who had treated Molly, gave the reason in Noah's records: "Sudden deaths 4 siblings, age 4 weeks to 2½ years not explained by clinical and autopsy findings. This baby being transferred to Upstate Medical Center for evaluation. At present seems very normal."

Chapter Four

On May 13, 1971—Neta's twenty-fifth birthday—
Noah was admitted to Upstate Medical Center. Federal
funding for the Children's Clinical Research Center
had been cut back, so Noah was admitted to the pediatrics ward, where Dr. Alfred Steinschneider studied
the four-day-old baby. He ordered a medical course
similar to Molly's: Keep Noah on an apnea monitor set
to trigger an alarm at fifteen seconds and watch him
closely.

Noah fared nicely on the ward. He breathed normally, his color looked good, he slept soundly and
steadily gained weight. His medical records were remarkable only for the number of times they noted
malfunctions of the apnea monitor.

May 15: "Patient continued to do well. We are having trouble with the apnea alarm on the monitor. It
keeps going off but the child is not apneic. No documented apneic spells."

May 16: "Condition unchanged. Patient supposedly
had one apneic episode; but on close questioning of
the nurse, it appears that there was a malfunction of the
monitor."

May 17: "Status quo except that the monitor malfunctions more frequently now. . . . No documented apneic episodes yet."

Although Noah appeared to be perfectly normal on
the ward, Steinschneider concluded from lab studies
that the baby was experiencing apnea more frequently

during sleep and appeared to have trouble coordinating his breathing during bottle feeding. The feeding problem disappeared, and the doctor tried giving Noah different drugs and changing his sleep position to reduce the apnea. By early June, Steinschneider took Noah off research status. He planned to send the baby home as soon as he could find an apnea monitor for the Hoyts.

Tim and Neta arrived at the pediatrics ward at one o'clock on June 15. Steinschneider told them to keep Noah hooked up to the apnea monitor and to bring him back in five days. The couple took the one-month-old baby home for the first time. By the next day, Noah was back at the Upstate Medical Center, brought in by a Newark Valley ambulance.

Neta told Steinschneider she was in the kitchen when the monitor sounded. Noah was lying in his bassinet, pale and not breathing, but he perked up when she shook him. She told Steinschneider that when she tried to call him, Noah fell asleep in her arms and turned a dark blue. Once again, she saved the life of one of her children with mouth-to-mouth resuscitation.

Steinschneider ordered more tests, which showed that Noah was apparently in good health. He took Noah back to the lab, where the baby was examined at temperatures ranging up to ninety degrees. Noah remained on an apnea monitor in the pediatrics ward. Clinically he appeared to be fine, but Steinschneider said he had documented fifteen spells of prolonged apnea.

By the time of Noah's second hospitalization, Tim had come to the painful conclusion that whatever was killing his children might be hereditary and that he and Neta shouldn't have any more babies. On July 2, 1971, he underwent a vasectomy.

Steinschneider sent Noah home after a second month in the hospital. He told Tim and Neta to bring the baby back in a week, but Noah returned to the hospital the next day. This time Neta told Steinschneider that she had been feeding Noah when he began to cough, turned blue, and stopped breathing. He started breathing again after Neta made him gag.

The nurses who witnessed Noah's return to the pediatrics ward began to form the same suspicions that had troubled the nurses who treated Molly upstairs in the Children's Clinical Research Center. They wondered if Neta had tried to kill her baby and changed her mind; Noah had never needed resuscitation in the hospital. Neta seemed jealous of Noah. When Tim held Noah, Neta would sit next to her husband and rub his leg, ignoring the baby.

Gail Dristle, a twenty-one-year-old nurse's assistant, couldn't understand Neta's lack of interest in the pretty, rosy-cheeked baby who seemed to delight in being around people. "You'd walk in the room and he'd look at you when he could, as soon as you were in his sight," she said. "He'd lay there and want attention."

Dristle recalled that Neta stiffened when she tried to hand her the baby. When Neta finally took Noah, she held him away from her body. Another time, Dristle found Neta standing with her arms crossed, glaring at Noah in his crib ten feet way. Dristle walked toward Neta and their eyes met, but neither said a word. That image of Neta hovering by the crib bothered Dristle for years. "Anger was in her face," she said.

Julia Evans was one of the few nurses who took care of both Molly and Noah. Knowing what had happened to Molly, she watched Noah more closely and became concerned about Neta's pattern of indifference.

"I saw that there was no warmth between the mother and her babies," Evans said. "I would try and give the mother the bottle to feed the babies and she would never take it. The father would always take the bottle and feed them."

Tim didn't seem to find Neta's behavior strange. Nurses saw him as a loyal husband, always holding his wife's hand or caressing her shoulder. Dristle thought of Tim as "the big, dumb dog."

Evans had known Steinschneider for years and felt comfortable taking her concerns to him. She said she told Steinschneider that Neta had neglected her babies and did not appear to love them, but the doctor said she couldn't prove anything was wrong.

Steinschneider had observed only one prolonged apnea spell during Noah's week at the hospital but decided to test him again before sending him home. On the afternoon of July 27, 1971, a nurse fed Noah formula, burped him, and laid him down for a nap in the autonomic lab so he could be tested for sleep apnea. He nodded off about two-thirty, but was very restless. Steinschneider examined Noah when the baby awoke shortly after six. Tim and Neta arrived soon afterward and played with Noah until they left the hospital at seven-thirty.

Evans bet Steinschneider a quarter that Noah would not come back. Steinschneider laughed at her and shrugged it off. It was a bet that Evans's colleagues hoped she would lose.

Tim Hoyt's neighbors couldn't help noticing when he left for work the following morning. His pickup truck had a broken muffler, and they heard the engine's roar as Tim drove off to his job building Route 17, the Southern Tier Expressway. Wednesday, July 28, was the kind of sunny day meant for outdoor work. Once again, Neta was left alone with her baby.

Neta would say later that she heard the alarm sound on Noah's apnea monitor after she put him down for a nap. By the time she got to the baby, he was blue. But this time she could not bring him back to life.

Dr. John Scott was standing in the kitchen of his large colonial home overlooking the southern bank of the Susquehanna River when a dispatcher for the Tioga County Sheriff's Department called. There was a medical crisis up north in Newark Valley. Would Scott go?

The forty-nine-year-old doctor didn't hesitate. "I'll meet your car," he said and rushed out to an emergency he would never forget.

Scott headed across the river to the sheriff's department in Owego, where a deputy with a patrol car waited to take him on the ride of his life.

On Route 38 the deputy and the doctor left the village behind. Once he hit open country with his lights flashing and siren wailing, the deputy let the engine unwind. Scott watched the radar gun on the dashboard clock the accelerating speed. 105 miles per hour. 107. 108. As the car flew up the narrow two-lane road, Scott hoped they wouldn't end up victims themselves. They covered the seventeen miles to the Hoyts' trailer on Davis Hollow Road in roughly fifteen minutes.

Inside, Scott faced Tim and Neta for the first time. Tim seemed calm, but Neta looked distraught. Then he saw the source of her anguish: a baby boy lying motionless on the couch.

Scott moved quickly, checking Noah's vital signs. He found no sign of breathing. No heartbeat. No response to pain. He checked the eyes: pupils dilated. There was no need for a doctor. Noah was dead. But whoever decided to call Scott that morning had chosen wisely—he also served as county coroner. Unable to save Noah's life, Scott now set about trying to determine what caused his death.

There wasn't much to go on. The baby looked to be a couple of months old. Affixed to Noah's chest were electrodes sprouting cables for an apnea monitor. Scott decided Noah hadn't been dead long. Rigor mortis hadn't set in; the tiny body was still limp. There was no sign of *livor mortis*—the purplish discoloration caused by blood pooling in the lowest parts of the body after death. Scott could see no injuries. The blue-eyed boy with fine brown hair appeared normal in every way. The absence of any obvious cause of death suggested that Noah had fallen victim to SIDS.

Neta didn't cry, but she looked agitated, rocking from foot to foot, her twitching hands broadcasting distress signals. Scott tried to talk to her, but he got no response.

Tim, who had rushed home from work, kept himself under control enough to tell Scott that Dr. Steinschneider had discharged Noah from Upstate Medical Center the day before. Scott called Steinschneider from the trailer.

Steinschneider told Scott that Noah had spent nearly his entire life in the hospital. But Scott didn't understand the depths of the tragedy he'd walked into until Steinschneider told him that Tim and Neta had lost four other children.

Steinschneider told Scott he was very interested in having Noah's body autopsied at the medical center, and Scott agreed.

The hospital's pathologists didn't have any better luck in finding a cause of death than Scott did. They noted that Noah had grown three inches and gained three pounds since birth. Minor inflammation in the lungs and some excess fluid were attributed to bronchiolitis, a respiratory infection. That may have been a factor, Scott noted in his coroner's report, but it wasn't a cause of death.

"This is best described scientifically as 'sudden unexplained death,'" Scott wrote, "but this has not been widely accepted as a cause of death for use on Death Certificates by registrars and by some people in the medical profession."

Following accepted practice, Scott listed acute bronchiolitis on the death certificate, but he believed that Noah had died of SIDS. He would still hold that belief twenty-three years later, when others began to suspect that something else had caused the boy's death.

"I looked at it as . . . a medical problem, which

seemed to be evident with the appearance of the body and the medical electrodes, the fact that the child had been in the hospital for respiratory problems right up until shortly before he died," Scott said. "The other four [deaths] certainly pointed toward a crib death."

The case was closed without a police investigation. Nobody noted that although Noah never had a medical emergency during the seventy-eight days he spent in hospitals, he faced a crisis on each of the three days he was at home with his mother.

At the age of twenty-five, Neta Hoyt prepared to bury her fifth child. MacPherson Funeral Home again handled the arrangements. A private service was held at the funeral home. Noah was dressed in a light-colored, short-sleeved jumper, a cloth diaper, and rubber pants. As they had with Molly, Tim and Neta placed keepsakes in the baby's Styrofoam casket: an orange plastic giraffe, a stuffed toy with a windup music box, and flowers.

The Rev. Donald Washburn, the new minister of the United Methodist Church in Newark Valley, officiated at the gravesite in Highland Cemetery. As Noah was buried with the four brothers and sisters he'd never known, Neta fainted.

"I thought we had lost her right there," Washburn said. "Fortunately, after a while she was revived, but it was a very traumatic experience."

At Upstate Medical Center, the nurses cried when Steinschneider told them another Hoyt baby was dead. Julia Evans said to him, "I told you so."

But Steinschneider saw the deaths of Molly and Noah Hoyt in a larger context. They were part of a group of five children whom he had been studying in his lab. These five "very, very important babies," as Steinschneider called them, all fit his theory that prolonged apnea might lead to the sudden death of an otherwise healthy baby.

Like Molly and Noah, the other children in the

study—a brother and sister, and a premature baby from a third family—all suffered episodes in which they stopped breathing and turned blue, a condition called cyanosis. And like Molly and Noah, the other children were apparently healthy.

Steinschneider published a research paper about the five children in the October 1972 issue of *Pediatrics,* a leading medical journal. The eight-page article, which included more than a dozen graphs, identified the children only by their initials.

"The five patients participating in the present study demonstrated frequent episodes of apnea while asleep," he wrote. "Although the majority of these apneic episodes were brief and self-limited, a number were sufficiently prolonged to be associated with cyanosis and were of sufficient severity to prompt vigorous resuscitative efforts."

Although the three other children survived, the fact that Molly and Noah died the day after they were sent home on apnea monitors seemed to confirm Steinschneider's hypothesis that prolonged apnea was part of the final pathway of SIDS.

Steinschneider's clinical findings contained stunning implications for the understanding of SIDS. This was the first time that infants who had suffered prolonged apnea spells had been closely studied before they succumbed to SIDS. His account of the other Hoyt children's sudden and unexplained deaths indicated that the disorder might run in families. The article suggested that doctors might be able to identify infants at risk of becoming victims of SIDS and therefore might prevent it.

Steinschneider's study helped to launch a revolution in SIDS research. A report published in New Zealand in 1983 traced the influence of the 1972 article on nearly one hundred other SIDS studies during the 1970s. Although Steinschneider published other SIDS studies during that decade, none surpassed the 1972 paper as a reference for other researchers.

Many researchers quickly accepted the sleep apnea theory, in part because it offered hope that SIDS could be prevented. But some of Steinschneider's other ideas weren't so readily accepted. He came to believe that babies born to parents who had lost a child to SIDS faced a greater risk of succumbing to the syndrome. Although large-scale epidemiologic studies found little evidence of SIDS among subsequent siblings, Steinschneider spent the next twenty years promoting the use of home apnea monitors to prevent tragedy from striking families a second time.

While many doctors were inclined to accept Steinschneider's account of the Hoyt children's deaths, a few looked at his evidence and reached a different conclusion. *Pediatrics* published a letter from Dr. John Hick, a pediatrician from Winona, Minnesota, challenging Steinschneider's reading of this "unparalleled family chronicle of infant death."

Hick picked up on the same point that the nurses at Upstate Medical Center had grasped: neither M.H. nor N.H., as the article referred to Molly and Noah, required resuscitation in the hospital; they suffered life-threatening episodes only when they were at home with their mother.

"Despite the circumstantial evidence suggesting a critical role for the mother in the death of her children, Steinschneider offers no information about the woman," Hick wrote. "The potential for child abuse inherent in family history and the danger of hospital-acquired infection are two variables which could have been more adequately controlled in this study, had Steinschneider chosen a foster home as his laboratory for the investigation of the youngest sibling. Perhaps the outcome would have been different?"

Steinschneider's response, published at the same time, insisted that the children had suffered prolonged

periods of apnea and cyanosis in the hospital and required vigorous stimulation before they could resume
breathing. He scoffed at Hick's suggestion that studying the children in a foster home might have produced
a different outcome, saying the idea "denies the importance of parental wishes and feelings as well as the
needs of a developing child."

An accompanying editor's note endorsed Steinschneider's willingness to give parents the benefit of
the doubt in cases of sudden unexplained death.

"Failure to define the cause of a sudden death can
never be used as support for the diagnosis of child
abuse," Steinschneider argued. "Humanity as well as
logic dictates the need for positive evidence as well
as extreme sensitivity in the collection of such information. No such evidence was available in the family
Dr. Hicks [*sic*] refers to."

Steinschneider also rose to the defense of Mr. and
Mrs. H., as the Hoyts were identified. The couple frequently drove an hour and a half to see their children
in the hospital, he said. They would sit next to the crib
and had to be encouraged to touch the baby. But
Steinschneider's observations led him to a different
impression than the one formed by nurses who cared
for the children.

"It was my impression that they feared becoming
too attached emotionally with either infant because
they anticipated a tragic outcome," Steinschneider
wrote. "Mrs. H. expressed, on a number of occasions,
considerable guilt over the death of her children and,
because of the inability of physicians to define the
cause of death, felt there must have been something
she did or failed to do that was responsible."

Steinschneider's willingness to accept Neta's de-
scriptions of the life-threatening episodes that Molly
and Noah experienced at home was seen as an enlight-
ened approach to the study of SIDS. SIDS research
was becoming distorted by a crusade to spare the feel-

ings of grieving parents. The tendency among SIDS parents to fault themselves for the deaths of their children came to be regarded as a disease second only to SIDS in gravity. Expressions of guilt were interpreted as symptoms deserving treatment, not scrutiny. Allowing doubts to persist about the cause of a child's death only added to the parents' suffering. The mere suggestion that a diagnosis of SIDS didn't necessarily preclude child abuse provoked outrage.

Steinschneider also defended his article in a private exchange of letters with Dr. Stuart Asch, a professor of psychiatry at Mount Sinai School of Medicine in New York City. Although Asch's conclusion echoed Hick's, he had little interest in challenging Steinschneider publicly. Asch had grown cautious after SIDS parents expressed outrage over a study he reported on in 1968. That study, the results of which Asch published in a journal with a small readership to avoid publicity, suggested that a large proportion of crib deaths were actually infanticides committed by mothers suffering from acute postpartum depression. Asch had tried to enlist Steinschneider's help in his research before Steinschneider published the article linking SIDS to prolonged apnea. Now he felt compelled to write Steinschneider that the deaths of M.H. and N.H. looked suspiciously like infanticide.

"I was struck by the fact that neither of these infants had serious apneic episodes while under observation in the hospital despite long periods of hospitalization," Asch said. "Serious apneic episodes, and the eventual deaths all occurred within 24 to 48 hours *after* discharge and while at home. One can't help wondering why these would occur only at home, and so soon after discharge, and presumably with a clean bill of health. . . . Your first case is also suspicious in view of the similar deaths of three siblings."

Steinschneider's response bristled with indignation. "By way of clarification, *all* of the infants described in my article in *Pediatrics* had a number of prolonged apneic and cyanotic episodes *in the hospital* which were sufficiently severe to precipitate resuscitative procedures by the nursing staff," he wrote. "Consequently, your conclusion is incorrect that the two infants who died had severe episodes *only* after discharge from the hospital."

He went on to belittle Asch's research and lecture him on his responsibility to SIDS parents: "You are certainly aware of the tremendous sense of guilt in parents who lose a baby to SIDS. The premature publication of the 'infanticide' hypothesis, which was based solely on highly theoretical grounds and without adequate documentation and proof that it is truly relevant to SIDS, can only serve to support and magnify the sense of guilt within these families and to provide the needed 'expert testimony' for unfounded accusations leveled against these families by segments of the community."

Steinschneider had reason to be defensive. The 1972 article had given him instant respect as a SIDS researcher. The National Foundation for Sudden Infant Death named him to its medical advisory board in 1972. The International Guild for Infant Survival, another leading parents' group, put him on its advisory board the same year.

Steinschneider eventually left Upstate Medical Center to head a new SIDS research program at the University of Maryland.

By then, Steinschneider had joined the crusade to console parents by eliminating any vestige of infanticide from the discussion of SIDS, and he enlisted Waneta Hoyt in the cause. He had Neta attend one of the early meetings of Sudden Infant Death Syndrome of Central New York, the support group for SIDS parents that Steinschneider founded in Syracuse.

Neta had the tragic presence that SIDS groups often used in a deliberate attempt to win sympathy for their views. Beverly Whitney, who had lost a son to SIDS, sought Neta out during a meeting at Upstate Medical Center. Neta's plight left an indelible impression on her.

"Sorrowness enveloped her," Whitney said more than twenty years later. "It emanated from her being."

Chapter Five

People in the valley were left with conflicted feelings about Tim and Neta Hoyt's plight. Sympathy, doubt, and fear swirled among the couple's acquaintances. Some women worried that their babies were at risk of some obscure disease, while others felt ashamed for daring to think that the deaths of Eric, Julie, Jimmy, Molly, and Noah might involve something more appalling.

"Everybody thought murder after the third one died," said Yvonne Lane, Neta's hairdresser at the time. "Then it happened again and again, and you thought, 'Aha.' But then the coroner's report would come out; poor Waneta and Tim lost another baby to SIDS. I mean we're small-town, we're a farming community, but we're not stupid. It may look like Hicksville, but underneath that surface these people are not stupid.

"But nobody in a small town wants to point a finger and be wrong. You just don't want to be wrong."

A week after Noah's death, Tim and Neta were back at the Tioga County Department of Social Services, trying to adopt a child. Dr. Alfred Steinschneider had encouraged them to adopt immediately, but their names went on a waiting list. Later, in the fall of 1971, caseworker Alberta Weisz prepared a report on the Hoyts' application.

Weisz had frowned on the couple's earlier applications because she thought they needed a child more than a child needed them. Their pattern of abandoning adoption plans as soon as Neta became pregnant bothered her, as did their insistence on producing more babies only to watch them die. Neta's need to adopt so soon after her children died made Weisz uneasy.

"I felt like every time a child died she wanted to go to the dog pound and pick up another puppy, and she wanted it quickly, she wanted it right then," Weisz said. "The child wasn't even in the ground a week and she was applying for something to replace him."

But this time might be different, she thought. The couple wanted to adopt because Tim's vasectomy prevented them from having another child of their own. They seemed to have resolved their emotional need for a natural-born child.

As Weisz worked up her study on the couple, she was struck by the contrast between Tim and Neta. Tim seemed shy and quiet. He answered questions with one or two words, despite Weisz's attempts to draw him out. Neta started answering questions before Weisz could get them out. She was aggressive, demanding, and outspoken.

"So much grief and turmoil has made their family the target of [so] much community talk and comment that she at times is defensive," Weisz noted.

The caseworker made a surprise visit to the Hoyts' trailer to see what kind of home an adopted child would grow up in. Neta gave Weisz a tour, showing where the family would eat its meals and where the baby would sleep.

The tidy home gave Weisz a feeling of warmth. Tim and Neta kept a house cat; a beagle stayed in a kennel outside. The trailer sat on an acre of land, with flower beds and a vegetable patch tended by Neta.

"Although not fancy or ornately landscaped, the yard offers ample opportunity for a child's outdoor play," Weisz noted in her records.

The caseworker also noticed Tim and Neta's closeness. They belonged to no community groups, choosing to spend most of their time together at home, working in the yard, watching TV, or playing cards. They were together whenever Tim wasn't working.

"During their years of marriage, they have gone through many sessions of grief and problems," Weisz said in her study. "It is felt that these difficult periods have strengthened their bonds, giving them a stable marriage filled with thoughtfulness and understanding."

The Hoyts had solid references, their health was good, the home was clean, and Tim was working. Weisz brushed aside her misgivings and approved the adoption. She set out to find Tim and Neta a baby in time for Christmas.

"Since Mr. and Mrs. Hoyt have had so many grievous experiences with unhealthy children born to them, destined to live awhile, only to expire, it is vital that they have an older baby, past the formula complications, etc., which often arise with newborns," Weisz concluded. "Intellectual potential, national background, coloring, or sex seem not important factors. Just a normal healthy child is all that is necessary."

On November 19, 1971, the social services agency found such a child, a nine-month-old boy named Scottie. Tim and Neta picked up the baby at the agency and took him home to the valley on a six-month trial basis. They were parents again.

Weisz checked on Scottie three days later. "I worried about him because he was nine months old," she said later. "You pick up my cat and he's going to know you're a stranger: 'You don't belong here, you're different.' A nine-month-old boy was going to be the same way. He might give them a hard time."

But Tim and Neta told her everything was fine with them and Scottie. It wasn't, however. Not for Neta.

Two days later, on the eve of Thanksgiving, Tim called the emergency line for Tioga County Community Psychiatric Services. He told psychologist Miriam Elkin that Neta was distraught and needed help right away. Elkin had Tim bring his wife to the office in Owego, where Neta told the psychologist she'd had wicked thoughts about Scottie. She was worried she might hurt him.

"What might you do?" Elkin asked.

"I feel as though I would like to wring his neck," Neta said. Given time, she might come to love Scottie, she said, but not now.

Dr. Mokarram Jafri, a psychiatrist, suggested that Neta admit herself to a hospital; it would relieve her of the stigma of having to return Scottie. Neta refused; she wanted medication instead. Because Tim was going to be home for the holiday weekend, Jafri relented and prescribed Stelazine to treat Neta's anxiety and Elavil for her depression.

Neta called Weisz at her home on Thanksgiving Day to ask her to take Scottie away. She had talked to a psychiatrist, she said, and now wanted to wait one or two years before trying to adopt. When Weisz arrived at the Hoyts' trailer, Neta had Scottie dressed and packed to leave.

"I don't know what to say to you," Neta said. "I'm very confused."

Scottie reminded her of her birth children, she said, and she feared she might harm him. Weisz took the baby back to the foster home he'd left the week before.

Neta went back to the psychiatric clinic the following Monday and told Jafri she had given Scottie back to the county. The psychiatrist consoled her, saying she still might be able to adopt one day. Neta continued seeing Jafri for the next year and a half.

"She has been feeling better since returning the adopted child to the social services department, though still she feels she hasn't gotten over the loss of her five children and mostly in some ways she feels responsible, as if she has herself killed them," Jafri wrote after one session.

In counseling, Neta continued to find the attention she craved. Each session gave her a chance to discuss the latest turmoil in her life. Although she and Tim had been without children for nearly two-thirds of their seven-year marriage, she complained that they never spent time together because of the kids. Now that they had delayed their plans for adoption, she told Jafri, she and Tim were going to pay more attention to each other. Once she got over her grief, she said, they would start a family again. Her relationship with Tim, money woes, and her desire to have more children became recurring themes.

In April 1972, Tim went to a counseling session at which Neta told Jafri she was growing more depressed and was fighting with her husband. She thought her depression could be traced to living in the trailer where two of her children had died. Less than a year later, the trailer was destroyed by fire. The fire started underneath the trailer, according to newspaper accounts, but firefighters never determined the cause. Neta was treated for possible smoke inhalation.

An appointment with her gynecologist triggered another crisis in the spring of 1972. She called Jafri's office, upset about her chances of having more children. She was angry at Tim for having a vasectomy and complained that he was cold and superficial.

Neta demanded attention incessantly, especially from Tim. After Tim left for work, Loretta Hoyt, Chuck's wife, would get calls from a relative saying Neta had threatened to kill herself. Loretta recalled rushing over to the trailer the first time to make sure Neta didn't hurt herself.

"I was on pins and needles," Loretta said. "I'm sitting there, 'Oh, my God, how is she going to do this?'" But Neta smiled, and the two women began playing cards. After a while, Loretta wondered why she was there; Neta seemed fine.

After about three suicide watches with Neta, Loretta got a call from Tim: Neta was again threatening to kill herself.

"Tim, I'm not going to stop her," Loretta said. "You have to call her bluff. You can't let her continue this way. She needs help. Get her help."

"Well, what if she does it this time and I'm not there?" asked Tim.

Loretta saw Neta's threatened suicide as a cruel ploy to use on a man whose father had hanged himself. "No matter what she does, she has her own mind," Loretta told her brother-in-law. "It's not your fault, and don't you take the blame." Neta never followed through on her threats.

Having children remained Neta's paramount concern. She told Jafri in February 1973 that she had put her name on a waiting list with a private agency to adopt two children but preferred having her own. Neta's attitude about children had swung back and forth since Noah's death. She once mentioned artificial insemination as an option if Tim's vasectomy couldn't be reversed. Now she talked about having a hysterectomy if they decided to adopt.

"The only reason that came out seems not as a measure of contraception, but, in my opinion, in self-mutilation, especially the organ which did not give her what she wanted," Jafri noted in his records.

The psychiatrist recommended against the operation. With Tim's vasectomy, he reasoned, Neta had no need for contraception, unless she got involved with other men. Neta, who had told the psychiatrist she occasionally thought about having an affair, went ahead with the hysterectomy later that year.

By the time of her last meeting with Jafri in June 1973, Neta seemed to have put her life in order. She and Tim had bought a new trailer, and Tim was working regularly, allowing them to catch up on their bills. The couple also pressed ahead with plans to adopt a child through the private agency in Ithaca that they had tried before. The agency contacted Weisz, who related the couple's experience with Scottie.

"Our relationship with one another has been damaged," Weisz said. "We find the Hoyts most difficult to work with, considering the numbers of fine applicants on our waiting list, yet it is sad to deny them the joys of parenthood should their strengths be gaining."

The agency put the Hoyts' name on a waiting list, where it remained for years while the couple endured periodic upheavals, like a neighbor's alleged rape of Neta.

The neighbor's wife remembered Neta's showing up on her doorstep the day she and her husband moved in across the street from the Hoyts in the fall of 1973. The couples soon arranged an evening to play cards together. The woman found her new friend's behavior unnerving. Neta always seemed to be at the center of events, vying for the attention of men in the room.

The couples kept up a neighborly relationship. When Neta said she needed bedroom furniture for the baby she expected to adopt, the woman told her about a dresser that her in-laws had stored at their home in neighboring Broome County. On June 14, 1974, the woman's husband drove Neta to look at the dresser; the woman stayed behind to do chores around the house. On the way, the husband stopped the car.

"He told me he had a birthday coming up and he wanted a birthday kiss," Neta later told police. "I tried to resist his kissing, but he kept pulling me to him, and he was also fondling me about the breasts and legs. I tried to get him to stop, and told him I didn't want him to touch me. He said he didn't care and that I excited him and he wanted me."

When Neta threatened to walk home, the man drove on to his parents' home, where they looked at the furniture. On the way back, he turned down a dirt road, Waneta said. He stopped the car by a dirt pile, locked the doors, and turned on the radio. Neta said he raped her while the radio played.

"He asked me not to tell my husband because he didn't want a shotgun to his head by my husband or his wife," Neta told police. "I told him I was going to tell my husband, and that maybe it would take a couple days."

The neighbor didn't sense anything was amiss when her husband and Neta returned. Neta came into her house and had a cup of coffee. Neta invited her to go shopping, but the woman said she was busy. Neta went home, showered, and went shopping in Owego, where she bought an electric razor, a Father's Day present for Tim, the childless father.

Neta didn't mention the alleged incident in the car until four days later, when she and Tim visited Art and Natalie Hilliard, their best friends. She then told her minister, who went with her and Tim to file a complaint with the state police in Owego. Afterward, Neta called neighbors to tell them what had happened, and people started talking about a rapist being loose in the valley.

Police charged the man with rape, but the case was dismissed after Neta refused to pursue it. The man told police that Neta was a willing partner; he believed she accused him of rape to draw attention to herself. Not long afterward, the couple moved away.

Some members of Neta's family didn't know whether to believe her story. If the man had forced himself on Neta, why weren't her clothes torn or her skin bruised? Chuck and Loretta Hoyt wondered. Her reaction didn't ring true, either.

"When a person is raped, usually, how do they react? What do they do? They feel ashamed," Loretta Hoyt said. "Would you call the whole neighborhood and tell them?"

Neta would later say she had been so distraught that she tried to kill herself by overdosing on aspirin. "He took my life . . . you didn't think your husband would want you," she explained.

But later that year she stopped at the Newark Valley service station run by Bill Evans and told him she'd had dreams about him. Neta said she wanted to start a relationship with Evans, but he refused.

Tim told his friend Mike Harbac that Waneta claimed men tried to break into their home to rape her. Tim thought she was just acting out what she had seen on the soap operas that day.

On September 20, 1976, the adoption agency in Ithaca came through with the baby Tim and Neta had waited nearly four years to adopt, a two-month-old boy with dark hair and dark eyes. They named him Jay Timothy and took him home to Davis Hollow Road. The nervous parents had the baby sleep in their bedroom for nearly a year.

The responsibility of caring for a baby again made Neta tense. Ella Hoyt spent a lot of time at the trailer next door, changing Jay's diapers, giving him his bottle, and pacifying him when he fussed. Without her mother-in-law's help, Neta said, she never would have coped.

For the Hoyts, life was an exercise in survival. Tim and Neta lived on the edge financially as well as emotionally. Tim's wages from construction work fluctuated with the seasons. Little money came in during long winter layoffs. Medical bills from their first five children and Neta's chronic ailments put them in debt early on. They remortgaged their first trailer to pay bills from Upstate Medical Center and took out bank loans to cover other obligations. True to his word, Tim continued to pay a couple of dollars here and there for Molly's and Noah's funerals, and funeral director David Cooley eventually forgave the balance.

In more than twelve years of marriage, Tim and

Neta had been unable to lift themselves out of the ranks of the working poor. A week before bringing Jay home they filed for bankruptcy. The new family started out nearly $8,000 in debt. Of the fourteen businesses or individuals they owed money to, one was a hospital and four were doctors. Except for $30 in Tim's Christmas Club account, they had no money in the bank.

Life didn't get any easier after Jay arrived. In the early 1980s, fire destroyed the Hoyts' trailer. Neta claimed the furnace exploded, just as she said it had in their other trailer. The family eventually settled in a trailer park in the town of Berkshire, between Richford and Newark Valley. They lived there nearly five years, until a bank repossessed their trailer. Tim and Neta filed for bankruptcy again.

This time their debts topped $11,000. They had no money in the bank, a 1969 Dodge Charger worth $75, and a 1968 Chevrolet pickup truck with nearly half a million miles on it, worth $50. In 1989, the family moved into a rented farmhouse along Route 38, not far from Davis Hollow Road.

Over the years, the Hoyts came to rely on help from the United Methodist Church in Newark Valley. The church hired Tim to do odd jobs during his layoffs. The family received food from the church pantry and emergency cash allotments of $25 and $50, enough to keep their phone from being disconnected.

The Rev. Lisa Jean Hoefner, pastor of the church, visited the Hoyts one winter and found a cot in the kitchen; Jay slept there because his parents couldn't afford to heat the upstairs. The family's misfortune, so typical of life in the valley, touched her.

"You wouldn't have any luck at all if you didn't have bad luck. That was the Hoyt family," Hoefner said.

Neta continued to lurch from one emotional crisis to the next. In March 1987 she made an emergency visit to the psychiatric clinic in Owego where she'd received counseling fourteen years earlier. Jay, now eleven, was getting on her nerves with his newly acquired dog, she said, and she feared she might lose control.

As part of her screening, Neta filled out forms describing what bothered her and provided a medical history. She circled the word "yes" for twenty-three of the thirty-two ailments listed on the form, including high and low blood pressure. She circled "yes" for all nineteen mental health problems.

Neta complained about family problems, recurrent dreams of accidents and fires, and a loss of sexual desire. Most specifically, Jay's dog bothered her. She was afraid she might hurt the pet or commit some other irrational act. Dr. George Primanis's evaluation revealed no severe psychiatric disorders, such as delusions or hallucinations. But the psychiatrist found she suffered from anxiety and depression.

When Neta met with Primanis a month later, she had some news: Jay's dog was dead, apparently run over by a car. Neta felt both guilty and relieved. She also talked about her continuing problems coping with Jay and mentioned the possibility of getting a part-time job at her son's school, a step that the psychiatrist encouraged as a way to meet mothers who had similar problems with their children. Neta was supposed to see Primanis within two weeks but never went back. She didn't get the job either.

Neta drifted from one unhappy moment to the next. Her mother, Dorothy, died September 1, 1989, from injuries suffered in a car accident. The next month, she and Tim filed for bankruptcy a third time. Nearly a third of the twenty-four creditors were owed for medical expenses. At one point Neta was seeing at least four doctors.

"She'd get a prescription from this one but wouldn't tell this one," Chuck Hoyt said. "She was interacting drugs and stuff, and I think that's where her health went to hell."

In March 1993 Neta said she suffered a cluster heart attack. Six months later, an ambulance crew went to the house on Route 38 to treat Neta for breathing difficulty.

Her behavior seemed to get stranger each passing year. Tim's brother George once saw her parked in a notch along Route 38 where truckers often pulled over to rest. He honked his horn as he drove past, but Neta didn't react. She sat frozen behind the steering wheel, with the vacant gaze that others had seen.

Neta, now forty-seven, draped herself in sadness the way an old woman puts on sweaters in a cold house. People looked at Neta and felt sorry for her. But acquaintances also avoided her gaze when they passed in the grocery store or the post office. They knew that the courtesy of asking about her health was the cue for an endless tale of woe.

More and more, Neta retreated into her narrow world at home. She skipped family gatherings. Tim and Jay took over much of the housework, while Neta bundled up in an afghan and soothed her back with a heating pad. She sat as if waiting for the next crisis to strike.

PART TWO

The Prosecutor

Chapter Six

A lonely light burned on the twelfth floor of the Onondaga County Civic Center in Syracuse as Chief Assistant District Attorney William Fitzpatrick Jr. put in another late night preparing for a murder trial. The thirty-three-year-old prosecutor was nearing the end of an exhausting year. He'd already taken seven homicides to trial in 1985 and won convictions on the highest charge in every case. Now he sat behind the desk in his cramped office, poring over the file on yet another murder.

Prosecuting killers was more than a job for Bill Fitzpatrick; it was a calling. In his nine years with the district attorney's office, Fitzpatrick had earned a reputation for winning tough cases. Cops loved him. They saw this Brooklyn-born son of a cop as one of their own. That's why two investigators from the Onondaga County Sheriff's Department turned up at Fitzpatrick's office on this winter night. They wanted Fitzpatrick's views on an arson in which two young children had died.

Fitzpatrick put aside the case he was working on and took the investigator's file. A believer in destiny, Fitzpatrick would later see the significance of this tiny gesture. But at the time he had no way of knowing that he had picked up the case that would lead to the end of his career as an assistant district attorney. And shape his life afterward.

As the investigators sat watching, Fitzpatrick went

through the file. It contained a sheet of yellow legal paper bearing a note scrawled in green ink, the trademark of Fitzpatrick's boss, District Attorney Richard Hennessy, Jr.: "There's always hope."

Fitzpatrick put the cryptic note aside without giving it much thought. He was more interested in the investigators' report about the fatal fire.

The investigators suspected that the fire had been set by a woman who was having an affair with the children's mother. The suspect had a record of forgery, larceny, and prostitution. More important, she had set fire to three other homes over the last eight years. One of those fires happened after she'd had a spat with another lover. Although she wasn't charged with any of the fires, the woman was committed to a psychiatric hospital after the last one, in 1983.

"For Christ's sake, it's a homicide," Fitzpatrick snapped. "What the hell's the problem?"

The investigators exchanged looks as if to say, "Oh, we're glad you feel that way." They seemed almost disappointed that they didn't have to argue the merits of their case.

Fitzpatrick promised to pick up the case as soon as he finished the one he was working on. But when he presented the arson investigation to a grand jury in January 1986, his boss blew up.

Unbeknownst to Fitzpatrick, Dick Hennessy had reviewed the investigation and decided not to seek an indictment until the suspect confessed. That's what Hennessy's note meant: "There's always hope" she'll confess.

Fitzpatrick had clashed with Hennessy before, but the disputes had always been professional. This fight got personal. Hennessy accused Fitzpatrick of going behind his back and threatened to withhold his signature from the indictment.

The woman had never admitted she set the earlier

fires, and Fitzpatrick was convinced she wouldn't confess to starting the blaze that killed the two children.

"Dick, the bottom line is this: She's going to be indicted," Fitzpatrick said. "This woman killed two kids. She's a psycho. She's going to set a fire again. I don't know if she's going to kill somebody again, but she's going to set another fire. I guarantee you that."

Hennessy finally relented. "You better hope you convict her," he said.

"I guarantee you I'll convict her."

Fitzpatrick expected the disagreement to blow over when Hennessy signed the indictment. That's how Fitzpatrick saw his job: Push the tough cases, the ones nobody wanted, and win convictions.

But the fight left deeper wounds than Fitzpatrick knew. In February he received a memo from Hennessy announcing his reassignment: Fitzpatrick would oversee cases in Family Court and would handle homicides every other month. Another assistant DA would handle homicides that occurred during the other months.

The memo came as a bitter blow. Fitzpatrick felt he was being punished for doing his job. The *Post-Standard,* Syracuse's morning newspaper, took the same view.

An editorial cartoon pictured Fitzpatrick, legal folder and briefcase in hand, casting a huge shadow. Hennessy, throwing a tiny shadow, stood next to him, saying, "Move over please, Fitzy!"

An accompanying editorial questioned whether Hennessy had demoted Fitzpatrick to eliminate a rival: "Was Fitzpatrick moved out of the spotlight because he was doing his job too well? Is it just coincidence that Dick Hennessy's term expires next year, and that Fitzpatrick has expressed interest in the district attorney's job?"

Looking back at his career in the district attorney's office, Fitzpatrick asked himself the same questions.

Bill Fitzpatrick wanted to work as a prosecutor before he entered Syracuse University's law school. During his second year in law school, he started working as a clerk in the district attorney's appeals unit. He researched cases, wrote briefs, and occasionally argued before the state appellate court in Rochester.

A case won by Hennessy, then an assistant district attorney, gave Fitzpatrick his first courtroom experience. He argued the appeal against F. Lee Bailey, and the court upheld the conviction. It was the first of many successes that Fitzpatrick turned from the opportunities Hennessy gave him.

In 1976, Hennessy was elected district attorney, promising a "get-tough" approach to crime. Under his predecessor, only about one-third of the trials produced convictions on the top charge; another third ended in outright acquittal. Hennessy needed a staff of aggressive prosecutors to make good on his promise. In February 1977 he hired Fitzpatrick fresh out of law school.

"He wanted to try cases more than anything else," Hennessy recalled. "And there was no doubt in my mind that he was going to be good at it."

Hennessy put Fitzpatrick on a fast track. Instead of spending the usual two years in city court disposing of misdemeanors and violations, Fitzpatrick worked six months in the appeals unit, then vaulted to the felony trial unit, where he prosecuted every kind of serious crime short of murder.

As an outsider from Brooklyn, Fitzpatrick felt indebted to Hennessy for giving him a start in Syracuse, a conservative, industrial city where the cold, snowy winters fostered a hardy insularity among the inhabitants. Although just an hour's flight from New York City, Syracuse seemed more a part of the Midwest. It stood at the center of Onondaga County, which had 463,000 residents and covered a chunk of central New York more than half the size of Rhode Island.

Working in the district attorney's office also gave Fitzpatrick an introduction to Diane Langenmayr, a

young defense lawyer with an engaging smile and
dark, soulful eyes. Like two courtroom adversaries,
they would never agree on how they met, but Fitzpatrick recalls being smitten by Diane's poise and exotic beauty the first time he saw her in court. They got
to know each other during pretrial negotiations in a felony case and started dating a few months later. They
married May 2, 1981.

Later that year, Hennessy made his twenty-eight-
year-old protégé the youngest senior assistant district
attorney in Onondaga County history. By then, Fitzpatrick was prosecuting murderers.

Just five years out of law school, Fitzpatrick felt as
if he'd made it into the big league. He could think of
no greater test of a lawyer's skills than trying a murder.
He soon earned a reputation for prosecuting cases with
the passion of a grand inquisitor.

The role came naturally for Fitzpatrick. He looked
like a stern young priest, tall and lean, with dark hair
and strong glasses that magnified the intensity of his
icy blue eyes. Conducting cross-examinations in a
deadpan voice that retained traces of a Brooklyn accent, Fitzpatrick could make even routine questions
sound tough. He could play hardball, too, using blunt
accusations and stinging sarcasm against witnesses he
thought were lying.

Fitzpatrick worked hard, and he played hard, and he
pursued both with a cocksure attitude. Colleagues
might have found him overbearing if his pugnacity
hadn't been leavened by a wacky sense of humor.
Fitzpatrick delighted in zany escapades—like joining
another prosecutor for a late-night competition to see
who could hit the longest tee shot on a downtown
street or playing the theme from *Rocky* at full volume
before going into court.

While Hennessy's indulgence for such capers won
Fitzpatrick's affection, Norman Mordue's reputation as
a trial lawyer won Fitzpatrick's admiration.

Mordue had worked his way up the ranks of the DA's office to become chief assistant and head of the trial unit. A master of trial preparation, Mordue preached a simple creed: You win cases by outworking your opponent.

Fitzpatrick learned to sweat the details. He preferred handling cases from the beginning, often getting involved in the police investigation, playing hunches that more than once produced a crucial piece of evidence. In one case, he noticed some fuzz clinging to a velour shirt seized from a suspected rapist. Nobody knew where the strange material came from; the shirt had been sealed in an evidence bag.

During a routine interview with the victim, Fitzpatrick asked her about the attack. "I want you to describe to me the area where you were raped," he said, "and I want you to pretend that I'm blind."

The victim started describing her bed—the sheets, the blankets, the pillow. There was a hole in the pillow, she said, and foam rubber leaked out. Her description clicked in Fitzpatrick's mind. He asked the crime lab to compare the foam filling to the fuzz on the suspect's shirt. The fibers matched.

In the weeks leading up to a trial, Fitzpatrick would sharpen his case with single-minded purpose—a guilty verdict. He would spend twelve hours a day and more reading police reports, autopsy results, and witnesses' statements until he had them memorized. He would bring the case file home and read it in bed.

Diane Fitzpatrick marveled at her husband's ability to shut out everything around him and focus on a case.

"I can sit down and concentrate on a case for a couple of hours and then I need to get up and walk around and let everything sink in," she said. "But he doesn't do that. I mean, he just goes on and on. He knows a case inside and out by the time he's going into the courtroom."

When a case hinged on an arcane discipline such as

ballistics or forensic pathology, Fitzpatrick immersed himself in the topic so he could challenge the opinions of defense experts.

In the final stages of preparation, Fitzpatrick forged the bare facts into a passionate prosecution. He made the case personal, venting his anger at the defendant, and often the defense attorney, sometimes railing against both in the same breath. He wanted to feel the outrage he hoped to evoke from the jury, and he wasn't above using courtroom theatrics to get his point across.

Before one rape trial, Fitzpatrick gave up his habit of biting his nails, letting them grow long. In his summation, he held up a blown-up photo of the defendant's back, showing where the victim had scratched her attacker.

"She left her signature on his back," Fitzpatrick said, screeching his nails across the photo. The jurors cringed, then reached a quick verdict of guilty.

Defense lawyers who didn't like his style accused him of overzealousness. But Fitzpatrick took this as a compliment. He saw himself as a crusader for justice, secure in the righteousness of his cause.

He became a favorite of the media. His in-your-face style made good copy, and provocative statements seemed to roll off his tongue with quotation marks around them. But his outspokenness sometimes got him in trouble.

Tommie Blunt, the local president of the NAACP, criticized remarks that Fitzpatrick made after an all-white jury acquitted a black man of the shooting death of another black man. Fitzpatrick, speaking to reporters, said the verdict may have said to the black community, "we're so used to people on the South Side settling things in their own way, that they can take the law into their own hands."

Blunt accused Fitzpatrick of being a racist and demanded his resignation, but Hennessy leapt to his assistant's defense.

"Mr. Fitzpatrick expressed fear that the verdict itself was racist," he explained. "Rest assured that Mr. Fitzpatrick continues to enjoy my full confidence as a young, brilliant trial attorney."

It was gestures such as this that made Fitzpatrick revere Hennessy, a feisty politician with a shock of silver hair and a winning smile. But Fitzpatrick saw another side to Hennessy when his boss demoted Mordue from chief homicide prosecutor.

"Mordue gets assigned to burglaries," Fitzpatrick said. "I can remember sitting in Mordue's office laughing about it, but we were laughing on the outside, crying on the inside."

Mordue, who compiled a one hundred percent homicide conviction rate over eight years, longed to be DA. His chances of getting the job now seemed remote; Hennessy was in the middle of his second term and showed no signs of relinquishing the job. In January 1983, Mordue became a county court judge, and Fitzpatrick emerged as chief homicide prosecutor. The murder of millionaire James Pipines the next month quickly thrust Fitzpatrick onto center stage.

The fifty-eight-year-old businessman was shot to death in the master bedroom of his luxurious suburban home on his thirty-third wedding anniversary. A single .38-caliber slug had ripped through his head as he lay in bed.

Pipines's nude body was found by Cynthia Pugh, the comptroller of his roofing company and, the state police soon learned, his mistress for more than a decade. Two weeks later, the state police arrested the forty-five-year-old Pugh. Investigators identified the murder weapon as a derringer owned by the man Pugh lived with.

The Cynthia Pugh case aroused curiosity in Syracuse like no other in recent memory. A wealthy victim. A younger mistress. Infidelity. Murder. The pressure of handling the sensational case put Fitzpatrick on an emotional roller coaster that would last more than a year.

The trial opened August 1, 1983, and played out like a soap opera into autumn. Spectators lined up outside the courtroom to gawk at the key players.

The case pitted Fitzpatrick, ten weeks shy of his thirty-first birthday, against seventy-six-year-old Paul Shanahan, who in a career spanning fifty years had made a reputation as the best lawyer in Syracuse. Shanahan possessed a voice that Shakespearean actors could envy, and he used it to full effect to sway juries. One prospective juror said she was glad she'd been picked for the Pugh trial because she wanted to see Shanahan work.

Three days before the start of the trial, Hennessy reaffirmed his support for Fitzpatrick by naming him chief assistant district attorney. But the promotion didn't improve his chances in the courtroom; Fitzpatrick had a spotty, circumstantial case.

The trial dragged on for eight weeks as Fitzpatrick and Shanahan called nearly seventy witnesses. Fitzpatrick got so wrapped up in the case that he stopped eating and dropped fifteen pounds. After fifty hours of deliberation spread over five excruciating days, the jury remained deadlocked eleven to one for acquittal. A mistrial was declared. Fitzpatrick's roller coaster plunged.

Fitzpatrick took responsibility for presenting a confusing case. He wouldn't have blamed Hennessy for giving the retrial to someone else, but his boss stuck by him. Hennessy's support meant all the more because he faced reelection in less than a month, and this time he looked vulnerable.

Hennessy's popularity had waned since 1979, when he won reelection to a second term by nearly 70,000 votes. Feuds with the press came back to haunt him when both of Syracuse's daily newspapers endorsed his opponent. When Hennessy squeaked back into of-

fice by a 602-vote margin, one newspaper columnist
dubbed him "Landslide" Hennessy.

Six months later, Fitzpatrick repaid Hennessy's confidence by convicting Cynthia Pugh of murder.
Fitzpatrick's roller coaster ride was over.

"It was an emotional thing," he said. "I had never
been through anything like Cynthia Pugh, ever. Nor
will I ever in my life. I don't think physically I could
stand it. It was an incredible, incredible experience to
have won that case, when a jury had voted eleven to
one to acquit six months earlier."

The victim's family gave Fitzpatrick a plaque inscribed: "To Bill Fitzpatrick, the greatest prosecutor
we'll ever know."

Others shared that view. Lawyers began talking
about Fitzpatrick as a future district attorney. In January 1985, the Syracuse *Herald American* featured him
in a roundup of movers and shakers in fields ranging
from the arts to law. He spoke publicly for the first
time about his ambition to become DA. Ever the loyal
assistant, he deferred to his boss's plans, saying,
"When and if Mr. Hennessy should call it a day, I
would like to run for district attorney."

Without realizing it, Fitzpatrick had become a political threat to Hennessy. The newspaper profile held the
first clue. After praising Fitzpatrick for being "as tal-
ented [an attorney] as we've ever seen in a courtroom
in Syracuse," Hennessy added: "The only other person
to beat Shanahan more times than him is me." The
message was clear: However important Fitzpatrick had
become, Hennessy still considered himself the best
prosecutor in town.

Fitzpatrick didn't begin to sense the depths of the ri-
valry until the blowup over the fatal arson case. When
Hennessy reassigned him to Family Court in February
1986, Fitzpatrick saw it as a replay of the falling-out
with Mordue.

Fitzpatrick thought about quitting on the spot, but a

thread of loyalty tugged at his conscience. For nine years, Hennessy had been a great boss, giving him every chance to excel as a prosecutor and sticking by him during tough times. Now Hennessy faced a crisis: His wife, Ellie, was dying of cancer. Fitzpatrick was fond of Ellie Hennessy. He didn't feel he could walk out on her husband and leave cases like the fatal fire unresolved. He decided to put off his resignation until the end of the year.

The fatal arson case kept Fitzpatrick busy into the summer of 1986. The defendant was found guilty of murder, just as Fitzpatrick had promised. In August she was sentenced to the maximum, twenty-five years to life.

Shortly afterward, Hennessy transferred one of his cases to Fitzpatrick. Ellie Hennessy was near death, and her husband needed time to be with her.

Fitzpatrick took *People* v. *Stephen Van Der Sluys* without complaint; he knew it would be the last case he handled for Hennessy. He also knew it would be a formidable challenge.

Stephen Van Der Sluys was accused of the most ruthless act imaginable, killing his baby daughter. Although it had taken more than ten years to bring charges against Van Der Sluys, Fitzpatrick had less than a month to prepare for trial. During that time, he had to master a subject he knew nothing about—sudden infant death syndrome.

Chapter Seven

Something told Bob Chase he should take special care in preserving the body of the baby girl laid out before him in the tiny white casket at Dunn Funeral Home. He'd performed all the customary procedures to prepare her for viewing by her family: He'd done an arterial embalming, injecting a formaldehyde-like solution into the body's circulatory system; he'd preserved the internal organs separately; he'd then performed what undertakers call a "shake and bake," placing the body in a plastic bag with Hexaphene, a pink, viscous embalming chemical, and letting it sit overnight while the fumes penetrated and preserved tissues. Now, just before closing the lid, Chase opened a jar containing a little Hexaphene and tucked it into the bottom of the casket. Once he sealed the casket lid, the Hexaphene fumes would envelope the body in a protective shroud.

The extra step took a mere fifteen seconds, but somewhere in the back of his mind, Chase suspected that this casket wouldn't stay buried. And if it was ever exhumed, he wanted the little girl dressed in the blue corduroy smock to be perfectly preserved. According to her death certificate, the baby died of sudden infant death syndrome. But something about this child's death had troubled Chase since he'd been called to pick up her body two nights before.

The phone rang at Dunn Funeral Home around one o'clock on the morning of January 12, 1979, waking Chase and his wife, Patti. The Chases lived in an apartment above the funeral parlor at 319 Park Avenue in Mechanicville, New York, a city of 5,000 that had grown up around a railroad junction on the Hudson River, about half an hour north of Albany. Chase had managed the funeral home for about a year and a half, since moving east from Syracuse, 150 miles away. As a funeral director and a volunteer firefighter, Chase had trained himself to snap awake for such late-night calls; he picked up the phone before the third ring. The police officer on the other end told Chase the coroner wanted him to handle a body removal—a baby. He gave Chase the address—411 Park Avenue—an apartment house just four doors away.

"What's up?" Patti Chase asked as her husband hung up.

"Jeez, that's funny. There's a baby call up the street and the name is Van Der Sluys." A sudden chill passed between them.

The unusual Dutch name, meaning "house of Sluys," drew Chase back almost two years to the day, to the John G. Butler Funeral Home in Syracuse. Chase had worked around the funeral home while attending mortuary school. In return for his labor, he and Patti got to live above the casket house next door. That's how he came to help with the funeral of a two-month-old girl named Heather Van Der Sluys, who died of SIDS on January 7, 1977.

Another student working at the Butler Funeral Home recognized the name. "We've worked for this family before with a baby," he told Chase. "They've lost another one to SIDS."

He was only partly right. Chase checked the funeral home's records and found that Stephen and Jane Van Der Sluys had lost their first child on October 8, 1976, exactly three months before Heather's death. But sixteen-month-old Heath Jason Van Der Sluys hadn't died of SIDS; he apparently choked to death on a quarter.

Three years later, as Chase dressed to go out into this wickedly cold night, he braced himself for the grim task of removing a dead baby. His every move bespoke the particular tact of his profession. Even at such a late hour he took time to put on a suit coat and tie before bundling up in a ski jacket.

Chase drove up the street in his dark-green station wagon and parked in front of a large, three-story apartment house with a gambrel roof and a wraparound porch. The night was clear and quiet except for the sound of the hard-packed snow crunching under Chase's shoes. He carried a baby-removal case, an inconspicuous black wooden box the size of a small footlocker. To anyone on the street, he looked like a salesman getting home late with his sample case.

The mechanics of the job usually helped keep Chase's mind off the tragedy at hand, but tonight the prospect of facing another baby named Van Der Sluys preoccupied his thoughts. Just before reaching the apartment on the third floor, he paused on the landing and set down the baby-removal case; he didn't want the sight of the box to shock the family. Inside the apartment, he encountered a quiet knot of people who had been drawn there in ones and twos by the events of the last few hours.

Chase's entrance marked the final act in a drama that had begun around eleven P.M., when Jane Van Der Sluys left the apartment to help her father and mother with one of their cleaning-business jobs—washing the floor at the Grand Union supermarket just around the corner. She left Steve alone with their baby, Vickie Lynn. Not long afterward, Judith Fantauzzi, a downstairs neighbor, heard noises from the Van Der Sluyses' apartment and went upstairs to check. She saw Steve bending over Vickie Lynn's crib and asked if everything was okay. Steve assured her that all was well and asked her to leave. Years later, Fantauzzi would tell police that as she left she saw Steve pick up Vickie Lynn; the baby looked blue.

Fantauzzi and Abel Aldrich, another downstairs neighbor, heard Jane Van Der Sluys return home shortly after midnight. A few minutes later, Jane ran down the stairs, screaming. Aldrich raced to the Van Der Sluyses' apartment and saw Vickie Lynn lying motionless in her crib. Jane collected herself enough to call her parents, Jim and Anita Bowers, who had just returned to their home, less than three miles out of town. Jim Bowers called the Mechanicville Police Department, then headed to Steve and Jane's apartment.

Patrolmen Tom Salvadore and Ralph Peluso arrived first, and Jane directed them to Vickie Lynn's crib; the baby was obviously dead. Members of the John Ahearn Rescue Squad arrived, checked Vickie Lynn, and left, saying there was nothing they could do. Frank Kearney, Saratoga County's coroner, came next. Kearney was an elected official, not a trained medical examiner. Emergency workers at death scenes sometimes kidded Kearney about confusing his part-time coroner's duties with his full-time job—auto mechanic. He would approach a body, lift an arm, and somebody would say, "Jeez, you checking for ball joints or seeing if it's rigor mortis?" Kearney took the ribbing goodnaturedly, but nobody was heartless enough to crack jokes in the Van Der Sluyses' apartment.

Chase focused on the family members sitting around the kitchen table in a tableau of grief. Jane Van Der Sluys was sobbing. Her father sat with her. Steve Van Der Sluys, standing behind his father-in-law, nodded to Chase. The look of recognition in Steve's red-rimmed eyes confirmed Chase's suspicion: This was the same couple who had lost two children in Syracuse.

Officer Salvadore led Chase to Vickie Lynn's bedroom. As soon as they were out of earshot of the family, Chase confided in Salvadore.

"Look," Chase said in a low voice, "you better do your homework on this because they lost two before."

The family had explained all that, Salvadore said: The other two children died of SIDS, and this probably was SIDS too. An autopsy had been ordered because the death was unattended. Salvadore's lack of concern did little to reassure Chase.

Chase found the baby with the light brown hair lying on her tummy in the crib. He saw no blood, no sign of injury, only sadness. With her pastel yellow blanket pulled up around her, Vickie Lynn looked like any other sleeping infant.

He returned to the silent kitchen and asked if anyone wanted to spend a few minutes with Vickie Lynn before he took her away. While Steve and Jane and her father headed into the nursery, Chase went to get the black box.

By the time he made his way back to the nursery, everyone had left the room. He closed the door and went to work, opening the black box and arranging Vickie Lynn's quilted blanket inside. He handled the baby as if she were alive, gently lifting her from the crib, placing her in the box, and wrapping the blanket around her.

The task of removing Vickie Lynn from her nursery could have easily overwhelmed Chase. He closed caskets on adults almost every day without a second thought, but the death of a child still affected him, no matter how many he handled. The baby-removal box could retract from three feet to eighteen inches, but even at its smallest, it seemed too big for Vickie Lynn's body. As Chase closed the box, he tried to think of something else. But his mind came back to the troubling pattern of deaths in the Van Der Sluys family. Three infant deaths in one family just didn't set right. Chase's vain warning echoed in his head: "You better do your homework on this."

Chase stopped in the kitchen on the way out.

Kearney, the coroner, had left. Chase gave Jim Bowers his card and suggested the family call in the morning to make the funeral arrangements. He then drove to Saratoga Hospital, twenty minutes away, and left Vickie Lynn's body at the morgue.

That afternoon, Steve and Jane Van Der Sluys came to the funeral home with Jim Bowers. Chase sat them in his office and began to gather information for Vickie Lynn's death certificate and an obituary. Jane seemed still in shock, so Steve did most of the talking. Once again, Chase saw the look of recognition in Steve's eyes, but neither of them spoke of their earlier encounter in Syracuse.

The meeting went quickly. Steve and Jane arranged for Vickie Lynn's funeral two days later, a Monday. They chose to have an open-casket service at the funeral home. Burial would have to wait; Mechanicville was in the grip of a cold snap, and the ground at Hudson View Cemetery had frozen rock-hard.

After the family left, Chase ordered a casket, a Wilbur Company "Cherub" model, made of indestructible plastic. It cost a little more than other models, but Chase wouldn't bury a baby in a casket he wouldn't have used for a child of his own. He then drove to Saratoga to pick up Vickie Lynn's body and death certificate.

Dr. Jack Paston, a pathologist at Saratoga Hospital, had done an autopsy and found nothing remarkable. He had listed the cause of death as SIDS. Chase kept his suspicions to himself.

That evening, Chase began the toughest part of his job: preparing Vickie Lynn's body for viewing. Chase hated working with babies, and an autopsy made the job more difficult. He spent a couple of hours performing an arterial embalming and repairing the damage from the autopsy. Finally he placed the body in a plastic bag with Hexaphene-soaked gauze and left it overnight.

The next morning, Steve and Jane returned to the funeral home with clothes for Vickie Lynn to wear at the viewing. In a conversation that Patti Chase would remember for years, Steve insisted that the Chases return the sleeper Vickie Lynn was wearing when she died, along with her blanket. They wanted them for their next child, he said.

But Steve Van Der Sluys had run up against one of the Chases' inviolable rules: Babies need a blanket to take to the grave. The Van Der Sluyses hadn't brought a blanket to replace the one Vickie Lynn had been wrapped in, and the Chases wouldn't put a baby in a casket without one; it just didn't look right.

"The blanket goes with the baby," Bob Chase explained.

Jane Van Der Sluys agreed. "We need to have a blanket, and I know that's clean," she told her husband.

As soon as the casket arrived, the Chases began preparing for the funeral. Patti dressed Vickie Lynn as if she was her own child, right down to a diaper and a pair of socks. After they arranged Vickie Lynn in the casket with her blanket and a pink pillow for her head, Bob Chase set up the viewing room.

A thin stream of mourners arrived the next morning, walking down the street from Steve and Jane's apartment. Bob Chase nodded to the dozen or so relatives who entered the funeral home. The mourners filed into the viewing room, where music played in the background. They peered into the open casket and then, weeping, moved on to take a seat or find an empty patch of carpet.

As Chase expected, there was little talking. Babies' funerals tended to be quiet affairs, and in his view that made them all the sadder. At an adult's funeral, the mourners' spirits eventually lighten with conversation. But not at a baby's. If anything, the grief grows worse. The sudden, unexpected death of a healthy baby poses so many unanswered questions, especially for the parents. How? Why? Why us? And in the silence, Chase knew, a lot of young parents lost faith—in God, in each other, in themselves.

Chase moved into a side room, where he half listened to a Jehovah's Witness elder lead the prayer service. Half an hour later, the mourners drifted toward the door, leaving Steve and Jane in the viewing room. Chase stood back, hoping the couple wouldn't pick up Vickie Lynn's body. Grieving parents sometimes snatched their baby's remains from the casket. It didn't happen often, and Chase saw nothing wrong with such desperate gestures, but each heartbreaking scene had been burned into his memory and he didn't need another.

After a few minutes, Steve and Jane left, and Chase found himself alone again with Vickie Lynn. He moved the casket back to the embalming room and began working a space-age sealer into the grooved lip of the casket. As he focused on the task, the thought that he would see this baby again hovered somewhere beneath the surface of his consciousness. Just before closing the lid, Chase tucked a nearly empty jar of Hexaphene into Vickie Lynn's casket. He placed a weight on top of the casket to make sure the lid set in the sealer and left it overnight. Inside, the protective fumes surrounded Vickie Lynn. The next day, he took the casket to Hudson View Cemetery, where it would be stored in a vault until burial.

As January wore on into February, Bob Chase couldn't shake his doubts about Vickie Lynn's death. It didn't seem possible that one family could lose three infants, one after another. He talked to Patti about his concerns, but they found no easy answer. Then he came across a fact sheet from the National Sudden Infant Death Syndrome Foundation that seemed to confirm his suspicions.

"According to the best available data, SIDS is not hereditary, and any future babies in the family will run no more than a one per cent risk of recurrence," the pamphlet said.

Chase took the pamphlet and his misgivings about the Van Der Sluys children's deaths to Harvey LaBar, a state police investigator he knew through the Mechanicville volunteer fire department. LaBar was a twenty-year veteran of police work with a gruff, John Wayne manner and the six-foot, three-inch, 230-pound bulk to match. In his forties, he still cut an imposing figure, but as an investigator he relied more on brains than brawn. Born and raised above his grandfather's grocery in Mechanicville, LaBar knew the area so well he did most of his investigating by phone. He started to make calls about Steve Van Der Sluys, jotting information in a stenographer's notebook. He never imagined he would be facing retirement by the time he closed the book on this case.

LaBar didn't have to go any farther than James Bowers to confirm Chase's suspicions. The best Bowers could say about his son-in-law was that he was a good talker who made a good first impression. That's what attracted Bower's daughter Jane to him in the first place.

Friends introduced Jane Bowers and Steve Van Der Sluys in the spring of 1970 at a Jehovah's Witness Kingdom Hall in Troy, a small city between Albany and Mechanicville. Jane was fourteen, Steve was four years older. Five feet, five inches, he had thick, dark hair and blue eyes, and Jane thought he looked cute. His good manners and piety charmed the impressionable girl, and she dated him for the next four years. On May 18, 1974, five days after Jane's eighteenth birthday, they got engaged.

James Bowers thought his future son-in-law seemed shady. He tried to warn his daughter, but she was a high school senior in a hurry to grow up and didn't listen. She married Steve on August 10, 1974, in the Kingdom Hall in Troy.

The Kingdom Hall in Mechanicville, where the Bowers family had worshiped for years, accepted Steve into the fold shortly after he married Jane. But, as Bowers explained to LaBar, the church suspended Steve several months later for making sexual advances toward Jane's younger sister, Sue.

Bowers tried to help the struggling couple by setting Steve up with several of his floor-cleaning accounts. But Steve didn't do the work and lost most of the clients. He just wasn't dependable.

Bowers told LaBar he suspected that Steve had something to do with the children's deaths but didn't feel he could condemn his daughter's husband without proof.

LaBar's suspicions grew when he received reports on two bogus burglaries reported by Steve. Steve told Mechanicville police that somebody entered the front door of his Park Avenue apartment on August 8, 1977, and took a nineteen-inch color television and a clock radio. He said he found a key on the kitchen table with a message: "We have revenge." Officers found the TV set and clock radio in a garage behind the apartment house.

Three months later, Steve reported another break-in. This time, more than $6,500 worth of property was missing, Steve said, including television sets, jewelry, and expensive electronics, all insured. He filed a claim with the insurance company and submitted canceled checks to prove he owned the missing property. But the insurance company quickly traced the checks to other purchases, and Steve dropped the claim rather than take a lie-detector test.

LaBar learned that Steve also had claimed several disabilities as a result of auto accidents and on-the-job injuries.

What bothered the investigator more were the reports that Syracuse police sent about the deaths of the Van Der Sluyses' first two children.

Jane got pregnant soon after her wedding, and she and Steve moved to Syracuse. The couple moved into a basement apartment not far from the home of his parents, Jack and Hazel Van Der Sluys. On May 26, 1975, after sixteen hours of labor, Jane delivered her first child, a seven-pound, ten-ounce boy. They named him Heath Jason.

Later that year, with Steve out of work again, the struggling family cut expenses by moving in with Steve's parents. Steve returned to his parents' home at a difficult time: Hazel had liver cancer. Her death in July 1976 at age forty-four disturbed Steve deeply. Jack Van Der Sluys compounded the hurt when he quickly fell in love with Jane's oldest sister, Debbie. Steve thought his father's affection for Debbie Bowers betrayed the memory of his mother. The crises in Steve's life began to mount. Jane was pregnant again, and as autumn came, Jack and Debbie talked about getting married.

At 3:33 P.M. on October 8, a Syracuse police dispatcher broadcast a Signal 78—baby choking—at 3808 South Salina Street, the Van Der Sluys home. Officer Bruce Kiggins was parked in Valley Plaza, almost directly across the street. He entered the house a minute later and found Heath on a couch in the living room. The child's face had turned blue.

An off-duty officer saw Kiggins's patrol car and stopped to help perform cardiopulmonary resuscitation. They worked on Heath for nearly twenty minutes, until an ambulance crew arrived and rushed the baby to Community-General Hospital, less than three miles away. Heath Van Der Sluys was pronounced dead on arrival at 4:05 P.M. The body was taken to the Onondaga County medical examiner's office.

A hasty investigation followed. Kiggins questioned the parents, who said Heath had gone down for a nap around noon. Steve said he went into Heath's room about ten minutes later to put some loose change in a jar he was using to save money for his son. Worried that the dropping of coins in the jar might wake Heath, Steve put the change on a plastic diaper pail next to the crib.

Steve said he returned to the room about three-thirty to awaken Heath. He shook the baby, but he didn't wake up. He said he got scared, picked Heath up, shook him hard, and a quarter fell out of the baby's mouth. When Heath still showed no signs of life, Steve called the police.

Two Syracuse police investigators talked to Kiggins at the medical examiner's office. A cursory examination of Heath's body showed no signs of physical abuse; the baby was clean, and there were no cuts or bruises. "Closed Pending Results of Autopsy ..." the investigators said at the bottom of their report.

The next day, Dr. Martin F. Hilfinger Jr., the Onondaga County medical examiner, signed the death certificate. A few days later, another investigator added three lines to the report: "Learned from Medical Examiner's Office that victim's death was due to ASPHYXIATION DUE TO OBSTRUCTION IN AIRWAY. Death accidental ... Cleared and Closed."

Hilfinger did not perform an autopsy. The investigators didn't question Steve. Nobody took evidence from Heath's room. As far as the world was concerned, the baby had choked to death on a quarter. Heath was buried in White Chapel Memory Gardens two days later. Eleven days after the funeral, Jane went into labor.

Although this labor lasted only ten hours, Jane had a more difficult time. The doctor had to use forceps to deliver the baby girl, who emerged with the umbilical cord wrapped loosely around her neck. She looked a little blue, but they gave her oxygen, and within a few minutes she looked like any other eight-pound, one-ounce newborn. They named the baby Heather Joy.

Heather developed normally, gaining almost three pounds by the time of her six-week checkup on December 3. Jane told the pediatrician, Dr. Robert Chavkin, that Heather was nursing well. She was a little fussy in the evening, but had slept up to nine hours at night.

Jack and Debbie got married later that month, and this put a strain on the living arrangements in Jack's house. With Steve working again cleaning businesses, he and Jane could afford to move out. They found a $150-a-month apartment with a working fireplace on the second floor of a house at 376 Bryant Avenue on Tipperary Hill, Syracuse's Irish-American enclave.

Jane and Steve set to work painting Heather's nursery and moved her bassinet to the kitchen. The baby was sleeping in the kitchen when Jane and Steve went to bed around ten-thirty on the evening of December 30, a Thursday. Jane woke about an hour later and found Steve standing beside the bed with Heather in his hands, saying something was wrong with the baby.

Heather looked pale and limp, her eyes open but unfocused. Jane took her into the dining room and gave her mouth-to-mouth resuscitation. Between breaths, she told Steve to call for help. Syracuse police broadcast another Signal 78.

Officer Joseph A. West arrived with an ambulance crew and found Heather breathing shallowly. Edward Moser, an ambulance attendant, grabbed Heather and administered first aid as he carried her into the back of the ambulance. Steve and Jane rode in the front to Upstate Medical Center.

By the time Heather reached the hospital, her temperature had dropped from a normal 98.6 degrees to 97. Fearing a serious infection, the hospital staff performed a spinal tap to test for meningitis and began treatment with antibiotics as a precaution. The test came back negative and by midnight, Heather was breathing normally.

Steve told the police that he had been getting ready for work around 11:20 when he heard Heather whimpering in her bassinet. When he checked on her, she was having trouble breathing. The case was closed with no further investigation.

Heather's hospital stay passed uneventfully over the New Year's weekend. Dr. Chavkin, her pediatrician, saw her on Sunday, January 2, and sent her home the next day with an appointment for a routine checkup three days later.

During the office visit, Jane said Heather had experienced no problems since leaving the hospital. Chavkin examined Heather, gave her an oral polio vaccine and sent her home a normal, healthy baby. The next day, she was dead.

Jane had left the apartment around four-thirty p.m. on Friday, January 7, to buy a curling iron. Heather was asleep in her bassinet, and Steve said he was going to shower. Jane returned less than an hour later and found Heather motionless in the bassinet. She called to Steve to phone the police, but she knew from the moment she picked Heather up that the baby was dead. While Jane held Heather in her arms and paced, the Syracuse police broadcast another Signal 78 for 376 Bryant Avenue.

Officer Brian Murphy found Steve and Jane waiting outside with Heather. Murphy and another officer, John Kerwin, tried to resuscitate the baby until the ambulance crew arrived and took her to Community-General Hospital. Heather arrived with no vital signs, and except for an apparent injection of chemicals directly into the heart, no attempts were made to revive her. She was pronounced dead at 6:45 P.M. in the same emergency room where her brother Heath had been dead on arrival three months earlier.

The police report said Heather apparently died of

natural causes, and the body was turned over to the medical examiner's office. The next morning, assistant medical examiner Dr. William D. Alsever performed an autopsy. Alsever found some blood in the membrane encasing the heart, probably as a result of the injection administered at the hospital. He noted tiny hemorrhages in the lungs and heart and signs of a possible respiratory infection, but none of these findings indicated how Heather died. Her death certificate listed sudden infant death syndrome as the cause.

On January 21, a note was added to the police report on Heather's death: "Natural, Case Cleared and Closed." By that time, Heather had been buried beside Heath.

Distraught by the death of her second baby, Jane wanted to be closer to her family. She and Steve returned to Mechanicville and picked up their lives. In October, Vickie Lynn was born. Because of Heather's death, Vickie Lynn was considered to have a high risk for SIDS. She underwent tests at Albany Medical Center, a teaching hospital in the state capital, to determine whether she suffered from apnea. LaBar later learned the evaluation showed Vickie Lynn was in perfect health, but fifteen months later, she was dead, too.

The investigator saw a pattern emerging in the deaths of Heath, Heather, and Vickie Lynn: Each had been a normal, healthy baby; each had experienced a sudden breathing problem; and each had been alone with Steve Van Der Sluys. Even if Heath's death was an accident, the deaths of Heather and Vickie Lynn remained suspicious. A doctor working on a SIDS study for the state health department told LaBar that the odds against SIDS occurring with two, three, or more infants in the same family were astronomical. And SIDS usually struck children less than eleven months old. Fifteen months—Vickie Lynn's age—was too old for SIDS.

LaBar suspected that Steve, with a history of insurance scams, had killed the children to collect on insurance. But the insurance industry's policy of confidentiality frustrated the investigator's efforts to nail down greed as a motive.

By April 1979 LaBar's steno notebook bulged with information. He and his partner, Senior Investigator Robert Bryan, thought they had enough on Steve to take the case to Saratoga County district attorney David Wait. The investigators asked Wait to subpoena a host of insurance companies to see whether they had sold any policies to Steve. They also asked Wait to have Vickie Lynn's body exhumed and reexamined. Wait refused both requests.

Under New York law, a district attorney can't issue subpoenas without launching a grand jury investigation. Although Wait agreed that the investigation had raised suspicions about Stephen Van Der Sluys, there was no hard evidence on which to base a criminal proceeding.

LaBar and Bryan pushed ahead to the next option: questioning Stephen Van Der Sluys. The investigators wanted to bring Steve to the state police barracks in Malta, Saratoga County, where they could interview him in a controlled setting. By the end of April 1979 they had everything they needed except Steve Van Der Sluys; he and Jane had left Mechanicville. Not even James Bowers knew where they'd gone.

Chapter Eight

Harvey LaBar kept up with the Van Der Sluys case by periodically punching Steve's name and date of birth into the state motor vehicle computer to see if he had filed a new address. Steve's driver's license eventually expired, but LaBar kept checking. On August 11, 1981, more than two years after he opened his investigation, LaBar got a break. Steve had renewed his New York license four months earlier; the computer showed he now lived in Victor, a town in Ontario County, in New York's Finger Lakes region.

LaBar pulled together all the information he had on Stephen Van Der Sluys, ripping dozens of pages out of his notebook, and sent the material to the state police barracks in Canandaigua, the Ontario County seat. Investigator William Morshimer picked up where LaBar had left off.

After Vickie Lynn's death, Steve and Jane moved to Tulsa, Oklahoma, so Steve could attend school for specialized welding. In 1981 they relocated to Victor, where a friend was going to get Steve a welding job. But like so many of Steve's plans, this one didn't pan out. For Steve and Jane, life went on as before: Steve scraped along by running a cleaning business; Jane prayed to have more children; together they professed their faith as Jehovah's Witnesses at a nearby Kingdom Hall.

Four months before LaBar located them, on April 24, 1981, Jane gave birth to a son, Shane Jessie. Morshimer learned that the baby underwent a SIDS evaluation at Strong Memorial Hospital in Rochester, the nearest major city. Like Vickie, Shane was considered a high risk because a sibling had died of SIDS—in his case, two. Extensive tests revealed that Shane had a minor breathing abnormality, and he was sent home on an apnea monitor.

Morshimer tracked down the respiratory specialist who examined Shane at Strong Memorial. Dr. John Brooks was suspicious about the deaths of the other Van Der Sluys children, especially after Morshimer told him Steve had been alone with each child. The investigator took the precaution of asking the local rescue squad to notify the state police about any emergency calls to the Van Der Sluys home.

Then Morshimer got a lead on the motive LaBar had suspected from the start: An informant told him that Vickie Lynn's life had been insured. The state police eventually learned that Heath's and Heather's lives were insured for $10,000 each. For Vickie Lynn, Steve Van Der Sluys upped the insurance to $30,000. He had used the money to buy cars and cleaning equipment and a stereo.

At that point the investigation ground to a halt again. The state police still had only circumstantial evidence, and their case wasn't likely to get any stronger without a confession. Fearing that Steve might ask for a lawyer if they confronted him prematurely, the state police waited for an opportunity to get him in a controlled setting where they could interview him at length. It took almost four years, but Steve finally gave them the chance. On April 3, 1985, he was charged with raping a sixteen-year-old foster child.

The girl was the daughter of a troubled Jehovah's Witness couple Steve and Jane had known for several years. Social workers placed the girl in the Van Der Sluyses' home in 1984, after her father struck her dur-

ing a family argument. She and Steve soon began
having sex, and in early 1985 the girl got pregnant.

When the girl's mother found out about the pregnancy, she reported Steve to the police. Then thirty-
three, Steve admitted having sex with the underage girl
and was arrested on thirty-six counts of statutory rape
and sodomy. For the second time in Steve's life, a Jehovah's Witness congregation stripped him of member-
ship. His predicament was complicated by the fact that
Jane now had two children at home and was pregnant
with a third.

Steve's arrest suddenly revived interest in the deaths
of Heath and Heather in Syracuse, where the police department had been quietly tracking the state police investigation. John Brennan and Danny Boyle, the
Syracuse Police Department's top homicide investigators, were assigned the case.

As long as the rape charges were pending, Steve
could not be questioned without his lawyer's consent.
While that case worked its way through court, Brennan
and Boyle brought themselves up to date on the nine-
year-old investigation of the children's deaths. They
spent weeks canvassing the Syracuse and Mechanicville neighborhoods where Steve and Jane had lived.
They interviewed Bob Chase at his funeral home and
quizzed the Syracuse patrolmen who rushed to the Signal 78s for Heath and Heather.

The legal shield protecting Steve from police questioning fell in July, when he pleaded guilty in the rape
case and was sentenced to one year in the Ontario
County Jail. Brennan and Boyle, who had the freshest
information on the deaths of the three children, got the
first shot at talking to him.

On the morning of September 6, 1985, they drove to
Canandaigua, seventy miles west of Syracuse, where
they met Robert Beswick, the state police investigator
who had handled the rape case. Beswick took Brennan
and Boyle to the jail and introduced them to Steve.

Steve seemed surprised to see the Syracuse investigators, especially when they said they wanted to talk about the deaths of his children.

The initial interview didn't go anywhere; Steve denied any involvement in the children's deaths. Brennan and Boyle switched gears and asked him if he would take a polygraph test. Steve agreed, but by the time they got him to the state police barracks and set up with a polygraph expert, he'd changed his mind. Brennan and Boyle went into the interview room to try to question him again.

"We get in there and he's physically nervous. He's shaking and he had a tough time looking at us," Brennan said. The investigators quickly sized Steve up as a wimp, but they also detected a hint of remorse and decided to take advantage of it.

"We weren't playing good cop/bad cop or anything like that," Brennan said. "We weren't going to get hard with him about the insurance or anything like that till we got him to roll over. We were the window, we were the way out, and we were just going to give him an out.

"We just started talking to him: 'Hey, look, you're a young guy. You were left alone with the children. You probably couldn't handle it.' "

After twenty-five minutes, Steve broke down in tears and began talking. Although he insisted that Heath's death had been an accident, he admitted in vague terms that he was responsible for the deaths of Heather and Vickie Lynn. Steve denied that the insurance money was a motive. He said he just couldn't handle being left alone to care for the baby girls.

"When he started crying, we knew we had him," Boyle said. "He said: 'I've been waiting for years for somebody to come talk to me about this.' "

But after the initial breakdown, Steve's confession slowed to a trickle. Brennan and Boyle and two state police investigators took turns questioning him. After a few hours, Brennan and Boyle tried another tack. At 5:20 P.M., they gave Steve a pen and paper to write a statement.

"We wanted to get something in his own writing to show that we didn't coerce it out of him," Boyle said. "He started to write, then we realized it was going to be a long time."

Steve began writing an essay on his troubled life: "My mind and heart has [sic] many problems to deal with. Problems such as rationalization, having a hard time distinguishing between reality and fantasy, lack of confidence and total indecisiveness. For years I have had an extreme amount of difficulty making decisions. Until today.... I feel like a man again. The weight has been lifted off me. All these years I have been pummeled into submission by indecisiveness."

He continued to write as the investigators took his order for dinner from a McDonald's restaurant. He took a twenty-minute break to eat, then resumed writing. After nearly two hours, Brennan and Boyle called a halt to the exercise in penmanship; Steve had written nothing in his four-page statement about killing his children.

Brennan and Boyle went back to questioning Steve. Brennan used a typewriter to take down the statement.

"I was home alone with Heather because my wife had gone out. I went to check on Heather and I noticed that she had difficulty breathing and it seemed that her breathing was getting worse. At first I was indecisive and I had this intense feeling that she was going to die. I felt that there was nothing I could do and I felt that she should die. I had Heather in my arms and I took her and laid her face down into the crib. I laid her face on something white, but I do not remember if it was a pillow or a bassinet. I watched her for a few minutes and Heather was making noises like she could not breathe. Finally she stopped the noise and I thought that she was dead. I then went into the bathroom and took a shower."

Steve implicated himself more explicitly in Vickie Lynn's death.

"Shortly after Jane left the apartment, Vickie started screaming and crying loudly. I went to see what was wrong and Vickie was standing in her crib and screaming. I picked her up and put her on the dressing table and she was still screaming. I then took my hand and put it over Vickie's mouth and kept it there about a minute, trying to get her to calm down.

"I picked her up and she was still crying and I knew that Vickie was going to die. I put her head against my shoulder and held her head against my shoulder with her nose and mouth against my shoulder. I wanted her to stop crying and I held her like that for about five minutes. I held her like that for about five minutes until she stopped crying and then I felt her go limp. I put her in my arms and cradled her and held her a while. I knew that she was not breathing and that she was going to die. I then took Vickie and laid her face down in her crib and put her face into the pillow, just like I had done with Heather. I stood there looking at Vickie and thinking, 'This was the way it had to be and that she was going to die anyway.' These are the same feelings I had when Heather died. I then went into the bedroom and laid there and waited for Jane to come home."

Brennan finished typing at 9:20 P.M. and Steve signed the two-page statement. Although Steve admitted playing only a passive role in Heather's death, the Syracuse investigators saw the statement as a start.

In the following days, Dr. Erik Mitchell, the Onondaga County medical examiner, suggested that the investigators get Steve to describe how he killed Heather—and Heath, if they could get the suspect to budge on his denial. Mitchell came up with the idea of having Steve use a doll to demonstrate what he did to the children. A week later, Brennan and Boyle returned to jail, hoping to videotape a reenactment, but backed off when jailers warned them that Steve might have retained a lawyer. The follow-up interview could wait. The statement they'd already obtained was strong enough to give them the opening denied to Harvey LaBar six years earlier—exhumation of the children's bodies.

The sky over Mechanicville looked threatening on the morning of October 2, and Bob Chase put on blue jeans and a raincoat, expecting rough work. Harvey LaBar had called Chase the night before to remind him about the exhumation of Vickie Lynn. "I'll be there," Chase had said.

The funeral director met LaBar and more than a dozen state and Mechanicville police at the cemetery overlooking the Hudson River. Chase led the group to a large oak tree, where he knew he would find the small metal plaque marking Vickie Lynn's grave. Three cemetery workers started digging and uncovered a Styrofoam casket.

"That's not her," Chase said. "She's in a 'Cherub.' "

"Well, are you sure it's in here?" LaBar asked.

"It's here, Harvey, it's here."

Someone probably removed the marker to mow the grass and didn't put it back in the right spot, Chase thought. The gravediggers widened the hole. About a foot and a half farther from the oak tree, they found Vickie Lynn's white-plastic casket. Chase lifted the two-foot-long box out of the ground, put it in the back of his station wagon, and drove to Albany Medical Center.

At the morgue, Chase worked a pry bar around the casket lid that he had sealed more than six years earlier with super-bonding glue. LaBar watched anxiously. Although the police had Steve's statement about killing Vickie Lynn, that wasn't enough. Under New York law, prosecutors must have corroboration—independent evidence that proves a crime has been committed. The law is intended to prevent the convictions of mentally ill people who confess to crimes that they had nothing to do with or that never occurred. LaBar knew he needed something to show that Vickie Lynn had been smothered. He watched Chase struggle to open the casket, wondering how long it took for a body to decompose.

"What are we going to find when we open it up?" he asked.

"You are going to find a perfectly preserved body," Chase said.

"Are you sure?"

"Not a doubt in the world."

And Chase had no doubt that if Vickie Lynn's remains held a clue about how she died, Dr. Jack Davies, a pathology professor at the medical center, would find it. After nearly an hour, Chase broke the seal.

"The cover wasn't even off all the way and I knew I was safe," he recalled.

Vickie Lynn's body looked as if it had just been brought from the funeral home. LaBar was relieved; the well-formed body reminded him of a Cabbage Patch doll.

Dr. Davies, standing across the room with Dr. Jack Paston, the Saratoga Hospital pathologist who performed the original autopsy, saw something else.

"Jack, you're a good pathologist, but you missed this one," Davies said in his pronounced British accent.

It was the kind of avuncular remark that colleagues expected from Davies, a round little man with a white goatee who had been performing autopsies for forty years. He intended no insult. As a hospital pathologist, Paston relied primarily on autopsy findings to establish a cause of death. Davies specialized in forensic pathology, or the legal aspects of death, especially homicide. Forensic pathologists consider a wider range of evidence before reaching their conclusions. In this case,

Davies had read Steve's statement and was looking for evidence that Vickie Lynn had been smothered.

Davies had seen the first telltale sign of homicide from fifteen feet away: the baby's nose looked as if it had been pushed in or, as he put it, "squidged." Chase didn't remember seeing any compression of the nose when he prepared the body for burial. And Davies might not have noticed it either if a brownish discoloration hadn't thrown the misshapen lines of the nose into contrast. The pressure marks on the nose fit with Steve's account of holding Vickie Lynn's face to his shoulder until she stopped breathing.

Davies spent two and a half hours performing the second autopsy. During his examination of the head, he removed cotton that Chase had used to pack the nose. "Look at this, chaps," he said, peering into the nostrils with a magnifying glass.

Chase watched Davies's forceps pull out tufts with yellow fibers that looked like they came from the blanket the body had been wrapped in. The implication was clear: Vickie Lynn, struggling for breath, had inhaled fibers from her blanket. The same blanket Steve had asked the Chases to return. The same blanket the Chases had insisted Vickie Lynn carry to the grave.

With the autopsy over, Chase placed Vickie Lynn's body back in the casket and resealed the lid. He drove back to the cemetery knowing he'd done his job. He'd had a hunch and it was right. Vickie Lynn didn't die in vain.

"Nobody should have to go through that," he thought, "especially a baby."

Chase returned the casket to the grave beneath the oak tree. A chill wind had kicked up, and Chase headed home before the caretaker finished covering the casket with earth.

Patti Chase appeared from the kitchen when her husband got back to the funeral home.

"We got him," he said.

The exhumation of Heath's and Heather's bodies the day before hadn't worked out so well. The manager of White Chapel Memory Gardens outside Syracuse had no trouble finding the children's graves, but the bodies had deteriorated too much for Dr. Mitchell, the Onondaga County medical examiner, to find any evidence of how they died. That put John Brennan and Danny Boyle in a bind.

By coaxing Steve Van Der Sluys to describe smothering Vickie Lynn, the Syracuse investigators had paved the way for the exhumation in Mechanicville. The evidence from Dr. Davies's autopsy gave Saratoga County district attorney David Wait the corroboration he needed to back up Steve's confession. Wait could now push ahead and charge Steve with murdering Vickie Lynn.

But once that happened, Brennan and Boyle would be barred from talking to Steve about the deaths of Heath and Heather, and that would leave the case in Syracuse on shaky ground. Dr. Mitchell was hardpressed to corroborate Steve's statement without physical evidence. He urged the investigators to get a description of the children's deaths. And they had to get it before an indictment came down in Saratoga County.

Two days after the exhumation of Heath's and Heather's bodies, Brennan and Boyle returned to the Ontario County Jail and interviewed inmates who said Steve had told them about the children's deaths. The investigators didn't learn much more than they already knew. When they found out Steve did not have a lawyer, they decided to talk to him again.

Steve seemed to crave the attention, but he continued to give vague answers to the investigators' questions. After two hours of getting nowhere, the partners prepared to leave. Then Steve asked to speak to Brennan alone.

Once Boyle left the interview room, Steve admitted

that he'd held Heather against his shoulder until she stopped breathing—the same way he'd smothered Vickie Lynn.

"At that time, Stephen said that he decided that he should kill her and then he said that he took the child, put the child's face against his shoulder, covering the nose and mouth, put his hand on the back of her head and held it in that position for approximately three minutes," Brennan said.

"He stated after about three minutes he cradled the child in his arms and said that he could tell that the child was dead."

But when Boyle returned, Steve refused to give a signed statement. The investigators were left with only Brennan's word that Steve had confessed to smothering Heather. As the investigators retreated to Syracuse to plan their next move, events began to overtake them.

During the first week in October the teenager Steve had impregnated gave birth to a girl. A week later Jane Van Der Sluys delivered a boy, Corey. The same day, October 9, a grand jury in Saratoga County handed up a sealed indictment charging Steve with murdering Vickie Lynn.

On October 16 Brennan and Boyle obtained a court order to bring Steve to Syracuse for an interview. After several hours of fruitless questioning, an arrest warrant arrived from Saratoga County. They stopped the interview and placed Steve under arrest, foreclosing any hope of getting him to sign a confession about smothering Heather. The next morning in Saratoga, Steve pleaded innocent to murdering Vickie Lynn.

It took another two months to pull together the pieces of the Syracuse investigation. In December, Onondaga County district attorney Dick Hennessy presented it to a grand jury. Hennessy didn't try to make a case on Heath's death. He had no confession, no evidence to show Heath hadn't choked on a quarter, only a $10,000 insurance policy pointing to a motive. John Brennan told the grand jury about Steve's description of smothering Heather. Mitchell told the grand jurors the baby's death was a homicide.

The grand jury decided Hennessy had enough evidence to charge Steve with murdering Heather. But a prosecutor's burden of proof is much heavier during a trial, and the Van Der Sluys case didn't get any stronger by the time it landed in Bill Fitzpatrick's lap in August 1986.

Fitzpatrick faced the task of proving that Heather did not die of SIDS. Despite Steve's statements about smothering Vickie Lynn and Heather, Fitzpatrick knew that Van Der Sluys would try to argue that both children died of SIDS. After all, doctors had put the Van Der Sluyses' three surviving children on apnea monitors. And for all Fitzpatrick knew, SIDS really did run in families.

As Fitzpatrick started preparing for trial, he came to a dire conclusion: He had only half a case. The missing piece was corroboration.

Unable to determine a cause of death from the examination of Heather's remains, Dr. Mitchell had apparently relied on Steve's statements to conclude that the baby's death was a homicide. Fitzpatrick saw that there was no independent evidence to show Heather had been smothered. Worse, Stephen Van Der Sluys's lawyer, Edward Z. Menkin, knew it.

"You don't have a cause of death," Menkin told Fitzpatrick.

Menkin, who had once worked with Fitzpatrick in the DA's office, had developed an elaborate strategy to show that the prosecution did not have independent evidence to corroborate Steve's confession. He planned to use Mitchell's collaboration with Brennan and Boyle to show that the medical examiner did not conclude Heather's death was a homicide until Steve confessed. If Menkin could show that Mitchell had merely rubber-stamped the investigators' findings, the prosecution's case would fall.

Believing that a judge would be more likely than twelve laypeople to demand independent corroboration, Menkin had persuaded Steve to agree to a nonjury trial.

"If this case isn't further prepared," Fitzpatrick thought, "this case is a loser."

Beth Van Doren had the same concern.

Pressed for time, Fitzpatrick had asked Hennessy to assign an assistant district attorney to help him prepare for trial. The job went to Van Doren, a twenty-nine-year-old prosecutor who worked in the appeals unit. Van Doren thought that relying on Mitchell would play into Menkin's strategy. Fitzpatrick agreed.

"Find me a topflight, competent pediatric pathologist anywhere in the United States of America who's familiar with SIDS and any related fields," he told Van Doren.

She already had someone in mind: Dr. Linda Norton, a forensic pathologist with a private practice in Dallas.

Norton was best known for her work on the exhumation of Lee Harvey Oswald. She and three other pathologists identified the remains as Oswald's, putting to rest a theory that a Soviet agent's body had been substituted for his. But most of Norton's experience involved investigations of fatal child abuse.

John Brennan had given Van Doren an article on child abuse that Norton wrote in 1983 for *Clinics in Laboratory Medicine*. The twenty-two page article traced research into child abuse back to a 1946 study that first described a curious pattern of broken bones and deep bruises in six infants. The condition baffled the doctor treating the children, but Norton thought he simply failed to recognize the true nature of his observations.

In retrospect, she wrote, "All six cases represent

classic textbook examples of repeated assaults on these infants."

Similar cases puzzled researchers in the 1950s. The innocent mishaps that parents said their children suffered did not explain the severity of the injuries doctors saw on X-rays. Overlooking the obvious, if painful, conclusion that adults were covering up abuse, researchers concentrated on finding an underlying medical condition that might make some infants susceptible to chronic fractures.

The first suggestion that children with these injuries might be victims of abuse did not come until 1955. It took seven more years for doctors to recognize the chronic injuries as evidence of battered child syndrome and to hold their colleagues responsible for stopping the abuse.

Despite a proliferation of laws requiring doctors to report suspected abuse, "an uncomfortable number of cases are still missed, only to be discovered when the child is finally killed," Norton wrote. "It is the continued refusal of the physicians to disbelieve the clinical history given by caretakers that allows child battering and even more subtle forms of child abuse and homicide to go undetected. If the physician is to assume an active role in treating this problem, he must first come to grips with the fact that parents who, for whatever reason, injure or kill a child, will lie."

Norton saw history repeating itself in the reluctance of many doctors to face the fact that some deaths attributed to SIDS were homicides. She agreed with the bulk of SIDS research, which pointed to apnea, or the cessation of breathing, as the final pathway to death. But there were many causes of apnea, not all of them natural. An adult could place a hand or a pillow over an infant's nose and mouth and stop the child from breathing. The pressure needed to smother an infant often left no telltale signs, Norton explained.

"There is no way for the pathologist at autopsy to

distinguish between homicidal smothering and SIDS," she concluded.

Norton worried that homicides were being passed off as SIDS because many doctors held the erroneous belief that SIDS ran in families. They ignored large-scale studies that had shown no genetic tendency toward SIDS. Flouting conventional wisdom, Norton warned that the sudden, unexplained death of a SIDS victim's sibling should be treated as a possible homicide.

She felt like an abolitionist preaching against slavery in the antebellum South. Although many forensic pathologists agreed with her, theirs was a minority view. Many more doctors, especially pediatricians, chose to believe that siblings of SIDS victims faced a higher risk of succumbing to SIDS. This view had become an article of faith, providing a handy rationale for the unexplained deaths of subsequent siblings. The idea of recurring SIDS held a powerful appeal for doctors who were reluctant to question parents who had already lost an infant.

Norton traced the conventional wisdom to a 1972 study involving a couple who lost five infants to sudden, unexplained deaths. She dissected the case and concluded that the children probably had been smothered. Like the doctor who first identified the curious pattern of fractures in 1946, the author of the SIDS study failed to recognize the true nature of what he had observed, Norton believed. Her reference notes identified the author as Dr. Alfred Steinschneider.

Norton's insight on multiple SIDS deaths caught Beth Van Doren's eye. It addressed one of Fitzpatrick's key concerns: The similarity between Heather's and Vickie Lynn's deaths suggested a common medical problem, and that seemed to confirm the notion that SIDS ran in families. But if a series of unexplained infant deaths indicated foul play, as Norton suggested, the prosecution could use the evidence in Vickie

Lynn's death to bolster the argument that Heather didn't die of SIDS either.

Van Doren called Norton and told her about the Van Der Sluys case: the insurance, the ages of the children, the intervals between their deaths, the fact that Heather had been in and out of the hospital before she died but was fine while she was in the hospital.

"Honey, you don't have SIDS. You have a homicide," Norton said.

Van Doren didn't know which startled her more: being called "honey" by another professional woman or the speed with which Norton reached her conclusion.

The Van Der Sluys case contained some intriguing elements for Norton. She had found that children usually were smothered by women, especially mothers. The insurance angle interested Norton too; most child abusers didn't have such a calculated motive.

Yes, Norton said, she was interested in reviewing the case and testifying. She mentioned her fee—$1,600 per day—and Van Doren said she would get back to her. The doctor's self-assurance impressed her.

"Where's Bill?" Van Doren thought. "I can't wait till he hears this."

Fitzpatrick felt an instant rapport when he talked to Norton on the phone. They traded quips with the same brash confidence.

"I'm expensive," she said.

"I'm not intimidated by your fee," he replied. "How do I know you're worth it?"

But he already knew from Norton's clear, authoritative explanation of Heather's death that the Dallas pathologist was worth every penny. Fitzpatrick had his topflight medical expert and more: He had the germ of a trial strategy.

Then Saratoga County district attorney David Wait threw Fitzpatrick a curve. The day Steve was to go on trial for the murder of Vickie Lynn, Wait agreed to a plea bargain. Steve pleaded guilty to manslaughter in return for a sentence of eight and one-third to twenty-five years in prison. The deal cut in half the minimum prison time Steve would have served if he'd been convicted of murder.

The plea bargain outraged Fitzpatrick. Wait had the stronger case, and Fitzpatrick thought he should have held out for a murder conviction.

"If he pleads in Saratoga to murder and pleads to spitting on the sidewalk here, only uninformed people are going to say we dropped the ball," Fitzpatrick reasoned.

Wait's decision put added pressure on Fitzpatrick to win a murder conviction in Syracuse. Nothing less would do.

"I've been prosecuting murder cases for the last four years," Fitzpatrick thought. "This is the worst murder case I've ever seen."

Chapter Nine

Stephen Van Der Sluys's murder trial began on the morning of September 23, 1986, in the gray Beaux Arts courthouse next door to the modern Onondaga County Civic Center. Courtroom 311, with bright yellow walls and ornate white molding, could seat about fifty people, but only a handful of spectators turned out for this trial.

What happened in court would be decided by one man—Judge William Burke. In a nonjury trial the judge is responsible for ruling on questions of law, which determines which evidence he'll hear, and for deciding the defendant's guilt or innocence. In two decades on the bench, Burke had earned a reputation for working attorneys hard.

Bill Fitzpatrick didn't expect any breaks from the fifty-seven-year-old judge; they'd had run-ins in the past. The prosecutor thought Burke was so concerned about higher courts criticizing his decisions that he tended to rule in favor of the defense on procedural issues. Fitzpatrick was prepared to do some heavy lawyering.

He began his opening statement with a straightforward presentation of the facts, referring to a chart that outlined events spanning nearly a decade. He took advantage of his leadoff position to defuse Ed Menkin's defense.

"The last question, then, facing the court is the cause

of death, and I suspect that that will be an issue of some importance raised by the defense," he said.

Fitzpatrick wanted to lay the groundwork for overriding the 1977 autopsy that had classified Heather's death as SIDS. SIDS, he told Burke, was nothing more than "an attempt to give a name to that to which a name cannot be given. . . .

"You will hear evidence from an expert witness from Dallas that many cases, many cases have been documented where the original diagnoses by a medical examiner or pathologist of SIDS have later proved to be, in fact, asphyxial deaths, either accidental or homicidal."

With a carefully worded reference to Dr. Erik Mitchell, Fitzpatrick invited Menkin to believe that the prosecution's case hinged on the medical examiner's corroborating Steve's confession.

"Dr. Mitchell, if allowed to look at the total picture . . . will render an opinion as to the cause of death of Heather. If he is unable to do so because of a shortage of proof, or whatever ruling the court may make at that particular time down the road, that does not preclude this court finding that . . . this defendant caused the death of Heather Van Der Sluys."

The defense wasn't required to make an opening statement, but Menkin took the opportunity to prepare Burke to discount any medical opinion that was based on Steve's statements.

"Judge, I only have one thing to say, and that is that you, by virtue of your experience and your oath, you are the arbiter of credibility. A doctor cannot pass on somebody's credibility."

When Menkin sat down, Fitzpatrick called Jane Van Der Sluys to the witness stand.

Jane had never been a serious suspect in her children's deaths, but the way she stuck by Steve had left questions in the minds of investigators John Brennan and Danny Boyle. She gave them a handwritten statement saying that after Steve was charged with rape, he told her he felt responsible for the children's deaths. But the Syracuse investigators still had doubts about where she stood on her husband's guilt.

Fitzpatrick needed Jane as a leadoff witness to present an overview of the case. Working off typed notes, he asked her about her life with Steve. He started with the couple's financial problems, then worked his way around to Heather's and Vickie Lynn's deaths.

Jane answered questions about the night Steve awakened her holding Heather's limp body and told how she revived the baby. She then recalled the night a week later when she returned home from buying a curling iron and found Heather dead in her bassinet. She answered more questions about Vickie Lynn's death in Mechanicville. Her testimony established that Steve had been alone with the children in each case. Her words betrayed no emotion.

Months earlier, her father had broken down in tears trying to convince her that Steve was guilty. She seemed unable to believe that the man she'd fallen in love with as a teen, the husband who professed to be a Jehovah's Witness, could have murdered their children. James Bowers realized then that nothing less than a guilty verdict in open court would force his daughter to let go of her love for Steve.

When Fitzpatrick got to the question of insurance, he ran up against a legal restriction that prevents prosecutors from asking about conversations between a husband and wife. He tried to have Jane explain that it was Steve's idea to insure the children, but Menkin made repeated objections and Burke sustained them. Fitzpatrick vented his frustration by scrawling "fuck you judge" in his notes.

Menkin's cross-examination focused on Heather's health. He asked Jane about chemicals she and Steve kept in the apartment for their cleaning business; the temperature of the apartment; the proximity of the fireplace to the kitchen where Heather slept; the number of colds the baby had and whether they caused breathing problems. He also asked about Heather's treatment at the hospital the night Jane revived her.

His questioning was gentle, but his point was clear: If SIDS simply meant that doctors didn't know what caused a baby's death, then here was a host of factors that might have affected Heather's health.

Menkin also tried to use Jane's testimony to suggest that Steve's statements to the police were merely expressions of the guilt that many SIDS parents felt. Jane acknowledged that she used to belong to a SIDS parents' group.

"Is it fairly common for those parents to feel guilt over the death of their children?" Menkin asked.

Fitzpatrick objected on the grounds that this was irrelevant. Burke agreed, and Menkin tried a different approach: "Are the guilt feelings of the parents who are members of these support groups discussed?"

Fitzpatrick objected again, and Burke sustained.

"Judge," Menkin argued, "I think it's relevant on the question of interpreting the defendant's statements of September 6th and October 3rd, which the district attorney wants you to construe on a psychological level."

The judge gave him a one-word answer: "No."

The first day ended with the testimony of Joseph West and Brian Murphy, the Syracuse police officers who handled the Signal 78s for Heather. Neither remembered much about the calls, but Fitzpatrick needed them to testify so he could enter their reports as evidence.

Menkin's cross-examination of West finished on a melancholy note that could only remind Fitzpatrick of how the passage of time had dulled the poignancy of Heather's death.

"Does reading the report refresh your recollection of the event at all?" Menkin asked.

"No, sir."

"Lost in memory?"

"In time, yes, sir."

The next day Fitzpatrick continued building his case
piece by piece. The testimony of Dr. Robert Chavkin,
Heather's pediatrician, showed she was a normal,
healthy baby before she died. Two insurance agents
testified that they had sold Steve life insurance policies
for his children.

Fitzpatrick then called Investigator Donald
Wentworth, the state police polygraph expert who had
tried to examine Steve at the Canandaigua barracks.
Wentworth went through the various statements that
Steve gave during the marathon round of interviews
that followed.

Menkin wanted to make sure Burke understood that
John Brennan was the only investigator who had ever
heard Steve say he smothered Heather and that that admission came later, during a jailhouse interview. The
defense lawyer grilled Wentworth to show that during
the first interview, Steve gave a different account of
the baby's death.

"With respect to what he told you about Heather, the
sum and substance of it was that . . . she had difficulty
breathing, he picked her up, he didn't know what to do,
he put her down. She was breathing when she was
down in that crib. He knew she was going to die and
he let her die. Is that what he told you, the long and the
short of the whole day?"

"Yes, sir."

Fitzpatrick took up the jailhouse confession when
Brennan took the stand. He asked what Steve said after
Danny Boyle left the interview room.

"He told me that the day that Heather died, that he
went to check on her and he noticed that she was very
blue and that she kept making these exhaling sounds.
He stated he picked her up from her bassinet and said

at that time he was torn whether ... whether she should live or whether he should kill her. At that time, Stephen said that he decided that he should kill her and then he said that he took the child, put the child's face against his shoulder covering the nose and mouth, put his hand on the back of her head and held it in that position for approximately three minutes. He stated after about three minutes he cradled the child in his arms and said that he could tell that the child was dead. At that time, he took the child and put her face down in the bassinet and put her head into the pillow."

Steve's confession was on the record; Fitzpatrick had one leg of his case in.

It was past five o'clock by the time he finished with Brennan, but Menkin was eager to get into his cross-examination—and start laying his trap for Mitchell. He wanted to pin Brennan down on his collaboration with Mitchell during the investigation, which would put the medical examiner in a box when he tried to explain later how he determined the cause of Heather's death. Burke gave the defense lawyer twenty minutes to get started.

Menkin knew Brennan well. He was a hardworking cop, with good looks and a low-key style. That was one of the reasons Menkin had decided on a bench trial; he knew he had no chance of convincing a jury that Brennan had coerced a confession from Steve. Now Menkin was counting on the investigator's honesty to help snare Mitchell.

Menkin launched his strategy by asking Brennan whether he had contacted Mitchell between the time Brennan was assigned the case and Steve's first interview.

"I believe we may have contacted Dr. Mitchell, but we didn't get any reports from him or anything like that," Brennan said.

"Did he tell you he thought it was a homicide?"

"No, sir, he didn't."

"Did you leave that meeting with Dr. Mitchell with
the impression that Dr. Mitchell thought that foul play
was involved in this case?"

"I got no impression from Dr. Mitchell. He couldn't
give us any real information."

"All right," Menkin said. So far, so good.

Menkin kept the cross-examination conversational,
referring to Brennan by his first name. But the investigator became wary as Menkin kept pressing him about
Mitchell.

Brennan said he spoke to Mitchell about a week after the September 6 interview at the barracks, and
again on October 1, after the exhumation of Heather's
remains showed no evidence of foul play.

"That's why you went back to Van Der Sluys on
October third, isn't it, John, because you needed an explanation as to how Heather died? Isn't that so?"

"We wanted to reinterview him to get any more information that we might have omitted on the sixth [of
September], yes, sir."

"And you needed to know how Heather died because the case with Vickie was made, isn't that so?"

Fitzpatrick objected, and Burke sustained. Menkin
continued for a few more minutes, but his cross-
examination began to run out of steam.

"I'd sort of like to regroup, Judge. There's a lot I
want to know, and it might be a good time to break."

Burke agreed: "Nine o'clock tomorrow morning."

Fitzpatrick needed time to regroup, as well. Dr.
Linda Norton had arrived in Syracuse while court was
in session, and Fitzpatrick needed the evening to prepare her testimony.

Beth Van Doren felt responsible for bringing Fitzpatrick and Norton together, and she worried about
how they would hit it off. She wanted their first face-
to-face meeting to go well, but she knew she was dealing with two people who each liked being in control.
Van Doren braced herself for a test of wills as they

gathered in a conference room in the DA's office. She didn't have to wait long.

Fitzpatrick, already caught up in the trial, wanted to get down to business. "I'd like to have you review . . ."

Norton cut him off: "I'd prefer to have dinner, then work."

"I like to work, then eat," Fitzpatrick insisted, and they forged ahead. Van Doren took note: Fitzpatrick was in charge.

Burke had ruled that the prosecution could bring in evidence about Vickie Lynn's death but not Heath's, and Fitzpatrick needed to make sure that Norton based her opinion only on admissible evidence. Straying from that path could result in a mistrial, so Fitzpatrick had made an inventory of all the documents Norton could consider: the original police reports, which contained Steve's initial accounts of Heather's and Vickie Lynn's deaths; the girls' original autopsy reports and death certificates; Steve's confession; the indictment in Heather's death; the indictment in Saratoga County; and Steve's manslaughter plea.

Norton began going through the documents, explaining how each supported her conclusion that Heather did not die of SIDS. Being in Syracuse and discussing SIDS reminded Norton of Dr. Alfred Steinschneider's study on the couple who lost five children. Steinschneider had done his research at Upstate Medical Center, just a few blocks from the DA's office.

"Oh, by the way. You have another homicide here in this county," she said. "You have a serial killer right here in Syracuse. It's a famous case. Take a look: *Pediatrics,* October 1972."

The mention of Steinschneider's study had no more impact on the discussion than a hiccup, but Norton didn't press the issue. For her, Fitzpatrick was just another in a long line of prosecutors who had ignored her warning about Steinschneider's study. She'd made a point of telling authorities who were looking at multiple infant deaths that they shouldn't accept the theory that SIDS ran in families. The police often accepted her view that the sudden, unexplained death of more than one infant should be treated as a suspected homicide.

"But then the DA says, 'Now wait a second. I really need something more substantial here,' " Norton said. "And the first thing you know, they talk to a pediatrician or they talk to another forensic pathologist, and lo and behold, we discover that, 'Oh, no, Mr. DA. It's well known that SIDS occurs multiple times in families. In fact, what you really need to do is call Dr. Steinschneider.' "

Fitzpatrick had noted Norton's reference to a serial killer, but he was too caught up in the complexities of preparing her testimony to pay much attention. He was more concerned about not tipping his hand to Menkin.

Criminal procedure laws require prosecutors to give the defense any material generated by expert witnesses, but Fitzpatrick had made sure there was nothing from Norton to disclose; she did not prepare a report, and he kept no notes of their conversations. Working without a script carried risks for Fitzpatrick, but he was counting on his courtroom savvy and Norton's expertise to produce a compelling presentation.

Once Fitzpatrick was satisfied with their preparation, he took Norton to an Italian restaurant for a late dinner. They talked shop as they ate, swapping stories about homicides in the matter-of-fact way of professionals all too familiar with the evil wrought by human hands.

The next morning Menkin resumed his cross-examination of Brennan. He wanted to know one thing right off the bat: Had Brennan discussed his earlier testimony with Fitzpatrick?

Brennan said he had just asked the prosecutor why

Menkin was interested in his conversations with Dr. Mitchell.

"Did he give you some idea of where he thinks I'm going with that line of questioning?"

"Yes, sir. He gave me some type of idea."

"Have you thought about that overnight?"

"No, sir, not particularly."

After clearing up a few details about the initial interview at the state police barracks, Menkin asked Brennan whether he spoke to Mitchell before trying to question Steve in jail a week later. If Menkin expected resistance, he was disappointed.

"Yes, sir. I have thought about it, and I do believe I did talk to Dr. Mitchell before the thirteenth of September."

Now they were getting somewhere. "And can you tell us what you told Dr. Mitchell?"

"Well, I briefly explained to him what we had gotten from Mr. Van Der Sluys on the sixth, and just told him vaguely, you know, I believe I even showed him a copy of the confessional affidavit at the time."

Mitchell told him to get more details about Heather's death, Brennan said.

"What kind of details?"

"Exactly how he killed her, just have him go through the actions if you can, and get him to demonstrate how he killed Heather."

Menkin closed in for the score.

"Now, is it fair to say, John, that Dr. Mitchell's statement to you was, at least in part, one of the reasons you brought the doll and the videotape equipment?"

"Yes, sir, it is."

Done. Menkin got what he was looking for on that point.

But Brennan didn't have much more to say about Mitchell. He said he didn't discuss Steve's statements with Mitchell when he got the medical examiner's signature on an affidavit for the exhumations. They didn't talk about the statement on the day the remains were unearthed, either. And he and Dan Boyle went back to interview Steve two days later at the direction of their boss and Dick Hennessy, he said, not Mitchell.

Menkin questioned Brennan closely about the jailhouse interview, zeroing in on the statement that Boyle started typing after Steve spoke to Brennan in private.

"And isn't it a fact, John, that in the affidavit form that you were drafting, Stephen Van Der Sluys did not tell you on October third that he held Heather against his body until she died and then he put her back in the crib; is that a fact, John?"

"Yes, sir. He had stopped before we had gotten that far in the affidavit."

Menkin had what he needed: Brennan's word was the only source for the belief that Heather had been smothered. The trap was set to spring on Mitchell— and the prosecution. But Fitzpatrick had an escape plan, and it began with his next witness.

Chapter Ten

Dr. Linda Norton cut an impressive figure on the witness stand. Sitting upright in her understated suit and speaking with a Southern drawl, she delivered a lengthy recitation of her credentials as a forensic pathologist: her education; her experience as a medical examiner in Alabama and Texas; the number of autopsies she had performed—roughly ten thousand.

Bill Fitzpatrick's questions let her highlight her experience in distinguishing between child abuse and SIDS. If Judge William Burke was to accept Norton's explanation of Heather Van Der Sluys's death, Fitzpatrick had to build the doctor's credibility as an expert.

"There are many cases where an autopsy alone will simply not give you any hint as to the manner of death," Norton explained. "For example, a contact gunshot wound to the head is something that one can easily determine during an autopsy. The cause of death is a contact gunshot wound to the head. Unless you know something about the circumstances surrounding the death, it would be impossible to know whether that contact wound was delivered by the person intentionally and, therefore, is a suicide; whether someone else shot the person in the head, making it a homicide; or whether it was a reckless game of Russian roulette and, therefore, could be categorized as an accidental death."

Ed Menkin let this primer continue uninterrupted until it edged toward issues related to corroborating

Heather's death. When Fitzpatrick asked Norton if she had ever amended a death certificate that originally gave SIDS as a cause of death, Menkin lodged his first objection—irrelevant. Burke overruled him.

"I, and I think my fellow medical examiners, never consider a death certificate to be carved in stone," Norton said. "Therefore, when you sign a death certificate you are placing your opinion on the best evidence you have at that time. If, later on, further investigation reveals information that causes you to change your mind about either the cause or manner of death, then I consider it a moral obligation to go ahead at that point and change the death certificate to reflect the new information."

Norton's clear, authoritative responses set the tone Fitzpatrick was looking for. Fending off niggling objections from Menkin, Fitzpatrick posed a series of questions that Norton used to give Burke a crash course on SIDS:

FITZPATRICK: Would you define SIDS for the court, Dr. Norton?

NORTON: Okay. SIDS, S-I-D-S, stands for sudden infant death syndrome. It is synonymous with the term "crib death," and in England the terminology they use is "cot death," c-o-t. . . . The term was designed to define a specific category of infant death for which we had no known cause and still don't know the exact cause. But strictly defined, the limits are as follows:

The death occurs in an infant from age one to nine months, with the most common age group being from two to six months. The child dies during sleep. In other words, they are found after they've been put down for a nap, or they are found after they've been put down overnight for sleep. The child has been in all respects relatively healthy. We're not talking about they haven't had earaches or runny noses or little colds, or something like that in the past. But we're talking about the child does not have any history of major illness, like congenital heart disease or anything of that sort.

The child normally . . . not just normally, but there is no outcry. In other words, the parent, who may be in the next room while the child is napping, does not hear any outcry from the child. There is usually no evidence of any particular struggle that the child has been through when the child is found dead. And when . . . this is very important: When a complete autopsy is done, there is no anatomic cause of death found. In other words, children who are found to have pneumonia, viral pneumonia, meningitis, or other natural causes of death cannot be considered SIDS deaths, and so, therefore, the important aspect is a complete examination, including microscopic toxicology, bacteriologic examinations, are negative, so that no anatomic cause of death is found at autopsy. And these deaths are categorized as sudden infant death syndrome.

Twenty to thirty years ago, all these deaths used to be considered homicides and parents were . . . there was usually a witch hunt, and parents were accused of killing these children, and I think we have come to realize that most of these deaths are, in fact . . . they are not homicidal deaths. They are some form of non-suspicious and unfortunate, you know, type of death.

FITZPATRICK: Aside from age, are there any other common denominators or characteristics that apply to SIDS victims?

NORTON: There are certain epidemiologic characteristics, and by "epidemiologic" all we're saying is that there are certain groups that seem to be at higher risk of having SIDS death than other groups. For example, if the mother is under twenty years of age, she's more likely to have a SIDS death. If she is unmarried, if the father is under twenty years of age, if they are a low socioeconomic group. The highest incidence of SIDS occurs in the poor black population in this country.

So these are epidemiologic characteristics. This does not mean that a thirty-year-old mother with a thirty-year-old father to whom she's married, white, and upper class cannot have a SIDS death occur in their family. We're simply defining characteristics where SIDS is more common than it is in other particular groups.

FITZPATRICK: And have there been occasions that you're familiar with in your experience where other types of deaths are misdiagnosed as SIDS?

NORTON: Yes.

FITZPATRICK: And can you give us examples of those?

NORTON: All right. There are many individuals who, rather than performing a complete autopsy, simply, a child, a dead child, is signed out as SIDS. I mean, there are individuals, particularly in counties where a coroner system abounds, the term SIDS will be uniformly applied to basically any death in a child. And so, any time a complete autopsy examination is not performed on an infant found dead, there is a margin for error.

There are many people who do not use the standard cutoff of nine months.... I've actually seen death certificates where a child four years of age was signed out as sudden infant death syndrome, and this is, obviously, an inappropriate use of the terminology.

So SIDS has, for many, become a wastebasket term, so that you don't really have to do much in the way of investigation. You don't bother with a complete autopsy examination, and you have something that you can put on the death certificate that seems to be satisfactory, or satisfies the powers that be, whoever they might be.

When Fitzpatrick returned to the question of whether the onset of SIDS caused babies to cry in distress, Menkin objected again. The defense lawyer thought he saw where his opponent was headed.

"I think that what the prosecution is doing, at least up to this point, seems to be going towards impeaching the conclusion of, in this case, a 1977 autopsy," Menkin argued. "In that respect, I don't know that Dr. Norton is a competent witness."

Burke overruled him. He wanted to hear Norton's response.

NORTON: Now, this is not to say that a child who may be put down for a nap or put down for bed may not have been fussy during that particular day, or crying or manifesting any of the behavior that normal infants, you know, may manifest when they are teething or they have a, you know, a little viral infection or something like that. So, I'm not trying to imply that infants who end up dying of SIDS do not cry, or cannot cry, or cannot be fussy during a period of time before they're put down for their nap or put down for their, you know, bedtime at night.

Menkin's repeated objections began to frustrate Fitzpatrick. When Menkin challenged Norton's testimony on the various theories surrounding SIDS, Fitzpatrick fought back.

"I really object to the lengthy objections which are arguments to the court," he complained. "I would like to proceed in an orderly fashion with this witness's presentation."

Burke agreed. "Go ahead."

FITZPATRICK: Doctor, can you tell us, then, what are some of the theories that have been proffered relative to the cause of SIDS?

NORTON: I'd be happy to. All right. There are many things that have been pursued in trying to figure out why normal, healthy infants can be put down for a nap and wake up dead, as it were. The various things that have been investigated and. have been discounted at this point, are things like anaphylaxis to cow's milk, allergic reactions, overwhelming viral infections, things that are wrong with the conduction system of the heart, and exotic things like that.

Theories that seem to still have fairly wide acceptance—and my opinion is that these theories probably comprise, in other words, every one of these is probably responsible for a certain percentage of what we call sudden infant death syndrome, but we are not able to differentiate at autopsy which of these causes are actually responsible. One theory that came right out of Syracuse, New York, and has gotten a fairly wide contingency behind it, is one by Dr. Steinschneider right here in Syracuse, and that is the sleep apnea theory. Normal infants when they sleep and, in fact, adults when they sleep, but infants more so than adults, will have periodic cessations of breathing. They stop breathing for a period of time and then normal breathing mechanisms take back over and the infant or the adult starts to breathe again. Dr. Steinschneider's theory is that if one of these periods of apnea becomes prolonged, the child stops breathing altogether, and death ensues. So, sleep apnea theory is one that is . . . I think it's still widely held by a large proportion of the medical community.

There are other theories that have been proposed that I think also account for a certain percentage of what we call sudden infant death syndrome. For example, most children of that age group are obligant nose breathers. If their airway is cut off nasally they will not open their mouth to breathe. Therefore, one theory is unilateral choanal atresia, which is a very fancy ... or congenital anomaly, where one half of the nasal passage is not completely developed and you get a very high obstruction, and so, you only have one nares open. If the child happens to get into a position during sleep where they close off the one open nasal passage and they are an obligant nose breather, which means they will not breathe through their mouth, then they will die.

Infants, both human and monkeys, do not have the same reaction to anoxia that human adults do. If someone were to cut off an adult's airway while they are sleeping, it would wake us up. It has been shown in experiments, quite accidentally with human infants, but deliberately with infant monkeys, that cutting off of the airway in a sleeping infant will not even wake them up. They simply continue to sleep and they die, whereas, as you grow older you develop a stimulus. When your airway is cut off, the stimulus wakes you up so that you change positions or you do something to restore your breathing. So choanal atresia is another one.

There are a certain number of deaths that are categorized as sudden infant death that are probably what we call accidental overlayings. The adult rolls over on the child during the night and accidentally smothers the child to death.

There are a certain percentage of SIDS deaths, and I happen to believe that it's probably the highest percentage, are due simply to the fact that children of that age almost constantly have some sort of nasal congestion in that age group. The number of SIDS deaths increases during that time of the year when colds and flu are rampant in the society, and I believe that a certain ... and I think a high percentage of SIDS deaths are simply due to the fact that you put a child down, they have a stuffy nose, they may have one side of their nose completely blocked because they've got a little bit of cold or quite a cold, they happen to turn their head, they block the other airway, they are obligant nose breathers, they will not open their mouth to breathe, and so they die.

A certain very small percentage of sudden infant death syndrome deaths are probably homicides, and they're probably isolated cases where this particular infant is actually deliberately smothered by an adult.

The problem is that, at autopsy, you cannot differentiate between an asphyxial death, regardless of which of the causes. You cannot, by autopsy examination, tell whether you have simply a blockage of the airway because the child has a little cold and accidentally blocked its airway.

Most autopsies are not extensive enough because of the extensive damage that one would have to do to the face in order to discover choanal atresia, so you're not going to be able to differentiate choanal atresia.

Overlying, unless you get a history of the child sleeping with a parent, you're not going to be able to differentiate a smothering [by] overlying from the accidental type of smothering that, you know, the infant does himself by having to block a nasal passage.

The prolonged apneic episode that's proposed by Dr. Steinschneider cannot be differentiated from an asphyxial death of any other means. And a deliberate smothering death, unless you have some sort of other injury, is not going to be able to be differentiated at autopsy. And, of course, an infant being so much smaller than an adult, it is very, very uncommon to find injuries due to smothering in infants or in debilitated old people—debilitated old people are the other group of folks that can rather easily be smothered without leaving any trace of anything.

Fitzpatrick felt as though he had been working with Norton for years. Her responses flowed like water, sweeping the courtroom along in the current. His questions kept her headed in the right direction.

FITZPATRICK: While we're on the subject of theories, are there monitors that are used to attempt to predict or prevent the onset of SIDS?

NORTON: Okay. The monitors were developed and are still being produced specifically for those people who believe in the sleep apnea theory for SIDS. The monitors would, of course, also, if it were a matter of the child blocking a nasal passageway and stopping breathing for that reason, would also pick up those children. . . . The monitors are basically designed to try to detect a prolonged period of cessation of breathing while the child is asleep.

FITZPATRICK: Are they successful in doing that?

NORTON: They basically are not, and, of course, the reason they're not very successful is because it's very . . . we don't have any way to predict which child is going to die from SIDS and which one is not.

We cannot afford to monitor every infant that comes into this world. So far, the studies would indicate that there's no genetic predisposition, so therefore, to simply just select children to monitor because they've had a child, or a sibling, die, is, I think, very unfair to the parents who have already been traumatized by a sudden infant death.

There's no way to predict, prospectively, which infant is going to die. You can't monitor every infant. Therefore, you have to select out of a particular population, and, of course, the population that we have tended to select is [the] population where a child has already died of SIDS, they've already had one death. If that death has been a nonsuspicious, natural type of death, then the sibling who is being monitored is being unnecessarily monitored because their chances of dying are no greater than anyone else's, and the parents are being subjected to a device which is so sensitive that virtually any normal infant will set it off.

And in large studies where infants have been monitored to try to determine whether or not infants who have prolonged apnea during sleep are at higher risk than those who don't, we have not shown any difference in the number of SIDS deaths between those infants who have prolonged periods of apnea.

So, we have no prospective way at this time to reliably pick the infants that are at high risk ... and so, what we're doing, basically, is a very random monitoring that probably is doing more trauma to the family than it is doing anybody any good, and it's costing a lot of money.

FITZPATRICK: Now, this term, Dr. Norton, "near-miss SIDS," is there such an accepted term?

NORTON: There are many who accept the term "near-miss" SIDS.

FITZPATRICK: And what is it?

NORTON: All right. Those who believe that such a thing exists believe that near-miss refers to episodes where the child has a prolonged apnea spell. In other words, a period where they stop breathing, and by sheer luck and circumstance, the parents happen to walk into the room or happen to be present when this occurs. And if an apnea spell or cessation of breathing is interrupted and resuscitation is begun, then the child can, in many instances, be successfully resuscitated.

FITZPATRICK: Do you accept the existence of cases of near-miss SIDS?

NORTON: I am never going to say that, you know, anything is not possible or anything of the sort. However, there is also a malady among some human beings where the deliberate induction of apneic episodes is performed so that the child can be rushed into the hospital and receive medical care, and the individual gets a secondary benefit from having a sick child. There are many reported cases where these people have actually been caught in the act of putting their hand over the child's nose and mouth in a hospital setting in order to deliberately induce periods of cessation of breathing. And, in my opinion, I think probably most of what are considered near-miss SIDS are apneic episodes that are deliberately induced by a parent or by an adult.

Menkin piped up again when Fitzpatrick hit the question of parents smothering their children. But Burke seemed caught up in the lesson and let it continue.

FITZPATRICK: Can you give the court, Dr. Norton, an example of how an apnea spell could be induced in an infant?

NORTON: It has been shown, experimentally, in both infants and in infant monkeys, that if you block their airway for a certain period of time—and the length of time it takes to block the airway and induce a spell varies from one child to another, but we're talking about a fairly short time, we're talking about minutes—that if you induce, by blocking their airway, a spell of cessation of breathing, or an apnea spell, that once you remove your hand, the child will not spontaneously start to breathe again. In order to get them to start breathing again, you have to actively resuscitate them. You have to do mouth-to-mouth resuscitation and actually get their breathing started. So, in other words, you don't have to keep your hand over the infant's nose and mouth for the full five minutes that it takes to kill. You can actually hold your hand long enough to induce a spell of apnea that they will not spontaneously resolve once you remove your hand.

Having laid his foundation, Fitzpatrick moved to the heart of his case—corroboration. He had Norton identify the records she had reviewed, then asked her what they had to say about Heather's death.

Taken alone, Norton said, the original autopsy findings were consistent with either SIDS or intentional smothering.

When Fitzpatrick asked whether Stephen Van Der Sluys's original explanations of Heather's first brush with death and the final crisis were consistent with SIDS, Menkin unleashed a barrage of objections. Burke turned his arguments aside and let Norton answer.

"The sequence of events described in those three statements do not fit the syndrome we accept as sudden infant death syndrome," she said. "The sequence of events describes respiratory distress of some kind in the infant that is perceived and noticed by the adult, in which case there must be an underlying respiratory problem, and those deaths, therefore, would not fit into the category of sudden infant death syndrome."

Fitzpatrick felt a rush of excitement as he guided Norton to her conclusion. He asked a couple of questions to shore up his foundation; he wanted to make sure Burke understood that Norton's opinion was based on the records she cited, not on Steve's confession. Then, he asked the crucial question: "And what is your opinion as to the cause of death of Heather Van Der Sluys?"

Menkin objected, as Fitzpatrick had expected he would. But his opponent's argument didn't register. Fitzpatrick was locked in anticipation. All his preparation came down to this—an answer he knew but had never heard. Finally, Burke's voice broke through—"overruled"—and Norton spoke.

"In my opinion, Heather was smothered to death."

The sound of Heather's name reached Fitzpatrick like a cry from the grave. He felt a lump in his throat and turned away from the witness stand. Here was his client, the victim, like so many others, he'd never known. In a single sentence, Norton had made Heather real. And sent her away again in the same breath. The thought of all the tomorrows Heather never would see overwhelmed Fitzpatrick. He busied himself with a water pitcher so nobody could see the tears in his eyes.

Fitzpatrick wrapped up quickly. What else could Norton add? Her testimony was terrific. If this were a jury trial, he thought, Stephen Van Der Sluys would already be halfway to prison.

Menkin had to react quickly. Whatever his plans were for Dr. Erik Mitchell, he couldn't let Norton's testimony stand unchallenged. He tried chipping away at the foundation of her opinion, working a variation of his Mitchell strategy. He tried to show that Norton had relied on Steve's statements to reach her conclusion about Heather's death. But the doctor shot him down.

"I have no interest in talking to the defendant in order to formulate an opinion," she said. "They tend to lie, and so, therefore, talking to defendants has never gotten me anywhere in particular, and so I don't do it."

Fitzpatrick admired Norton's professionalism on the stand. She kept her composure and gave honest answers to Menkin's questions, even when she didn't necessarily like the implications. She conceded that Heather exhibited some characteristics that were common among SIDS victims: Heather was the right age;

she'd had a cold; she came from a poor household. But Norton hung tough on the question of SIDS running in families.

"Statistically, quote, SIDS has been reported to occur more than once in a family. There have been families where ... SIDS has been reported as a cause of death up to four times," she said. "A careful review of cases where this is reported to have happened would tend to indicate that those cases represent the fairly small percentage of cases where the SIDS is due to homicidal smothering, and that is why it is recurring in the same family."

Menkin made a few more stabs at trying to undermine her opinion before calling it quits. Norton may have held fast, but Menkin was confident he could dismantle Mitchell on cross-examination. And Mitchell, not Norton, was the authority in Onondaga County.

Fitzpatrick led Mitchell through a brief recitation of his credentials, then asked him to identify Dr. William Alsever's 1977 report on Heather's autopsy.

"What conclusion did he reach as to the cause of death of Heather Van Der Sluys?" Fitzpatrick asked.

"He decided upon sudden infant death syndrome."

"And is that reflected on some death certificate, as far as you know?"

"Yes, sir."

"Okay. Thank you very much, doctor."

Menkin's jaw dropped. "Is that it? Really? Is that it?"

"Yes," Fitzpatrick said.

Menkin's elaborate strategy had just fallen apart. Cross-examination is limited to matters raised by a witness on direct examination. By confining Mitchell's testimony to a mere technicality, Fitzpatrick had robbed Menkin of the opportunity to grill the medical examiner about his opinion on Heather's death. Menkin realized his opponent had pulled a fast one.

While he had been gearing up to demolish Mitchell on cross-examination, Fitzpatrick had used Norton's testimony to corroborate Steve's confession.

"Judge, I'd ask for a fifteen-minute adjournment," Menkin said. "I'd like to consult with myself."

The defense lawyer asked to meet privately with Burke in chambers. Fitzpatrick fumed at being excluded, but he would have been elated if he could have heard what Menkin was saying.

"I think that it is obvious to the court that I have been pursuing a line of inquiry which has been directed over many witnesses toward building a foundation to impeach the testimony of Dr. Mitchell," Menkin told Burke.

"Quite frankly, the district attorney's extremely abbreviated direct examination of Dr. Mitchell took me by surprise, and I ought to also state for the record that I certainly admire the brilliance of the move."

Menkin, who prided himself on always having another ace up his sleeve, had run out of options. The corroboration that the prosecution needed to show that Heather's death was a homicide now rested on Norton. He decided to tackle her opinion in closing arguments and wanted Burke's assurance that the court stenographer would give the defense a copy of the doctor's testimony without alerting Fitzpatrick.

Menkin returned to court for another round of gamesmanship with Fitzpatrick. He questioned Mitchell briefly about the handling of tissue samples from Heather's autopsy, but he asked nothing about the medical examiner's discussions with Investigator John Brennan. Nothing about getting Steve to reenact Heather's death with a doll.

When Mitchell stepped down, Fitzpatrick rested his case. The third day of the trial was over.

Menkin rested his case the next morning without

calling a witness. He began his closing argument with
a nod to his opponent's skill.

"I find it more than passingly interesting," Menkin
said, "I find it absolutely brilliant, that this prosecutor
didn't ask Erik Mitchell what he thought the cause of
death was, because it ... was obvious to Mr. Fitzpatrick as to where I was going when I'm talking to
brother Brennan over here."

He also acknowledged Norton's expertise without
conceding the corroboration issue.

"If you take Dr. Norton's opinion out of this, you
don't have an explanation for cause of death," he argued. "You just don't. Unless you take a look at what
the defendant said."

Menkin quoted Norton's testimony, trying to show
that she didn't have any more medical evidence than
Mitchell did to refute the original finding that Heather
died of SIDS. But Menkin hedged his bets, arguing
that even if Heather was smothered, it could have been
an accident.

Fitzpatrick insisted there was nothing accidental
about Heather's death: "The evidence is crystal clear
this is a killing for greed, and it's a killing because of
inadequacy."

He didn't want to play into Menkin's hands by em-
phasizing Norton's testimony, so he organized the
other evidence into a patchwork of guilt—Steve
smothering Vickie Lynn, his selfish use of the insurance money, his jealousy.

Fitzpatrick thought of Heather, and his passion rose:
"What we look at as a child that today should be looking forward to her tenth birthday, he looks at as competition for the affections of his wife, and God help us,
he looks at her with a dollar sign on her head, ten thousand dollars ...

"And, Judge, I urge you to do justice ... stand up
and tell this community that on January the 7th, 1977,

that little girl, that helpless little girl, was smothered to death by this defendant."

Four days later, Burke delivered a written decision finding Stephen Van Der Sluys guilty of murder.

Fitzpatrick felt that he'd proven himself again; he'd taken a lousy case and used his skills as a trial lawyer to make it a winner. He took satisfaction in knowing he'd helped bring a child-killer to justice.

The victim was still on Fitzpatrick's mind at Stephen Van Der Sluys's sentencing three weeks later. Fitzpatrick pointed out to Burke that Heather's birthday had passed two days before.

"She would have been celebrating her tenth birthday, probably in fourth or fifth grade, looking forward to a new school year, probably asking her mother all kinds of questions about boys and clothes and music and any one of a thousand other things that little girls wonder about, and she hasn't had those opportunities and she never will." He asked for the maximum sentence.

When his turn came, Steve complained he was the victim of a conspiracy. Fitzpatrick stared straight ahead, but inside he seethed over the self-pitying speech. Steve held an envelope containing drawings and letters from his surviving children.

"They're the most valuable and precious things that I own," he told Burke. "You see, you've torn my world apart. You've ripped my children away from me to try to prove your lies, to back up your hunches. For do what you may, say what you may, I love all my children. I've always loved all my children and I will always love all my children."

Burke wasn't moved. He sentenced Steve to twenty-five years to life on top of the sentence he got for killing Vickie Lynn. Stephen Van Der Sluys wouldn't be eligible for parole until he was nearly seventy.

As usual, Fitzpatrick got the last word. "It totally made me nauseous to sit there and listen to that crap about how his children love him," he told reporters. "His children don't even know him, and the only reason they're alive is his wife wouldn't let him take out any more insurance."

Chapter Eleven

The Van Der Sluys case drew Bill Fitzpatrick into another tangled investigation involving SIDS, this time in Schenectady, a once-thriving General Electric company town near Albany. As the fourteen-year history of the Schenectady investigation became clear, Fitzpatrick saw disturbing parallels with the Van Der Sluys case.

Schenectady police began asking questions about Marybeth Tinning after three of her children died in quick succession in early 1972. Jennifer died first. She was Marybeth Tinning's third child.

Jennifer was born the day after Christmas 1971 with hemorrhagic meningitis, an infection apparently contracted in the womb. She stayed in the hospital and died three days into the new year. Years later, doctors, police, and prosecutors remained convinced that Jennifer died of natural causes. But they could never agree if, or how, the trauma of the newborn's death had twisted Marybeth into a serial killer.

Seventeen days after Jennifer's death, Marybeth's two-year-old son, Joseph, died. Five weeks later, while Marybeth was pregnant with her fourth child, her firstborn, Barbara, died. The girl was just shy of her fifth birthday.

Marybeth's fourth child, Timothy, died three weeks after his birth. After that death, on December 10, 1973, the investigators appealed to the Schenectady County district attorney's office for help. They got the same answer Harvey LaBar got when he first asked the Saratoga County DA for an investigation of Stephen Van Der Sluys: You don't have enough evidence to initiate an official inquiry.

Over the next eight years, the death toll of Tinning children rose. Marybeth's five-month-old son, Nathan, died September 2, 1975. Four-month-old Mary Frances died February 22, 1979. Jonathan was about the same age when he died a year later. And on March 2, 1981, Marybeth's adopted son, Michael, died. He was two and a half. Some of the younger children's deaths were attributed to SIDS. Two of them—Nathan and Mary Frances—had been put on apnea monitors as a precaution.

Although Schenectady police suspected that Marybeth Tinning was doing something to her children, lapses by doctors, prosecutors, and others prevented a proper investigation. The county had a part-time medical examiner, and the police had no way of knowing when another Tinning baby died. Most of the babies were buried before the investigators knew they were dead, eliminating any chance of collecting medical evidence. Some weren't autopsied.

That changed when four-month-old Tami Lynne Tinning died December 20, 1985. Schenectady police learned about her death within hours and persuaded an assistant district attorney to take action. A forensic pathologist familiar with the history of deaths in the Tinning family was called in to perform an autopsy. He could find no obvious cause for Tami Lynne's death.

Almost fourteen years after Marybeth Tinning's children began dying, Schenectady County district attorney John Poersch assembled a task force of prosecutors, police, and pathologists to start an investigation. The Schenectady police department agreed to call in the state police.

The state police were eager to help. They had a new forensic sciences unit they wanted to put to work on a big case, and they had just wrapped up a similar inves-

tigation in neighboring Saratoga County that led to
Stephen Van Der Sluys's indictment for killing his
fifteen-month-old daughter, Vickie Lynn. Once forensic pathologists on the task force became convinced
that Marybeth had killed Tami Lynne, the state police
began working up a strategy for interviewing her. They
turned to LaBar.

The senior investigator had learned about the Tinning investigation after Tami Lynne's death, when state
police colleagues warned him that Marybeth and her
husband, Joe, were planning to move to Saratoga
County. The task force investigators later drove to the
barracks in Malta to ask LaBar about the Van Der
Sluys case.

It was an obvious step. The Van Der Sluys case had
received wide publicity in the capital region. The Tinning investigators hoped LaBar could given them some
insights into handling a suspect who seemed as depraved as Stephen Van Der Sluys.

Marybeth was full of contradictions, by turns outgoing and insecure. She reveled in melodrama, staging
her children's funerals in a way that cast her in the
starring role. Some of her scheming mirrored Steve
Van Der Sluys's unsavory behavior. Several Tinning
children had burial insurance, and Marybeth, like
Steve, used the proceeds to go on selfish spending
sprees. Schenectady police also suspected Marybeth
had staged a burglary at her home to cover up the theft
of cash she held for her husband's bowling club, much
as Steve had faked break-ins at his apartment in
Mechanicville. They also shared a weakness for adul-
terous affairs.

LaBar believed that Marybeth had a pathological
craving for attention and that she took to the outpouring of sympathy from Jennifer's death the way a junkie
takes to dope. With each succeeding child's death she
got another fix. Jane Van Der Sluys had noticed how

much her husband enjoyed the attention he got talking about his children's deaths, a topic she tried to avoid.

The task force also wanted to talk to Joe Tinning, the husband whom Marybeth had tried to kill with an overdose of phenobarbital. Investigators never considered this meek, General Electric production specialist a suspect. He seemed as much a captive of docile loyalty to his spouse as Jane Van Der Sluys was to hers.

On February 4, 1986, task force investigators took Marybeth to the state police barracks in Loudonville, an Albany suburb. After hours of fruitless questioning, an investigator Marybeth had known since childhood was called in to help. He got her to admit she had smothered Tami Lynne with a pillow. She also said she had killed two of her other children, Timothy and Nathan, but the police charged her only with the murder of Tami Lynne.

The investigation continued throughout 1986 as the task force grappled with the question of whether to pursue charges against Marybeth in the other children's deaths. Poersch and Alan Gebell, one of the senior prosecutors leading the investigation, eventually visited Fitzpatrick to ask him about the Van Der Sluys case.

Fitzpatrick told them the Van Der Sluys case probably wouldn't be appealed in time to provide case law that would help their prosecution, but offered the research he used in trial preparation. He recommended that they hire Dr. Linda Norton as an expert witness and urged them to have all the Tinning children's bodies exhumed.

"You never know what you'll find," he said, remembering the remarkable preservation of Vickie Lynn Van Der Sluys's body.

Poersch opposed the idea. Under pressure from Dr. Michael Baden, the forensic pathologist for the state police, Poersch had reluctantly approved the exhumations of Nathan and Timothy Tinning. Nathan's body had deteriorated too much to provide any evidence. Timothy's remains were never found. Because of a mix-up with the grave markers, Jennifer Tinning's body was dug up by mistake. Poersch refused to give Baden another chance to exhume Timothy's body, which probably lay buried under Jennifer's grave marker.

Fitzpatrick urged them to exhume all the bodies because he thought Poersch should prosecute Marybeth Tinning for the eight deaths. He had an ally in Gebell.

"Any advice I gave them about Tinning, Gebell was saying, 'Yeah, that's what we should do,' and Poersch was saying, 'No, I don't think so. We're going to keep it simple. It's one; it's just Tami Lynne. She confessed to Tami Lynne, and we have a pathologist who says it's murder.' "

Fitzpatrick thought justice demanded more. He was guided by a promise he'd made to himself years earlier: People aren't entitled to one or two free murders throughout their career. Just because we don't catch you right away doesn't mean you can get away with it.

The Van Der Sluys case had reinforced that view. And maybe because he had no children of his own, the death of Heather Van Der Sluys had given Fitzpatrick a profound appreciation for the preciousness of a child's life. He continued to press Poersch to make a case with the other Tinning children's death.

"If not for justice's sake, then just for letting the jury see the whole picture," he said. "The jury is going to find it incomprehensible that this woman, completely out of the blue, suffocates a perfectly healthy baby. You've got to let them know about the other seven babies."

Poersch disregarded Fitzpatrick's advice. He didn't hire Dr. Norton, either. After a six-week trial, Marybeth Tinning was convicted in July 1987 of murdering just one of her children—Tami Lynne.

For Fitzpatrick, the rejection of his suggestions was not nearly as painful as knowing that nine children had died before the authorities in Schenectady recognized Marybeth Tinning as a threat. Looking at the Van Der Sluys and Tinning cases together, he saw a tragic sequence of events. Senior Schenectady and state police officials were widely quoted as saying that publicity surrounding the Van Der Sluys case triggered the Tinning investigation in the next county. But Stephen Van Der Sluys was indicted in Saratoga County two months before Tami Lynne died.

"They said, 'We got suspicious of her after we heard about the Van Der Sluys case,' " Fitzpatrick said. "I read that and I'm thinking, 'Jeez, couldn't you have gotten suspicious a couple of weeks earlier? Maybe the last child would've been saved.' "

The same could be said about the Van Der Sluys case. In hindsight, nearly everybody viewed Heath Van Der Sluys's death with suspicion. At the time, however, the Onondaga County medical examiner, Dr. Martin Hilfinger, signed off on it as an accidental death without performing an autopsy, and the Syracuse police investigation didn't go beyond filing the required paperwork.

But what about when Heather died three months later? Shouldn't the sudden, unexpected death of another child have caused Hilfinger and his assistant, Dr. William Alsever, to call for an investigation of the family? And if they had looked at the two deaths together, shouldn't they have concluded that Heather did not die of SIDS?

Fitzpatrick knew the implication. Ed Menkin had pointed it out during his cross-examination of Norton.

"Well, they could have saved the life of another child, couldn't they?"

"Yes," Norton said. "I don't know exactly what to say about that sort of professional conduct."

Fitzpatrick was left to ponder the judgment involved in other infant deaths. The Van Der Sluys trial taught him how easily an adult could snuff out the life of a baby. Marybeth Tinning had done it too—by her own admission, more than once.

"How many of these people are out there?" Fitzpatrick wondered. But he already feared there was at least one more close at hand. He remembered Norton's reference to a woman who had lost five children. "You have a serial killer right here in Syracuse," she had said.

Fitzpatrick asked a law clerk to get him a copy of the article Norton had cited. Reading Dr. Alfred Steinschneider's landmark study in the October 1972 *Pediatrics* confirmed his worst fears.

"I knew right away the kids had been murdered," Fitzpatrick said. "If you show me an article about five kids that died under mysterious circumstances in the same family, I would say to you those kids were murdered until you prove otherwise to me. It just doesn't happen.

"Now, you tell me some more things. All five of the kids died of some type of respiratory problem. Now, the convincing level goes from ninety percent to ninety-five percent. Now, you tell me that some of the kids had been registered in a hospital before for near-death episodes, and had been revived heroically by the mother. Now, I'm up to ninety-nine percent. Now, you tell me that all five of the kids only had breathing difficulties when they were in the custody and the care and the control of the mother. Now, I'm up to one-hundred percent. And all of those factors were present in the article."

Fitzpatrick couldn't understand how the last two children could have been killed while they were under Steinschneider's care. Didn't knowing about the three earlier deaths make Steinschneider suspicious when the next baby died? Why didn't he alert the authorities after the fifth death?

Fitzpatrick assumed that the family lived in the Syracuse area because the children were treated at Upstate Medical Center. Based on the date of the article, he could surmise that the last child died at least fourteen years ago, making the case older than Tinning's or Van Der Sluys's. But he had no way of knowing whether this woman had borne more children. Were they in danger? And if not her own, what about other children? Did she baby-sit nieces and nephews, or her neighbors' children?

The article didn't give him much to go on. In it, Steinschneider had identified the children by initials—M.H. and N.H. The doctor referred to the mother as "Mrs. H." Fitzpatrick didn't even know the age of "Mrs. H." Could she still bear children? He decided to track down Steinschneider. He got as far as the University of Maryland before the thread ended. Steinschneider had left Baltimore in 1983; the university invoked confidentiality and would not say where he'd gone. Then time ran out.

Fitzpatrick knew he couldn't stay in the district attorney's office any longer. The friction with Hennessy would only grow worse. He'd made plans to go into private practice with a Syracuse law firm. All that remained was to break the news to his boss. Hennessy surprised him by seeming genuinely upset.

"Aw, get out of here, go back to your office. You're not really leaving."

Hennessy's bluff attempt to talk him out of going reminded Fitzpatrick of the bond they had once shared, but he couldn't turn back.

"Dick, I'm really gone. I'd like to leave at the end of the year, if that's okay. I'll do whatever you need to wrap things up."

Before he left, Fitzpatrick said, he told two other

prosecutors about the woman with the five dead children.

The resignation of Syracuse's top homicide prosecutor made front-page headlines when word leaked out. Fitzpatrick called a news conference on December 18, 1986, to announce his departure, and reporters focused on the prospects for a fight between him and Hennessy for the DA's job.

"While I have disagreed with him, I will not challenge him," Fitzpatrick stated. But he made it clear that he wanted the job if Hennessy decided not to seek reelection.

Everybody seemed to understand that Fitzpatrick was giving up a job he loved. He tried to lighten the moment with a joke about how much he looked forward to defense work. "I understand my first assignment is to get ready for tomorrow's Christmas party."

Fitzpatrick found it difficult to let go. On New Year's Eve, he made a last visit to the district attorney's offices on the twelfth floor of the civic center. It was late; the place was empty. He wandered among the offices, alone with his thoughts. He looked back over his career as a prosecutor, the excitement of being close to the action, making a difference, the big cases. Nine good years, he thought, one bad. The last one.

He unlocked Hennessy's large corner office with its commanding views of Syracuse and looked around. Fitzpatrick had known good times here, too. Hennessy had given him great opportunities, and Fitzpatrick had rewarded his confidence. Their bond had once bordered on love. Fitzpatrick's eyes grew moist, but before he could complete the sentimental journey, his sense of humor kicked in. He spotted a microphone on Hennessy's desk, picked it up, cocked his head, and, in his best impression of Gen. Douglas MacArthur, announced: "People of the Philippines, I shall return."

Fitzpatrick wanted to make a faster comeback than

MacArthur, but he refused to go to war with his former boss. Instead, he hoped that Hennessy, still stuck with the nickname Landslide from his slim victory in the last election, would step aside and clear the way for him to run.

The winter of 1987 passed with no word from Hennessy on whether he would seek reelection. Fitzpatrick began to worry that his deferring to Hennessy's decision had unnecessarily tied his hands. If he continued to delay his plans while Hennessy made up his mind, other candidates could get a jump on the Republican nomination.

Spring came, and Fitzpatrick got tired of waiting. He announced his candidacy on March 26. He stuck by his pledge not to challenge Hennessy but pointed out a loophole: If he won the Republican nomination before Hennessy announced his candidacy, his former boss would be the challenger, not him.

"I think that three and a half years is long enough to wait to see if somebody is going to run for reelection," Fitzpatrick said.

His announcement didn't spur Hennessy's decision. The district attorney didn't reveal he was running until a month later, at a Sheraton hotel where party officials had arranged the first in a series of candidate debates.

The former colleagues used the forum to trade barbs that left no doubt that each thought himself better qualified than the other for the job.

But Hennessy had an edge. Fitzpatrick had set himself up for a question he didn't have an answer for: What about your promise not to challenge Hennessy if he decided to seek reelection?

Fitzpatrick got a laugh by thanking a Hennessy supporter, a DA's investigator, for asking the question, then tried to deflect the issue with another jab: "It wasn't until twenty minutes ago that I learned I'd have an opponent."

Hennessy wouldn't let him off the hook. "I'll let Bill hang out on his word."

Back home, Bill Fitzpatrick realized Hennessy had boxed him into a corner. He and Diane talked late into the night. His resignation from the district attorney's office had freed Diane to clerk for a county court judge. His election as district attorney would create a conflict of interest for them, but Diane didn't let that complicate the question.

"You do what you think is right," she said, "and whatever you do, whether you stay in or drop out, I'll back you one hundred percent."

The next night, during the second candidates' forum at a suburban church, Fitzpatrick withdrew from the race.

"In January, I announced I would not attempt to run against Dick Hennessy, and I'm going to keep my word," he said. He gave his support to Hennessy, and the Republican committee people rewarded him with a standing ovation.

In the darkness outside the church, doubts lingered. "Did I make the right decision?" Fitzpatrick thought. "Did an opportunity slip by that may never present itself again? I've been saying since I was a kid that I wanted to be in law enforcement, and to me, law enforcement is being DA."

Five months later, allegations of Hennessy using his staff to run personal errands hit the newspapers. Similar ethical allegations had dogged Hennessy for more than a decade, but the revival of the charges less than six weeks before the election took its toll. Hennessy lost to Robert Wildridge, a Democratic convert whom Hennessy had narrowly defeated for the Republican nomination eleven years before.

Although many thought Fitzpatrick made the wrong choice by dropping out of the race, he never regretted his decision. He saw his career shaped by a larger force, a power that imbued life's infinite variables with purpose. Fitzpatrick had no doubt that he would serve as district attorney someday.

"I'm a great believer in destiny," Fitzpatrick said. His mother likes to say he was born that way.

Chapter Twelve

At first, Anne Fitzpatrick couldn't understand why her obstetrician was giving her a choice of dates for her second cesarean section—October 13 or 15.

"In case you're superstitious," the doctor explained.

"No," she said, "the sooner the better."

The surgical delivery was scheduled for nine o'clock in the morning on the thirteenth, a Monday, at Brooklyn Hospital. When maternity nurses started prepping her about six-thirty that morning, they became alarmed: They couldn't hear the baby's heartbeat.

"They called the doctor and, God, he was there like in seconds," Anne recalled decades later. "He asked me if I was upset. I said, 'Hysterical.' "

"Do you trust me?"

"I trust you."

With that endorsement, the doctor went to work, and at 8:13 A.M. October 13, 1952, he pulled William John Fitzpatrick Jr. from his mother's womb—alive.

"He had been choking on the umbilical cord," Anne said. "Had I waited until the fifteenth . . ."

The child would grow into a man awed by the mere fact of his existence.

"We—everybody on earth—were meant to be," Bill Fitzpatrick said, "by the fact that it's beyond our control. If you went back a thousand years, and went through all the possibilities of being born, there isn't a number long enough to account for that."

Another figure who survived long odds to factor into

that equation was William J. Fitzpatrick Sr. Raised in Brooklyn, Bill Sr. came of age during the Depression and served in the Seabees during World War II. In 1947, at the age of twenty-six, he joined the New York City Police Department. He walked a beat in the Eighty-eighth Precinct in the Bedford-Stuyvesant section of Brooklyn.

Bill Sr. and Anne had grown up three blocks apart, but they didn't meet until after the war. They were married in 1948 and settled into a four-room apartment on Willoughby Avenue in Brooklyn. Their first son was born a year later. They named him Barry, after the actor Barry Fitzgerald. Bill Jr. came along three years later.

Bill Fitzpatrick Jr. grew up in a household where family responsibilities were divided along traditional lines: His mother stayed home and saw to the needs of the children; his father brought home the paycheck, usually two. Bill Sr. had started moonlighting to earn enough money to move his family to a more comfortable home.

In 1955, the Fitzpatricks bought a row house on Seventy-third Street in the Bay Ridge section of Brooklyn, across from Staten Island. The gray brick house had a small backyard where the boys could run around, and traffic was light enough for children to play stickball in the streets. The Fitzpatricks lived on the first floor; Bill Sr.'s mother, his sister, and her husband lived upstairs.

"On the day the moving van pulled away, I think our cash capital was sixty cents," Bill Sr. said.

The Fitzpatricks never questioned the sacrifice. They had found an ideal spot to raise their children. Bay Ridge was a solid, middle-class neighborhood populated by families of Irish, Italian, German, Swedish, and Puerto Rican descent. There were so many families with fathers who wore NYPD blue, they almost counted as a separate ethnic group.

Bill Jr. remembered that his parents always put the children first. When he was two, his parents noticed that his left eye had turned. The next year, they took him to Mother Cabrini Hospital in Manhattan for the first of two operations to correct his eyesight. Billy, as they called him, lived in darkness for ten days, with both eyes swathed in bandages. Anne and Bill Sr. took turns staying with him.

Billy never forgot how safe his parents made him feel. At their twenty-fifth wedding anniversary, he told family and friends how his parents' touch had quelled his fears in the hospital.

"I had my patches on for ten days. I would like everyone just to close your eyes for a second. I was only little. Ten days of that. But when I put my hand out, Mom and Dad were right there."

Billy never touched his dressings, never cried. The only time he complained was when a nurse told him to turn over so she could bathe him, then gave him a shot in the bottom instead. The needle didn't bother him; his mother didn't brook any fussing over shots. But Billy didn't like the trick the nurse played on him. She had told a fib, and Billy knew his mother didn't stand for that either. He was already showing the influence of his mother's moral certitude.

Anne Fitzpatrick had definite ideas about right and wrong. Her outlook didn't allow for gray areas, and she saw no point in sugarcoating life's hard lessons for her children. Sometimes doing the right thing hurt, like a shot in the fanny. Her judgments came wrapped in the warm embrace of a mother's love, and Billy took her word as gospel.

Anne Fitzpatrick's matter-of-fact discipline became the source of a special bond between her and her younger son. He grew up knowing he could tell his mother anything without risking the loss of her affection.

The nuns at Our Lady of Angels grammar school down the street reinforced the lessons taught at home.

Family and parish life merged every day. After packing her boys off to school, Anne Fitzpatrick went to the eight forty-five a.m. Mass. Barry and Billy joined the parish Cub Scout pack. Later, they served as altar boys. The depth of Barry's faith showed early. By the time he was eight, he was saying Mass at home on a makeshift altar draped in blankets. Always a dutiful older brother, Barry let Billy help.

Even when he worked two jobs, Bill Sr. tried to get home in the evening in case the boys needed help with their lessons. Good grades were expected, not rewarded. When Billy came home excited by a ninety-six average, his mother said, "Well, who got ninety-seven? Ninety-six doesn't look so good if there are six or eight others in the room who got ninety-seven."

The gentle push didn't hurt. Both boys' names turned up regularly on the honor roll. Barry even skipped a grade in grammar school.

Sports also helped shape the boys' character from an early age. They inherited a love of baseball from their father, who had played with major leaguers in the Pacific during World War II. When the family gathered in front of their small television set to watch ball games, the boys stood and saluted during the national anthem.

Barry was a gifted athlete who eventually shot up to six-four. Billy hustled to keep up with Barry and the older kids on the baseball diamond. He could pitch, but his glasses made hitting difficult.

Glasses had been the bane of his existence since his eye operations. Whenever anyone called him "four eyes," his glasses came off and his fists went up. The size of his tormentor didn't matter.

Whatever Billy lacked in talent, he made up for in scrappy competitiveness. Some of his fondest memories summon images of playing summer baseball for the Police Athletic League. He remembers his father, always pressed for time, taking him to a park one day to teach him how to hit.

"We were out there for two or three hours. I was in heaven. He said, 'Get the elbow out,' and do this and do that. And the next game was one of the best games I ever had."

Billy also inherited his interest in law enforcement from his father. He was ten when his father took him to the police academy and an officer gave him a finger-print kit. Billy used it to dust for fingerprints all over the house.

"I was afraid to go to sleep at night, for fear he'd be dusting my nose," his father said.

Billy set up his desk like a crime lab with the dusting kit, and within weeks closed his first investigation. Bill Sr. saw the evidence labeled with an index card: "Rock from a Famous Case."

"Explain this one to me," the father said.

"Oh, remember the one I hit Barry with the other day?"

Bill Sr. never pushed his sons toward police work, but the influence was hard to avoid. The NYPD served as an extended family. The Fitzpatricks went to the beach and on picnics with other officers' families. They vacationed at a police recreation center in the Catskills, where the staff played "Mockingbird Hill" over the public address system each morning to summon the cops' families to a communal breakfast.

Bill Sr. became a safety-warrant officer in 1953 and spent the next fourteen years tracking down thousands of people who failed to show up for court. He avoided talking about the gritty part of his work at home, but Billy liked to hear his father explain the different methods he used to bring in defendants.

"A favorite trick I used to use was writing letters . . . suggesting they had won prizes in order to get them to come in," Bill Sr. said.

Billy raced through Hardy Boys mysteries, but none of their adventures excited him like the real-life drama in *Kidnap,* George Waller's 1962 account of the abduction and murder of the Lindbergh baby. The painstaking collection of evidence pointing to Bruno Hauptmann's guilt so captivated the twelve-year-old sleuth that he read the book three more times as he got older.

While the Fitzpatricks could only guess at their younger son's future, their firstborn had a clear idea of what he wanted to do. Barry left home at sixteen to join the congregation of Francis Xavier. Brother Barry Fitzpatrick later became principal of St. Joseph's High School in Baltimore.

Bill Jr. followed Barry to Xaverian High School in Bay Ridge, where he took an interest in journalism. He and a group of friends published *The Third Rail,* an underground paper that mixed campus muckraking with satire that poked fun at their teachers' quirky habits. The group put the paper to bed in the Fitzpatricks' basement and printed it on the school mimeograph machine.

Bill Jr. graduated from high school in 1970 eager to change the world. He thought he would do it as a crusading reporter, and so he began taking journalism classes at Syracuse University. He went to school on scholarships and earned money during the summer supervising baggage handling for Pan-Am at JFK Airport.

His career plans started to change when he spent the spring of 1972 in Washington, D.C. He worked as an intern for U.S. Sen. James Buckley, the brother of conservative columnist William F. Buckley Jr. and later a federal judge. Fitzpatrick registered for an undergraduate constitutional law class the next semester. He did well, and his professor encouraged him to go on to law school.

Even then, Bill Fitzpatrick Jr. knew he wanted to work as a prosecutor, and that pleased his father, who retired from the New York City Police Department in 1967.

Law enforcement connected father and son as adults

the way baseball did when Bill Jr. was a kid. As an assistant district attorney, Bill Fitzpatrick often called his father to discuss cases. He clung to that bond when he started defending criminal cases, occasionally telling jurors his father had been a cop for twenty years. But as Bill Jr.'s exile from law enforcement dragged on, the two men found another tie to bind them—fatherhood.

Diane and Bill Fitzpatrick began to rethink their lives after he left the district attorney's office. They'd spent the first five years of their marriage building their legal careers. But with Diane settled into a comfortable private practice and Bill free of all-consuming homicide prosecutions, they began to talk about having a family.

They already had an ideal place to raise children. Just before the Van Der Sluys trial, they had moved into a sprawling raised-ranch with a broad front lawn in LaFayette, a rural town south of Syracuse best known for its annual apple festival. During their first year in LaFayette they talked more and more about having children.

"I wasn't ready until just about then," Diane said. "We just had too many things going. Then I started looking at our ages and said, 'Whoa, we've got to start getting serious.'"

When Diane had difficulty getting pregnant, her gynecologist referred her to Dr. Nabil ElHassan, a fertility specialist who had helped dozens of couples conceive.

"He always made me feel special," Diane said, "I think he made everybody feel that way." ElHassan quickly corrected Diane's problem, and she became pregnant.

The birth of the Fitzpatricks' first child came with a reminder that life's intricate equation carries a quotient of loss. Diane's long labor began on the afternoon of May 16, 1989. ElHassan spent time with her in the labor room early the next morning, but left when he became ill. He collapsed at 4:00 A.M. and died. He was forty-five.

Ninety minutes later, Diane delivered a healthy tenpound, two-ounce boy. She and Bill named him Daniel Barry. Even as they celebrated the birth, the couple mourned the death of the doctor who had made it possible.

Bill Fitzpatrick shared the anxieties of many new parents. He and Diane put a speaker in Danny's room so they could hear when he stirred from his naps, but sometimes that wasn't enough. Bill Fitzpatrick would wake to silence in the night and go to his son's room. Listening to the sound of the infant breathing reminded him of the fragile thread by which life hangs. From time to time he thought about the woman he knew only as "Mrs. H," and the five children who slept forever.

Fitzpatrick's new career in defense work had taken off. His reputation as a prosecutor helped him build a lucrative private practice, and soon he was making more than twice the $55,000 salary he had earned as a prosecutor. He attributed his success to luck, but skill played a part.

He'd spent years as a prosecutor preparing for trial by devising defenses that exposed weaknesses in his case. Now he could put those lessons into practice as a defense lawyer. He walked away from three murder trials with his clients convicted of lesser manslaughter charges.

Such successes didn't endear him to his friends in law enforcement, however, especially when they were the target of one of his grueling cross-examinations. Fitzpatrick was unapologetic. Defense work had given him a broader view of the criminal justice system. He began to see some gray areas. He even found he liked some defendants, although he didn't necessarily admire them.

But the novelty of working on the other side of the

courtroom soon wore off. Fitzpatrick missed the action of the district attorney's office. He found himself in a bar one night helping a young prosecutor prepare a summation in a murder trial. Diane Fitzpatrick realized that defending criminal cases would never engage her husband's passions.

"He would work hard, and he obviously did well on them," Diane said, "but I think defending a case is significantly easier because a lot of times you don't have to do anything except punch holes in the prosecution's case. Something was missing in his life, and you could tell. He wasn't happy."

Part of the problem lay in Fitzpatrick's law-and-order values. He found it difficult to reconcile his sympathy for victims with the right of a defendant—however notorious—to a vigorous defense. He wasn't cut out for the ethical hairsplitting needed to justify representing a client he knew in his heart was guilty. Bill Fitzpatrick Sr. heard his son's doubts.

"He had a case involving some drug pusher and he said, 'I know this guy is probably the biggest bum that God ever created, and he knows he's going to jail. And he says the only reason he's retaining a lawyer is that by virtue of exercising the proper postponements and appeals I can give him some more time on the street. What I'm afraid of is that while he's on the street, he's never going to turn an honest dollar and he's probably turning over more narcotics, and kids are going to be affected.'

"I said the big thing is that you have got to be able to look yourself and your family in the face. 'Don't worry,' he says, 'I will always be able to do that.' "

Bill Fitzpatrick Jr. saw only one way out of his problem. Not surprisingly, he found the answer in his family. In December 1989, he told a group of influential Onondaga County Republicans he didn't want one day to have to tell six-month-old Danny that he defended killers. He used his platform to criticize the murder conviction record of Dick Hennessy's successor, District Attorney Robert Wildridge. When a reporter remarked that his address sounded like a campaign speech, Fitzpatrick said, "It did, didn't it?"

Almost two years before the election, Bill Fitzpatrick had a plan for winning the district attorney's job. His blueprint called for getting an early start, raising plenty of money, and spending it to scare off any potential challengers for the Republican nomination. The last step would pit him against Wildridge, the likely Democratic candidate, who already looked vulnerable.

Wildridge had gotten off to a shaky start as district attorney. His office lost three murder trials in a row, and he alienated the police by prosecuting an accused cop-killer himself, although he had never tried a homicide. His future as district attorney looked even dimmer in 1990, when he ran a distant fourth in a state court race.

Fitzpatrick's plan worked better than he expected. On March 27, 1991, Wildridge announced he would not seek a second term as district attorney. In June, Fitzpatrick received the Republican nomination. Shortly afterward, the Democrats decided not to field an opponent, thus ensuring Fitzpatrick's victory.

Rather than coast into office, Fitzpatrick decided to maintain his head start. He put together a list of overdue investigations he wanted to launch when his term began and started to organize his staff-in-waiting. Fitzpatrick also made it clear that his office would be responsive to victims and their families.

"These are human beings we're dealing with," he said in a newspaper interview before the election. "You can't allow a situation to happen where a woman's house gets burglarized and she never hears anything from the DA's office about what happened to the defendant. Or a guy loses a limb or an organ or something, or gets stabbed, and he reads about the disposition of the case in the newspaper."

On November 5, three weeks after his thirty-ninth birthday, Fitzpatrick was elected district attorney. He moved into the corner office on the twelfth floor of the civic center in January. With his staff busy at work, he took hold of the microphone he'd spoken into on New Year's Eve five years earlier and made an announcement that only he understood: "People of the Philippines, I have returned."

PART THREE

The Investigation

Chapter Thirteen

Bill Fitzpatrick wasted no time putting his imprint on the district attorney's office. If ever a place reflected the interests of the person who inhabited it, the spacious suite that Fitzpatrick occupied on the twelfth floor of the Onondaga County Civic Center was it. The corner office looked like an exhibit from the National Baseball Hall of Fame and Museum in Cooperstown, with pictures of ballparks lining the walls and autographed balls arrayed on shelves. Law books, mementos from his cases as an assistant prosecutor, and plaques from police agencies represented his other passion. He indulged the wacky side of his personality by installing a jukebox loaded with an eclectic selection of hit singles, including "I Fought the Law and the Law Won," by the Bobby Fuller Four. But Fitzpatrick had more in mind for the district attorney's office than redecorating. One of the first possessions he unpacked was a list of cases that other prosecutors had overlooked or given up on.

In his first year, District Attorney Bill Fitzpatrick would reopen five murder cases, including one that had sat untouched for nine years. Never afraid to get his hands dirty or hide his sentiments, Fitzpatrick would try one of the cases himself, winning a murder conviction after delivering a tearful summation. High on his agenda was file 92-100—the case of "Mrs. H."

Fitzpatrick was determined to use his newly acquired authority to force this investigation to a head.

Though he had a vast network of contacts in law enforcement circles, Fitzpatrick would always remain vague about the initial steps he took to identify the children Dr. Alfred Steinschneider had written about twenty years earlier. But this is known: The last to die was the first revealed. The baby boy Steinschneider referred to in his article as "N.H." was Noah Hoyt.

Armed with that name and the scanty clues in Steinschneider's article, Fitzpatrick started piecing together the story behind the five children's deaths. He had a grand jury secretly subpoena Noah Hoyt's medical records from University Hospital, known as Upstate Medical Center when Steinschneider worked there. As Dr. Linda Norton had suspected years earlier, the records showed the baby had been healthy until he died suddenly at home in 1971. Noah's records also identified his four brothers and sisters, who had died from 1965 to 1970, and named the parents. The father was Timothy Hoyt; "Mrs. H" was Waneta Hoyt. Nearly three months after entering office, Fitzpatrick finally knew the secret identity of the family Steinschneider had studied.

For Fitzpatrick, the hospital records contained another revelation: The family he had been pursuing in his mind for five years didn't live in Onondaga County. Although two Hoyt babies had been treated at a Syracuse hospital, they had all died at home in Newark Valley, a town seventy miles south of Syracuse, in Tioga County.

Fitzpatrick had his staff track down the children's death certificates before he conceded what he already knew: the case that had become his obsession wasn't in his jurisdiction; it belonged to Tioga County. If Fitzpatrick knew little about the rural county bordering north-central Pennsylvania, he knew even less about the district attorney empowered to enforce the law there—Robert J. Simpson.

Fitzpatrick was reluctant to turn his case over to

someone he didn't know, and Bob Simpson was one of the few district attorneys in New York State that he had never met. He gave the task of checking out Simpson's reputation to Pete Tynan, a former Syracuse police sergeant whom Fitzpatrick had hired as his chief investigator. Fitzpatrick trusted Tynan like a brother. They had solved cases together as prosecutor and cop, and they spoke the same street-tough language. Tynan was his backup on the Hoyt investigation, but more important, he had a cousin who worked as chief investigator for the district attorney in Broome County, next door to Tioga County.

"How's this Simpson guy? Is he all right?" Tynan wanted to know.

Simpson was fine, his cousin assured him.

As much as Fitzpatrick hated to give up the Hoyt case, he knew he had to tell Simpson about the suspected murders in his county; he would expect the same if the roles were reversed. In late March, Fitzpatrick called the Tioga County district attorney's office to hand over what could have been the biggest case of his career. He backed into the conversation, telling Simpson he was the new district attorney in Onondaga County and was wondering if Simpson ever attended the statewide DA conventions. He tried to feel Simpson out—"Bob, how's everything going down there? How long have you been in office?"—then got down to business.

"We have kind of an unusual situation here," Fitzpatrick began.

He walked Simpson through the Van Der Sluys case, explained Norton's suspicions about Steinschneider's article, and said he believed that the five Hoyt children had been murdered in Tioga County. He ticked off everything he had done to that point: identifying the family; gathering Noah's hospital records; finding medical experts who could review the case.

"OK," Simpson said. "Send me the records and we'll get working on it."

"OK?" Fitzpatrick thought. Just OK? Although he knew next to nothing about the person on the other end of the line, Fitzpatrick expected to hear more excitement from a prosecutor who'd just had five unsolved homicides dumped in his lap. He started having second thoughts about turning over the complex case to a small-town DA. Fitzpatrick hustled to preserve a role for himself in the investigation. "I'm available," he told Simpson. "You need anything, I'm available." That got an OK, too.

Bob Simpson and Bill Fitzpatrick were about as different as two white, male, forty-something upstate New York Republican DA's could be. Simpson was as low-key as Fitzpatrick was brash. While Fitzpatrick courted the media and would soon launch his own public affairs television program, Simpson shunned the limelight.

The contrast extended to their looks. Fitzpatrick was tall, thin, and pale, while Simpson, a compact five-seven, had the robust appearance of a latter-day Teddy Roosevelt. With a neatly trimmed thatch of brown hair and a bushy mustache that concealed a gap-toothed smile, Simpson looked a decade younger than his forty-eight years. He often appeared to be deep in thought, his brow furrowed, as he walked with long, splayfooted strides that made the heels of his shoes click on the floor.

The Tioga County district attorney worked out of a renovated antique office building in the village of Owego, the county seat. His rarely used desk took up little more space than a closet in Fitzpatrick's office. Simpson did most of his work at a ten-foot-long table in his law library. The room came equipped with a mini-refrigerator, and Simpson kept a jar of peanut butter and a two-foot-tall container of hard pretzels at hand to snack on.

The offices the two district attorneys ran were as different as the places where they worked. Simpson was the only full-time prosecutor serving fifty thousand people scattered among nine rural towns and a handful of villages. The county gave him a $250,000 budget to prosecute criminals, and he secured indictments in 125 cases annually. He had no investigators and only three part-time assistant district attorneys to help with his caseload, which meant that Simpson himself handled everything from speeding tickets to homicides. Fortunately, Tioga County wasn't a murderous place. The county usually saw one homicide a year. There hadn't been four homicides in one year since 1979, let alone five at once, and Simpson hadn't taken any murder to trial in two years.

Fitzpatrick's jurisdiction encompassed a city with 165,000 residents, plus suburbs and towns with half again as many people. He had a legion of forty-five full-time assistants, fourteen investigators, and a $5 million budget. His office secured indictments in roughly 1,300 cases a year, about 20 of them homicides. Fitzpatrick might prosecute one or two cases by himself, but he never handled traffic court.

Although Simpson's twenty-two years as a prosecutor gave him the edge in seniority, he had little experience with the kind of complex or high-profile cases that Fitzpatrick had handled. Simpson had grown up in nearby Ithaca, the son of a state Supreme Court judge. He started as a part-time prosecutor in 1970, right after he graduated from the State University of New York at Albany's law school. When his boss became County Court judge in 1978, Simpson was elected DA, which was then a part-time job. In Tioga County, district attorneys traditionally moved up to the bench. Simpson was the heir apparent when his former boss retired from the bench in 1992, but he decided to stay in his post, which by that time the county had made a full-time position.

While high-powered lawyers working in large criminal court systems often approach their work as mortal combat and measure themselves by win-loss records, justice in Tioga County was a more familiar affair. Nobody paid much attention to the score, and slick gamesmanship would have appeared unseemly; neither Simpson nor the tight circle of defense lawyers he almost daily encountered could afford to harbor grudges.

Simpson didn't put much stock in courtroom theatrics, and he seemed unperturbed by his adversaries' occasional bombast. He was methodical, not flashy. For Simpson, even the routine of ordering lunch was an exercise in deliberation. Nearly every day, he went to the Parkview Restaurant around the corner from the courthouse, and he always ate the same lunch. He could have walked in and called for "the usual," but he always spelled out the order: a bacon, lettuce, and tomato sandwich with very little mayonnaise—no pickles and no chips—split pea soup and iced tea.

The cautious prosecutor wasn't overwhelmed by Fitzpatrick's hunch about the Hoyt children. "I'll certainly have to be convinced," he thought after hanging up from Fitzpatrick's call. "All I have is a fellow district attorney who calls me up and says you have five deaths under bizarre circumstances."

He remained skeptical after receiving a fax of Steinschneider's article from Fitzpatrick later that day. Simpson knew the people of his county. They had zero tolerance for criminals and were not immune to the horrors of child abuse, rape, and murder that seemed to be daily occurrences in big cities. He had trouble believing that five babies had been murdered and no one had done anything. Not doctors, not neighbors, not family, not the police. Simpson had been an assistant district attorney when the last two children died, and he couldn't recall hearing about any suspicions, much less an investigation.

Did Fitzpatrick know what he was asking? Was

Tioga County's only full-time prosecutor supposed to go after a local family who had suffered the loss of five children to what doctors had said were natural causes because Onondaga County's district attorney had a hunch the kids were murdered? Fitzpatrick's audacious request also came at a crucial time in Simpson's life: Already divorced once, he had just separated from his second wife.

Fitzpatrick had picked up on Simpson's doubts during the phone call. He held on to the vain hope that Simpson would see that the investigation was beyond his means and ask to have his colleague from Syracuse appointed as a special prosecutor. But Simpson had no intention of shirking his responsibility. He may not have seemed as aggressive as Fitzpatrick, but Simpson had a competitive streak. As with Fitzpatrick, it showed in the sports paraphernalia that Simpson kept in his office. But the hockey stick and other gear that were piled up in the corner weren't for show; the prosecutor, fast approaching fifty, still played ice hockey every Monday night against men years younger.

Investigator John Sherman thought he was being set up for a joke when Bob Simpson called him at the state police barracks in Owego. During his eight years as an investigator, Sherman had often seen Simpson turn his dry wit on waitresses at the Parkview. His teasing usually began with deadpan comments.

"I've just got some paperwork out of Onondaga County," Simpson said. "I've got five homicides for you to investigate."

"Yeah. OK, Bob," said Sherman. "Good, Bob. When I get around to it, I'll look into it."

Simpson assured Sherman he wasn't joking. He explained Fitzpatrick's hunch about Steinschneider's medical article and Fitzpatrick's belief that these five babies had been murdered. Soon afterward, Simpson and Sherman sat down to figure out how to verify Fitzpatrick's tip. They knew they had to poke around quietly; they didn't want to start any talk that might get back to the Hoyt family or to their friends and relatives in the valley.

Sherman didn't see the Hoyt case as a priority; he was too much involved with current investigations to worry about events from decades ago. His partner's retirement had left him as the only investigator in the barracks, and he would see his caseload in 1992 nearly double, to 221 investigations. A few months after Simpson's briefing, he got around to talking to Robert Bleck, the trooper who patrolled the valley where the Hoyts lived.

To the residents of the valley, Bob Bleck *was* the New York State Police. From the close-cropped hair beneath his Smokey-the-Bear hat, to the solid middle-weight's build clad in a slate-gray uniform, Bob Bleck looked every inch an authority figure. Only his easygoing manner and the genial nickname "Bubba" softened the picture.

Bubba Bleck grew up in the valley in the 1960s and attended the same high school where Tim and Waneta Hoyt had gone years earlier. He served two hitches in the army before joining the Owego Police Department in 1978. Nine months later, he joined the state police. His early assignments took him to various posts upstate, but he continued to live in Tioga County. For the past eight years, Bleck had worked out of a storefront office in Berkshire, his hometown.

The outgoing trooper became a popular figure patrolling the valley's crossroad settlements, which line Route 38 like loosely strung beads. People stopped by to strike up conversations as he sat in his car, and he looked out for them like a big brother.

One bitterly cold day prompted a typical Bleck lecture to a woman whose family he knew. "Hey, why don't you have your scarf on?" he called to her as she headed to her car. "It's minus-thirty degrees out and you're walking around with just a coat. You get something on your head right now."

The woman dug into her pocketbook for a scarf.

Bleck's visitors kept him up on the local gossip. In the valley, everybody seemed related—by blood, or marriage, or the invisible bonds of small-town life. That's why Bleck had known who Waneta Hoyt was when she approached him a couple of years earlier in the parking lot of a bank. Her husband was working nights, she said, and she suspected that somebody was peeking in her windows. That night Bleck swung by the Hoyts' home on Route 38. He spoke with a man walking along the road, but found nothing suspicious going on.

That was Bleck's last official interest in Waneta Hoyt until one day when Sherman asked if he knew the Hoyt family. There were a lot of Hoyts in the area, Bleck explained. Sherman said he wanted to know about Tim and Waneta Hoyt, that the DA in Syracuse had read something that supposedly involved the couple.

Bleck said Tim Hoyt was hardworking, and Waneta was in poor health. They had an adopted son. That was it. The trooper wouldn't hear any more about the case for another year.

Sherman decided to talk with one more person, Dr. John Scott, the physician who was called to the Hoyts' trailer for a medical emergency in July 1971 and ended up signing Noah Hoyt's death certificate. Scott lived about two miles down the road from the barracks, and Sherman asked him to stop by.

"No, no, there's nothing there," Scott told Sherman. "It's all natural." The investigator didn't press him. Scott was a doctor; he must have known what he was talking about.

The Hoyt investigation seemed to be going nowhere, and Sherman wasn't surprised. He shared Simpson's doubts about whether five children could have been murdered in a tight-knit place like Tioga County without somebody getting suspicious. Neither he nor the district attorney saw any need to light a fire under the Hoyt case.

But Bill Fitzpatrick did. After four months had passed with no word from Simpson, he started to worry. In July 1992, he wrote to Simpson to find out what was going on, and made another polite pitch to help. The response he received three weeks later wasn't encouraging. Simpson said a state police investigator had been working on the case but was now on vacation.

Simpson plugged away, subpoenaing the Hoyt children's medical records and obtaining their birth certificates. Because the children's deaths were originally attributed to natural causes, Simpson needed a medical expert to review the records for evidence of murder. "I understand bullet wounds, and I understand knifings, and I understand poisons and stuff like that," Simpson said. "But I had no knowledge of apnea or SIDS or any of these things."

Fitzpatrick suggested that Simpson send the records to a pathologist he'd consulted before, Dr. Michael Baden, the head of the New York State Forensic Sciences Unit in Albany. Baden had earned an international reputation in the 1970s as the forensic pathologist who led congressional inquiries into the assassinations of President John F. Kennedy and Dr. Martin Luther King Jr.

Months passed with no more word from Simpson. Fitzpatrick called occasionally, but the Tioga County DA had little to report. Fitzpatrick tried to remain patient. He respected his colleague's authority to proceed as he saw fit, but the delay started to weigh on him. He thought of the Marybeth Tinning case; if the investigation in Schenectady had moved quickly, her last child might have been saved.

"There's all kinds of different speeds you can play

Eric Allen Hoyt, born October 17, 1964; died January 26, 1965. (*Courtesy New York State Police*)

James Avery Hoyt, born May 31, 1966; died September 26, 1968. (*Courtesy New York State Police*)

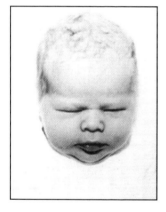

Julie Marie Hoyt, born July 19, 1968; died September 5, 1968. (*Courtesy New York State Police*)

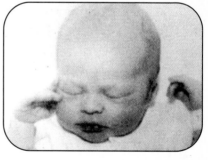

Molly Marie Hoyt, born March 18, 1970; died June 5, 1970. (*Courtesy New York State Police*)

Noah Timothy Hoyt, born May 9, 1971; died July 28, 1971. (*Courtesy New York State Police*)

Waneta and Tim Hoyt on their wedding day, January 11, 1964. (*Courtesy New York State Police*)

Waneta and Tim Hoyt with Molly shortly after her birth in March 1970. (*Courtesy New York State Police*)

James Avery Hoyt, who lived 2½ years, the longest of the Hoyt children (*Courtesy Tioga County Court*)

Waneta Hoyt holds her second child, James Avery. (*Courtesy New York State Police*)

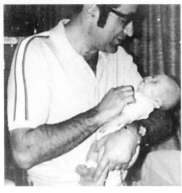

Dr. Alfred Steinschneider holds Noah Timothy Hoyt at Upstate Medical Center in Syracuse in June 1971.
(*Courtesy New York State Police*)

Tim Hoyt holds Noah at Upstate Medical Center in Syracuse in June 1971. The nurses, from left, are Shirley Bacon, Julia Evans, and Pearl Dowdell.
(*Courtesy New York State Police*)

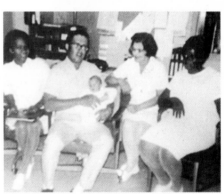

Tim Hoyt holds Noah Timothy, with lead wires from an apnea monitor still attached, at Upstate Medical Center in Syracuse.
(*Courtesy New York State Police*)

Waneta Hoyt holds her fifth child, Noah Timothy, at Upstate Medical Center.
(*Courtesy New York State Police*)

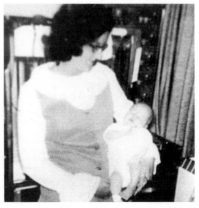

State police use a backhoe to dig up the graves of the Hoyt children in Richford, New York, in January 1995. (*Courtesy New York State Police*)

State police forensic pathologist Dr. Michael Baden, right, with investigators at the January 1995 exhumation of the Hoyt children's graves. (*Courtesy New York State Police*)

State Police Senior Investigator Robert Courtright kneels beside the exhumed casket of Julie Marie Hoyt. (*Courtesy New York State Police*)

Senior Investigator Robert Courtright, Onondaga County District Attorney William Fitzpatrick, and Tioga County District Attorney Robert Simpson at a news conference the day of Waneta Hoyt's arrest. (*Randi Anglin*)

State troopers escort Waneta Hoyt to a hearing in Newark Valley, New York, a week after her arrest. (*Frank Ordoñez, Syracuse Newspapers*)

Dr. Alfred Steinschneider, testifying for the defense in Waneta Hoyt's murder trial in Owego, New York, in April 1995. (*Dennis Nett*)

Tioga County Court Judge Vincent Sgueglia, presiding over Waneta Hoyt's murder trial. (*Dennis Nett*)

Waneta Hoyt's lawyers, Robert Miller and Raymond Urbanski, at her murder trial. (*Dennis Nett*)

State police investigator Susan Mulvey, who held Waneta Hoyt's hand as she confessed to murdering her children (*Photo by Randi Anglin.*)

Waneta and Tim Hoyt on the first day of her murder trial.
(*Dennis Nett*)

Jay, Waneta, and Tim Hoyt listen to her guilty verdict being
announced April 21, 1995. (*Dennis Nett*)

Testifying in her own defense, Waneta Hoyt cried as she described how each of her five children had suddenly lost consciousness and died, despite her efforts to revive them. After her conviction and sentencing, she told the judge, "God forgive all of those who have done this to me. . . . I didn't kill my kids." (*Dennis Nett*)

the record at—33⅓, 45, 78," Fitzpatrick said. "If you move too fast, you tip your hand, and the case goes down the drain. But what if another baby dies? This type of crime is not something that goes away with the passage of time. It goes away with, 'I haven't had any more babies,' or 'I haven't had access to babies.' " Fitzpatrick didn't know whether Waneta Hoyt had access to children.

Fitzpatrick felt the horror of infanticide more sharply as his personal life gave him a deeper appreciation of the bond between parent and child. His son, Danny, was now three. He and Diane had had another child, Sara, in July 1991, during his election campaign, and she had already celebrated her first birthday. In December, Diane would give birth to their third child, Sean.

As 1992 dissolved into 1993, Fitzpatrick could not understand why Simpson wasn't moving faster. Eventually, it was March 1993—one year since Fitzpatrick and Simpson had first talked. Then another three months. By the summer of 1993, Fitzpatrick's patience had worn thin. "I haven't heard anything, goddamn it," he complained at home one night. "I can't believe I handed this guy the case of his life and I haven't heard anything."

Fifteen months after his first call to Simpson, Fitzpatrick decided he'd had enough. On July 7, 1993, he wrote to Simpson, thanked him for his help, and said he would investigate the children's deaths himself. Fitzpatrick believed he had legitimate, if tenuous, grounds for snatching the case from Simpson. If anyone challenged his jurisdiction over the matter, he could argue that the Hoyts had taken two of their children from a hospital in Syracuse with the intent to harm them.

Simpson scrambled to mollify Fitzpatrick. He sent him the documents he had gathered and said he was already looking for a second expert to review the medi-

cal records. Fitzpatrick had recommended Dr. Linda
Norton, but Simpson told him Tioga County officials
would balk at paying the Dallas pathologist's $1,500
fee. Simpson assured him everything was on track; he
just needed more time. The Tioga County DA had no
interest in giving up now that state police Senior Investigator Robert Courtright was taking over the Hoyt investigation.

Courtright's uncanny ability to solve major crimes
had earned him the nickname Dalai Lama. Two days
before Fitzpatrick fired off his letter to Simpson,
Courtright completed an assignment as head of the state
police narcotics unit charged with investigating drug
trafficking throughout the Southern Tier. Courtright's
team capped his tenure by shutting down a cross-
country drug ring, arresting five dealers and seizing
about $1 million in marijuana. Members of his team
posed for a photograph with Courtright standing behind
a table laden with marijuana. In a prank mixing humor
with admiration, everybody else crouched to make
Courtright, barely five-nine, appear to be the tallest in
the crowd.

Courtright was reassigned to the Owego barracks,
where he had worked off and on over the years.
Simpson welcomed his return. The prosecutor had
deep respect for the bantam investigator with carefully
groomed white hair and a preference for dapper suits.
The fifty-four-year-old grandfather exuded the quiet
confidence of a cop with nearly thirty years on the job.
Although the Lama's experience had given him an in-
tuitive ability to solve crimes, he shared Simpson's af-
finity for the methodical approach to police work. If
anyone stood a chance of getting to the bottom of the
Hoyt case, Simpson believed, it was Courtright. Besides his investigative skills, he brought another asset
to the task: He'd lived among people like Tim and
Waneta Hoyt nearly all his life.

Bob Courtright grew up in modest circumstances in

Waverly, a village tucked into the southeast corner of
Tioga County, on the Pennsylvania line. His father
worked for the railroad, and his mother stayed home to
look after Courtright and his two brothers. He admits
he was a hellion, quitting school at sixteen to get married and becoming a father at seventeen. Enlisting in
the Marine Corps turned his life around.

"It's the best thing that ever happened to me, being
in the Marine Corps, especially boot camp," Courtright
said. "It's changed a lot now, but back when I was in
there, in fifty-eight, them drill instructors were very
creative people. Very creative. My first day there, I got
punched by the drill instructor, who chipped my tooth.
He just didn't like New York boys. Knocked me right
down. I said, 'This is going to be a long four years.' "

Courtright spent much of that time aboard the carrier
Essex, guarding the brig, dodging hot shell casings
from a five-inch gun, and shooting at sharks menacing
downed pilots. But the boy from Waverly also sailed
twice to Europe and through the Suez Canal once, and
got to turn out with the honor guard at various ports of
call to welcome kings and queens, and even two movie
stars, James Cagney and Robert Montgomery.

Courtright's Marine training still shows in the $10
globe-and-anchor tattoo on his right arm, his salty language, and his spit-and-polish appearance. He wears
suits—he had nineteen at one point—like a set of dress
blues. He won't even bend his knees to pick up a piece
of evidence off the floor for fear of breaking the
creases in his trousers. The investigator's strict sense
of discipline serves a purpose: "If your daughter is
raped, when I come to your door I want to look professional and to let you know that I take this very seriously. I want you to know that I am on the job."

Courtright's first law enforcement job was with the
ten-member Waverly police force in 1963. His first
homicide involved a former high school classmate who
suffocated his own child with a washcloth. Courtright

passed the state police exam three years later, but fell
a quarter-inch short of the five-nine height require-
ment. When he passed the exam again two years later,
a doctor told him to have his height measured in the
morning because the spine shrinks as the day wears on.
This time Courtright measured up; he became a trooper
in October 1968.

His military bearing served him well in the troopers'
paramilitary culture, where officers carry ranks of lieu-
tenant, captain, major, and colonel. He spent much of
his time working drug cases after his promotion to investigator in 1974, but he also investigated some fifty
homicides. In 1989, he made senior investigator, the
highest noncommissioned rank in the state police.
Troopers accorded seniors the kind of respect Marines
reserved for veteran sergeants.

Courtright was working with the narcotics unit in
Binghamton in early 1993 when he stopped by the
Owego barracks and overheard John Sherman talking
about five children in one family who had died under
suspicious circumstances more than twenty years ago.
"I'd been a policeman a long time and I'd never heard
anything like this," he recalled. "I thought it was just
fascinating that these five children would die like that,
as opposed to all five dying in a car accident at the
same time."

From time to time, Courtright checked in to see
whether Sherman was making any progress. As a senior, he got his pick of cases, and when he was transferred to Owego, he claimed the Hoyt investigation as
his own. Like Fitzpatrick, the Lama had a hunch. But
unlike the Syracuse district attorney, Courtright knew
the lay of the land.

Chapter Fourteen

Senior Investigator Bob Courtright began his investigation of the Hoyt children's deaths with a blank slate and a firm belief that painstaking police work could uncover the truth that had lain buried in the valley for nearly thirty years. His methodical approach ran through his paperwork: Bob Courtright was the rare cop who could produce flawless reports with two-finger hunt-and-peck typing. The first page of his file on the Hoyt case neatly spelled out the challenge that lay ahead: "Complaints 1. Weapons 0. Documents 0. Witnesses 0. Victims 5."

Courtright worked the investigation as if he were peeling an onion, removing one layer of information at a time until he approached the core. He had to contend with the same problem that Investigator John Sherman had faced when he first looked into the case in 1992: If he moved too far too fast, he ran the risk of tipping his hand to the Hoyts. If the couple knew they were the targets of an investigation, they might hire a lawyer who could shield them from questioning. At some point, Courtright knew, he would need to confront Tim and Waneta Hoyt.

Unlike Sherman, Courtright had the time to devote to a painstaking investigation. The Hoyt inquiry was the only major case on his desk, and he made it a priority. He proceeded cautiously, working from the outside in, relying on the methods that had sustained him for twenty years as an investigator. Over several months, he unearthed scores of personal records on Tim and Waneta Hoyt and their children. Those documents that he couldn't obtain from open sources he got with some of the two dozen grand jury subpoenas that District Attorney Bob Simpson issued during the investigation.

Courtright checked Tim's and Waneta's driving records, employment records, birth and marriage certificates, high school records, credit reports, medical charts, telephone and gas and light bills, and real estate records. He also checked the children's obituaries. Courtright didn't necessarily expect the background check to reveal any clues about the children's deaths; he was more interested in getting a feel for the Hoyts. Details gleaned from such records often gave investigators insights on how to question a suspect.

"When I talk to a blue-collar worker, I am going to be on his level, so we can relate to each other," Courtright said. "I'm not going to use fifty-cent words with a blue-collar worker, because he might not understand it."

A profile of the Hoyts quickly emerged from the documents: They were life residents of the county; they had never been arrested for a crime; they had struggled financially throughout their marriage; they were not socializers. Their son Jay was now a seventeen-year-old senior at Newark Valley High School. Courtright checked Jay's medical records but found no evidence of child abuse. Except for the deaths of their five children, Tim and Waneta Hoyt had lived unremarkable lives amid the valley's familiar hills.

The investigator also culled the records for names of people who knew the Hoyts and might remember the deaths of their children—doctors, nurses, neighbors, ambulance crew members, social workers, funeral directors. All were potential witnesses, but Courtright held off interviewing them because he didn't know whether one of them might tell the Hoyts about his investigation. Even talking to a neutral source was risky because the person might mention his inquiry, and in the tight-knit valley, word would soon get around to Tim and Waneta. An informant wasn't likely to honor a request not to discuss such a scandal either. Courtright methodically listed the names on sheets of paper and set them aside to pursue later.

The passage of time had taken its toll on the body of evidence. Many old documents had been destroyed; medical records for Eric, Julie, and Jimmy, the first children to die, were particularly scarce. Moreover, several people who had figured prominently in the Hoyts' saga were dead: Dr. Noah Kassman, the physician who delivered the five children; Dr. Arthur Hartnagel, the coroner who signed the death certificates for the first three children; Howard Horton, the town cop who became suspicious after Jimmy's death. A number of the volunteer ambulance workers who tried to revive the children at the trailers on Davis Hollow Road also were gone. Courtright knew, too, that the memories of surviving witnesses probably had faded.

Records from Upstate Medical Center on Molly and Noah Hoyt—the foundation of Dr. Alfred Steinschneider's suspect article—gave the most complete account of what had happened to any of the children. But Courtright couldn't see any clues to the children's deaths amid the endless references to formula feedings, vital signs and apneic spells. For that, he needed an expert.

The Hoyt children's records spoke volumes to Dr. Michael Baden, a former New York City medical examiner who had earned a reputation as one of the nation's leading forensic pathologists. During the 1980's, he lifted his career out of the ash heap of New York City politics to become known as "the celebrity pathologist."

In 1979, Mayor Ed Koch demoted the veteran pathologist from chief medical examiner to deputy at the request of Manhattan district attorney Robert Morgenthau, a move that Baden saw as a reaction to his unwillingness to conform to the prosecution's point of view. Baden remained in the medical examiner's office until 1986, when he became head of the state's newly created Forensic Sciences Unit, which went into operation just in time to help with the investigation of Marybeth Tinning.

Paid $40,000 a year by the state, Baden commanded as much as $200 an hour for consulting on civil and criminal cases involving the deaths of celebrities such as John Belushi, Andy Warhol, and New York Yankees manager Billy Martin. His hectic schedule often left the fifty-eight-year-old pathologist looking disheveled in public, and his coworkers tried to improve his image by periodically sending his dingy, wrinkled raincoat to a dry cleaner. It seemed a hopeless effort. Baden's untamed hair and drooping mustache gave him the woolly look of a Koren cartoon character the moment he stepped out of his Manhattan apartment.

However unkempt his appearance, Baden had a flair for wrapping up mysteries in tidy packages. His review of the Hoyt case proved no exception. In a conclusion carefully worded to meet the standards for admissibility in court, Baden said, "It is writer's opinion, beyond a reasonable degree of medical and scientific certainty . . . that the five children did not die of natural causes. To the contrary, these findings are typical of deaths due to homicidal asphyxiation."

Baden had seen other cases where babies had been smothered, only to have their murders buried under the label of SIDS. He identified several suspicious factors in the Hoyt deaths: All the children were born healthy and normal; Waneta Hoyt described several episodes in which she alone saw the children have breathing difficulties and turn blue; and each child died suddenly and unexpectedly in her presence.

Baden's opinion added weight to Bill Fitzpatrick's hunch. It also helped Courtright focus on Waneta Hoyt as the main suspect. Whether Tim Hoyt had known what was happening to his children remained an open question, but he apparently didn't cause their deaths.

Courtright and Simpson still wanted a second opinion to confirm Baden's findings. A circuitous route through the medical literature and a few phone calls led the investigator to Dr. Janice Ophoven, a little-known pediatric forensic pathologist at the Midwest Children's Research Center in St. Paul, Minnesota. Ophoven was excited about reviewing the Hoyts' medical records and Steinschneider's work.

On November 24, Fitzpatrick and his chief investigator, Pete Tynan, drove to Owego to join Simpson, Courtright, and other investigators in a conference call with Ophoven. She agreed with Baden: The children didn't die from SIDS or some other mysterious illness, they were killed. Like Baden, Ophoven found Waneta Hoyt's description of cyanosis suspect. A SIDS baby's heart and lungs shut down at the same time, which means the child doesn't turn blue, she explained. Cyanosis occurs when the heart continues to pump blood after the oxygen supply is cut off. That's what happens when babies are smothered.

Dr. Steven Boris, an expert on apnea who worked at the same research center as Ophoven, also reviewed the medical records, and he found no evidence of hereditary breathing disorders in the Hoyt children.

Ophoven's findings gave the investigation a boost, and Fitzpatrick left the meeting confident that they were on the right track. On their way back to Syracuse, he and Tynan stopped at Highland Cemetery in Richford to pay their respects to the victims who had almost been forgotten. In the ground hardened by autumn frost Fitzpatrick found Eric and Jimmy Hoyt's tiny grave markers near the headstone of their grandmother, Dorothy Nixon. Nothing marked the graves of the other children. In the gathering darkness, Fitzpatrick offered the words he prayed whenever he passed a cemetery: "Eternal rest grant unto them, O

Lord, and let perpetual light shine upon them. May they rest in peace. Amen."

Few would have guessed the Hoyt children's deaths could touch Bob Courtright as deeply. Squinting through the blue haze of the Merit Lights that he chain-smoked like a condemned man, Courtright didn't seem the type to admit tender feelings over the loss of five tots. His square jaw, gravelly voice, and flashy gold jewelry added to the impression of a hard-bitten cop. But his soft heart showed in the gruff affection he expressed for the passions in his life—his pet cat, Sammy, bass fishing, and growing Hungarian wax peppers.

"Fucking great," was how he described his peppers, which he kept pickled in a jar on the windowsill in his office. "I love my fucking garden."

And in his stoic way, Courtright mourned the Hoyt children's deaths. Watching his two young grandchildren reminded him of the precious lives that had been lost. The cop in him wanted to find out why.

His investigation had already uncovered two of the three elements of murder. Waneta Hoyt had the opportunity to kill her children when she had them home alone. And she had any number of means to kill; it took little effort to snuff the life out of a helpless child. But Courtright hadn't come up with a motive. He scoured banking records from the 1960s and 1970s, but found no evidence that the Hoyts had received the kind of windfall that Stephen Van Der Sluys had reaped from the insurance policies on his children.

"They didn't get any money from these deaths," he said. "I was satisfied with that. But I'm looking for the goddamn motive. You got to have a motive in every crime. I'm thinking, 'What the hell is the motive here?' "

Ophoven's and Baden's findings forced him to consider an explanation far more complicated than greed. Both pathologists believed the evidence pointed to Munchausen syndrome by proxy.

The name of the syndrome was inspired by Karl Friedrich Hieronymous von Münchhausen, an eighteenth-century German baron and mercenary officer in the Russian cavalry. When he returned from the Russo-Turkish wars, Baron von Münchhausen beguiled his friends and neighbors with outlandish tales of his military adventures. Two hundred years later, medical researchers would think of the baron while trying to explain the behavior of patients who went to extraordinary lengths to receive treatment for fictitious ailments. A doctor in the 1950s first noted patients who had the habit of concocting imaginary symptoms and seeking medical attention. Their convincing presentations often led to exhaustive medical investigations, lengthy hospitalizations, and, once in a while, unnecessary surgery. The condition of fabricating illnesses became know as Munchausen syndrome.

In the late 1970s, doctors noticed a variation of the syndrome: a parent, almost always the mother, would secretly make a child ill to get medical treatment that fed the parent's need for attention. This became known as Munchausen syndrome by proxy.

Courtright started poring over medical articles about the disorder. He also talked with researchers, psychiatrists, child protection agencies, and other cops, and soon understood why Ophoven and Baden saw Waneta Hoyt's behavior as a classic example of Munchausen syndrome by proxy.

Although Munchausen syndrome by proxy occurs mainly among the middle class, it was not unknown in poor families like the Hoyts. The abusive mother often has some knowledge of medicine, and Waneta Hoyt had been known to read medical books. Like the Hoyt children, the victims are usually too young to speak of the abuse. Abusers sometimes exhibit signs of Munchausen syndrome, inventing illnesses for themselves as well as their children. Waneta Hoyt's fainting spells and litany of complaints about everything from breathing difficulty to cancer fit the picture.

Courtright also learned that researchers had drawn a connection between apnea and Munchausen syndrome by proxy. Doctors had seen cases of mothers' smothering their children and then resuscitating them to create the appearance of recurring apnea spells. The children typically underwent extensive and often painful testing that revealed no underlying problem. Once the children left the hospital, the apnea recurred. Occasionally children died, and their deaths usually were attributed to SIDS. The children's mothers often fed their need for attention by repeating the pattern of abuse with subsequent children. And like Waneta Hoyt, they passed off the appearance of the same symptoms in later children as evidence of a hereditary disorder.

The investigator recognized the parallels to the Hoyt case: Waneta Hoyt reported several of her babies' having life-threatening apnea spells that only she witnessed; she told doctors she had to resuscitate the children on several occasions; her children had no critical apnea spells in the hospital; she was more than willing to have her babies undergo extensive testing.

The succoring environment of hospitals seems to exert a powerful pull on Munchausen mothers, and they have a knack for making doctors and nurses unwitting collaborators in fostering the belief that a child is sick. The lengthy hospitalizations of Molly and Noah Hoyt looked like a web of deceit spun by a woman with Munchausen syndrome by proxy.

Researchers believe that some Munchausen mothers derive satisfaction from matching wits with the best hospitals and doctors. Other mothers apparently abuse their children to build closer relationships with their distant husbands. From time to time, Waneta Hoyt had complained that she and Tim were drifting apart. The fathers of children abused by Munchausen mothers are usually oblivious to the abuse and steadfastly support their wives. Tim Hoyt's blind loyalty added to the pattern.

Munchausen syndrome by proxy wasn't described until five years after Steinschneider published his study linking apnea and SIDS. But when doctors looked at his 1972 paper in light of the later research, they wondered whether the Hoyt children had been victims of this form of abuse.

Drs. Dominick and Vincent Di Maio, father and son who worked as medical examiners, referred to the cases of M.H. and N.H. in their 1992 book *Forensic Pathology*. "The presentation of the two deaths in Steinschneider's article, in conjunction with the family history, suggests that these may represent the malignant form of Munchausen syndrome by proxy and that these cases are actually homicides," they said.

Shortly before Courtright took over the Hoyt investigation, a team of researchers from Canada wrote an article recommending a reevaluation of Steinschneider's 1972 article. The doctors suspected that Case 1, as Steinschneider had referred to Molly Hoyt, was a victim of Munchausen syndrome by proxy.

The Hoyt case came to a crossroads at the beginning of 1994. Courtright and Simpson called for a meeting on January 14 to pull together the threads of the investigation. They invited Fitzpatrick and Tynan.

Some fifteen people gathered in a conference room at the Treadway Inn in Owego on the bitterly cold Friday; the group included the two district attorneys, Courtright, Tynan, and half a dozen investigators and high-ranking state police officers. Trooper Bubba Bleck, who patrolled the section of the valley where the Hoyts lived, was supposed to be there, but other duties kept him away. Ophoven and her sister, Judy Olein, a microbiologist, had flown in from Minnesota the day before. Dr. Michael Baden was characteristically late.

The Hoyt task force, as it became known, sat around

a wide table. A fire burned in the fireplace to keep out the cold from an arctic air mass that had buffeted the region with thirty-mile-per-hour winds and pushed the wind-chill factor to minus thirty. Simpson called the meeting to order and turned it over to Courtright. The unassuming Tioga county DA saw no need to posture; he was more interested in learning what others had to say.

Courtright gave an up-to-date briefing on the Hoyts' background. Waneta Hoyt was a housewife, he said. She had talked publicly about the deaths of her children from SIDS. Tim Hoyt had bounced around factory and construction jobs before Pinkerton Security and Investigation Services hired him as a guard. He now worked thirty hours a week at Cornell University in Ithaca, guarding the Herbert F. Johnson Museum of Art's extensive collection of Asian, African, Pre-Columbian, European, and American works. Tim's income was supplemented by his wife's disability checks. Still, they managed to have only about $5 in their checking account.

Courtright mentioned leads that needed checking and then wrapped up his presentation so they could get to the primary purpose of the meeting—hashing out the medical evidence.

Doubts lingered about whether the Hoyt children had been murdered. Simpson and the state police wanted to make sure they weren't jumping to conclusions. They needed assurance from the experts that they were dealing with homicides rather than simply unexplained deaths. The task of persuading them fell to Ophoven.

The forensic pathologist reviewed her findings, stepping to a blackboard to trace the history of SIDS. She spoke confidently in a voice carrying a hint of a Minnesota twang. The big-boned Midwesterner had a cherubic face that made her look younger than her forty-eight years. She wore tortoiseshell glasses, and her short brown hair was cut in a wedge that swept up on the sides. Her sister sat at the table, taking notes on a laptop computer. The sisters, whose father was an organic chemist at the University of Minnesota Hospital, had been working in tandem for five years and often traveled together.

Ophoven was in the midst of explaining apnea and other breathing disorders when Baden joined the group. Although Ophoven had once heard her famous colleague lecture, the two had never met, and her presentation proceeded awkwardly for a few minutes while Baden asked questions and offered comments.

"I sort of had this sense that he was concerned about my qualifications to make some of the statements that I was making," Ophoven recalled. "I'm not sure he knew I was a pathologist."

Simpson sensed Ophoven's discomfort and interrupted the discussion. "I think it would be appropriate if we reintroduced Dr. Ophoven for Dr. Baden," he said.

In fact, Ophoven was no ordinary pathologist. She was one of a handful of forensic pathologists in the country who specialized in pediatric cases. She had consulted on homicides in the United States and Canada, and had become a leading expert in Munchausen syndrome by proxy, developing a list of warning signs for the FBI that advised police on how to spot the behavioral disorder. The pathologists' dialogue became much more relaxed after Ophoven's credentials were established.

"Simpson might have hit a home run here," Fitzpatrick thought, listening to Ophoven. "She would be a fabulous witness." He liked the firm but polite way in which she made her points. Her folksy manner was in sharp contrast to Baden's big-city style, and Fitzpatrick thought she would play well with jurors in a rural place like Tioga County: "She would be very

polite with someone, whereas Baden would conde-
scend."

The prosecutor's mind ran ahead to trial strategy. He
remembered how he had won the Van Der Sluys trial
by letting the defense believe the Onondaga County
medical examiner was his star witness when he really
planned to rely on an out-of-state expert.

"Maybe Ophoven is the person to bring in, hit the
home run," Fitzpatrick thought.

While Fitzpatrick was planning for trial, Simpson
was still trying to decide whether he had a case at all.
He cross-examined Ophoven like a witness, challenging her to explain how she concluded from the medical
records that the Hoyt children had been murdered. "If
you can convince me, I can probably convince a jury,"
Simpson said.

Ophoven took the questions in stride. She had worked
with police officers and prosecutors before and understood that they needed to be convinced they were dealing with infanticide before they confronted the parents.

"You just don't walk up to people and say, 'Boy, I
think you did this terrible thing,' " Ophoven said.

Baden and Ophoven took the group through the
medical records and explained how they had found
nothing to indicate Molly and Noah had ever suffered
life-threatening apneic spells. Ophoven pointed out all
the places in the record where Steinschneider mentioned apnea, and she said they showed nothing more
than normal breathing. She and Baden said they found
no evidence of heart problems or any other diseases
that would have caused the children's deaths.

"That was the common denominator between her
and Baden: These were murders. This is not a gray
area. This is black and white. These kids were suffocated," Fitzpatrick said.

"It was good for the people there to see this occur.
People from, as far as I knew, completely different
backgrounds, from different sides of the continent es-

sentially, saying that in this small community twenty
years ago, these five kids were murdered. I think it
gave a little adrenaline boost to some of the cops that
might have been thinking, 'Hey, why should we believe this doctor as opposed to Dr. Steinschneider?' "

Courtright felt the boost most of all. "I have two pathologists here who, in my opinion, are probably two
of the best in the nation, who support what I think," he
said—"these five babies were murdered."

The next step seemed obvious: questioning Waneta
Hoyt.

Ophoven saw herself as a full partner in the investigation, and she didn't hesitate to suggest areas that investigators should touch on during the interview. Take
Waneta through each of the children's deaths and get
her to describe any life-threatening episodes, the pathologist said. That way, if Waneta stopped talking at
some point during the interview, they would have her
version of events, which they could try to disprove
with evidence from the medical records.

She wanted them to probe for details that would help
show the children hadn't died of SIDS or some other
natural cause. "I want to know about the frequency and
severity of these events," she said. "I want to know
what the babies looked like. I want to know if they
were sweaty. I want to know if they were blue. I want
to know a lot more about what happened with James
because the holes in that one were so big."

Ophoven briefed the task force on Munchausen syndrome by proxy, which she described as a behavioral
disorder, not a mental illness, and therefore not a legal
defense. But she warned the investigators not to get
caught up in trying to show that Waneta was motivated
by Munchausen syndrome by proxy; it was just a fancy
name for an awful form of child abuse. By any name,
the deaths of the Hoyt children were murders.

Now Bob Courtright had to get Waneta Hoyt to admit that she committed them.

Chapter Fifteen

Bob Courtright prepared for the interview with Waneta Hoyt with the same care he'd given to every other aspect of the investigation. Courtright knew he needed every advantage he could get: with no witnesses to the Hoyt children's deaths and no physical evidence from the crime scenes, getting Waneta to admit what she had done was critical, maybe even indispensable, if they hoped to charge her with murder. After a supervisor in the state police Bureau of Criminal Investigation mentioned the similarities between the Hoyt case and the prosecution of Marybeth Tinning in Schenectady, Courtright read up on the earlier state police investigation. He dissected *From Cradle to Grave*, British author Joyce Egginton's 1989 account of the Tinning case. He made notes and compiled a list of leads from the ominously familiar story. The Lama was trying to crawl into Tinning's mind in hopes of discovering what made Waneta Hoyt tick.

Marybeth Tinning's nine babies began dying in early 1972, eight months after Noah Hoyt died. The last one, Tami Lynne, died in 1985. All the deaths were attributed to SIDS or some other mysterious cause. The last three babies, Mary Frances, Jonathan, and Tami Lynne, were sent home from the hospital on apnea monitors. After Mary Frances died in 1979, Tinning told a tale that was remarkably similar to what Waneta Hoyt had said after Molly and Noah died. Mary Frances had been fed and put down in her crib for a nap, Tinning said. Then the apnea alarm sounded. By the time Tinning got to the baby, Mary Frances was unconscious.

The book revealed other intriguing parallels. Tinning adopted a baby boy, but unlike Waneta's adopted child, this one died. Tinning's husband, Joe, seemed cut from the same cloth as Tim Hoyt, indulging his wife's aberrant behavior even after she tried to poison him. Marybeth Tinning was also suspected of setting fire to a trailer home that she and Joe had been planning to move into. As with the fires that destroyed the Hoyts' two trailers, the cause was never determined.

Courtright went to the next step in his studies. He and Investigator John Sherman drove to Schenectady to interview retired state police investigator Bill Barnes, who had gotten Tinning to admit she killed three of her children.

Barnes had gone to school with Marybeth Tinning and knew her family, and he thought that familiarity helped him get through to her when other investigators were unable to get past her denials. He suggested that Courtright get a trooper whom Waneta Hoyt was familiar with to sit in on the interview. He also told Courtright he should have Tim and Waneta Hoyt picked up and questioned separately. Investigators had made a careful plan to approach Marybeth Tinning when her husband was at work, Barnes said. He recommended that Courtright make sure that Waneta was provided with food and water when she wanted it; defense lawyers had tried to say police coerced Tinning's confession by wearing her down and not offering her something to eat and drink. Barnes also mentioned how the sound of cops rushing in and out of the barracks created a distraction during the Tinning interview.

Courtright also looked up Schenectady County district attorney Alan Gebell, the assistant prosecutor in the Tinning case who had asked Bill Fitzpatrick to share the lessons he had learned from Stephen Van Der Sluys's trial. While Courtright was in the courthouse,

Gebell introduced him to a security officer who had
served on the jury that convicted Tinning. The woman
told Courtright that the Tinning jurors found much of
the testimony from medical experts confusing. They
were more impressed by what ordinary people had to
say about the Tinning children. She suggested that
Courtright find people who had spent time around the
Hoyt children and could describe them as normal,
healthy kids. She had another piece of advice for the
investigator: Get someone else to interview Waneta
Hoyt. Courtright's voice was too powerful and intimidating, the woman said. He might scare Waneta.

Her advice bore the added weight of history. The
Tinning investigation stood as a proud chapter in the
history of the New York State Police, the first big case
its Forensic Sciences Unit and Dr. Michael Baden had
helped crack. But it wasn't a complete success. Although she admitted killing three of her children,
Marybeth Tinning only described what she'd done to
one child, Tami Lynne, her last. Lacking detailed confessions on the other children's deaths, prosecutors
decided to charge Tinning with just one murder. Courtright had four fewer chances to stick a murder charge
on Waneta Hoyt, and none of the deaths was as fresh
as Tami Lynne's death had been at the time Tinning
confessed. Although he firmly believed in his skills as
an interviewer, Courtright had to consider giving the
honors to another investigator.

Courtright asked a psychologist at the state Office of
Mental Health for tips on questioning Waneta, and he
toyed with the idea of interviewing Marybeth Tinning,
who was serving twenty years to life in the state's
maximum-security prison for women in Bedford Hills,
thirty miles north of New York. He eventually rejected
the idea. Seven years after she was convicted, Tinning
continued to maintain her innocence, and Courtright
doubted she would reveal anything to him.

That posed another problem. Some doctors believed

that Tinning's behavior, like Waneta Hoyt's, fit the profile of Munchausen syndrome by proxy. Researchers had found that Munchausen mothers often refuse to admit harming their children, even when confronted with evidence of abuse. The Lama could only hope that was one trait Waneta Hoyt didn't share.

Courtright's meticulous mind began to shape a strategy for questioning Waneta Hoyt. He distilled her children's deaths to a few lines of notes, which he neatly typed on five sheets of white paper, one for each victim:

NUMBER 1
ERIC HOYT

Born 10/17/64
Died 01/26/65
3 months—10 days old
bled from mouth & died suddenly

NUMBER 2
JULIE HOYT

Born 07/19/68
Died 09/05/68
1 month—18 days old
choked on rice cereal

NUMBER 3
JAMES HOYT

Born 05/31/66
Died 09/26/68
2 years—4 months old
came into house from playing and said "Mommy"
and bled from nose and mouth and died suddenly

NUMBER 4
MOLLY HOYT

Born 03/18/70
Died 06/05/70
2 months—18 days old

died at home
died the day after being released from hospital

NUMBER 5
NOAH HOYT

Born 05/09/71
Died 07/28/71
2 months—19 days old
died the day after being released from hospital—
died at home

Like the bare-bones scorecard that Courtright typed at the outset of the investigation, the scant notes served as a reminder of how far the case still had to go. He left the balance of each page blank for whatever details his new partner could wrest from Waneta Hoyt. After going back and forth on whether he should question Waneta himself, Courtright had decided the risk of putting her off with his personality was too great. He planned to sit in on the interview because his knowledge of the case might come in handy, but another investigator would take the lead in questioning her. The state police had a host of topflight homicide investigators from which Courtright could pick, and he approached the decision with typical deliberation.

Courtright wanted an experienced cop, preferably someone he knew and had worked with. The interrogator needed the personal skills to put Waneta at ease, win her confidence, and get her talking. In March, Courtright decided he also wanted a woman, and he picked Investigator Susan Mulvey, a thirty-seven-year-old member of the Hoyt task force.

"She's a mother and has her own kid," Courtright said, "and this was to be a woman-to-woman interview."

Mulvey, a fifteen-year veteran of the state police, came from a family of cops. Her father and an uncle were former troopers, and her father was sheriff of Broome County while she was growing up. Still,

Mulvey didn't consider going into police work until she found her college degree wasn't enough to get her into veterinary school.

A friend's mother gave Mulvey an application for the state police exam. "I took the test and the next thing I knew, I was being sworn in."

The state police had been hiring women for barely five years when Mulvey entered the academy in 1979, one of twenty women in a class of two hundred. Years later, Mulvey could laugh about the rigors of the academy, which included boxing.

"The academy, for me, was not that much different than going to Catholic school," she said. "It's the same thing, just not as much plaid. You could switch the nun for the head trooper very easily, except maybe the nuns were tougher. At least they didn't hit us in the academy."

She survived with the encouragement she received in weekly letters from her father, and when she graduated, he gave her a little plaque with the bar he'd earned on the state police shooting team.

Mulvey started out on road patrol, but an undercover assignment with the major-crimes unit quickly moved her onto a fast track. The youthful blonde with fresh-scrubbed looks and a love of horses was sent out to make drug buys. She learned the nuances of investigations by watching experienced investigators such as Courtright work.

In 1987 Mulvey both earned her sergeant's stripes and became one of the few women investigators in the state police. She soon gained a reputation as a leading investigator of child abuse. Along the way, she married another trooper and had a baby. The marriage broke up, leaving her a single, working mother.

Mulvey's experience investigating child abuse and her familiarity with Munchausen syndrome by proxy earned her a spot on the Hoyt task force. But her reputation as an interviewer recommended her for the critical task of talking to Waneta. Courtright had heard she had a gift for talking to abused children, as well as to their abusive parents.

Mulvey didn't see interviewing Waneta Hoyt as a particularly daunting assignment. She'd listened to Courtright, Ophoven, Baden, and others describe Waneta Hoyt at the January 14 meeting and felt she already knew her subject.

"A lot of times when you do the interview you don't know what happened and you kind of fish," Mulvey said. "We knew so much about her, and her family, and the events, and the medical possibilities."

But first they had to hook Waneta, and that's where Trooper Bob Bleck came in. Courtright took a page from the Tinning case and picked the trooper who knew Waneta best to make the all-important initial contact.

With his starting lineup set, Courtright scheduled the confrontation with Waneta Hoyt: Wednesday, March 23, almost two years after Bill Fitzpatrick had called Bob Simpson about the case. On Tuesday, Courtright and Simpson had the cops working the case come back to the Treadway Inn to go over the plan. Once again, they asked Fitzpatrick and his chief investigator to attend the meeting.

Simpson began the briefing shortly after two o'clock that afternoon and gave Courtright the floor. The senior investigator methodically reviewed the steps he had taken during the previous nine months and then turned to his plan for bringing in Tim and Waneta Hoyt.

The idea was simple enough in outline. Bubba Bleck would accompany Sue Mulvey to the Hoyts' home around ten o'clock the next morning. They wanted Waneta alone, and they figured Tim Hoyt should have left for his security job at Cornell University by that time. Bleck would make the first contact, then introduce Mulvey, who would tell Waneta she wanted to

ask some questions about the deaths of the five children. She would try to persuade Waneta to return with
them to the Owego barracks, where Courtright would
join the interview. But if Waneta wouldn't budge,
Mulvey was prepared to question her in her living
room.

Investigators John Sherman and Bill Standinger
were assigned to pick up Tim Hoyt at Cornell and interview him at the Ithaca barracks. They would go to
the campus security office, where Tim would be summoned on the pretext that the state police were investigating a theft.

The plan depended on how well each team handled
the nuances of the initial encounters, and that left room
for countless missteps. Courtright gave each team
specific instructions on what to say when they picked
up Tim and Waneta. He cautioned them not to lie to either one.

At Tuesday's meeting he also coached Mulvey on
how to interview Waneta. Knowing that crafty lawyers
might later try to accuse them of putting words in
Waneta's mouth, Courtright told his partner not to introduce the word "suffocation."

"The pathologists say they were suffocated. I want
her to say that word," Courtright said. "If she starts
saying, 'I poisoned one and I drowned one,' I know
something has gone wrong."

The tension was high in the room, and Courtright
puffed on one cigarette after another to calm his
nerves. He had tried to think of every contingency.
Backup teams were assigned to take over the interviews if the first investigators didn't click with Tim
and Waneta. A state police polygraph expert would be
on hand at the Owego barracks in case Waneta denied
any wrongdoing and agreed to take a lie-detector test
to prove it.

Courtright's worst fear was that Waneta would simply refuse to talk. If that happened, there was a fall-

back plan: Investigators would immediately rush into the valley to start interviewing the Hoyts' relatives, friends, and neighbors. Courtright had compiled a list of people they needed to interview before the tight-knit community could close ranks. He also had a list of local public records that investigators could check once word of the investigation got out. Courtright wanted whatever information police, fire, and ambulance agencies had on the Hoyts. Margaret Drake, an assistant prosecutor in Simpson's office, had helped prepare another list of possible witnesses who could be interviewed later. Drake had read the medical records, looking for the names of nurses who had seen Molly and Noah Hoyt when the two were healthy babies.

Earlier on the day of the meeting, a judge granted the state police permission to tap Tim and Waneta's home telephone with a device that would record the numbers called. The pen register could lead investigators to people who might have heard the couple make incriminating statements. At the post office, all the mail Tim and Waneta Hoyt sent or received would be held so investigators could check the names and addresses.

Fitzpatrick sat across the meeting table from Courtright, encouraged by the thoroughness of the plan. The prosecutor had acquired a deep respect for the Lama. "When he says things, he says them with a ring of authority, like, that's the way it's going to be," he said. "I felt good about him being involved in it, and I was anxious about Sue Mulvey."

Fitzpatrick had met Mulvey briefly at the January meeting and they shared a laugh over one of the investigators' uncanny resemblance to John Wayne Bobbitt, the Virginia man whose wife cut off his penis. But Fitzpatrick knew little about her as a cop. He chided himself for questioning Courtright's choice, but he couldn't stop worrying. His personal crusade had come to this moment of reckoning. He wanted to make sure nothing went wrong.

Simpson could sense Fitzpatrick's uneasiness and invited him to Owego for the confrontation.

Near the end of the meeting, Fitzpatrick put aside his doubts and rose to speak. He drew on his experience to give the investigators an idea of what to expect the next day. Waneta probably would not admit that she killed all of the children, he said. He remembered that Stephen Van Der Sluys admitted killing only two of his three children, and Marybeth Tinning admitted killing just three of her nine.

Fitzpatrick also predicted that Tim Hoyt would loom large in his wife's thinking. "My suspicion is he's probably a Caspar Milquetoast kind of a guy," he said, "but she's got to know at some point during the interrogation that he's going to be there to support her."

Fitzpatrick knew that Waneta could ask for a lawyer, stopping the interview cold. But he wanted to give the investigators encouragement; he predicted that Waneta would confess, just as Van Der Sluys and Tinning had. Then he took it a step further: He guaranteed it.

Watching TV in bed that night, Fitzpatrick brooded over the unknowns. At the center of all his doubts stood Waneta Hoyt. After eight years, the case hinged on whether she would freely confess to killing the five children she'd borne. Would the troopers spook her? Would she ask for a lawyer? Would Bob Simpson refuse to prosecute if she didn't confess?

Fitzpatrick fell asleep after midnight, telling himself that Waneta would talk.

Chapter Sixteen

Investigator Sue Mulvey took pains getting dressed on the morning of March 23, 1994. She picked out an eighteen-year-old blue suit and a white blouse that buttoned up to her chin. Her only concession to fashion was a Mickey Mouse watch.

"I wanted to dress simply; not a lot of jewelry because Waneta's rural and not very well-off," Mulvey said. "I wanted to be very low-key, wear something she's not going to notice. You try to give yourself every advantage."

Mulvey's wholesome looks enhanced her chances of appealing to Waneta. The investigator wore her ash-blond hair in a sensible, collar-length cut, with neatly trimmed bangs. She had wide, prominent cheekbones and deep-set brown eyes that took on a mischievous look when she smiled.

She had already arranged to drop off her three-year-old daughter, Jackie, at her mother's house. Mulvey's daughter was the most important part of her life. She had even kept her ex-husband's last name so it would be the same as her daughter's. Mulvey had found it increasingly difficult not to think about Jackie while investigating child abuse cases: "I put her face right on all the little kids."

With a job that often required odd hours, Mulvey relied on her family to help look after Jackie. Everyone pitched in—her father and mother, brothers and sisters, and Jackie's father.

Dressed and ready to go, Mulvey tried to dispel the tension she'd felt the night before. "What am I going to say?" she'd thought. "How am I going to do it?"

Compared to Bob Courtright, she looked the picture of calm.

Courtright had dressed carefully too, choosing a gray suit that made him look like he'd just stepped off the cover of *GQ*. He got to the Owego barracks early, eager to complete last-minute details. He remembered the advice from the investigator in the Marybeth Tinning case and used a pocketknife to dismantle the bell that chimed every time the barracks' door opened. He didn't want any distractions during the interview with Waneta and ordered troopers to stay away from the barracks unless they had an emergency.

Trooper Bubba Bleck didn't have to spend much time over his wardrobe that morning. He arrived at the barracks wearing the gray uniform that Waneta knew so well as a symbol of quiet authority.

The rest of the team assembled around eight o'clock, giving Courtright a chance to go over the plan one more time. Two hours after gathering at the barracks, the team set out to get Tim and Waneta Hoyt.

Bleck and Mulvey rode in a gray, unmarked Chevy Caprice, followed by Courtright, who was driving his white Cutlass Cierra. Bleck and Mulvey had known each other since they were classmates at the state police academy. Mulvey had tormented Bleck during their training by stepping on his freshly polished shoes. The two continued to tease each other like brother and sister.

The two cars headed north on Route 38, following the course Dr. John Scott had taken twenty-three years earlier to respond to the death of Noah Hoyt. Just beyond the village of Newark Valley they bypassed the turnoff for Davis Hollow Road, where all the children had died.

The Hoyts' two-story bluish-gray house sat in a depression off the east shoulder of Route 38. A long, weather-beaten shed stood at the back of the lot. A sign on the corner of the house warned about the black and brown hound the Hoyts kept chained to a wooden shelter next to the shed. Bleck's car slowed as it approached the driveway, but he didn't stop. His car rolled past the house and continued up Route 38. Bleck thought he'd seen Tim Hoyt's Chevy Chevette parked in the yard. Courtright's well-laid plan had hit its first snag: apparently, Waneta wasn't alone.

The unmarked cars continued north three more miles, to Bleck's outpost in Berkshire. The state police satellite office and the Berkshire post office occupied half of what looked like a large suburban house. A green bench on the porch in front of Bleck's office added to the homey atmosphere. A green-and-white highway sign on the door told visitors: TROOPERS ARE ON PATROL. TO CONTACT STATE POLICE CALL 657-8030. A hand-lettered note in the window directed visitors to the phone at the Citgo station next door.

Courtright wanted to regroup, call the other members of the investigative team and figure out what to do next. The first task was to locate Tim Hoyt. If he hadn't shown up at work, Courtright figured they could call the Hoyt home on some pretext to see if he was there. If Tim was home with Waneta, they would postpone the operation.

But as they pulled into the satellite parking lot, Bleck spotted Waneta leaving the post office next door. Courtright gave him the OK to make his approach.

The last time they'd met, Waneta hadn't been feeling well, so Bleck struck up a conversation with one of his standard inquiries: Why wasn't she wearing a scarf on her head? After exchanging pleasantries, he asked Waneta if he could talk to her for a moment in his office. Once inside, he introduced Mulvey.

The trooper improvised the introduction to needle the investigator about using her ex-husband's last name instead of her maiden name. "This is Sue Mulvey—or is it Sue Andrews? Oh, yes, Sue Mulvey," Bleck said. "She's an investigator. I went to the academy with her."

Then Bleck shifted gears. He told Waneta that Mulvey wanted to ask her a few questions about the unfortunate deaths of her children.

Mulvey began a carefully worded explanation of her interest. The case first came to her attention in an article written by Dr. Alfred Steinschneider, she said. She also had talked about the case with a pediatrician in Minnesota, a woman who specialized in determining how children die.

"We'd like to talk to you about how your children died," Mulvey said. "You'd be the best person to talk to because you were there. The records aren't around."

Then Mulvey gave Waneta a reason to cooperate: "We want to know as much as we can about how your children lived and died to prevent this from happening again."

Waneta agreed to help. She had taken Tim to work that morning and didn't need to pick him up until later. "I don't have anything to do till four," she said.

Mulvey asked Waneta to come to the Owego barracks, where she had her paperwork.

"Fine," Waneta said. But she wanted Bleck to come too, she said, she was nervous.

When Waneta said she needed to stop at home to make sure that Jay got off to school, Bleck offered to follow Mulvey and Waneta to the house and then drive them to Owego, "so we can use state police gas instead of yours."

As they headed out, Waneta mentioned a photo album she wanted to pick up at home. Looking at the babies' pictures would help her remember, she said.

Mulvey made small talk during the ride to Waneta's house. Waneta hadn't been read her rights, and Mulvey didn't want to stumble into a tainted conversation about the case. She and Bleck followed Waneta into the house, where Jay was getting ready for school. Waneta told him she was going to Owego to talk about the deaths of his brothers and sisters, but Jay showed no interest in the siblings he'd never known.

Waneta took the album from the living room, gathered arthritis medicine for stiffness in her arms and legs, and picked up an old bottle of heart medication. With her pocketbook and cane in hand, she was ready to go. Bleck offered to give Jay a lift to school, and they set off in the unmarked car with the men in the front seat, the women in back.

Bleck dropped Jay at the high school and headed back to Owego with Waneta and Mulvey. They filled the time with small talk. Bleck speculated about Jay's chances of becoming a NASCAR driver, and Mulvey discussed whatever came to mind—a recent trip to Disney World, the weather, anything to start establishing rapport with Waneta.

Investigators John Sherman and Bill Standinger had driven to Ithaca to carry out Courtright's plan for Tim Hoyt. No one believed Tim Hoyt had murdered his children, but Courtright needed to make sure. Even if Tim didn't have a hand in the killings, he might have known that Waneta did, and his failure to step in and save his children might leave him open to a charge of criminally negligent homicide. At the very least, Courtright thought, interviewing Tim might give them new leads. He wanted Sherman and Standinger to find out whatever Tim knew.

The investigators met Tim at Cornell University's security office. Tim was wearing his Pinkerton security uniform—a blue blazer with a gold badge, a white shirt, and a black tie. With his light brown hair slicked down and aviator glasses, Tim could have passed for a moonlighting trooper. At fifty-one, he was four years older than Waneta but looked ten years younger.

After introducing themselves as cops, Standinger

and Sherman used the same approach Mulvey had used to win Waneta's cooperation: They were looking at the deaths of the five children because doctors had questions about what happened.

Tim became defensive almost immediately. "These are all SIDS," he said. "Why are you looking at it now?"

The chances of getting Tim to agree to an interview began to look dim, and Standinger tried appealing to the security guard's sense of duty.

"The DA asked us to," the investigator said. "We're just doing our jobs. We're cops like you." The gambit worked; Tim agreed to go with them to the state police barracks outside Ithaca.

The investigators took him through each of the children's deaths, but they knew more than he did. Tim said he'd been at work when each child died. At one point, he got confused and said Julie had been treated at Upstate Medical Center.

As far as Tim knew, all the children died of natural, if unexplained, causes. He and Waneta had searched their souls about whether to have more children, he said, but Dr. Steinschneider had assured the couple there was no evidence of a hereditary problem.

Tim agreed to give them a formal statement, and Sherman began typing it.

Having seen Bleck and Mulvey reach their first goal by isolating Waneta, Courtright rushed back to the state police barracks in the Owego town office building overlooking the Susquehanna River. Courtright briefed Tioga County district attorney Bob Simpson and the rest of the investigative team. About twenty minutes later, Bleck and Mulvey brought Waneta in and introduced her to Courtright.

Mulvey showed Waneta to the bathroom and got her a cup of coffee. Shortly after ten-thirty Courtright led them to a standard interview room, about six feet wide and eleven feet deep. Four chairs were arrayed around a six-foot table that had been pushed sideways against one wall. They'd hoped to steer Waneta to a seat in the middle so they could flank her, but she picked a chair at the far end of the table, what Mulvey thought of as the power seat. Bleck took the chair next to Waneta, Mulvey sat along the length of the table and Courtright sat at the other end, opposite Waneta.

Courtright asked Bleck to read Waneta her rights, and the trooper held up the card bearing the Miranda warnings so she could follow along. Waneta waived her right to a lawyer and began to answer questions. Courtright's operation had reached its second objective: Waneta was talking. Now they faced the tougher task of getting her to admit she'd murdered her children.

Courtright and Mulvey followed the plan they had worked out at the strategy session the day before. Instead of the good-cop, bad-cop routine, they used a soft approach—nice cop, very nice cop. Mulvey asked most of the questions, trying to establish a rapport with Waneta. She took Waneta through her medical history, the background on her family and Tim's family, the course of her pregnancies, the births of the five children, and how they died.

Waneta said she had met Tim in high school and married him after a whirlwind romance when he returned from out of state. They lived with Tim's mother—Mom Hoyt, she called her—on Davis Hollow Road when they were first married. Waneta chuckled softly a couple of times, but otherwise remained impassive.

As Mulvey asked about each child, Waneta pointed to the ghostly images of her children in the photo album. All the children died of SIDS, Waneta said. When the babies were young, she or Mom Hoyt would find them blue in the crib or on the couch. Jimmy's death was different. Waneta said she was in the bathroom when she heard an awful scream. Jimmy ran to her, collapsed in her arms, and died. He was bleeding from his mouth and nose, she said. Waneta had a lot of pictures of Jimmy, who was almost two and a half when he died.

Mulvey questioned Waneta intently but never challenged her story, never accused her of lying. When Waneta spoke sadly about her children's funerals, Mulvey said how sorry she was. Waneta craved sympathy and attention, and Mulvey was only too happy to supply it. She worked to win Waneta's trust. When Waneta made a remark about Mulvey's foot bumping her leg, the investigator apologized, kicked off her black flats, and continued the interview barefoot. Her message was clear: I'm not going to hurt you.

Courtright interrupted occasionally to clarify a point. He'd brought along his five typed pages to take notes on each child. He jotted down a few details, but he hadn't heard much new information; Waneta was sticking to the story she'd been telling for more than twenty years.

The investigators tried to keep Waneta talking, knowing that if she didn't confess they still might be able to disprove parts of her story and use that against her. Mulvey had already picked up on subtle changes in Waneta's account of Jimmy's death.

They took a break shortly before noon. Bleck stuck with Waneta. Mulvey and Courtright went to the office where Simpson had been waiting out the interview. The investigators were summarizing the results when Bill Fitzpatrick and Pete Tynan, his chief investigator, walked into the barracks.

Fitzpatrick's anxiety about the confrontation with Waneta had been growing steadily since he set out from home. He knew that if everything was going according to plan, Bleck and Mulvey should have been approaching Waneta about the time he and Tynan were leaving. Fitzpatrick wore his beeper, expecting Bob Simpson to page him with news about the outcome.

But as Tynan drove Fitzpatrick's black Jeep Cherokee along the back roads toward Owego, the news blackout grew unbearable. Fitzpatrick used the car phone several times to call his office, but Simpson hadn't left word there, either.

Tynan picked up Route 38 in Cortland and continued south into Tioga County, toward Berkshire. As they passed Waneta's house, Fitzpatrick saw several cars in the yard.

"Oh, shit! They must be talking to her in the living room," Fitzpatrick said. "All those cars there? Got to be one of them is a state police car." Not wanting to attract attention, Tynan kept going, only to get lost in Owego.

Tynan wound up near the Treadway Inn, where they'd attended the strategy session the day before. He stopped twice to ask for directions and found the barracks around noon. Fitzpatrick's outlook brightened as soon as he heard Courtright and Mulvey describe what Waneta had said.

Courtright summarized Waneta's statement in his usual laconic style while Mulvey paced the office, interrupting as striking impressions came to mind. Fitzpatrick had never seen her so supercharged.

"Oh, yeah, yeah," Mulvey said. "She asked me to take my shoes off. She asked me to take my shoes off because I bumped into her, and I did it." Mulvey was most excited about the details surrounding Jimmy's death. Waneta had once told doctors Jimmy died after playing outside. She now said he was stricken after eating, while she was getting dressed in the bathroom.

Fitzpatrick, in the awkward role of guest observer, tried to rein in his emotions, but Mulvey's excitement became infectious. "This is great stuff," he blurted out, his heart racing. "You're grabbing great stuff from her."

Courtright continued his methodical report to Simpson, steering the briefing to the next move. As long as Waneta was talking, they decided to proceed with another round of basic questions. They would try to draw out all the details they could, look for contradictions and hope Waneta would give them an opening.

Mulvey and Courtright went back to the interview room with Bleck and Waneta. They returned to their places around the table, and Mulvey began to rekindle the conversation.

Another investigator showed Fitzpatrick and Tynan to an adjacent room where they could watch through a one-way mirror. The closet-size space had been designed so witnesses could identify suspects without being seen. But it also held the barracks' copying machine, which Fitzpatrick had to squeeze alongside to get to the window. With no microphone in the interrogation room, Fitzpatrick and Tynan strained to hear the muffled conversation coming through the wall. They spoke in hushed tones, worried that any noise from their side might tip Waneta off to their presence.

They kept the lights off to get a better view through the tinted glass. Fitzpatrick couldn't wait to see what Waneta looked like. He craned his neck trying to catch a glimpse of her, but Bleck sat blocking his view. Still, it was the best spectator seat in the place, and for the next hour Fitzpatrick watched Mulvey's and Courtright's work with a studied eye.

The investigators' teamwork reminded Fitzpatrick of docking an ocean liner: Mulvey worked like a tugboat, steadily pressing Waneta for answers; Courtright acted as the pilot, correcting the course with an occasional question. The effect looked simple, but Fitzpatrick knew it required tremendous coordination and energy.

Fitzpatrick also admired the discipline Bleck brought to his supporting role. His quiet presence not only reassured Waneta, it reinforced the inescapable authority of the law.

As the group around the table rose for a break shortly after one o'clock, Fitzpatrick saw Waneta clearly for the first time through the looking glass. The years had not been kind to her; at forty-seven she looked a decade older. Overweight and hobbled by arthritis and osteoporosis, she moved heavily toward the door. She dressed plainly in dark slacks and a short-sleeved blouse open at the collar. Large glasses with clear-plastic frames gave her an owlish look. One of her many ailments had produced massive swelling in the lymph glands under her right arm. Waneta's drab appearance fit the picture Fitzpatrick had formed in his mind. But he had not expected her most striking feature: She was nearly bald. The wisps of short gray hair covering her pale scalp gave her matronly looks a garish twist.

Mulvey and Courtright used the break to report again to Simpson. They'd exhausted Phase One of the interview, they said. They'd gotten Waneta to cooperate, they'd kept her talking, but she was sticking to the script she'd been using for twenty-three years. They wanted the OK to confront her.

"Hey, let's take her," Fitzpatrick said, unable to contain his excitement. He switched into cheerleading mode, trying to pump up Mulvey and Courtright. "She's gonna go for it. I can feel it. I'm telling you, she's gonna go now. This is it; it's the moment of truth. Let's go."

Simpson showed no emotion. Whatever his colleague's stake in the case, the decision to confront Waneta remained in Simpson's hands. As did the risks. If Waneta balked now, the investigation would blow up in his face. Fitzpatrick might get singed, but Simpson would get burned. Simpson deliberated a few moments, then said, "Yeah, let's go."

As Courtright and Mulvey regrouped for the showdown, Fitzpatrick's doubts resurfaced. He'd guaranteed Waneta's confession to boost the investigators' confidence, knowing she could balk at any time. Even now she could lie, ask for a lawyer, or simply walk away.

Or just maybe tell the truth and prove him right. Fitzpatrick knew this was his moment of truth as much as Waneta's. He had pursued Waneta from Steinschneider's specious theory about the Hoyt children's deaths, through his own political exile, to his comeback as Onondaga County district attorney. It had taken him two more years to prod Simpson to investigate his hunch and bring Waneta to the edge of the abyss. Now he stood on the sidelines, a spectator, powerless to affect the outcome of the final confrontation. He stacked his faith in Sue Mulvey against all that. This Brooklyn-born son of a cop had become a believer in the shoeless investigator. She shared his sense of mission. He knew if she didn't take Waneta over the edge, it wouldn't be for lack of effort.

As Fitzpatrick and Tynan took up their posts behind the one-way mirror, Mulvey quietly executed a simple maneuver that changed the dynamics of the interview: She eased into Bleck's chair, putting herself next to Waneta. Bleck took Mulvey's place, and Courtright returned to his spot, poised to take notes.

Mulvey closed quickly. She took Waneta's right hand in hers and said, "Mrs. Hoyt, we know what you told us about the deaths of your children is not true. We know you caused the deaths of your children."

Waneta bristled for the first time. Redness rose in a wave from her chest to her face. "That's not what you told me this morning," she said. "You tricked me."

"No, no," Mulvey said, keeping her voice low and even. "I told you the doctors told us that there were some problems, and that's what we wanted to talk to you about."

Mulvey pressed the point. "Now I'm telling you it's the doctors' opinion . . . that you caused the deaths of your children."

Waneta shook her head. She'd always made sure her children got the best care, she said. They all died of SIDS. "Go ask Dr. Steinschneider, he'll tell you."

Mulvey remained firm. "I want you to tell me the truth," she said. Long pauses shifted the conversation into slow motion.

Tynan left the observation room, struggling to suppress a nagging cough. Fitzpatrick remained hunched over the copying machine, his ear pressed to the one-way mirror, straining to hear the interview over the sound of his own heartbeat.

"I've been trained as a state police investigator to assist in things like this," Mulvey said, her voice soft and consoling. "We can understand how things like this might happen. You might have had some problem that caused this." She reached out and caressed Waneta's shoulder. "It must have been a terrible burden to carry all these years."

Waneta wept. "I don't know how many times I've asked God to forgive me," she said.

Fitzpatrick felt instant exhilaration. "It was like being underwater and all of sudden breaking through the surface and sucking in a deep breath of fresh air," he recalled later. "It was a feeling of comfort that flows through your body when you get oxygen back.

"You're happy, but you're not happy in the sense it's your child's birthday and you're happy, or it's a wedding and you're happy. You're happy in the sense you've crossed one of the last thresholds of the case. You're not some crazy person who read an article and went off on a completely illogical tangent for eight years."

Fitzpatrick rushed out and found Tynan listening wide-eyed at the door to the interview room. They punched fists in silent celebration. Then they went to get Simpson.

Although she had spent nearly two hours questioning Waneta, it had taken Mulvey less than fifteen minutes to take her over the edge. Waneta hung her head and cried softly. When she spoke, her first words were not about the tragedy of her children's deaths, but about what others would think of her. "You're all going to hate me," she said. "Everyone's going to hate me."

Waneta feared the loss of Tim's affection the most. "Tim will hate me," she declared. "He'll just throw me in the gutter."

Bleck held up a hand. "That's not true," he said. "I'll speak to Tim."

The pathos of Waneta's anguish touched Fitzpatrick as he watched again through the mirror. He always felt a pang of sympathy for the defendants he prosecuted, but this ran deeper. He was the relentless inquisitor who had exposed the truth of her past. He had brought her down. And now he grasped what Waneta could only dimly see: He couldn't have done any worse to her if he'd asked for the death penalty. Life as Waneta Hoyt knew it was over, she was ruined. She had plunged into the abyss and the only way out was confession. Mulvey showed her the way.

Mulvey produced a state police form. She filled in the spaces at the top with Waneta's biographical information and explained the formatted waiver of constitutional rights. Courtright gave Waneta a chance to ask questions, but she had none. Mulvey wrote the time—1:45 P.M.—and began asking questions, printing Waneta's statement on the form in longhand. After three hours of questioning, the task might have seemed anticlimactic if Waneta's words weren't so chilling.

"I caused the death [*sic*] of all my five children," she began.

Waneta described how she smothered her firstborn child, three-month-old Eric, with a pillow.

"He was crying at the time and I wanted to stop him. I held a pillow . . ."—Mulvey interrupted to ask what kind—". . . It might have been a sofa throw-pillow—over his face while I was sitting on the couch. I don't remember if he struggled or not, but he did bleed from the nose and mouth. After he was dead, I picked him up and went to my neighbor's house—Rodney and Betty Lane. They called the ambulance for me.

"Julie was the next to die."

Waneta described how three years later, she smothered her one-month-old daughter in her arms.

"She was crying and I wanted her to stop. I held her nose and mouth against my shoulder until she stopped breathing."

Mulvey picked up another sheet of paper and asked Waneta how two-and-a-half-year-old Jimmy died three weeks later.

"I was in the bathroom getting dressed and he wanted to come in. He came in the bathroom and I made him go out. He started crying 'Mommy! Mommy!' I wanted him to stop crying for me, so I used a bath towel to smother him.

"We were in the living room when I did this. He got a bloody nose from struggling against the towel. After he was dead, I picked him up and flagged down a garbage truck for help."

Jimmy's cry echoed in Fitzpatrick's mind. "Mommy! Mommy!" Fitzpatrick couldn't help thinking how often his toddlers pestered him and Diane in the bathroom. He pictured his two-year-old son, Sean, knocking on the door, trying to get in. And then he saw Waneta chasing Jimmy down a hall with a towel in her hands. Fitzpatrick suddenly grasped the particular horror of Jimmy's death. Waneta's other children were babies; they died unaware. But two-and-a-half-year-old Jimmy must have known as he gasped for breath that his mother was killing him.

"The next one was Molly," Waneta continued. She described smothering two-and-a-half-month-old Molly on June 5, 1970, the day after the baby was released from observation at Syracuse's Upstate Medical Center.

"I used a pillow that was in the crib to smother her.

After she was dead, I called Mom Hoyt and Dr. Stein-schneider.

"Noah was the last child that I killed."

Waneta killed the two-and-a-half-month-old boy July 28, 1971. Like Molly, it was the day after he was released from Upstate Medical Center.

"He was home from the hospital and was in his crib and crying. I could not stand the crying.

"It was the thing that caused me to kill them all, because I didn't know what to do for them," she said.

"I held a baby pillow over his face until he was dead. I then called for Mom Hoyt and Dr. Steinschneider. I remember it was a hot day in July."

Mulvey asked about Jay crying when he was little. "Jay went through some of those crying spells," Waneta explained, "but Tim was always there for that."

Waneta stopped after twenty minutes. The investigators had what they needed. Mulvey noted the time—2:04—and handed the two-page statement to Waneta. She spent fifteen minutes reading it and made one correction, changing the word "his" to "Noah," to make it clear she had not smothered Jay.

Then Waneta balked, just as Fitzpatrick had feared. "I want my husband here before I sign anything," she said.

Fitzpatrick had predicted that Waneta would turn to her husband for support in the end. And he had privately worried that it would take too long to bring Tim Hoyt to her if the state police interviewed him in Ithaca, an hour's drive away.

The delay put Courtright and Mulvey in a bind. Waneta's statement had not been tape-recorded or videotaped. Without the signature, the investigators had only their say-so that she'd spoken the words written in Mulvey's hand. And the longer they waited to get that signature, the more time Waneta had to consider the implications of what she'd said.

Mulvey maneuvered Waneta into connecting herself to the statement by asking her to write down what she wanted. Waneta picked up the pen and in a tight scrawl wrote: "I want to wait until my husband Tim comes to sign anything."

Mulvey explained it was a common defense tactic to say that police bullied a defendant. She asked Waneta to write something about how they had treated her.

"The people here have been kind in this matter," Waneta wrote.

Courtright called the barracks outside Ithaca and told Sherman and Standinger to bring Tim to Owego. Waneta had confessed and wanted her husband.

By the time Courtright called, the investigators were convinced that Tim knew nothing about his wife's killing their children. Like the doctors and family and neighbors, Tim had believed what Waneta told him for nearly thirty years.

"If every expert in the world came in and said it's obvious, it's a medical fact that your children were killed by your wife, I don't think he would buy it," Sherman said. "Love is blind, I guess sometimes, and in that case it must have been."

Tim signed a typed, two-page statement at 2:20 P.M., and Standinger and Sherman put him in their car for the drive to Owego.

With more time to fill, Courtright called in stenographer Kevin Callahan, who had been standing by at the barracks since late that morning. Courtright told Waneta they wanted to clarify the circumstances surrounding her children's deaths. He and Mulvey took turns asking questions.

Courtright returned to the question that had puzzled everyone on the task force.

"And after causing the death of five of your children, why didn't this happen to Jay?" Courtright asked.

"I don't know," Waneta said. "I just felt maybe I was a sitter to him or something, and he needed a home and somebody to love him, which I was picked out to be that mother."

During a break, Mulvey got Waneta a cup of coffee and took her outside for some fresh air. It was a beautiful afternoon, Mulvey thought, soaking in the sunshine as she waited for the investigators to bring Tim.

The investigators brought Tim into the Owego barracks around three-thirty P.M. Courtright introduced himself and showed Tim into the interview room where Waneta was waiting. Mulvey had given Waneta the option of having the investigators tell Tim what happened, but she chose to do it herself.

Tim hugged Waneta when he entered the room. When she said she had smothered the five children, he refused to believe her. The ever-loyal Tim became protective and angry by turns.

"They made you say it," he said.

"No, it's true, I did it," Waneta said. "I suffocated my children."

"It can't be true," he said. "These troopers are just feeding you a bunch of shit."

Courtright spoke to Tim, and he quickly calmed down. "Why didn't somebody catch this?" Tim complained.

Tim and Waneta talked again, and she decided to add a line to her statement. "Mom Hoyt was with me when Molly die [sic], I thought she was still alive, but not sure," she wrote.

She signed her name—Waneta E. Hoyt—and Tim witnessed the statement with his own signature. Mulvey initialed the page, once again noting the time, 3:45 P.M.

But Waneta wasn't through. After talking with Tim for a couple of minutes, she decided to add to her statement again. Mulvey started printing on a third sheet of paper.

Waneta said she sought psychiatric help through Tioga County social services. "I was seeking their help because I knew that something was wrong with me," she said. "I feel that if I got help from them, it would have prevented me from killing the rest of my children. I feel I am a good person, but I know that I did wrong. I loved my children."

She loved Jay and Tim, too, she said. "I feel the burden I have carried by keeping the secret of killing my children has been a tremendous punishment. I most definitely feel remorse and regret my actions."

She finished by saying that Tim played no part in the children's deaths. "I was always alone." She put her cramped signature at the bottom of the page and Tim again signed as a witness. Mulvey noted the time—3:59 P.M.—and signed her name. "I still love you," Tim said, embracing Waneta. Courtright and Mulvey left them alone.

With Waneta's signed statement in hand, the barracks became a swirl of activity. Waneta was photographed and fingerprinted, and Simpson called the public defender's office to get her a lawyer. The Tioga County district attorney planned to charge Waneta immediately and have her arraigned. Tynan typed up the sheaf of forms they needed for the arraignment. Lawyers in Fitzpatrick's appeals unit in Syracuse supplied the wording of the murder statute on the books when the five children died.

Troopers got food from Burger King, but the Hoyts didn't like the selection. Tim said Waneta wanted candy bars, and Bleck got her two plain Hershey chocolate bars and two with almonds.

Bleck also went to get Jay Hoyt. The state police had adopted a protective attitude toward Jay, whom they saw as a victim, too. Nobody wanted him to hear on the street that his mother had been accused of murder. Bleck found Jay with some friends at a gas station in Newark Valley and brought him back to the barracks.

When Jay entered the interview room, Waneta

pointed to the photo album. "You know your brothers and sisters," she began, "I smothered all of them. I killed them. I hope you don't hate me." The investigators left the room to give the family time alone.

Waneta had grown so attached to Mulvey during the daylong questioning that she asked the investigator to accompany her to the arraignment in Newark Valley Town Court, and Mulvey reluctantly agreed. The interview had left Mulvey tired and hungry. Waneta hadn't wanted to eat, and therefore Mulvey, an inveterate snacker, couldn't eat either. But the investigator felt oddly responsible for the woman who had bared her soul to her, and she let Waneta hold her hand as the charges accusing her of murdering her children were read in court.

When Justice James Van Nordstrand ordered Waneta held in the Tioga County jail, Mulvey gave in to her request to stay by her side. Once Waneta was safely behind bars, Mulvey joined her colleagues at Bud's Place down the road from the barracks to celebrate with pizza and beer. She didn't stay long; she wanted to go home to her daughter, Jackie.

Bill Fitzpatrick also had some business to take care of before celebrating Waneta Hoyt's arrest. He called his wife, Diane, at her law office to give her the news.

"She went for it," he said. "She went for it all."

"I can't believe it," Diane said. "That's wonderful."

"I told you this would happen this way."

Only force of will kept Fitzpatrick's voice calm as he launched into an account of the showdown with Waneta.

Diane felt torn by the emotions of the moment. She wanted desperately to be with her husband, to hop in a car and drive to Owego and celebrate his triumph. But she couldn't do that; she didn't have a sitter for the kids. She had to settle for pumping Bill for details.

He went over the interview, but when he started to

describe how Waneta smothered Jimmy, Diane choked up.

"Stop. Stop. I can't hear any more," she said.

Joy at Bill's success and the description of Jimmy Hoyt crying "Mommy! Mommy!" combined to overwhelm her. Diane began to cry. She couldn't fathom a woman murdering her own child. Didn't mothers nurture their children, make them feel safe? Isn't that why children call for Mommy?

Fitzpatrick said he'd be late. Diane said he could tell her everything when they were together. Then she hung up and went home early. She needed to hold her children.

Chapter Seventeen

Tioga County public defender Robert Miller was getting ready to head out to dinner from his condominium in Fort Myers, Florida, when he received a call from Annette Gorski, the longtime paralegal at his office back home in Waverly. The only public defender Tioga County had ever known had grown accustomed to such interruptions, even on vacation. For twenty years, Bob Miller had worked part time for the county, representing people too poor to hire their own criminal defense lawyers. He took indigent defendants' pleas for help right along with calls from clients of his prosperous private practice. The urgency in Gorski's voice told him this matter needed immediate attention.

"Bob, a woman's been arrested for killing her kids thirty years ago."

Gorski quickly explained that District Attorney Bob Simpson had asked George Awad, one of Miller's two part-time assistant public defenders, to represent the woman at her arraignment in Newark Valley Town Court. The state police said Waneta Hoyt had admitted she smothered her five children, and she was due in court within the hour.

Miller's mind raced. He'd handled hundreds of criminal cases, including a couple of dozen homicides, but he'd never heard of anything like this. As the gravity of the case sank in, Miller realized that Simpson had him at an enormous disadvantage. Waneta Hoyt had already committed the worst mistake a suspect could make by agreeing to talk to police officers without a lawyer present.

Miller made a stab at long-distance damage control, telling Gorski to instruct Awad to reserve all of Waneta Hoyt's legal rights, make sure he put the mandatory not-guilty plea on the record, and get copies of every police and court document he could find.

Miller later called the DA's office and the sheriff's department in Owego and left word that no one should question his client further. He also called the Tioga County Jail and told Waneta not to talk to anyone.

Over dinner, Miller tried to sort out the case that had broken like a thunderclap back home. Something didn't sound right, he told his wife, Rose. He couldn't figure why Waneta Hoyt had been accused of murdering her children so many years after they died. Why had the state police started digging into the matter? What had Bob Simpson been up to?

The questions nagged at Miller until he found himself awake at three a.m. If Miller couldn't sleep, that meant Raymond Urbanski wouldn't either. Miller called his friend and former law partner at home in Elmira, a city fifteen miles west of Tioga County.

"You're not going to believe this," he told Urbanski. "I've got a woman down in Owego being charged with five counts of homicide for killing her children like between thirty and twenty-five years ago."

Miller needed to find out what was going on back home, and he knew the case would intrigue his friend. Urbanski agreed to visit Waneta in jail later that day. It was the first time the fifty-three-year-old Miller had ever asked for assistance in a criminal case.

Bob Miller was an imposing figure, brimming with confidence. The former Green Beret and son of an army brigadier general marched, rather than walked, into court. He held his tall frame erect, shoulders pinned back and chin jutting forward, as he addressed the court in a booming voice. He kept his dark hair in military trim, and the glasses perched on his putty nose gave his jowly face a pensive expression. Bob Miller looked like a man who enjoyed a good fight, and he had earned a reputation for combativeness as public defender, a largely thankless job in a law-and-order place like Tioga County.

Miller seemed an unlikely candidate to represent accused criminals at the government's expense. The Cornell University law school graduate had conservative views more in keeping with those of the county's bedrock-Republican authorities than those of a stereotypical liberal public defender. He didn't need the money either; the $35,000 he received for the appointment amounted to only one-tenth of his yearly income. Miller had become wealthy by winning multimillion-dollar settlements in a string of liability and malpractice cases. In addition to the waterfront condo in Fort Myers, Miller owned a fifteen-room mansion in the village of Waverly and Greenhills Land and Cattle Company, a 650-head cattle ranch on a thousand acres in Lockwood, New York, twenty miles west of Owego. Miller stuck with the public defender's job because he liked the challenges that came with it. He reveled in the opportunity to confront the power of government in defense of the little guy. He could be a powerful advocate.

The only person who ever seemed to have intimidated Miller was a flight attendant. Once, when he was on a flight with his wife, Rose, Miller helped himself to a can of V8 juice from the beverage cart. The flight attendant heard the sound of Miller opening the can and ran up the aisle yelling, "Hey, Buster! I'll serve the drinks around here!"

Miller cowered in his seat, too embarrassed to respond. From that day forward, whenever Miller got out of line, Rose called him "Buster."

In court Miller liked to fly close to the edge. He asked questions that ventured into subjects he knew were off-limits to the jury. When the court admonished him, Miller would back off, saying, "I'm sorry, Judge. I apologize." But he would have made his point. He also used his bulk to advantage during cross-examinations, charging a few steps toward the witness stand like an angry bull to ask a tough question.

His aggressive tactics helped him compile a stellar record defending accused killers. Of the twelve murder cases he'd taken to trial, only one ended with a murder conviction. Three times, juries acquitted his clients outright. The other eight were found guilty of less serious crimes, such as manslaughter or criminally negligent homicide. Another six or seven of his homicide clients pleaded guilty before going to trial. Miller had gone up against Simpson twice in murder trials and had come away with convictions on less serious charges. As dawn broke, Miller wondered how his well-known adversary, who had never intimidated him before, had come up with such a formidable case. He found the answer in the newspaper on his doorstep.

"Christ, there was a headline in the *Miami Herald,* that has all this shit with Fitzpatrick," he would say later.

The paper had published an Associated Press story about Waneta Hoyt's arrest that didn't even mention Simpson. The article said the investigation was instigated by Onondaga County district attorney William J. Fitzpatrick, and it traced the evolution of the case to Dr. Alfred Steinschneider's 1972 article. Fitzpatrick linked the Hoyt children's deaths to Munchausen syndrome by proxy, according to the story. Miller had never heard of Bill Fitzpatrick, but soon he couldn't get him out of his mind.

Miller decided to call Dr. John Scott. He had known Scott for twenty years and thought the physician might have heard about the case when he was county coroner in the 1970s. Not only did he know about the case, Scott said, he had ruled on the cause of death for one

of the Hoyt children. Scott, now seventy-two, recounted his high-speed ride in a sheriff's patrol car on
the morning Noah Hoyt died. The doctor stood by his
twenty-three-year-old opinion: The Hoyt children were
victims of SIDS, not murder. The out-of-town district
attorney who had stirred up such a fuss was wrong,
Scott said.

Miller cut short his vacation and caught the next
flight home. He arrived amid an avalanche of media
coverage, all of which involved Fitzpatrick and most
of which did his client no good.

Fitzpatrick had been part of a carefully orchestrated
state police press conference held the evening of
Waneta's arrest. Simpson and members of the state police task force were there, but the media-savvy prosecutor from Syracuse provided most of the sound bites.
Fitzpatrick's comments were televised with pictures of
Investigator Sue Mulvey and Trooper Bubba Bleck
leading Waneta out of the Owego barracks.

News of the case—and Fitzpatrick—spread in
waves. The *New York Times* ran a follow-up story by
the Associated Press. "There are a lot of mixed emotions on a day like this," the story quoted Fitzpatrick as
saying. "We brought to justice a killer who had preyed
on her own children." This story didn't mention
Simpson either, Miller noticed.

Miller believed Fitzpatrick was milking the case for
publicity at the expense of Waneta Hoyt's right to a
fair trial. Fitzpatrick gave interviews to the three major
television networks' nightly news programs, and CNN,
and explained his relentless pursuit of Waneta to three
of the nation's most influential newspapers—the *New
York Times*, the *Philadelphia Inquirer* and the *Los Angeles Times*.

Miller couldn't escape the media's feeding frenzy. In
the week following Waneta's arrest, his law office
logged 547 phone calls from the media. Reporters
started showing up at his home unannounced on week-

ends. "All the idiots were calling," Miller said. "It was all being generated by this guy Fitzpatrick."

More than for the intrusion on his personal life, Miller blamed Fitzpatrick for upsetting Tioga County's comfortable routine for administering justice. He decided to fight back under Fitzpatrick's rules of engagement—with a news conference.

Miller and Urbanski picked the Tioga County Courthouse as an appropriate backdrop for the message they wanted to get across. The lawyers told reporters from CNN, the *New York Times,* and the regional media that they would not talk about Waneta Hoyt's defense, but they had something else to say.

"For the last twenty years, there's been an unwritten policy between Bob Simpson and myself," Miller said. "We resolve criminal proceedings in this county right here in this courthouse. I want to address what I feel has been a very serious deviation from that unwritten policy by someone from outside the county."

He accused Fitzpatrick of whipping up interest in the case for personal gain. The prosecutor apparently was interested in making a movie or writing a book or hitting the television talk show circuit, Miller said.

"I'm sure Geraldo and Sally Jessy Raphael will want to fit him in between the transvestites who want to marry their mothers and whatever other garbage they put on," he said.

"I think I saw Miller on that show," Fitzpatrick responded later that day. "I don't give a crap what he says. He should stick to defending his client rather than making me the issue." He called Miller an amateur for complaining about pretrial publicity. He said that in doing so, Miller had shown the legal skills of a first-year law student. Months later, Miller would still feel the sting of Fitzpatrick's barbs.

The crush of national media attention didn't sit well with many others in Tioga County, where there was no daily newspaper and local news still traveled by word

of mouth. Out-of-town reporters were seen as obnox-
ious big-city types, who portrayed the county's residents, especially those in the valley, as backwoods
hicks. David Cooley, the owner of MacPherson Funeral
Home, which had buried the Hoyt children, sent one
reporter packing. The reporter, who said he was from
Vanity Fair magazine, pulled up in front of Cooley's
business in Newark Valley in a Jaguar. The reporter
said he had no problem finding the funeral home because it stood out as the nicest building in town.

"It kind of upset me a little bit when he said that,"
Cooley said.

Some of the fiercely loyal Hoyts reacted to the media with hostility. George Hoyt, Tim's oldest brother,
got into a shouting match with a TV cameraman, and
other family members muttered profanities about reporters.

Like Bob Miller, they blamed Fitzpatrick. The Hoyt
family and some of their neighbors in the valley believed the prosecutor had made false accusations about
Waneta because he had ambitions to be the state's attorney general or governor.

Miller and Urbanski escalated the battle with Fitzpatrick by filing a complaint with the New York State
Attorney Grievance Committee, accusing the district
attorney of misconduct.

"I am extremely concerned and dismayed by the
public exposition of what appears to be Mr. Fitzpatrick's own personal agenda," Miller wrote. "I feel it
would be a gross miscarriage of justice if he is allowed
to continue to make outrageous comments to the media
on the merits of this criminal prosecution."

Miller made a point of Simpson's silence.

"Despite Mr. Fitzpatrick's attempt to draw Mr.
Simpson into this matter, it is interesting to note that I
have not read or heard one single quote disseminated
in the press attributed to Mr. Simpson concerning the
guilt or innocence of my client," Miller said.

For the first time in his career, Fitzpatrick had to defend himself before the committee, which can recommend that a lawyer be disbarred, suspended, or publicly rebuked. Part of his duty was to protect children, Fitzpatrick said, and if publicity about Waneta's murder case saved one child's life, then he had done his job.

"Mr. Miller would be well advised to address his skills to the service of his client," he wrote. He went a step further, saying Miller and Simpson had an incestuous relationship.

The complaint dragged on for nine months before the committee decided Fitzpatrick had done nothing wrong. But Miller would later claim victory, believing that his complaint had shut up the DA from Syracuse. Through it all, Fitzpatrick and Miller agreed on one point: While the feud raged, Simpson had remained on the sidelines. Fitzpatrick believed Simpson should have come to his defense, and he wrote him a caustic letter.

"For eight months, I have to answer to this guy's unsubstantiated charges about my ethics when you keep going about your business," he said. "And this is after it takes me eighteen months to get you to make a move on the goddamn case."

Simpson never got the letter. Fitzpatrick's secretary told her boss it was too harsh, and she threw it in the trash.

As the national publicity died, only to flourish again with another story profiling Fitzpatrick, Miller became fixated on the idea that the prosecutor had gone outside normal channels to uncover the identity of the "H" family. In particular, Miller was bothered by a story in the *Los Angeles Times* in which Fitzpatrick said the name Noah Hoyt simply "popped up."

Miller had the germ of a legal argument. A failure to follow proper procedures to obtain the Hoyt children's records could have jeopardized the legal foundation for the investigation that followed. Although Fitzpatrick would never fully explain how he identified the Hoyts, Simpson had built a fire wall between his case and Fitzpatrick by subpoenaing the relevant records himself.

Miller and Urbanski worried most about the impact of the publicity on Waneta, who already had received a faxed contract at the jail from a television talk show seeking an exclusive on-air interview. The lawyers knew Waneta was having enough problems coping with life behind bars without having to field television offers. For the first time in her marriage, Waneta was separated from Tim and her family.

Waneta Hoyt wept as she sat with Tim and Jay by the booking desk in the Tioga County Jail the night of her arrest. Jail deputy Wayne Moulton recognized Waneta from his days as a bagger at a nearby grocery store. He tried to calm her. He told Waneta jail wasn't like she'd seen on television.

Between sobs, she told Moulton she hadn't meant to kill her children. She had put pillows over their faces to stop them from crying, she said. A deputy at the desk made a note of the remark.

Waneta was obviously distraught. During booking, she completed a standard one-page screening form, answering "yes" to eleven of the seventeen questions designed to detect suicidal tendencies or depression. A guard was stationed by her cell around the clock. Overnight, Waneta learned her first lesson as a defendant: She recanted the confession she had given the state police. The next day, Waneta told a mental health nurse she could not understand why she was in jail for something she didn't do.

Waneta seemed meek and spoke haltingly and in soft tones during the half-hour meeting, said the nurse, Nancy Erwin. Waneta said she was in a daze, but she seemed to perk up when Erwin asked about her medical problems. She ticked off a list of ailments; osteoporosis; arthritis of the spine; long-standing intolerance to smells, followed by coughing spells; hypertension; and postnasal drip.

Waneta spoke freely about her personal life, telling Erwin that Tim believed she didn't harm their children. Although Waneta said she didn't feel suicidal, Erwin asked guards to keep her under continuous watch.

Erwin saw Waneta five more times and found her gaining confidence with each visit. The guards took her off the twenty-four-hour suicide watch, returned some of her personal effects, and left her cell door open. "It makes me feel human," Waneta said.

Waneta said she drew strength from her family, friends, and faith in God. She began talking to other women inmates and took a young woman from Richford under her wing. She received visits from three ministers. But Waneta still had moments of depression. One evening she started crying because the jail's lasagne reminded her of better times with her family.

On the night of a preliminary hearing a week after her arrest, Waneta's family turned out in force at Newark Valley Town Court. They brushed past reporters and photographers to get to the rows of folding chairs that served as a gallery in the sparse courtroom. Waneta's youngest sister, Donna, arrived in a wheelchair. The woman who had ridden bicycles with Waneta as a girl now had inoperable spinal cancer. Tim and Jay Hoyt flanked Waneta in a vain attempt to block photographers from taking her picture. She had traded the orange jumpsuit she wore in jail for a purple silk short-sleeved shirt over a printed blouse and a pair of pants. She tucked her feet under her chair and stared straight ahead as James Van Nordstrand, a part-time judge who worked as a plumber by day, conducted the hearing.

In New York State, anyone arrested on a felony

charge is entitled to a preliminary hearing, in which a judge decides whether the prosecution has enough evidence to hold the defendant until a grand jury issues formal charges. Defense lawyers often use preliminary hearings to get a preview of the prosecution's case, so Bob Simpson faced a delicate task. He had to present enough evidence to hold Waneta without giving away everything he had. Waneta's confession wasn't enough. Simpson also had to offer evidence that the Hoyt children had been killed, just as Bill Fitzpatrick had once had to corroborate Stephen Van Der Sluys's confession about the death of his daughter Heather.

Simpson got the corroboration he needed from his first witness, Dr. Michael Baden, who said all five Hoyt children were suffocated. The forensic pathologist said the children's death certificates were wrong; they had not died of natural causes, they were murdered. It was almost a statistical impossibility for that many children in one family to die of SIDS, he testified.

Simpson called only one other witness, Investigator Susan Mulvey. In a soft, unwavering voice, Mulvey read the three-page confession Waneta had signed the day of her arrest. Simpson chose not to reveal the statement a stenographer had taken down at the Owego barracks the same day.

Waneta, who had held Mulvey's hand during her arraignment in the same courtroom a week earlier, listened to the investigator's testimony with disdain. "I didn't kill my kids," she muttered under her breath. "This isn't true."

Van Nordstrand ordered Waneta held until a grand jury could consider the charges. Nobody had seriously expected him to do otherwise, except, perhaps, some of the Hoyts. But as Waneta left the hearing at nine o'clock to return to her cell, family members noticed something odd: She was smiling. Once again Waneta seemed to enjoy being the center of attention.

When Tioga County judge Vincent Sgueglia (pronounced *Skwell*-ya) set Waneta's bail at $100,000 the next day, her supporters responded with letters urging him to lower it.

"She has always been a loving, kind, caring woman, always there with a hug and a smile. She held my boys when they were small and has always shown love for them," wrote Darlene Wait, who had married Waneta's nephew.

Waneta's pastor, the Rev. Lisa Jean Hoefner, told the judge that eight church people had volunteered to stay with Waneta at home while Tim worked, to ease concern that she might take her life. Hoefner remembered Waneta as the simple woman who'd offered to make afghans when she couldn't afford to donate money to the church.

The letter campaign worked. On April 15, Sgueglia lowered Waneta's bail to $75,000, and Waneta walked out of jail at 4:15 P.M. Family and friends had used their homes and other property as collateral for the bail bond that freed her.

Two weeks later, Waneta was indicted on ten counts of second-degree murder, two for each child. The grand jury charged Waneta under two distinct theories of murder. The first charge in each pair accused her of killing the child on purpose. This was known in legal shorthand as intentional murder. The second theory was known as depraved-indifference murder. This was a more serious version of manslaughter, in which a defendant is accused of recklessly causing another person's death.

Three months later, Simpson had to amend the indictment for Eric Hoyt's death to conform to the first-degree murder statute that was on the books at the time of his death. The higher degree had no practical effect; Waneta still faced the maximum sentence of twenty-five years to life if convicted of any of the ten charges.

The filing of formal charges had little impact on the

valley. Family and friends had already rallied to Waneta's defense. Many believed the police had preyed on a mother's guilt over the tragic deaths of her children and had tricked her into confessing to something she didn't do. They couldn't accept that the matronly woman who knitted afghans for neighborhood kids was a baby-killer.

Waneta Hoyt's arrest inevitably focused attention on sudden infant death syndrome and the 1972 study that pushed Dr. Alfred Steinschneider to the forefront of SIDS research.

Steinschneider had caught the crest of the campaign by groups such as the National Foundation for Sudden Infant Death to increase awareness of SIDS. Nine months before *Pediatrics* published his article about the Hoyt children, the foundation orchestrated a U.S. Senate hearing that led to a resolution urging the Department of Health, Education, and Welfare (later Health and Human Services) to make SIDS research a national priority. In 1973, the federal government awarded Steinschneider a $77,458 grant to study the possible role of sleep apnea in SIDS.

Continued lobbying by the foundation helped produce the Sudden Infant Death Syndrome Act of 1974, which dramatically increased funding for SIDS research. In the nine years following his article on M.H. and N.H., Steinschneider's projects received almost one in every four of the dollars that the National Institutes of Health awarded for SIDS research—nearly $5 million. The National Institutes of Health also asked him to review other researchers' applications for SIDS grants.

Steinschneider was a hot commodity. In 1977, he left Upstate Medical Center in Syracuse for the University of Maryland medical school, where he received a full professorship in the pediatrics department and was named director of the university's new SIDS research center. Steinschneider was looking for an improved ap-

nea monitor to use in Maryland and fell in with Parker
H. Petit, an engineer from Atlanta. Petit had lost a son
to SIDS in 1970 and channeled his grief into the devel-
opment of a home apnea monitor. His prototype didn't
suit Steinschneider's specifications, so Petit redesigned
it in a matter of weeks.

Petit had founded Healthdyne Inc. to manufacture
the machines and the company soon branched out to
make other medical devices. The venture took off in
the 1980s, in part because Steinschneider's research
had popularized the use of apnea monitors. By the
1990s, about forty thousand babies a year were hooked
to the machines, Healthdyne was reporting annual sales
of $260 million, and Steinschneider was known as the
"father of the apnea monitor."

In 1983 Steinschneider left the University of Maryland to help Petit establish the American SIDS Institute
in Atlanta. Steinschneider became president of the
nonprofit institute, which conducted academic and
clinical research on apnea and SIDS. Steinschneider's
position also allowed him to pursue his work without
the constraints of university or government oversight.

He started a push for corporate funding, chastising
the federal government for reducing research grants for
SIDS from a peak of nearly $5 million in 1979 to less
than $1 million in 1986.

"A million dollars will buy you ten cheap studies,"
Steinschneider said in 1989. "A million dollars is
equivalent to saying, 'It's not important.' "

But by then, many researchers had distanced themselves from Steinschneider's theories, and the routine
use of home apnea monitors was under attack. A British researcher who studied the breathing patterns of
nine thousand newborns reported in 1983 that none of
the children who later died of SIDS had suffered prolonged apnea.

Waneta Hoyt's confession to the state police accomplished what no researcher could. By undermining the

foundation of Steinschneider's work, she took the debate about apnea and SIDS out of the pages of obscure medical journals and put it onto the front pages of the nation's newspapers and prime-time TV.

Time magazine mentioned the case in a story illustrated with photographs of Waneta, Marybeth Tinning, and another accused child-killer, Gail Savage, of Waukegan, Illinois. Steinschneider's theory was in question, *Time* said, and so was the value of parents' using apnea monitors to prevent babies from dying of SIDS.

Nearly twenty-two years after publishing Steinschneider's study on the Hoyt children, *Pediatrics* took note of the interest that Waneta's arrest had generated in the popular press. "This is an incredible story," *Pediatrics'* editors wrote. "The whole apnea-home-monitoring-to-prevent-SIDS movement began with Steinschneider's original paper." The journal also printed an excerpt from Dr. John Hick's 1973 letter questioning whether Steinschneider had overlooked evidence of abuse.

Steinschneider would have preferred to keep the debate over his theories confined to medical journals, but the furor over the Hoyt case forced him to defend himself in the mass media.

"A district attorney read a paper about some unexplained deaths and proceeded to hold a press conference," he told one newspaper. "I just wrote a paper. It's a simple little paper. I would submit to you that every baby who dies suddenly and unexpectedly should be reviewed, should be looked at from the point of view of that possibility. But no accusation should be made until there's clear-cut evidence."

That district attorney was more than happy to debate Steinschneider in the media. Fitzpatrick believed the doctor's theories were dangerous, and he attacked them in every interview.

"In my opinion, awareness about this case is going to save a lot of babies," Fitzpatrick said.

The influential journal *Science* predicted that Stein-schneider's theory would fall if Waneta was convicted. The magazine posed a question Fitzpatrick had already raised: "Could Steinschneider have prevented the deaths of two of the Hoyt children?"

With the arrest of Waneta Hoyt and the attacks on Steinschneider's groundbreaking study, the media started to mention SIDS and murder in the same breath. The link SIDS activists had tried to suppress for thirty years suddenly loomed large. In June 1994, when CBS-TV newsmagazine *Eye to Eye with Connie Chung* prepared to broadcast a story about SIDS and cases of suspected serial infanticide, the SIDS Alliance in Columbia, Maryland, mobilized to influence the content. The alliance, the successor to the National Foundation for Sudden Infant Death, flashed a media alert to its chapters around the country.

"Apparently, the piece has already been taped. But, *we CAN still have an impact on the 'wrap-around' commentary,* which will be most likely handled by CBS medical reporter Dr. Bob Arnot or by Connie Chung," the organization told its members.

"We must seek recognition of the positive changes that have occurred over the past twenty-five years, and ask for sensitivity to the tens of thousands of affected families who must live with the repercussions of media attention focused on the rare criminal cases," the message said. "Tell your story—briefly. Were you unjustly suspected? And let them know how coverage such as this perpetuates a long-standing bias against SIDS families."

SIDS parents were urged to fax letters to CBS. "*Encourage at least twenty others in your group to do the same.* We would like to generate one thousand letters to CBS for impact!" the alert said.

Chung had interviewed Steinschneider at the American SIDS Institute outside Atlanta, and Fitzpatrick at his office in Syracuse, and the program offered the prospect of the first electronic showdown between the two men. In fact, the doctor and prosecutor had met on the phone almost a year earlier.

In July 1993 Bob Simpson let Fitzpatrick call Steinschneider to see if he had any records of his study of the Hoyt children. Steinschneider was guarded from the outset, Fitzpatrick said, and never uttered the name Hoyt. He became increasingly defensive as the prosecutor quizzed him about the 1972 article.

"This thing was thoroughly investigated back then," Steinschneider told him. "I don't know why anybody would be mentioning anything about it now."

"Well, doctor, wasn't it unusual that these things only happened while the babies were in the custody of the mother?" Fitzpatrick asked.

"Well, there's only three possibilities—the mother or the father or both," Steinschneider replied.

Fitzpatrick laughed to himself. "What? No fucking baby-sitters?" he thought. "No aunts, uncles, grandmothers, grandfathers, friends, relatives, neighbors, strangers? What kind of a moron is this guy? The baby can only be with the mother or the father, there's no other possibility? He didn't think it was odd that these things happened only when they were in the custody of the mother?"

Fearing that Steinschneider might warn the Hoyts about the investigation if he pressed, Fitzpatrick had cut the conversation short.

The *Eye to Eye* segment broadcast June 16, 1994, played like a teleconference of Steinschneider's critics. Dr. Linda Norton, who had first told Fitzpatrick about Steinschneider's 1972 study, called the doctor's paper "a scientific error. It should be purged from the literature."

Chung's producers also had interviewed the family of a Chicago woman whose six children had died in the late 1970s and early 1980s, apparently of natural causes. Years later, the medical examiner reclassified the deaths as homicides, but the state's attorney refused to prosecute because a consulting pathologist said the deaths could have been due to SIDS. The consultant based his opinion on Steinschneider's 1972 article.

Relatives of the babies' father, who was mysteriously killed at home, blamed the children's deaths on their mother, who was never charged. The family called Steinschneider's article a "license to kill."

When Chung put the charge to Steinschneider, he said, "I'm sorry to hear that. I'm truly sorry to hear that."

But the doctor, who continued to observe research etiquette by not identifying his subjects by name, made no apologies for his research on the Hoyt children.

"Do you think you could've saved the lives of the two children from the 'H' family?" Chung asked.

"Well, obviously I've thought about that," Steinschneider said. "I thought about it the day they died. I thought about that the day after they died, and I'm not sure what I could've done in 1972, or I would've done it."

When Chung pressed him on the influence of his paper, Steinschneider stammered, "No, no. That paper . . . I'm influential. I'm a big man, not the paper. The paper was the beginning."

Fitzpatrick, glowering on camera, told Chung that Steinschneider's responsibility was to his patients, not his theory. "His patients were Molly and Noah, and Molly and Noah are dead," he said.

The SIDS Alliance could take a measure of satisfaction from the follow-up segment by Dr. Arnot, which emphasized the tragedy of SIDS for parents. Arnot pointed with hope to a new government program urging parents to put babies to sleep on the back or side, which European studies had shown could cut SIDS deaths by half.

What the report didn't say was that Steinschneider's American SIDS Institute had sent the network a news release saying the initiative was premature. Steinschneider was the lead researcher on a new project to determine whether infants should be put to bed on their stomachs or backs. The release said the doctor planned to study infants who were at increased risk for SIDS— brothers and sisters of SIDS victims. Steinschneider had not given up his idea that SIDS ran in families.

When Fitzpatrick looked at Connie Chung's copy of the American SIDS Institute's news release, he saw it as further evidence of Steinschneider's arrogance. "I'm thinking to myself, 'Fuck this guy. Is he for real?' It cut SIDS down by fifty percent or more," Fitzpatrick said.

Steinschneider had no illusions about how Fitzpatrick felt. He told several people he was afraid to visit old friends in Syracuse because he thought the district attorney would prosecute him for the deaths of Molly and Noah Hoyt.

Chapter Eighteen

State police investigator Gary Gelinger's excitement grew as he pulled up to the small white house with a red-shingled roof and a well-kept lawn on a dead-end street. It looked like a place where an elderly woman might live, he thought.

Gelinger was looking for any clue that suggested he'd come to the right place. He and his partner had traveled from Owego to arrive at a strange address outside Syracuse where he hoped to find a retired nurse who might help convict Waneta Hoyt of murdering her five children. Their trip was part of the intensified investigation that the Hoyt task force launched the day after Waneta's arrest.

In the year leading up to Waneta's trial, prosecutors and state police assigned to the task force would pursue 154 leads that Senior Investigator Bob Courtright had developed during his initial investigation. Tracking down the nurses who had treated Molly and Noah Hoyt at Upstate Medical Center in Syracuse was lead number 60.

Tioga County assistant district attorney Peggy Drake combed through the children's medical records, trying to decipher the signatures scrawled after the nurses' hourly notes. The medical charts ran to hundreds of pages, and Drake eventually compiled a list of fifty-five names. The job of tracking down the people who went with the signatures fell to Gelinger and his partner, Investigator James Conzola.

Many of the nurses had signed the charts with just a first initial and last name, which the investigators tried to match with the hospital's employment records. That gave them some full names and addresses. But the investigators knew that after twenty-three years, many of the nurses probably had died or moved away, or had married and were using their husbands' last names. When they started thumbing through the Syracuse metropolitan telephone book, trying to locate nurses who had stayed in the area, they came across a listing for J. Evans. The telephone number and address matched the information in the employment records of Julia Evans, a practical nurse who had retired from the medical center eighteen years earlier.

Gelinger and Conzola knew they might have a key find: Evans was one of the few nurses whose name appeared in both Molly's and Noah's records. They also realized that if the person listed in the phone book was the same Julia Evans who had cared for Molly and Noah in the early 1970s, she was now seventy-nine and might not remember much about the children. The investigators figured she would respond better to a personal visit than a telephone call, so they drove to the address just south of Syracuse.

Something about the house just felt right, and Gelinger was convinced they would finally meet Evans when they went to the door. He was less certain about whether she would have anything useful to tell them.

"Hi. We're with the state police. I'm Investigator Gary Gelinger," he said. "This is Investigator James Conzola. Were you a nurse at Upstate Medical Center some twenty years ago?"

"Why, yes, I was."

"We're here to talk to you about the Hoyt babies."

"It's about time," Evans said.

The investigators had not only found the right Julia Evans, they'd found a witness who'd had suspicions about the deaths of Molly and Noah for more than two decades. Evans invited the investigators to sit with her on the front porch, and they talked for two hours.

Evans told them Molly and Noah were normal, healthy infants, and that she was bothered by Waneta's detached attitude toward them. "I never saw any other mother react to her babies the way Waneta did," she said. "I never forgot that."

Evans said she had been so convinced something awful was happening to the Hoyt children at home that she bet Dr. Alfred Steinschneider a quarter that Noah would not come back to the hospital alive. The doctor never paid up, she said.

Gelinger wrote out a statement about Evans's observations of the Hoyt family. But more important, Evans gave the investigators the names of other nurses who had worked with her and taken care of Molly or Noah.

From there, Gelinger and Conzola tracked down retired nurse Corrine Dower and her colleague Thelma Schneider, who had been head nurse in the Children's Clinical Research Center. Neither had forgotten Molly.

"I remember this family because of the bizarre way in which Mrs. Hoyt held the baby—not cuddling, but away from her," Schneider told the state police.

Joyce Thomas, another nurse who had cared for Molly, was traced to Tacoma, Washington. She recalled crying the night she put Molly in Tim and Waneta Hoyt's car to go home for the last time.

Gail Dristle was a twenty-one-year-old nurse's assistant when she helped take care of Noah. In November 1994, she read about Waneta's arrest in a *Newsweek* story with the headline "Why Parents Kill." She wrote to Bill Fitzpatrick's office, mistakenly believing Waneta had been arrested in Syracuse.

"The reason I remember Noah so long ago is because I lost several nights' sleep over his death, which occurred within twenty-four hours of his discharge home with an apnea monitor," she wrote. She signed her letter with her married name, Gail Pfeiffer.

Evans, Dower, Schneider, Thomas, and Pfeiffer had the kind of firsthand observations that Tioga County DA Bob Simpson and assistant DA Peggy Drake needed to breathe life into the medical experts' abstract opinions about the Hoyt children's deaths. The prosecutors were counting on the nurses' vivid memories to bring the victims to life and perhaps shift sympathy away from Waneta.

Task force investigators also tried to track down anyone in the valley who remembered the Hoyt children's deaths. They talked with Tim's and Waneta's former neighbors, former baby-sitters, ambulance attendants, the funeral director, the gravedigger, friends, and family.

Waneta's father, Albert Nixon, told the state police his family had had no idea that Waneta might have been killing her children. He described his daughter as a nervous woman but said she didn't suffer from any mental illnesses.

"I would like to say that Waneta grieved for each of her children after they died," Albert said in a written statement. "She acted like any other mother who lost a child."

Then he told investigators about his visit with Waneta in jail the night she was arrested. "I was talking to my daughter, but I cannot remember if I asked her or if she came out and told me that she did it," he said. "After that, she told me that she hopes that I was not mad at her for doing this."

Waneta's brothers and sisters said they did not believe she killed the children, although her older brother Archie wondered why she had kept having babies.

Waneta's in-laws told investigators the children had seemed normal and healthy. They described Waneta as a good mother who would never harm her children. The police did not talk to George Hoyt, the one member of the family who had voiced suspicions about Waneta. George had had an angry confrontation with a

TV cameraman the day of Waneta's arrest, and investigators thought it best to leave him alone.

The investigation in the valley ran into a few dead ends. Art and Natalie Hilliard, the couple who were so close to Tim and Waneta that they were practically family, refused to talk to the police.

Howard Horton, the Newark Valley police chief who started asking questions after Jimmy Hoyt's death, had died in 1983. If he had ever put his suspicions about Waneta in writing, the state police were not going to find the report: Three weeks before Waneta's arrest, Horton's son was cleaning house and burned three boxes of his father's police records.

"They all went up in smoke," Howard Jr. said. "Before the barrel had cooled off, the police wanted them."

With his evidence largely in place, Simpson started looking at how best to present it at trial. Courtright had told him about the juror from Marybeth Tinning's trial, who had given the investigator good tips on how to approach Waneta, and Simpson decided to go back for advice on trial tactics. In December, Simpson, Courtright, and Drake traveled to Schenectady, where they met with eight Tinning jurors in a room at the county sheriff's department.

The jurors told the prosecutors not to pick engineers for the Hoyt jury. Engineers tended to be too analytical and demanded a higher burden of proof, the Tinning jurors said. Select jurors who have children, they suggested, because parents would probably be less sympathetic toward Waneta.

Despite Tinning's hardened appearance, the jurors said, they had felt sorry for her. They had wanted to get her help, not punish her. Simpson had watched Tim Hoyt hold his wife's hand throughout pretrial hearings; the prosecutor wanted to know what impact the husband might have on a jury. Letting Tim sit next to Waneta during the trial would send the message that he believed she did not kill their children, the Tinning jurors said.

The jurors also gave Courtright a piece of advice: Don't wear your gold bracelet when you testify; it's too flashy and might distract Waneta's jurors.

By January 1995 Courtright and his team had exhausted all but one of their leads, lead number 154: Exhume the children's bodies.

With no fresh crime scene, no physical evidence, and inconclusive autopsy reports for three children, Simpson was looking for more evidence to corroborate Waneta's confession. Perhaps vital clues were entombed in the children's caskets, buried between the graves of their grandmother and great-grandmother in Highland Cemetery.

At a hearing six months earlier, Simpson had asked Tioga County judge Vincent Sgueglia for permission to dig up the children's graves. Dr. Michael Baden, the prosecution's only witness for the hearing, testified that new autopsies might yield useful evidence. No matter how badly the Hoyt children's bodies had decomposed, some parts—such as the bones—would have stayed intact, he said. The children might have been suffocated with enough force to break bones in the faces and necks, he said, or their breathing passages might contain fibers from a towel or pillow used to smother them.

Baden pointed to the remarkable findings from the exhumation of Mississippi civil rights activist Medgar Evers, who had been shot to death and buried in 1963—two years before Waneta's first baby died. Evers's body was dug up in 1991 for the retrial of a white supremacist accused of assassinating him, and Baden had helped perform a new autopsy on the body.

"The body was in excellent condition at the time of the exhumation," Baden said. "He appeared as if he died yesterday, the day before; just as a body would be in a funeral parlor the day after death."

Although Waneta and her lawyers did not oppose digging up the children's graves, Sgueglia denied Simpson's request. The judge found no compelling reason to justify the "serious invasion of the repose of the dead."

The judge's decision reflected the uneasiness that others in Tioga County felt about rooting around in events that had occurred so long ago. Every chance they got, Simpson, Drake, and Courtright asked their friends and family what they thought about the upcoming trial. Many people wondered why Waneta was being tried after all these years. Look at her, they said, hadn't she suffered enough?

Courtright and the prosecutors worried that prospective jurors might have similar concerns. Courtright had a stock answer whenever anyone questioned why he was investigating Waneta: "I can't give anyone five free murders."

Simpson knew that if he didn't appeal Sgueglia's decision, Waneta's lawyers could stand up in front of a jury and say the prosecution hadn't made every effort to prove that the children didn't die of natural causes. Maybe evidence that would exonerate Waneta had been buried with her children.

Simpson succeeded in having a state appeals court overturn Sgueglia's decision, and he got the go-ahead for the exhumations in January. The job took two days.

Baden and a team of state police investigators went to Highland Cemetery in Richford on Monday, January 9, and set up a green-and-white funeral tent around the graves. The temperature had dropped below zero, and the tent helped shelter the crew from the bitter wind that blew through the hillside cemetery. The team made slow progress. The hand-drawn map that cemetery caretaker Clarence Lacey had provided was not specific enough to locate the burial spots, and only Eric's and Jimmy's graves had headstones. The gravediggers used a jackhammer to break through the earth's frozen crust, then used shovels and garden tools to scrape away the dirt. They unearthed Molly's casket the first day. They returned the following day with a backhoe, and maneuvered around other graves to dig up the caskets of her brothers and sisters.

The five caskets were loaded into a hearse and taken to Albany Medical Center in the state capital for autopsies. Baden and other doctors found the toys Tim and Waneta had placed in each casket, but the bodies were badly decomposed. Eric and Jimmy had been buried in wooden caskets that had collapsed and filled with dirt. Water had leaked into Julie's lead casket. Noah and Molly had been buried in more durable Styrofoam caskets, and doctors thought their bodies might contain useful clues. But the autopsies performed by Baden and another forensic pathologist produced only one major finding: There was no indication from the remains that the children died of natural causes.

The autopsies showed no evidence that Waneta killed her children either, and Bob Miller and Waneta thought that supported her innocence.

The reburial of the five children on January 14 once again cast Waneta in the role of grieving mother. She had asked for a service to be held that morning at MacPherson Funeral Home. New caskets bought by Tioga County sat in a row in the funeral parlor for the ten-minute service attended by Tim's and Waneta's family and a couple of close friends. Funeral director David Cooley, who had buried Molly and Noah the first time, led the group in prayer.

Chuck Hoyt helped Cooley load the children's caskets into a hearse for the short drive up Route 38 to Highland Cemetery. Waneta had written a poem that she asked Chuck to read. Chuck looked at the tiny caskets holding his nieces and nephews and began to cry as he read her poem, "Goodbye My Little Family."

Waneta cried as cemetery workers placed receiving

blankets on each casket. Jay Hoyt had bought teddy
bears to be placed in the children's graves. Afterward,
Waneta's friends and family went home and turned
their attention to the next chapter in her life—the trial.

Waneta's arrest on March 23, 1994, marked the beginning of the defense investigation, and her lawyers,
Miller and Ray Urbanski, knew they had a lot of catch-
ing up to do. They hired private investigator Bill
Fischer, a former state trooper, who relished the opportunity to show up his former colleagues.

Fischer worked closely with Tim Hoyt to come up
with witnesses who could help Waneta win an acquittal. Fischer prodded Tim to remember people in the
valley who might recall the children's deaths. Tim
identified at least five Newark Valley ambulance crew
members who had responded to the children's medical
emergencies, and he helped Fischer track them down.

Tim tried to jog his family's memories to come up
with any information that might help Waneta. His
mother, Ella, dug out an envelope labeled "Jimmy's
first haircut." Jimmy was seven months old on Christmas Day 1966, when he had his hair clipped for the
first time. Ella had kept a lock of the boy's hair for
twenty-eight years. She gave it to Tim, hoping that
DNA tests might reveal a genetic illness that had killed
the boy. But the hair sample would never become evidence; there was no way to prove it was Jimmy's.

Tim took a leave of absence from his job as a security guard at Cornell University to work on Waneta's
defense, but he returned to the campus frequently to
conduct research with Waneta. The couple spent hours
in the university's medical library, looking for scholarly articles on sudden infant death syndrome. Their
teenage niece, Penny Hoyt, searched newspapers
nationwide for stories about SIDS and sleeping disorders. She found more than one hundred articles, not
knowing whether they would aid Waneta's defense.

Occasionally Penny found a story that bolstered Tim's and Waneta's spirits, such as a 1986 article from the *Detroit News* about twins who had died of SIDS. The story suggested a hereditary defect was the cause.

Miller and Annette Gorski, his paralegal, often arrived at his office in Waverly in the morning to find Tim and Waneta waiting to hand over the latest newspaper search or other scraps of evidence they thought would help. The couple sometimes created headaches for Miller and Urbanski. The biggest one was Waneta's insistence that her lawyers could not plea-bargain with Simpson. She had recanted her confession and was adamant in her assertion that she had not killed the children.

Miller wanted to put on a defense that would show Waneta was mentally ill and couldn't be held responsible for the deaths. He thought he could argue that she suffered from postpartum depression, which showed up as Munchausen syndrome by proxy. Any jury, he believed, would quickly sympathize with Waneta and decide she belonged in a psychiatric hospital, not prison. But Waneta would have none of it. There would be no defense based on Munchausen syndrome by proxy. Miller and Urbanski had to make an all-out effort to prove she hadn't killed the children.

The two Southern Tier lawyers wanted to split the task in a way that played to their individual strengths. By all accounts, they had been an odd couple since 1976, when Miller hired Urbanski out of Cornell University's law school.

Urbanski, the son of Connecticut factory workers, was a liberal Democrat. He wore his dirty-blond hair over his collar and dressed in stylish double-breasted suits and designer ties. With his thick-lensed glasses and protruding teeth, Urbanski had the look of a bookworm. He was the computer whiz; Miller still preferred a rotary-dial telephone.

Miller had decided to taper off his legal work after

a string of large settlements in civil cases made him financially secure. He split from the partnership in 1985, setting off an acrimonious breakup with Urbanski. Urbanski and another lawyer sued Miller for money they thought he owed them from a settlement. They eventually settled out of court, with Miller agreeing to pay Urbanski $20,000. The two lawyers didn't speak for six months. Although they eventually restored their brotherly friendship, the Hoyt case was the first criminal matter they'd handled together in nine years.

The two lawyers put in countless unpaid hours building Waneta's defense, but she seemed to get along better with Urbanski. While Miller was gruff and impatient, Urbanski paid more attention to her. The younger lawyer would throw his arm around Waneta's shoulder, hold her hand, and listen to her. She often called Urbanski at home to ask about her case or to chat about her everyday life. It seemed everything happened to Waneta.

Urbanski was more openly sympathetic than Miller. To him, the trial was one more tragic episode in Waneta's life. "Why are we doing this?" Urbanski asked, as if summing up the case for a jury. "You can get right down to the question of, what's the criminal justice system designed to do? It's not like having a serial killer running loose on the streets. There are some deep-seated questions in this case, and it goes beyond guilt or innocence."

Urbanski took charge of developing a defense for the portion of the prosecution's case that touched Waneta directly—her confession. The task seemed insurmountable after Sgueglia ruled in a pretrial hearing that the state police had legally obtained Waneta's statements and a jury could hear them.

Urbanski argued that the police had enticed Waneta to go with them to the Owego barracks, where they psychologically manipulated her to admit to crimes she never committed. He thought he could show that investigators had played mind games by using Bubba Bleck, a trooper Waneta considered a friend, to lure her to the barracks. Waneta had told Urbanski she agreed to talk to the police because they told her she would be helping a doctor from Minnesota conducting SIDS research.

Waneta was interviewed by a couple of psychologists before the defense team decided that one of them, Charles Ewing, was the expert they needed to explain to a jury how she had been tricked into confessing. Ewing, a forensic psychologist and law professor in Buffalo, interviewed Waneta ten times in the months leading up to the trial. He determined that she had three personality disorders, which, taken together, made her highly vulnerable to suggestions by authorities like the police.

Miller concentrated on countering the medical evidence the prosecution would use to corroborate Waneta's confession. He couldn't wait to cross-examine Baden, whose reputation as a celebrity pathologist had been bolstered when O. J. Simpson's defense team hired him as a consultant. Miller believed Baden's opinion that the Hoyt children were murdered was based on the assumption that five children from the same family cannot die of SIDS. The forensic pathologist's opinion wasn't scientific, Miller said, it was more a belief.

Given Baden's notoriety, his expertise, and his testimony at Waneta's preliminary hearing, Miller thought the prosecution probably wouldn't even summon Dr. Janice Ophoven from Minnesota to testify at the trial. That didn't concern Miller, because he knew Baden could be beaten. The public defender had done it twenty years earlier in his first murder trial.

Miller had defended a man accused of burying a fourteen-year-old friend alive along a riverbank in Elmira. The friends had been drinking heavily, and the boy passed out. Believing his friend was dead, the man buried him on the spot. Baden testified that the fourteen-year-old was buried alive.

Miller had to prove that the medical evidence showed otherwise. He sought the help of Dr. Eleanor McQuillen, a pathologist. McQuillen reviewed Baden's medical report and other evidence and concluded that the boy was dead when he was buried. The jury acquitted Miller's client of murder and found him guilty of the less serious charge of criminally negligent homicide.

As he prepared for his second encounter with Baden, Miller returned to McQuillen. She reviewed the Hoyt children's medical records, but she said she couldn't help Miller this time. No forensic pathologist in the country would testify that the children's deaths were anything but homicides, she told him. Jimmy, for example, was far too old to die of SIDS.

But she softened the blow by suggesting that Miller could poke holes in Baden's opinion by cross-examining him about contradictory details in the Hoyt children's records. McQuillen also recommended that Miller get an apnea expert, preferably Steinschneider, to testify about the possibility that the Hoyt children suffered from a congenital breathing disorder.

Miller and Urbanski flew to Atlanta, not knowing whether Steinschneider believed Waneta was innocent. As a matter of fact, Steinschneider said, doctors routinely consider murder in such cases. But, he said, he believed the deaths of the first three Hoyt babies had been fully investigated. As for Molly and Noah, Steinschneider said, their medical records showed they had breathing problems. They were not normal babies.

Steinschneider had buoyed Waneta's case. He didn't think she killed her children, and he gave them the name of another SIDS researcher who agreed with him.

Simpson also realized Steinschneider's importance as a witness: No doctor had examined Molly and Noah Hoyt more thoroughly. If Steinschneider still believed the children died of natural causes, despite all the evidence to the contrary, he could create reasonable doubt in the minds of jurors. The district attorney fished around, trying to find out whether Miller planned to call Steinschneider to testify. Simpson wanted to be prepared to cross-examine the noted doctor. On March 10, with the trial less than three weeks away, Simpson decided to call Steinschneider at the American SIDS Institute.

When Steinschneider asked about the exhumations, Simpson told him that the caskets contained mostly bones and flesh. Nevertheless, Simpson said, Baden's findings were consistent with Waneta's statements about suffocating the children.

"It also could be consistent with a lot of other things," Steinschneider said.

Simpson interpreted Steinschneider's comment to mean the doctor agreed that Waneta could have suffocated her children.

Later in the conversation, Simpson said, "I feel that what you have had to say is honest and forthright and I think you said, that based on what you know about the case, she could have suffocated her kids. And as a courtesy—"

Steinschneider cut him off. "No, I didn't say that."

"Yes, you did. And—"

"No, I did not."

"Yes, you did."

"You say I said that."

"Yes, you did. She could have, or she might not have. You don't know. There are four or five possibilities," Simpson said.

"You're being terribly dishonest," Steinschneider said, growing angry.

"OK."

"And I would say that in the courtroom, and I would say that now. We're through with that conversation. What you've done, you are showing your colors. You are a dishonest human being."

"Well, what did you say?"

"Now, I'll tell you. You're a dishonest human being . . . I had heard from other people that you were a nice person but you are a liar."

"OK, what did you say?"

"That you are a liar. I said that there are many, many possibilities."

"One was homicide."

"That there were other possibilities. That there were many possibilities. I did not say that it was consistent with, I said there were many possibilities. There is no evidence for any of them. That's what makes it an unexplained death. And I do not take kindly at all because you got to know: I don't like what you just did. And I think it's disgusting, and I now am convinced more than ever that it is your intention to fry somebody even though you believe they are innocent."

Steinschneider tried to turn the tables on Simpson, asking if it was possible that the police beat confessions out of suspects. That was possible, Simpson said, but it didn't happen to Waneta.

"You want the truth?" Steinschneider asked. "I think there is a real possibility that the investigators beat the shit out of her."

Steinschneider heard a clicking noise and asked Simpson if he was tape-recording the call. Simpson said he was, and Steinschneider quickly ended their conversation.

After this phone call, Simpson knew he had to be prepared for Steinschneider to testify at Waneta's trial.

Even with Steinschneider in their corner, Waneta's lawyers knew it would be difficult to win acquittals on ten murder charges. The prosecution could try to prove Waneta guilty under two theories: first, that she intentionally killed her children, or second, that she realized her actions were deadly but didn't care—so-called reckless murder.

Waneta's lawyers thought Simpson had scant evi-

dence to make the first set of charges stick; Waneta
had never said she meant to kill the children. But they
feared the prosecutor had enough evidence under the
second theory to prove to a jury that Waneta had acted
recklessly by covering her children's faces to stop their
crying.

Miller and Urbanski needed a fallback plan in case
their bid for a complete acquittal failed, and they found
one in a quirk of New York's homicide statutes.

The most serious homicide charge is murder, and it
carries no statute of limitations; district attorneys can
prosecute a murder no matter how long ago the homicide occurred. But the clock for prosecuting someone
for manslaughter, the second most serious charge for a
homicide, runs out after five years. Waneta Hoyt had
beaten the clock on July 28, 1976—the fifth anniversary of Noah's death.

Judges often agree to let juries hearing murder trials
consider lesser charges that may fit the facts, such as
manslaughter. Waneta's lawyers figured that if worse
came to worst, they could try to persuade the jury to
find Waneta guilty of manslaughter instead of murder.
The statute of limitations would invalidate the manslaughter conviction, and Waneta would walk away
free.

Miller believed that Waneta's pathetic appearance
would provoke sympathy among the jurors and that
might be enough to persuade them to let her off with
manslaughter. Miller decided not to discuss his fallback strategy with Waneta, who insisted on her innocence and wanted complete acquittal.

Simpson had figured out the same strategy, and it
worried him. He knew a manslaughter conviction
would be tantamount to an acquittal.

"We took the emotional, psychological fallback position that, even if she was convicted of manslaughter,
and in effect couldn't be sentenced for it, at least we

had vindicated the deaths of these children," Simpson said. "We were emotionally prepared for that."

Miller saw it as the perfect ending for everyone. Simpson would have a conviction. Bill Fitzpatrick could claim a moral victory. Waneta Hoyt wouldn't have to go to prison, and she could still claim she was innocent. "Everybody would be happy," Miller said.

All that remained was to pick a jury sympathetic to Waneta.

PART FOUR

The Trial

Chapter Nineteen

George Hoyt summoned his kinsmen to meet at 8:00 A.M. sharp at the Dunkin Donuts across from the Tioga County Courthouse. Word had filtered down to George that someone might take a shot at his sister-in-law, Waneta, at the start of her trial, and he wasn't going to stand idly by and let that happen.

Tim Hoyt's oldest brother had the rough-and-tumble aspects of a backwoodsman: craggy face, flannel shirt, camouflage cap, quilted vest, and surly disposition.

"You know that verse in church?" George liked to say, " 'Yea, though I walk through the valley of the shadow of death, I shall fear no evil.' That's me. I'm the meanest son-of-a-bitch in the land."

George was the son who'd stood up to the Hoyts' drunken father, the one who once put their dad through a kitchen window when he got rough with their mother.

"I don't threaten," George said. "I just tell you what I'm going to do and I do it."

Today, George was going to help form a human shield around Waneta Hoyt as she arrived to stand trial for the murders of her five children. Years ago, George had voiced suspicions about Waneta. Today, he said he was willing to take a bullet for her.

When Tim and Waneta pulled up in their car shortly after nine o'clock, the grim protectors formed a wedge to cut through the ranks of photographers and reporters waiting at the entrance on the south side of the courthouse. In the middle of the pack, Tim clutched Waneta's hand as he had since they started dating in high school. His loyalty was self-evident: Tim stood by the woman accused of smothering his children.

At the front of the phalanx marched Jay Hoyt, wearing a black jacket with gold lettering on the back reading, "Hoyt Racing #9." Jay sported the beginnings of a mustache, just one measure of how much he'd matured in the year since his mother's arrest. His place at the head of the party served as a reminder that whatever had happened to Waneta's other children, this one had survived.

The entourage escorted Waneta up the limestone steps of the courthouse where, thirty-six years earlier, a group of mob bosses were tried after the famous raid at Joseph Barbara Sr.'s estate in nearby Apalachin. George Hoyt's precautions had been unnecessary; Waneta entered the courthouse unmolested.

The building made an ideal setting for a trial that the defense hoped would boil down to forgiveness: With four square towers and narrow arched windows, the 123-year-old brick courthouse suggested a church. Only one feature made an awkward statement: The fountain at the north end of the courthouse square was topped by a statue of a firefighter cradling a stricken baby in his arms.

Inside, Waneta met a rare concession to modern times: a walk-through metal detector. On the other side stood the familiar figure of sheriff's deputy John Gregrow, one of Waneta's cousins. She had been named after Gregrow's mother, and as the trial went on, he would greet Waneta with a little wave from his thigh.

Once past the metal detector, Waneta stepped back into the nineteenth century. She climbed a winding stairway to the large second-floor courtroom, where the judge's ornate wooden bench sat like an altar before a gallery with long benches arranged like pews on each side of a center aisle. The front row on one side was reserved for reporters; Waneta's family congregated on the other side. Court attendants, prospective jurors, and spectators socialized in a back room, buying cups of coffee on the honor system. Photographers took pictures from one of two balconies that ran the length of the courtroom. Despite the unprecedented media coverage, nearly everybody noted the contrast between the informal atmosphere of the Tioga County Courthouse and the spectacle of the O. J. Simpson trial then playing on TV.

Tioga County was so small, state officials had decided it didn't need a commissioner of jurors. Neighboring Broome County picked the jury pool for Waneta's trial with a computer that randomly selected names of Tioga County residents from lists of licensed drivers, voters and taxpayers. Roughly 185 people were called for jury duty, including Albert Nixon, Waneta's seventy-five-year-old father, who was excused.

Waneta lowered herself into a seat at the far end of the defense table. Tim sat beside her, holding her hand. Nobody had objected when he took that position during pretrial proceedings, but District Attorney Bob Simpson wanted to put an end to the Hoyts' handholding during trial.

The Marybeth Tinning jurors had warned him that the presence of a supportive husband could help the defendant win sympathy. Simpson made a motion in chambers asking Judge Vincent Sgueglia to exclude potential witnesses from the courtroom. Because Tim was on the prosecution's list of witnesses, he would have to leave Waneta's side until after he testified. Sgueglia agreed to exclude all potential witnesses except Tim Hoyt. Simpson asked to have Tim barred from sitting next to Waneta, but the judge refused.

Coming from a judge who considered his job akin to fatherhood, the decision left no one surprised. The county's only criminal court judge brought more than a little compassion to the job. He'd been known to halt a proceeding involving a young person and say, "I need a photocopy. Come with me and help me." The judge would take the kid into his office, put his arm around him, and offer a few words of encouragement or a stern lecture: "That's pretty dopey what you did. Why don't you just think about it?"

The fifty-two-year-old Sgueglia seemed to wear a sympathetic expression whenever he wasn't smiling, which was not often. He treated the courtroom like his home, handing out doughnuts during a pretrial hearing in the Hoyt case. He broke with the tradition of having a bailiff call out "All rise" when he took the bench. The ritual seemed too pompous for a judge who liked to lounge on a bench in the gallery during breaks and shoot the breeze with spectators.

In his two years on the bench, Sgueglia had presided over only four or five criminal trials. The Hoyt case would be his first murder trial. Even as a lawyer, Sgueglia had never been involved in a murder trial. But Sgueglia gave no hint he felt out of his league. When the name of the first prospective juror turned out to be Ace, the effervescent judge couldn't let the moment pass without acknowledging the coincidence.

"Now, wait a minute," the judge shot in after the court clerk called the name. "Number one is named Ace? Do things like this happen to you often, Mrs. Ace?"

The clerk called twenty more prospective jurors for the first round of questioning—or voir dire—by Simpson and Waneta's lawyers, Bob Miller and Ray Urbanski. The opposing lawyers were looking for different qualities in the panel that would sit in judgment of Waneta Hoyt.

Remembering the informal surveys that members of the prosecution team had conducted, Simpson knew his primary task was to weed out Waneta sympathizers.

The tips from the Tinning jurors gave him other crite-
ria to consider. He didn't want any engineers; they
tended to overanalyze. He didn't want anyone who had
a beef with cops; it would be difficult to convince them
that Waneta's statement wasn't coerced. He wouldn't
seat anyone from the towns of Berkshire, Richford,
and Newark Valley; people from the valley were likely
to know Waneta or her family and might take pity on
her. Simpson wanted jurors with children and people
who could set aside any feelings of sympathy.

Miller looked for just the opposite. He wanted jurors
who would feel sorry for Waneta. Miller believed that
meant older jurors, people who would see that life had
pretty much passed Waneta by. He wanted people intelligent enough to grasp the legal concepts of corroboration and the prosecution's burden of showing that
Waneta had confessed voluntarily.

The common denominator was Waneta, who sat
across from the jury box looking like a harmless
grandmother dressed for church. She had traded her ordinarily drab attire for a pink-and-blue checked suit.
She wore a large gold cross around her neck and several colorful pins, including a blue sapphire heart that
held special meaning. The heart had come with a key
that Waneta pinned to her mother's clothing six years
earlier as Dorothy Nixon was laid out for burial.

"When we meet again, the key and heart will be together again," Waneta said.

Waneta's lawyers didn't see any need to coach Tim
and Waneta on how to look sympathetic at the defense
table. They'd seen the couple's intimacy in court before. During jury selection, Waneta looked helpless,
holding Tim's hand in her lap, blinking slowly, as if
she felt feverish. Tim let go of her hand only when she
asked him to pour her a cup of water from the pitcher
on the defense table.

This was the image that worried Simpson as he
stood before the jury box, asking questions in the flat

tones of a college professor reviewing a familiar subject. The potential jurors shook their heads when he asked if, having decided the prosecution had proven its case beyond a reasonable doubt, they would succumb to sympathy for Waneta because she had already suffered enough. He tried a different tack, asking one woman if she'd formed the opinion that Waneta was guilty.

"How could I get that impression?" the woman said. "She looks like a little old lady."

With other potential jurors, sympathy for Waneta lurked just below the surface. Two women who took up Sgueglia on his offer to hear private concerns in chambers were so astounded by Waneta's appearance that they asked to be excused.

"I thought I could be objective, but after coming in here and seeing that woman, I know I can't," one woman told the judge. "That woman has suffered. She's in God's hands."

"She's a wretch," the other woman said. "If she did this, she's lived with this all her life and suffered, and may suffer more in the afterlife. So why are we bothering with it?"

Waneta's lawyers took hope in the idea that if a handful of prospective jurors were expressing sympathy, others might harbor the same sentiments.

Simpson also asked whether anyone considered the murder charges against Waneta less serious because more than twenty years had elapsed since the children's deaths. Whether it happened twenty-five years ago or last week, it's all the same, one man said.

Miller used a different angle on the time lapse. He wanted assurances that jurors wouldn't expect the prosecution's evidence to be any weaker than if the crimes had been committed last week, and thus make allowances. He also wanted to plant seeds of doubt about how the police had obtained Waneta's confession. He asked members of the jury pool if they could accept the possibility that people differ in their self-esteem and submission to authority.

Behind him, Tim and Waneta seemed the epitome of low self-esteem. Waneta slumped in her chair, and she was now clutching Tim's hand and his forearm.

Miller used this first chance on stage to foreshadow his defense. In a voice that boomed in the spacious courtroom, Miller took his opening shots at Bill Fitzpatrick and Dr. Michael Baden.

"Anyone hear the name Fitzpatrick?" Miller said, spitting out the name. None of the prospective jurors had. Even though Fitzpatrick wasn't on Simpson's list of twenty-six witnesses, Miller promised a long-awaited confrontation.

"I guarantee you will hear and will have met him before this trial is over."

Once, Waneta leaned over and whispered to paralegal Annette Gorski that she didn't like something about a heavyset woman on the panel of prospective jurors. She didn't want the woman on her jury. The woman was excused. Otherwise, Waneta left jury selection up to her lawyers—and a mysterious figure sitting in the balcony.

When the attorneys recessed to confer over whom to exclude from the first panel, Miller looked up to the balcony, where a heavyset man with a flattop haircut sat watching the jury box. Miller turned his hands out at his sides and mouthed the word, "Well?" He and Urbanski met with the man in a corner of the courtroom before meeting with Simpson and Sgueglia.

The first five jurors were sworn in from the first panel. The foreman, chosen by luck of the draw, was Shawn Conway, a thirty-six-year-old IBM worker from Endicott with three children. To the surprise of everyone, the process went quickly. The lawyers had feared that jury selection might take a week. Four more jurors were seated by the end of the first day, including

Lynne Rocha of Spencer, a fifty-one-year-old waitress and mother of four.

The next day, Ray Urbanski continued to play up Waneta's vulnerability and gave jurors—prospective and sworn—an explicit summary of the defense strategy to challenge her confession.

"Will all of you be willing to consider a person's age, their health, that they were purposely separated from their family and support group, put in extremely unfamiliar surroundings, whether the subject they're being asked about is highly emotionally charged, and whether that person has been misled about the nature of the interview?"

The defense lawyers were frustrated by their choices on the second day. Miller joked about the last panel of seventeen: "A true cross section of Tioga County. They had a combined IQ of 10."

All three attorneys had become concerned about jurors' wandering in and out of conversations with spectators. During an afternoon recess, one of Waneta's relatives talked openly with a prospective juror in the middle of the courtroom. There was little Sgueglia could do; the courtroom was the only space large enough to hold a crowd. He excused the chatty potential juror and warned Waneta's family that he would ban them from the courtroom if there was another problem. But otherwise, he told the lawyers, they had to take people at their word: If they agreed not to discuss the case with anyone, read about it in the newspapers, or watch TV accounts, that should be enough.

It wasn't until the third day of jury selection that Simpson looked into the balcony and spotted the man with the flattop haircut.

"Oh, Judge, there is one more thing," Simpson said, waving his hand in the air. "May we approach the bench?"

The attorneys conferred privately with the judge.

"Phil Jordan's in the courtroom," Simpson whispered.

"Who?" Sgueglia asked.

"Phil Jordan. He's somewhat of a folklore hero around here. He's a real celebrity and everybody knows him and I'm afraid he's going to make the jury nervous."

The judge still didn't understand.

"He's a seer," the district attorney explained. "You know, one of those seers."

For the first two days, Jordan had peered over the balcony at prospective jurors undergoing voir dire. He was looking for green or blue auras.

Miller had called Jordan three weeks before the trial, asking him to work as a jury consultant. Miller had used him once before, in a murder trial twenty years earlier. The case had made national headlines as the first time a psychic had been used to seat a jury. It touched off a small furor. The Committee for the Scientific Investigation of Claims of the Paranormal, a group of college professors and scientists, sent a letter to the state bar association, attacking Miller.

"In calling a table-tipper into a court of law, the public defender has introduced charlatanry into the one place it cannot be tolerated," the letter said. The feisty lawyer kept the letter framed in his law office.

For Waneta's trial, Miller decided to seat Jordan in the balcony, out of Simpson's view. Jordan's job was to help the defense lawyers seat a sympathetic jury. Jordan sized up prospects not only by their jobs and ages but also by their auras. He said he could see an energy field of color around people. If he saw a band of pulsating red about someone's waist, for example, he knew the person felt pain in that area. For this case, Jordan was looking for green and blue auras—indicating people who would pay attention, judge the case with an open mind, and sympathize with Waneta Hoyt. Jordan was not only a psychic; he was also an ordained minister of a nondenominational church in Candor, a town in the northwest part of the county separated from the valley by the hills.

Jordan knew he had gotten under Simpson's skin. When Miller told Jordan afterward that Simpson wanted him out of the jury's sight, Jordan suggested that he simply move to the opposite balcony.

"You should've just waved up to me," Jordan told Miller. "I would have levitated across the courtroom." Instead, Sgueglia made Jordan sit in the gallery below.

Jordan had a key piece of advice for Miller and Urbanski: Be extremely careful whom you seat as the first alternate; one of the jurors is going to be injured during the trial. The lawyers were skeptical, but before the trial was over, Waneta herself would come to rely on Jordan more and more.

At the end of the third day, the jury was set—seven women, five men, and four alternates (one man and three women). It appeared to be a typical sampling of Tioga County: white, middle-class, backbone-of-America working types. Every one of them had children. Only one of them, a woman alternate, had never heard of the Hoyt case. Two of them were IBMers; others were waitresses, sales clerks, housewives, and the owner of a home building supply company. Eight of the jurors were older than thirty-five, two of them older than fifty-five. The youngest was thirty-two—just two years older than Eric Hoyt would have been.

Both sides thought they'd seated a jury to their liking. Simpson had all parents, no engineers, and no one with a grudge against cops. Miller had an older group of intelligent people who Jordan thought would sympathize with Waneta.

All her life, Waneta had convinced people that she deserved their sympathy. She had only these twelve men and women left to convince.

Chapter Twenty

District Attorney Bob Simpson watched with annoyance as Waneta Hoyt arrived in court the morning of his opening statement. She entered the courtroom holding hands with Tim and Jay, followed them up a side aisle like a child in tow, then made a slow circuit down the center aisle so she could accept hugs from family and friends. She gave her father a peck on the cheek and greeted her spiritual advisers before making her way to the defense table.

Waneta had four ministers—including Phil Jordan—attending the trial. One of them, the Rev. James Willard of the First Congregational Church of Berkshire, prayed every day for the judge, the jury, Tim, Waneta, and her lawyers. He even started praying for Simpson, then caught himself.

"I didn't like what I was praying," Willard said. "I was praying that he would not do a good job. Then I said, 'No, that's not really a good thing to pray.' "

Simpson didn't need any handicaps. Since he had first heard about the Hoyt children's deaths from Bill Fitzpatrick just over two years ago, he'd known this would be a difficult case. Waneta's forlorn appearance made the task even harder. Simpson saw Waneta's entrance as a big act, as part of a pattern: She had lied for attention, she had killed for attention, and now she was using the trial to get even more attention. "She is one cold bitch," he thought.

In the back of his mind hovered the fear that the jury

wouldn't see through her act. He knew that if the jurors took pity on Waneta, they could deliver a manslaughter verdict, not knowing that meant she would walk away unpunished. Simpson wanted nothing short of a conviction for murder.

To get that conviction, he had to overcome a thirty-year lapse that had dimmed witnesses' memories. His medical experts had to overturn the official findings on the deaths and convince the jury that the Hoyt children had been smothered. The state police had to show that Waneta had freely confessed to killing her kids. Most important, perhaps, Simpson knew he had to make the jury see that the victims were Eric, Julie, Molly, Jimmy, and Noah, not the pathetic woman sitting in court. Opening statements gave him his first chance to make his case.

For all his efforts to frame Waneta Hoyt's trial as a legal matter for Tioga County to resolve, Simpson was acutely aware of the case's broader implications. Only a week earlier, the SIDS Alliance had put out a national media alert, warning SIDS parents to brace themselves for the fallout from Waneta's trial. The prosecutor paused at the start of his opening statement to put those concerns to rest.

"SIDS is a tragic thing for a family," he told the jury. "We in no way, as we sit here prosecuting Mrs. Hoyt, are attempting to tell anybody that SIDS does not exist, and that people who lose children through SIDS are somehow, just for that reason, culpable, responsible for the death of their child. That is the furthest thing from the truth. We do not intend in any way during the course of this trial to make any kind of assertion with respect to the tragedy of SIDS, and that it does not exist. Because it does."

Beyond that, Simpson's thirty-five-minute statement was straightforward and mechanical, a map to help the jury travel through the trial. Standing behind a lectern, he read each of the ten murder charges in Waneta's indictment, as the law required. He touched on his two legal objectives in the order he planned to address them during the trial—corroborating the murder charge and showing that Waneta had voluntarily confessed to smothering her children.

Simpson challenged Dr. Alfred Steinschneider's two-decades-old assertion that Molly and Noah suffered prolonged apnea spells and needed vigorous stimulation to resume breathing in the hospital. Medical records showed that the children had normal interruptions of breathing, not prolonged apnea, Simpson said. The hospital pathologists who performed autopsies on Jimmy, Molly, and Noah did not see signs of murder because suffocation, performed properly, leaves no evidence on a child's body, he explained.

Knowing that Bob Miller would stand up in a few minutes and claim that the police had subtly coerced Waneta to confess, Simpson told the jury that she had willingly accompanied Trooper Bob Bleck and Investigator Sue Mulvey to the barracks in Owego. Once there, it didn't take much to get her to confess, Simpson said.

"She offered a natural cause of death for each one of these children," he said. "She was then confronted with the evidence that these children had died by other means. At that point, she admitted that she suffocated all five of these children.

"She was not abused, she was not coerced, she was not threatened."

Simpson periodically sauntered from the lectern, stopped in front of the jury box to make a point, then returned to consult notes on a yellow legal pad. Conflicting medical theories would be pitted against each other, he told the jury, but the case would come down to everyday logic.

"Common sense tells us that five kids don't die in the same family the way these kids died," he said.

"Common sense just doesn't allow us to make that kind of a jump."

Bill Fitzpatrick got only a fleeting reference. Fitzpatrick had told Simpson he wanted to testify to thwart Miller's attempt to paint him as the big-city bad guy. But Simpson didn't want the jury diverted by that. He wasn't going to call Fitzpatrick as a witness, and he'd asked his colleague to stay away from the trial, at least for now.

Miller didn't miss a chance to take a swipe at Fitzpatrick in his opening statement. Miller, who had promised the jury a confrontation with Fitzpatrick, said the out-of-town prosecutor had been dismayed to learn the case had landed outside his jurisdiction, which meant he couldn't stay in the limelight.

Miller's right eye was crimson, drooping, and swollen as he gave his forty-seven-minute statement. He'd had two cornea transplants in recent years, and the last one had become infected. Scar tissue had built up, and the pressure was causing glaucoma. The stress from the trial was worsening it, and he was having an allergic reaction to the medication he'd started taking. Hunched over the lectern like a bear, Miller fought through the pain and focused his one good eye on the jury.

Miller conceded that Waneta had confessed. But she gave the statement without understanding how she was being led along by investigators, he said.

"Mrs. Hoyt no more understood her Miranda rights than the chair she was sitting on," he said.

The confession wouldn't be enough to convict anyway, he said. The medical evidence had to be strong enough to back it up.

"You cannot simply at the conclusion of this case finish your deliberations with statements to yourself that, 'If she gave a statement incriminating herself, that's all we need to convict.' Because if you do, you violate your oath as jurors."

Waneta's defense focused on countering the testimony of Dr. Michael Baden with experts who would pronounce his opinion on the children's deaths unsound. Miller's voice rose as he told jurors that studies had shown that multiple SIDS cases occurred in families, that the National Institutes of Health said so, and that one study documented six unexplained infant deaths within a family. There had even been an article in that month's *Pediatrics* supporting Steinschneider, Miller said. He repeated Baden's name eleven times. He mentioned Dr. Janice Ophoven only once.

The difficulty Simpson faced in trying to prosecute murders thirty years after the fact became apparent when his first witness took the stand. Betty Lane barely remembered the day in 1965 when eighteen-year-old Waneta Hoyt ran across Davis Hollow Road, screaming that something was wrong with her first baby, three-month-old Eric. Lane wasn't sure of the year, or which child it was. She did remember a thick substance around the baby's nose.

Miller spent more time cross-examining Lane than Simpson took in presenting her direct testimony. But despite this, Lane still could not remember details of the day Eric died; she said she hardly knew the Hoyts when she and her husband lived on Davis Hollow Road.

Bob Vanek's memory wasn't much better. Vanek was one of the Newark Valley ambulance workers Tim Hoyt had tried to line up as defense witnesses, but Simpson called him to the stand first. Vanek said he responded to emergency calls for three of the Hoyts' stricken children, but he didn't remember which ones.

Carl Bonham, another former neighbor of the Hoyts', stayed on the stand just long enough to identify a picture of a little boy dressed in a red-and-black cowboy shirt, sitting on a kitchen chair. After twenty-seven years, Bonham recognized the boy with tousled light brown hair as Jimmy Hoyt.

The picture came from the photo album that Waneta had brought to the state police interview to help her recall the deaths. The police kept the photograph collection as evidence, but Jimmy's picture was the only one shown during the trial. The other children had died before they could develop distinguishing features, and Simpson felt it was too hard to identify them from their baby pictures. Those pictures also didn't make the point that Jimmy's picture made: Simpson was presenting tangible evidence that one of Waneta's victims had been a vibrant human being. Waneta muttered, "I don't believe he's doing this."

Dr. Bedros Markarian, the pathologist at Upstate Medical Center who performed the original autopsy on Noah, could only recall the case from his paperwork. Bronchiolitis and the other conditions he'd mentioned in the autopsy report were preliminary findings, he said; they did not add up to a cause of death.

But Dr. John Scott was emphatic about how he interpreted those findings in his 1971 coroner's report: Noah died of SIDS.

Simpson knew that Scott's testimony wouldn't help the prosecution, but he believed the jury would expect him to call the only doctor still alive who'd seen one of the Hoyt children within minutes of death. Simpson thought that if he didn't call the doctor to the stand, the defense would make an issue of it, and he wanted to avoid that. Simpson thought Scott came across as a physician interested in defending his work and willing to defy the accepted medical principle that an autopsy could not distinguish between SIDS and suffocation.

Miller used his cross-examination of Scott to bolster the defense's argument that the Hoyt children died of natural causes.

"These circumstances fit a SIDS death very well," Scott said. "This was a family who had a series of SIDS deaths."

The prosecution ended the first day of testimony

with a more effective witness, Joyce Thomas, one of the nurses who cared for Molly Hoyt at Upstate Medical Center.

Assistant District Attorney Peggy Drake had prepared for the testimony of the three nurses and a nurse's aide who had treated Molly and Noah. Given what the Marybeth Tinning jurors had said, Drake expected that the testimony of the women who had fed, cuddled, and changed Molly and Noah would leave a strong impression. These women had spent more time with the two youngest Hoyts than anyone else; more than Tim and Waneta, and more than Dr. Steinschneider.

Thomas was flown in from Tacoma, Washington, to testify about the second-to-last day of Molly's life, when the nurse had dressed the baby in a pink frock, put her in the car with Tim and Waneta, then returned to the Children's Clinical Research Center and cried. Thomas's vivid memories of her patient evoked the kind of response Drake had hoped for. Judge Vincent Sgueglia's eyes welled with tears when Drake asked the nurse to describe Molly's appearance.

"A pretty baby," Thomas said.

Thomas choked back the tears she'd bottled up for years. Her testimony not only helped build the prosecution's case after a slow start, it helped swing sympathy from Waneta to her children.

As Thomas testified, Waneta became visibly upset, muttering and shaking her head. "She was so good to me when I was there," Waneta said. "Why is she doing this to me?"

Thomas was still on the stand when court recessed at the end of the day. That night, she enjoyed an informal reunion with two former coworkers from the medical center, Gail Pfeiffer and Thelma Schneider. The prosecution had arranged for the three witnesses to stay at the Treadway Inn. They ate dinner together but intentionally avoided talking about the Hoyt children. Each knew why the others had been called to testify: more than twenty years ago, they'd had the same fears about what was happening to Molly and Noah Hoyt.

Corrine Dower, another nurse, joined them in court the next day. Simpson and Drake had also subpoenaed Julia Evans but decided not to call the former nurse, now eighty, because her family thought she was too frail to testify.

The nurses who testified said they never saw Molly and Noah stop breathing. All of them remembered having concerns about the way Waneta interacted with the children. Two of them described how Waneta sat on Tim's lap and held her babies at a distance.

Drake asked Schneider, the former head nurse, why she'd noted in Molly's records that Waneta's interaction with the baby was almost nil.

"Well, because I had talked to Dr. Steinschneider about concerns I had had because of the lack of mother-child interaction, and felt that I had to document it," Schneider said.

Waneta shook her head and grumbled. "Why didn't these people ever express any concern when I was there? I don't understand it. They were always very nice to me. I thought they liked me."

Pfeiffer, the nurse's aide who helped take care of Noah, cried when she testified about seeing Waneta glare into the boy's crib.

"It's not true," Waneta whispered from twenty feet away.

Miller had planned to handle all the medical testimony, but his eye had gotten worse and he had to travel two hours to Rochester for treatment. Raymond Urbanski stepped in and cross-examined the nurses.

Urbanski asked Thomas, Schneider, and Pfeiffer to identify notes in the medical records that suggested Molly and Noah had been ill. He asked about apnea alarms sounding, the children vomiting, and their hands appearing blue, but the questions did little to

blunt the impact of the nurses' memories of Molly and
Noah as healthy babies.

The nurses' testimony at the end of the trial's first
week had built a foundation for Simpson's next witness—Dr. Ophoven. The forensic pathologist arrived
from Minnesota on Sunday, April 2, and Simpson
called her to the stand the next morning.

Simpson took the no-nonsense Midwesterner
through the death of each Hoyt child just as he had at
the meeting at the Treadway Inn a year earlier. Ophoven disputed the significance of conditions such as
bronchiolitis and acute adrenal insufficiency, which
had been listed on the children's death certificates. If
any of those factors had been lethal, she said, then the
children would have seemed sick for days and would
never have been discharged from the hospital.

Simpson tried to drive home the agony of the Hoyt
children's deaths by asking Ophoven to describe the final moments of a suffocating infant. The plainspoken
doctor looked at the jurors as she explained the survival reflex of babies between two and four months
old.

"Little people, especially in the age group of sudden
infant death syndrome . . . don't really even know they
have hands and feet. If something gets in the way of
their face, or their breathing, they don't have the ability to kind of reach up and pull . . . If you do something to them that they don't like, they let you know
instantly. And if it's a big thing they don't like, they
arch their backs, they get mad right away. They use
their muscles, but it's kind of like this whole body reaction as opposed to a coordinated reaction. But even
little, tiny, premature infants will struggle if they're
uncomfortable or if something's happening that isn't
right.

"They may not have the power to do much about it,
but they will immediately react if they can't get air. An
infant will respond by moving as much and as hard as

they can in an attempt to get whatever is in the way out of the way."

Such infants will fight until they are overwhelmed by a lack of oxygen and an increase in the amount of carbon dioxide in the body, Ophoven said. If a baby can't reestablish the air passage after a couple of minutes, the child will pass out, she said. Death will occur in another two to four minutes.

Twice, Ophoven said, she had seen parents captured on videotape as they tried to suffocate their infants at the Midwest Children's Resource Center in Minnesota.

"Would a two-and-a-half-year-old resist differently?" Simpson asked, alluding to Jimmy Hoyt.

"Oh, Lord, yes," Ophoven said. "Whenever we have to do anything to a child that age we have to be prepared for what's kind of their fight-for-life reaction. They don't qualify it. A small boo-boo or a big boo-boo, they turn the whole thing on. And for a two-and-a-half-year-old, to draw blood, or start an IV, or to do a procedure, you may need two or three people to hold these folks down if they don't like what's happening. The kind of response they can mobilize can be quite amazing."

Ophoven went through an exhaustive assessment of Molly's and Noah's hospital records. She told the jury the charts showed no episodes of prolonged apnea. These children died from a cessation of breathing, she said, but it was not caused by apnea.

After Simpson had laid the foundation for her opinion, Ophoven told the jury that all of the five Hoyt children had been smothered.

Miller tried to chip away at Ophoven's opinion by asking about the disagreement between forensic pathologists and SIDS researchers over multiple unexplained deaths within a family.

"I don't think it's fair to characterize the SIDS people as all following the genetic theory," Ophoven said. "There are some pediatricians who are continuing to raise that question. There are a lot of SIDS experts who have the same opinion as the forensics community that SIDS is not a genetic entity."

"But there's been no medical proof to any degree of certainty regarding that, has there?"

"There's just a lot of experience, sir."

Ophoven hadn't expected her testimony to last more than a day, as was evident when she returned to the stand Tuesday wearing the same black skirt and jacket over a flowered blouse. Miller had court deputies roll out an easel and placed a three-foot-high flip chart on it. He told Ophoven he wanted to make a list of all the factors that went into her opinion that the Hoyt children had been smothered.

Miller promised Sgueglia it would be a short list, but Ophoven kept adding items. When Ophoven was done, she had listed thirteen supporting factors for her opinion, and Miller had covered three of the tall pages with notes. He had taken Dr. Eleanor McQuillen's advice and tried to attack the corroboration of Waneta's confession by delving into medical details. But he succeeded only in demonstrating how thoroughly Ophoven had reviewed the case. Miller realized he'd made a mistake; he never referred to the list again.

Under cross-examination, Ophoven talked about the connection between apnea and Munchausen syndrome by proxy without mentioning the disorder by name.

"There is documented experience in the literature, and that I have personally, of children at significant risk of death by homicide who present with infant apnea under circumstances such as this," she told Miller. "This is well established now. And that is a 1995 medical fact."

Ophoven's testimony ran seven hours. Toward the end she fanned herself with one of the documents while a storm kicked up outside. Hailstones pounded the courtroom windows, and Simpson had to shout questions on redirect to be heard over the din.

Ophoven's pleasant manner and command of the facts had dealt a blow to the defense, and Miller knew it. He gave Simpson credit for calling Ophoven before Dr. Michael Baden, the expert the defense was primed to attack.

"He knew she'd come across just the way she did—a Midwest gal who tells it like it is," Miller said. "Ophoven I couldn't attack."

Leading with Ophoven had been a lucky stroke; Simpson had expected Baden to testify first, but the state's forensic expert had a conflict in his schedule.

Ophoven's testimony had been so thorough that the confrontation between Miller and Baden later in the week seemed anticlimactic. Baden covered the same ground as Ophoven and reached the same conclusion: The Hoyt children had been suffocated. He offered a succinct explanation of why others had overlooked the possibility of homicide: Unlike forensic pathologists, other doctors were inclined to believe what the patient—or the patient's parents—told them.

Miller tried to back Baden into a corner on the exhumation and autopsies of the Hoyt children's bodies, which the doctor had said he needed to corroborate Waneta Hoyt's confession. Baden refused to concede that the autopsies didn't contribute to his opinion. Examination of the remains had ruled out natural disease, bone fractures, and malnutrition as causes of death, he said. Miller won one concession from Baden: The autopsies revealed no anatomical evidence of suffocation.

Simpson added another expert witness to the prosecution's lineup. Dr. John Brooks, a nationally known pediatrician at Dartmouth's medical school, testified that he had reviewed Molly's and Noah's medical records and found no episodes of life-threatening apnea.

Brooks, who had the tweedy look of an Ivy Leaguer, said he'd been involved in other cases where two children in a family had apparently died of SIDS.

"In fact, I've dealt with a family where I thought there were three for a while," he said. "It turned out that was not SIDS, that there was a conviction for infanticide."

"What's the name of that case?" Simpson asked.

"Van Der Sluys," Brooks said.

Brooks was working in Rochester, New York, in the mid-1980s, when he met Jane and Steve Van Der Sluys. Knowing that their first three children had died, Brooks advised the couple to put each of their three subsequent children on apnea monitors. Simpson had not known about the doctor's role in the Van Der Sluys case when he tracked Brooks down as a SIDS expert for the Hoyt trial.

The defense didn't even enjoy the usual satisfaction of getting the prosecution's expert witnesses to reveal their fees on cross-examination. Brooks, like Ophoven, took no money for testifying. Both saw their work as part of the effort against child abuse.

Miller had begun to doubt whether his experts could soften the impact of Ophoven's and Brooks's testimony. It was one more concern to add to the irritation of a painful eye. Medication and ice compresses hadn't given Miller much relief, and after Brooks testified in the morning, the lawyer went back to Rochester for treatment. His worries would only have multiplied if he'd stayed for the afternoon session, when Simpson took up the second half of his case, Waneta's confession.

Chapter Twenty-one

Senior Investigator Bob Courtright had prepared his testimony for Waneta Hoyt's trial with the same nervous compulsion that had driven his planning for her interview. He had summarized his twenty-one-month investigation in eighty-eight neatly typed paragraphs, starting with the tip from Bill Fitzpatrick. He also had reviewed Waneta's statements—her three-page signed confession, and the transcript of her stenographic interview, which had never been made public. Courtright went through each document fifty times. District Attorney Bob Simpson wanted him to read the statements to the jury, and the Lama didn't want to stumble on the words.

As the time to testify on Wednesday drew near, Courtright paced in a secluded office on the first floor of the courthouse, chain-smoking Merit Lights. He remembered the advice from the Marybeth Tinning jurors; he removed his gold bracelet and tucked it in his pocket. He looked natty enough with a silk handkerchief folded into the breast pocket of his brown suit and a gold chain holding his tie in place. He wore a stony expression when he arrived in the courtroom shortly before one-thirty p.m.

Courtright sat ramrod-straight in the witness stand as Assistant District Attorney Peggy Drake began with a series of questions about his investigation. Courtright gave a deadpan, Sgt. Joe Friday, just-the-facts-ma'am account of the biggest case of his career.

Drake took him through the plan to pick up Waneta on March 23, 1994, then turned his attention to the statements. Courtright had Waneta's three-page signed statement in hand, and he began to read aloud in his gravelly voice. Before he could get through the first page, his head dipped and his voice became huskier. Courtright labored to get out the words. Waneta's description of smothering her kids fought with images of the investigator's two grandsons. His voice cracked, and he stopped to clear his throat.

Courtright was fighting back tears, but Drake thought he was ill. When the investigator choked up a third time, Drake understood what was happening. She approached the bench to ask Judge Vincent Sgueglia for an adjournment. She needed time for Courtright to compose himself, or for her to find someone else to read Waneta's statements. But the judge said Courtright had to continue; taking a break then would only highlight his emotional reaction to Waneta's confession, and that could prejudice the jury.

Two women on the jury covered their eyes with their hands as Courtright picked up the narrative. Another wiped away a tear. The investigator's voice smoothed out as he started reading the twenty-four-page stenographic statement, but he would choke up again when he mentioned the children's names.

Courtright had asked Waneta a second round of questions to help kill time until Tim could be brought to the Owego barracks. What he got was a bonus. The words the stenographer had taken down were appalling enough on paper, but they sounded even more cold-blooded read aloud. Just as in the first interview, Waneta had started with Eric:

HOYT: He was just crying. He had a lot of—just cried a lot, and just, I couldn't handle the crying.
COURTRIGHT: What happened?
HOYT: I took a pillow and suffocated him, I guess. I

tried to get him to stop crying at the time, and I didn't—it was too late. When I checked him, he was gone.

COURTRIGHT: When you put the pillow over Eric's face, did that cause his death?

HOYT: I guess so, yes.

COURTRIGHT: He was dead right after that?

HOYT: Yes.

Next, she described James's death:

HOYT: He was the second to the oldest. He was two in May. And he died in September. So, he was two years, four months old.

COURTRIGHT: What year did he die?

HOYT: 1968.

COURTRIGHT: Where did that death occur?

HOYT: At my residence on a lot next to my mother-in-law's house. We had our own lot and trailer. He was the third death. Julie died secondly.

COURTRIGHT: Let's stay with James.

HOYT: Okay.

COURTRIGHT: He was the third death?

HOYT: Yes.

COURTRIGHT: Tell us how that death happened.

HOYT: I was getting dressed in the bathroom, and he wanted to come in, and I didn't want him to. I told him to wait out in the hall until I was done, and he kept yelling, "Mommy, Mommy," and screaming. And I took the towel, and went out into the living room, and I put the towel over his face to get him to quiet down, and he struggled. And once he finally got quiet, he was gone.

COURTRIGHT: He was dead?

HOYT: (Nods head)

COURTRIGHT: Was he lying on the floor, on the couch, when you were smothering him?

HOYT: On the floor.

COURTRIGHT: On the floor. Were you on top of him, straddled over him?

HOYT: No. I was just holding him cradle-type.

Then, Julie:

HOYT: She was crying, she wouldn't stop, and I cradled her to my shoulder until she quit crying. When she quit crying, I released her from my shoulder and she wasn't breathing.

COURTRIGHT: When you cradled her to your shoulder, do you know where her nose and mouth were?

HOYT: In my shoulder, right into here, in this area.

COURTRIGHT: You held her tightly?

HOYT: Yes.

COURTRIGHT: You held her—

HOYT: Until she stopped, was quiet.

COURTRIGHT: When you pulled her away, did you know that she was dead?

HOYT: I suspected that she was.

Molly was next:

HOYT: She was crying, wouldn't quit crying. She was in her crib, and I took the pillow from the crib, and laid it over her until she quit crying.

COURTRIGHT: What do you mean you laid it over?

HOYT: I laid it over her head until she quit crying.

COURTRIGHT: Did you have your hand on the pillow?

HOYT: No. I remember just laying it over her until she quit crying.

COURTRIGHT: Did you hold onto the pillow to keep it there, is what I'm asking, Waneta.

HOYT: No. I just laid it there and walked out of the room. When I went back a little while later, she— she quit crying, and she wasn't breathing then.

COURTRIGHT: She was not breathing then?

HOYT: No.

COURTRIGHT: Was she dead, in your opinion?

HOYT: In my opinion, she was, yes.

COURTRIGHT: And the reason that you did that, again, was because she was crying?

HOYT: Yes. I couldn't handle the crying all the time.

Then Noah:

COURTRIGHT: Okay. Now let's go to the last death, and that was Noah?

HOYT: Yes.

COURTRIGHT: What address did you live at?

HOYT: The same as the rest of the children.

COURTRIGHT: With the exception of Eric?

HOYT: Right.

COURTRIGHT: What year did Noah die?

HOYT: 1971.

COURTRIGHT: Tell us the circumstances surrounding his death.

HOYT: He just got crying. Anything that I did he wouldn't quit crying. So I took a pillow—it was on the sofa—until he quit crying, and I took a pillow, and he died.

COURTRIGHT: Okay. And this pillow, did you hold it against his nose and mouth, over his face?

HOYT: I don't remember holding. I just remember laying it over his face to get him to quit crying so I wouldn't have to hear him cry.

COURTRIGHT: How long was it before he quit crying?

HOYT: I don't know. I don't remember times.

COURTRIGHT: At some point you went back to check on him?

HOYT: Yes.

COURTRIGHT: Did you determine that he was dead at that time?

HOYT: Well, I wasn't sure. I did mouth-to-mouth resuscitation on him.

COURTRIGHT: Had he turned blue?

HOYT: Yes.

COURTRIGHT: Okay. What did you do then?

HOYT: I called my mother-in-law, and I called Dr. Steinschneider from Syracuse because he was the doctor that was checking him for apnea and so forth.

COURTRIGHT: What did you tell Dr. Steinschneider?

HOYT: That he had an apnea spell, and he wasn't breathing.

Courtright had gone back for details:

COURTRIGHT: Of all the five deaths, whom can you remember bleeding from the nose and mouth?

HOYT: James.

COURTRIGHT: Okay. What do you think that was caused from?

HOYT: I don't know. I just figured the towel, the pressure from holding it onto his face.

COURTRIGHT: Waneta, how much did James struggle?

HOYT: Not a lot, but he struggled some.

COURTRIGHT: Was he kicking and flailing his arms?

HOYT: Yes.

COURTRIGHT: He was?

HOYT: Yes.

COURTRIGHT: Probably in an attempt to what?

HOYT: To shake me off, I assume. To get me to stop holding him down.

Bob Miller learned about Courtright's testimony in a phone call from his co-counsel, Raymond Urbanski. Miller could only imagine how the investigator's emotional reading had affected the jurors. He had known Courtright for years and had never seen him crack.

Urbanski hadn't seen the jurors' reactions. He was trying so hard to avoid watching Courtright's struggle that he thought of crawling under the defense table. The only person at the table who appeared unaffected was Waneta Hoyt. During a break in Courtright's testimony, she broke into a smile. She smiled even wider a few minutes later, when she received a bouquet of pink roses from a former neighbor who had traveled from Florida expecting to testify as a character witness for her.

The stenographic statement presented a huge problem for Urbanski: How could he convince the jury that the police had suggested these acts to Waneta when the stenographer had made a verbatim record of her volunteering details? Urbanski wanted to show that although Waneta may have uttered those words, the investigators had cunningly coaxed them from her. He planned to use Courtright's finely wrought interview strategy against him.

On cross-examination, Courtright acknowledged that before he questioned Waneta, he'd asked a psychologist at the state Office of Mental Health about interviewing techniques. During the conversation with the psychologist, Courtright scribbled short notes for each technique. He couldn't remember why he'd written "Caspar Milquetoast" but said he knew the name described someone "with not a lot of initiative and ... prone to intimidation."

Courtright also said he couldn't remember why he'd written "tension-pressure" in his notes.

"You're telling the jury here today that, although you wrote down ... the two simple words 'tension-pressure,' as you sit here today you have no recollection of why you wrote that down?" Urbanski asked.

"That's what I'm telling the jury, yes, sir."

Urbanski asked what the psychologist had meant when he said, according to Courtright's notes, "sickly kids, first death rewarding, do it again."

"He was referring to ... cases where a mother will kill a child and, I believe, receive a lot of attention from that, finds it to be rewarding on getting that attention, and will do it again," Courtright said.

It was the second time during the trial that someone had described the behavior of Munchausen syndrome by proxy without naming the disorder.

Trooper Bubba Bleck, the next witness, described his role in picking up Waneta outside the Berkshire post office on March 23, 1994, and in the interview that followed. During his testimony, Bleck pressed his hands to his chest, reenacting a demonstration Waneta had given of smothering Julie.

Urbanski tried to show on cross-examination that Bleck was known and trusted by everyone in the valley, including the Hoyts. Urbanski wanted the jury to question the tactics the state police had used to lure Waneta to the interview, which she said had been represented as SIDS research.

But Investigator Sue Mulvey testified that she never told Waneta the state police wanted to talk with her for a SIDS research project. She said she told Waneta they'd read Steinschneider's study and had talked with doctors about the children's deaths. Courtright had instructed her to be sympathetic, compassionate, and low-key with Waneta, and had told her not to lie, she said.

Mulvey turned the tables on Urbanski when he questioned why she had told Waneta it was a common defense ploy to claim that a confession was coerced.

"What did you mean by ploy?" he asked.

She said, "You don't understand it?"

Urbanski could do little to lighten the burden that Waneta's statements had placed on the defense. The day's lineup of prosecution witnesses steadily added to the weight of her words. The stenographer who took down Waneta's second confession testified that Mulvey and Courtright had treated their suspect with tenderness. The prosecution also called the two Tioga County Jail guards who'd heard Waneta make incriminating statements after her arrest.

Dr. Michael Baden took the stand the next day, and

after Miller's cross-examination fizzled, Simpson rested the prosecution's case. The district attorney felt good about the way the evidence had gone in. In six days, the prosecution had taken the testimony of eighteen witnesses, none of which the defense seemed to have seriously undermined on cross-examination. Simpson had put the Hoyt children's medical histories into the trial record, as well as Waneta's statements. He thought he'd made strides in shifting sympathy away from Waneta, but he wasn't overconfident about that. Sgueglia had recessed the trial for three days, until Monday, April 10, and Simpson planned to use the time to prepare his attack on the defense's case.

Waneta's lawyers saw a small change that occurred on the last day of the prosecution's case as a good omen. Waneta's fourth minister, Phil Jordan, had told the lawyers during jury selection to be careful selecting the first alternate, because one of the jurors would become injured or sick during the trial. Miller and Urbanski had put little stock in the psychic's prediction because they'd never had a sitting juror excused in Tioga County. But that morning, Sgueglia announced that Juror No. 2, a saleswoman and mother of two, had injured her shoulder playing racquetball and could not continue. She was replaced by a seventy-one-year-old man the lawyers had picked as an alternate because they thought he would sympathize with Waneta.

"I'm a believer," Urbanski said.

Chapter Twenty-two

A blanket of new spring snow covered the lawn of the Tioga County Courthouse, as if to remind Dr. Alfred Steinschneider of the chilly reception that awaited him inside. The president of the American SIDS Institute in Atlanta had traveled 750 miles to testify in defense of both Waneta Hoyt and the SIDS theory he'd derived from her children's deaths more than twenty years ago. He'd had to brave more than Owego's subfreezing weather to get to court the morning of April 10, 1995.

In the year since Waneta was accused of murdering her children, Steinschneider's 1972 study in *Pediatrics* had been called a license to kill. His reputation had taken a beating at the hands of Bill Fitzpatrick and other critics. All along, the pediatric researcher had argued that the debate over what caused the Hoyt children's deaths belonged in scholarly journals, not a courtroom. He had little incentive to subject himself to cross-examination by District Attorney Bob Simpson. But in the end, Steinschneider couldn't say no when Waneta's lawyers asked him to testify.

Bob Miller and Ray Urbanski planned to put on a defense that mirrored the prosecution's case. First they would try to discredit the corroboration of the murder charges by calling medical experts and other witnesses to show that the Hoyt children died of natural, if still unexplained, causes. Then the lawyers would try to neutralize the impact of Waneta's confession by showing that the police had taken advantage of her pliable personality. Steinschneider was the defense's first witness. The doctor had brought along his wife, Roz, his 1972 study, and his best bedside manner.

Miller spent the first half-hour of his direct examination establishing Steinschneider's credentials. The lawyer wanted to leave no doubt that his witness was a SIDS expert. Steinschneider had come prepared with an eleven-page résumé that spelled out his qualifications: more than thirty years in medicine; board-certified in pediatrics; experience in dozens of academic, clinical, and research positions; consultant to the National Institutes of Health; author of sixty-eight medical articles.

Steinschneider, wearing a tweed jacket and tie, showed flashes of the genial personality that his colleagues at Upstate Medical Center in Syracuse remembered. The soft-spoken answers he gave to Miller's opening questions retained traces of a Brooklyn accent that more than a decade of Southern living could not erase. He turned on the charm, mentioning that he'd received advanced degrees in psychology from Cornell University in "beautiful Ithaca," a city in neighboring Tompkins County that jurors were sure to know. But a minute into the testimony, Judge Vincent Sgueglia broke in with a request that must have reminded the doctor he was in unfamiliar territory.

"Dr. Steinschneider, you have a beautiful, soothing voice. I'm sure your patients love it," Sgueglia said. "But no one can hear you in this courtroom. I'd like you to shout."

"OK. You got a deal," Steinschneider said, smiling first at the judge, then the jury.

Miller spent more time on Steinschneider's background than on the doctor's theory about the link between sleep apnea and SIDS. Holding the 1972 *Pediatrics* article in his lap, Steinschneider confirmed publicly for the first time that the "H" family described in his study was the Hoyts. He reiterated his findings:

Despite what his former nurses said, Molly and Noah had breathing troubles in the hospital.

"What I can say is that nurses reported episodes—alarms," Steinschneider testified. "They reported that the equipment was functioning, and on occasion they reported that they had to stimulate the baby."

Gail Pfeiffer, the nurse's aide who had cared for Noah Hoyt at Upstate Medical Center, frowned and shook her head. Pfeiffer lived a hundred miles away in northern New York, but she had returned to the trial nearly every day to hear for herself whether Noah and his siblings had died at their mother's hands. Now, sitting in the balcony across from the jury, Pfeiffer threw back her head and scoffed every time Steinschneider insisted that nurses had reported breathing problems in the babies.

In the balcony opposite Pfeiffer, purposely staying out of sight of the jury, was Bob Courtright. The investigator wanted to see Steinschneider testify, but he didn't want jurors to think he was trying to apply pressure with his presence. It was his first time in the courtroom since his testimony, and he was apprehensive about the outcome of the trial. Finding himself in a place where he couldn't smoke, the Lama jangled keys in his pocket.

Television reporters from Syracuse had come to the trial this morning expecting a double story: Steinschneider defending his life's work and Fitzpatrick staring him down from the gallery.

"I thought the cross-examination of him would be fun to watch, that he would be ripped up pretty good," Fitzpatrick said.

But Bob Simpson had spoken to him the night before and asked him to stay at home. Simpson didn't want the jury distracted by a possible flare-up between Fitzpatrick and Miller. Fitzpatrick agreed to stay away.

Miller used Steinschneider's testimony to attack the prosecution's assertion that the original findings in the

Hoyt children's deaths were wrong. There was no way to know that Eric Hoyt didn't suffer from a fatal heart abnormality, Steinschneider said. Miller had set up his witness to challenge the conclusions that Dr. Michael Baden had drawn from his autopsies.

"I don't think you can state that based upon a non-examination of the heart that there is evidence that there is no disease in that heart," Steinschneider said.

Then Steinschneider rose to Waneta's defense. Her lawyers hadn't shown Steinschneider a copy of her confession until the day before because they feared her description of smothering the children might force the doctor to alter his opinion. But Waneta's words didn't change Steinschneider's mind.

"Is there any medical evidence in this case, to your knowledge, to corroborate, independently corroborate, the statement of Mrs. Hoyt that she smothered these children?" Miller asked.

"No."

"And you don't know whether she did or not, do you?"

"No."

The cross-examination was less cordial. Even Simpson's seemingly innocuous first question had heat behind it.

"You and I have spoken before, is that correct?" he asked.

"That's correct," Steinschneider said.

Simpson was starting where he'd left off four weeks earlier during his contentious phone interview with Steinschneider. The doctor had drawn the battle lines when he called Simpson a liar and accused him of trying to convict a woman whom the prosecutor knew was innocent. Each had his guard up for the face-to-face confrontation.

"We have never met prior to today?" Simpson asked.

"Is that a question?" the doctor responded.

"Yes."

"No, we have not met."

Simpson asked a series of curt questions, fishing for any information that Steinschneider might have revealed to Waneta's lawyers. Simpson borrowed Miller's tactic of charging a few steps toward the witness stand to ask a question. In the gallery, Roz Steinschneider coached her husband by mouthing answers and signaling with her hands. Simple questions about a meeting between Steinschneider and the defense lawyers in Atlanta brought out the contempt on both sides.

SIMPSON: You recall whether they had a written script that they asked questions off from?

STEINSCHNEIDER: I do not believe so.

SIMPSON: Do you recall whether they came in with a briefcase, or with a knapsack, or anything that would have contained pens, pencils, note pads, things of that nature?

STEINSCHNEIDER: They did not have a knapsack.

SIMPSON: OK. How about a briefcase?

STEINSCHNEIDER: I believe they had a briefcase.

SIMPSON: They did have a briefcase?

STEINSCHNEIDER: I believe so.

SIMPSON: OK. Did you have a briefcase? Or a knapsack or something to carry papers in when you arrived at your attorney's office?

STEINSCHNEIDER: No.

SIMPSON: So you came empty-handed?

STEINSCHNEIDER: Well, I'm never empty-handed. But I came as you see me.

SIMPSON: Well, you look empty-handed to me right now.

Simpson's interrogation was more than verbal jousting. The prosecutor needed to make sure the doctor hadn't given the defense some previously undisclosed records that could be sprung as a surprise. Steinschneider said he had some notes and letters about the Hoyt case at home in Atlanta, but Simpson didn't see any point in asking to have them sent up. He figured Steinschneider would have brought the papers if they helped Waneta's case. Confident that the doctor had nothing besides Molly's and Noah's hospital records to support his twenty-three-year-old study, Simpson started to bore in on Steinschneider's findings.

The DA attacked Steinschneider's insistence that Molly and Noah suffered from abnormal breathing, and the doctor eventually conceded that there probably were times when the apnea monitor simply malfunctioned, as the nurses had said.

Steinschneider fidgeted under Simpson's cross-examination. He covered his mouth when he answered. He looked at his watch. He tried to fight back, challenging the way Simpson phrased his questions, but the prosecutor kept up the pressure.

Simpson zeroed in on Steinschneider's 1973 response to Dr. John Hick, the Minnesota pediatrician who had written a letter to *Pediatrics* suggesting that the "H" children had been victims of abuse. In his direct testimony, Steinschneider had referred to records showing that the babies required only stimulation, not vigorous stimulation, at the hospital.

SIMPSON: Were there any evidences in the record of vigorous stimulation of these children to arouse them out of this apnea state?

STEINSCHNEIDER: Not that I recollect.

SIMPSON: Yet when you wrote an article in response to Dr. Hick, you specifically mentioned in your defense that on two occasions the nurses were required to vigorously stimulate the children.

STEINSCHNEIDER: If I wrote it, it happened. But I didn't

see it in the notes. You were asking about the notes then.

SIMPSON: So which is the truth? There was a vigorous stimulation or there wasn't?

STEINSCHNEIDER: I wrote it, therefore it's true. I wouldn't have written it if it weren't true.

SIMPSON: So everything you write is true?

STEINSCHNEIDER: To the best of my knowledge, it is. Yes.

SIMPSON: Well, do you have a specific recollection in the record, Doctor, of a place where it talks about vigorous stimulation performed by a nurse?

STEINSCHNEIDER: No, I do not.

SIMPSON: And wouldn't it be important at your clinic that the nurses put such things down? Isn't that the reason the children were being studied?

STEINSCHNEIDER: Would it be important? It would be important.

SIMPSON: And when you questioned the nurses about vigorous stimulation—and I'm going to presume, based on your testimony, that they related to you orally that they had to vigorously stimulate these infants . . .

STEINSCHNEIDER: That's correct.

SIMPSON: And you recall that as though it was yesterday?

STEINSCHNEIDER: No, I do not recall. I recall it because it was in—I wrote it. I wouldn't have written it.

SIMPSON: Perhaps you wrote it in your letter to the editor in defense of your position as opposed to something that actually happened. Is that a possibility? You fabricated it in defense of your position?

STEINSCHNEIDER: No.

SIMPSON: You wouldn't do that?

STEINSCHNEIDER: No.

In the gallery, Roz Steinschneider gasped when Simpson accused her husband of making up the nurses' observations.

SIMPSON: Well, as you sit here today, you have no recollection of ever talking with a nurse about vigorous stimulation? As you sit here today, you have no recollection of that?

STEINSCHNEIDER: I have recollections of talking to nurses about their observations.

SIMPSON: I didn't ask you that, Doctor. I asked you if you had a recollection, as you sit here today, of a nurse advising you of vigorous stimulation?

STEINSCHNEIDER: No.

SIMPSON: And so it's possible that you simply put that in your letter to the editor to buttress a position that was perhaps not correct, isn't that true?

STEINSCHNEIDER: No.

SIMPSON: It's not true?

STEINSCHNEIDER: Absolutely not.

A minute later, Simpson returned to the subject:

SIMPSON: Did you use the words vigorous stimulation with respect to Molly and Noah in that letter?

STEINSCHNEIDER: The—

SIMPSON: Did you use the words, Dr. Steinschneider?

STEINSCHNEIDER: The answer is, yes. I said on these occasions vigorous stimulations were required before spontaneous respirations resumed and skin color returned to normal.

SIMPSON: And you got that information from where?

STEINSCHNEIDER: I got that from my notes, the nurses' notes, and talking to the nurses.

SIMPSON: OK. And you will be able over the lunch hour to find your notes and the nurses' notes as to where the term vigorous stimulation comes from when you review all these exhibits, won't you?

STEINSCHNEIDER: No.

SIMPSON: Why not?

STEINSCHNEIDER: The only notes I have are those that apply to the medical records. I've looked for that. I do not see in those particular babies where they said vigorous stimulation.

SIMPSON: So it's not in the medical records?

STEINSCHNEIDER: Not in—there were records that I kept following discussions with these nurses.

SIMPSON: And where are those records?

STEINSCHNEIDER: I don't have them.

What Simpson didn't know was that the witness had once claimed that Molly and Noah Hoyt needed more than vigorous stimulation. Steinschneider raised the issue in his private exchange of letters with Dr. Stuart Asch, the New York psychiatrist who warned Steinschneider in 1974 that his study of the "H" family looked like a case of serial infanticide. Steinschneider told Asch that the two babies he'd treated had to be resuscitated by nurses. Steinschneider testified that resuscitation, or mouth-to-mouth breathing, is required in more serious situations.

Steinschneider tried to dispel Asch's suspicions with information not contained in the babies' records, just as he had in his response to Hick.

Simpson and Steinschneider grappled over the definition of "prolonged apnea." Was it fifteen seconds, as Steinschneider said in his 1972 study, or twenty seconds, the alarm setting the doctor used on apnea monitors in 1995? When Steinschneider wouldn't give a firm answer, Simpson asked the doctor to tell him the difference between fifteen-second apnea and twenty-second apnea.

"Five-second difference," Steinschneider replied.

"Thank you, very much," Simpson said.

The sparring continued until Miller jumped to his feet and objected that Simpson wasn't letting Steinschneider answer.

"Sit!" Sgueglia told Miller. Then he turned to

Simpson. "Counsel, please count to one before you ask the next question."

"One," Simpson said.

"One," Steinschneider said.

"Go ahead, answer. I'm sorry, I don't mean to interrupt you. I tend to get that way."

"All right. Ask your question."

Like two rested boxers starting a new round, they went back at it.

SIMPSON: Now with respect to near-miss SIDS, as it applies to Molly and Noah Hoyt, is there any evidence in the hospital records, from the nurses or other caregivers in the hospital, of any near-miss SIDS?

STEINSCHNEIDER: In the hospital records?

SIMPSON: Yes, sir.

STEINSCHNEIDER: They stimulated the baby.

SIMPSON: I didn't ask you that. I asked if there was any evidence of near-miss SIDS?

STEINSCHNEIDER: In the sense in which that term was being used then, I would say at least those times when they felt the need to stimulate.

SIMPSON: Now, over the lunch hour I would like you to go through exhibits 16 and 17, which are the hospital records for Noah and Molly, and I would like you to pick out every instance where there was stimulation. Can you do that for us?

STEINSCHNEIDER: I will try.

Steinschneider spent an hour and a half in near panic, thumbing through the children's medical records. He had acknowledged that there would be no record of the babies' being vigorously stimulated. But he was looking for notes on simple stimulation.

"It's in here. I know it's in here," he said.

The doctor made a note of every point he thought Simpson would question. Miller said later he feared that Steinschneider might have a stroke. But after lunch Simpson let the matter drop. Instead, he asked the doctor which of the Hoyt children's deaths he would label SIDS. Steinschneider said he couldn't apply the term to Eric or Julie, because they'd never been autopsied. The term couldn't apply to James because the best information available showed that the boy had small adrenal glands, he said.

Molly and Noah, Steinschneider said, fit the definition of SIDS: After the police and coroners did their investigations, there were no known causes for the babies' deaths. Simpson asked if Steinschneider presumed the death scenes had been adequately investigated.

"I would hope that people are as thorough as I am," Steinschneider said. "If you're asking me whether or not I think a particular investigator did a thorough job—Lord have mercy, I'm having trouble talking about physicians doing an appropriate job. I'm certainly not going to pass judgment on whether you are doing an appropriate job, or they're doing an appropriate job, or the judge is. Forgive me, Judge. I wouldn't presume to pass on somebody else's expertise."

The doctor's response sent a clear message: He didn't think Simpson should presume to judge the physician's expertise.

Simpson took Steinschneider to the same question that had incited the doctor in their pretrial phone conversation. This time there was no confrontation.

"So for all you know, they could have been suffocated?" Simpson asked.

"For all I know, they could have been suffocated."

"Did you ever consider that as a possible cause of death of any of the Hoyt children?"

"Yes."

"And did you refer your thoughts to any police agency?"

"No."

Steinschneider said he didn't remember any nurses warning him that the Hoyt children might be dying at the hands of their mother. Simpson asked about one nurse in particular, Julia Evans. But Miller objected, saying the prosecutor could call Evans as a witness if he wanted to know what she'd told Steinschneider. The judge sided with Miller, and Waneta's jury never got to hear about Evans's twenty-five-cent bet with Steinschneider.

Steinschneider smiled gently when he stepped down from the witness chair after three hours and fifteen minutes. During the recess that followed, Steinschneider went to a conference room on the first floor of the courthouse, where he greeted Waneta Hoyt for the first time in twenty-three years. To Waneta, he was a hero who had comforted her after Molly and Noah died. Steinschneider hugged her.

"It's nice to see you," he said.

"Do you think I killed my babies?" she asked.

"No, I do not."

The doctor left quickly to catch a flight back to Atlanta. On the way to the airport, he restated his faith in Waneta. He attributed her confession to the tendency among SIDS parents to blame themselves for the loss of their children.

"I'll tell you right now—probably only Waneta and God know," Steinschneider said. "But I don't think she killed them. Those kids were sick."

Steinschneider did Waneta another favor by directing her lawyers to Dr. Dorothy Kelly, a pediatrician at the Southwest SIDS Research Institute near Houston, Texas, who supported his theories. Steinschneider believed that Kelly, who had published a study in 1987 about multiple SIDS deaths in Boston-area families, could provide the rebuttal testimony Miller was looking for.

Kelly testified later in the week. She said her review of records in the case showed four of the Hoyt children had symptoms of a central nervous system disorder that affects breathing and swallowing.

Multiple unexplained infant deaths in one family were not unheard of, Kelly said. Her 1987 study showed a one-in-five death rate among babies born to couples who had already lost more than one infant to SIDS, she said. One family, she said, lost four children.

Assistant District Attorney Peggy Drake was given the job of cross-examining Kelly. She remembered a warning from Fitzpatrick about the Boston-area study. Fitzpatrick believed that Kelly had been looking at victims of homicides, not SIDS, and he had passed his suspicions along to the district attorney in Boston.

Drake's questions dropped the same hints. She asked if Kelly would consider it significant if the children in her study had died in the company of the same parent each time. The doctor answered with the label that the prosecutors wanted to keep out of the trial.

"If you're alluding to Munchausen by proxy—" Kelly started to say, but Drake cut her off. The Hoyt jury would never learn what the term meant.

Drake couldn't shake Kelly's opinion on the Hoyt children's deaths.

"Is it possible that they could be the victims of homicide?" Drake asked.

"Any child could be," the doctor said. "But we are talking about children here who have symptoms of a disease that could lead to death."

Kelly's testimony buoyed Waneta's spirits. During a recess, Waneta smiled more broadly than she ever had during the trial. "When this is over, we will celebrate," she said.

But Kelly failed on several points, most glaringly her lack of an explanation for Jimmy's death. She never suggested what might have killed the Hoyt child who had survived the longest.

With Dr. Arthur King, Miller had another medical expert to tie with the three the prosecution put on the stand. But Miller's friend, Dr. Eleanor McQuillen, had been right: The defense could not find a forensic pathologist who would testify that the Hoyt children were anything but homicide victims. King was an eighty-year-old Pennsylvania neurosurgeon who had worked with Miller on medical malpractice cases.

King reviewed the findings of the exhumations and said it made no sense for Ophoven and Baden to say the Hoyt children's remains aided them in any way. Nothing in the children's records or the graves medically supported a finding of suffocation, he said. Therefore, there was no way of knowing that the children didn't die naturally.

"All we had were bones," King said. "It's impossible to exclude something that isn't there."

As King described the contents of the graves, Waneta wept. Tim wrapped his arm around her shoulder and whispered, "Everything's going to be OK."

Waneta's lawyers continued the assault on the prosecution's medical evidence with witnesses who recalled the deaths of the Hoyt children. Tim Hoyt and defense investigator Bill Fischer had tracked down three former ambulance workers who testified that they arrived at the Hoyt home in time to find a child alive. One of the witnesses, Henry Robson, said he gave mouth-to-mouth breathing to Jimmy Hoyt for forty-five minutes. The boy had no blood anywhere on his nose and mouth, he said, contrary to Waneta's confession.

Tim Hoyt's brother Chuck and sister Ann Schultheis also said they saw Waneta's babies alive at the emergency calls. Ann, who once made up diseases to see whether Waneta would claim she had the symptoms, testified that she'd seen her sister-in-law shake Molly's foot when the apnea alarm sounded.

Waneta thought the testimony of the ambulance workers and her in-laws on the second day of her defense helped. "Maybe things are going to be OK," she said after they'd finished. The next morning, she re-

ceived more encouragement when she met Phil Jordan
in the attorneys' conference room off the courtroom.
The psychic cupped Waneta's elbows as she placed her
hands on his outstretched forearms.

"I just was going to ask you, how do you think it's
going?" she said.

"It's going extremely well," Jordan said. "You have
to have faith and trust. You're a woman with a strong
faith, and you're going to do just fine."

In court that morning, Simpson seethed. The defense
had told him just two days before that Charles Ewing,
the Buffalo psychologist who had examined Waneta,
would be called to testify. Simpson claimed that
Waneta's lawyers had violated a court rule that re-
quires defense lawyers to notify the prosecution when
they intend to use a mental defense. The rule is designed to give prosecutors time to have their own psychiatrist examine a defendant. The late notice put
Simpson in the awkward position of having to stand
before the jury and ask for a delay.

"I look like the village idiot, the way they've perpe-
trated this fraud on me," Simpson argued without the
jury present. But Sgueglia refused the DA's request to
bar Ewing's testimony.

Both sides had argued the issue during an angry
meeting in the judge's chambers. Sgueglia reasoned
that if he barred Ewing's testimony because Miller and
Urbanski were late in notifying the prosecution,
Waneta could appeal a conviction on grounds that
she'd received ineffective assistance from her lawyers.

Urbanski bristled at the judge's comments. The noti-
fication rule didn't apply because Waneta wasn't
claiming mental illness as a defense, he said. Ewing
was to testify about whether her mental state affected
her ability to freely confess. Sgueglia called an early
recess to give Simpson time to find a psychiatrist to
examine Waneta over the Easter holiday.

Simpson asked state mental health officials for quick

advice on whom to call. He hadn't hired a psychiatrist to testify in eighteen years. The last time was in another murder trial against Miller. The defense lawyer had successfully argued in that case that his client suffered from emotional turmoil and ought to be convicted of a lesser charge of manslaughter.

Dr. Kelly's testimony Thursday finished the medical phase of the defense. Miller had done what he could to cast doubt on the prosecution's corroboration. It was Urbanski's turn to try to persuade the jury to disregard Waneta's confession.

Chapter Twenty-three

The Rev. James Willard rose early enough Easter morning to see the sun and the moon appear together over the valley. He would reflect on that image a few hours later, when he stepped to the pulpit of the First Congregational Church in Berkshire to deliver his sermon. In the transition from darkness to light, Willard had found a metaphor for the Resurrection, and a message of hope for two members of his congregation. On Monday, the dawn of the fourth week of her murder trial, Waneta Hoyt was scheduled to take the witness stand in her own defense, followed by Tim. They were counting on their testimony to renew Waneta's chances of acquittal. Willard's Easter service was the last stop in a hectic round of preparation.

On Good Friday, Waneta traveled to Rochester to be interviewed by the prosecution's psychiatrist, Dr. David Barry. Waneta's lawyers, Bob Miller and Ray Urbanski, and Assistant District Attorney Peggy Drake sat in on the two-hour session. Waneta emerged confident about her performance.

"There wasn't a dry eye in the house," she told Phil Jordan, the psychic who had advised the defense on jury selection.

On Saturday she spent nearly three hours at Miller's office in Waverly, practicing her testimony. Miller and Urbanski hit Waneta with the toughest questions they could think of, trying to give her a taste of what she could expect from District Attorney Bob Simpson. The dress rehearsal hit a snag when Waneta said she couldn't remember the second interview with the state police, the one the stenographer had taken down word for word.

Waneta needed to testify so she could disavow her earlier statements. But her lawyers were worried about what the jury would think if she buckled under cross-examination. Miller hit on a strategy to ensure the jury's sympathy if Simpson bullied Waneta.

"Listen," Miller told her. "All you've got to remember is: Cry and deny. Can you remember those two words? Cry and deny."

The next morning, Tim and Waneta went to the nine o'clock service at the United Methodist Church of Newark Valley, where their friends Art and Natalie Hilliard belonged. Two hours later, the Hoyts joined about a hundred other worshipers at Willard's church, just up the road from the couple's home.

The Hoyts held hands in the last pew. When the seventy-five-minute service began with the choir singing to recorded gospel music, Waneta clapped in time to the beat.

"This is a crucial week for Tim and Waneta," Willard told his flock. He asked that God grant the Hoyts mercy and encouraged the congregation to support Waneta by attending her trial.

"If you can't get down there," he said, "remember them in your prayers."

As the church emptied, well-wishers stopped to hug Waneta and whisper in her ear. She was the center of attention again, and that seemed to give her confidence.

"Tomorrow," Waneta told the last person she hugged, "is my day."

For her day in court, Waneta rose two hours before the sun. She had found sleep difficult since the trial started and had begun rising at four a.m. Tim often got up with her. Like a parent trying to soothe a colicky baby, he would drive his wife around the valley until she dozed off or it was time to go to court.

When they arrived at the Tioga County Courthouse that morning, Waneta was wearing a navy blue dress with white dots and the cream-colored jacket she'd worn to Easter services. The jacket carried the heart-shaped lapel pin that reminded Waneta of her mother. Waneta brought along a purse to hold her Bible and an embroidered handkerchief sent by a well-wisher.

The defendant had given herself a subtle makeover in the year since her arrest. She had lost fifty pounds and now appeared fit at 130 pounds. Her arms no longer looked flabby, and during the trial, she started wearing lipstick. Only her thin gray hair made her look older than forty-eight.

Inside the courtroom, Waneta faced the biggest crowd of the trial. About fifty people had come to hear her testify—not a full house but more than anyone could remember seeing at a trial in Owego. Tim's eighty-six-year-old mother, Ella, appeared in court for the first time. She and more than a dozen other relatives, friends, and ministers filled seven rows in the gallery. Albert Nixon, the only member of the Nixon family to regularly attend the trial, sat in the balcony.

Bill Fitzpatrick and Pete Tynan also made their first appearances at the trial—at Simpson's invitation. The friction between Fitzpatrick and Miller had eased, and Simpson felt he could no longer deny a seat in the gallery to the colleague who had initiated the Hoyt investigation. Fitzpatrick had kept up on the proceedings by calling Simpson and by listening to excerpts of testimony recorded on a dial-in news service at the Syracuse *Post-Standard*. He hadn't seen Waneta Hoyt since he watched her fall into the abyss during the state police interview. Now he would watch her try to climb out.

"Your Honor, we call Waneta Hoyt to the stand," Ray Urbanski announced at 9:38 A.M. Waneta released

Tim's hand and slowly crossed the courtroom to be sworn in. She steadied herself with a hand on Judge Vincent Sgueglia's bench as she climbed the three steps to the witness chair.

Urbanski was the obvious choice to ask the 107 questions the defense team had prepared for Waneta. She had never liked Miller's gruff personality. Urbanski had a gentler touch, and his sympathy for Waneta showed. She trusted him to help her win over the men and women in the jury box a few feet away.

Most of the jurors strained to hear as Waneta began testifying about her inventory of ailments. She continued to answer Urbanski's questions in a meek voice, although Sgueglia urged her to speak up. She seemed to explain her timidity when she talked about quitting her job at Endicott Johnson thirty years before.

"I don't like being in crowds," she said.

Urbanski laid open Waneta's life, asking about her childhood, falling in love with Tim, and coping with health problems and family tragedies. Albert Nixon leaned over the balcony railing as Waneta tearfully recalled her mother's death. She was still weeping when Urbanski led her through her children's deaths.

Waneta gave the children's birth dates and described how each had suddenly lost consciousness and died, despite her efforts to revive them.

As she spoke about the children, Waneta periodically dabbed her eyes with a handkerchief. Each gesture triggered a flutter of clicks from the news cameras trained on her from the balcony. At one point, Tim's older sister, Janet Kuenzli, swung her head up at the photographers and said, "Slimy bastards."

In an effort to show that social workers had considered the Hoyts fitting parents, Urbanski brought up the adoption of nine-month-old Scottie in 1971. Waneta said she and Tim had returned the boy because they were afraid of losing another child.

Waneta got another chance to explain her uneasiness

provoked by being in court when Urbanski asked why she had dropped charges against a neighbor she said had raped her in 1974.

"Because I couldn't handle the pressure of all you high-society people," she said.

A few minutes later, Urbanski started in on the confession. He asked Waneta to read the three-page signed statement, but she said she couldn't see the words without her reading glasses, which she'd left at the defense table. This was the same pair she'd left at home the day the state police took her in for questioning, she said. Without those glasses, she explained, she couldn't read her constitutional rights or the statements she gave.

When Tim Hoyt made a point of rising from the defense table and giving Urbanski the reading glasses to pass to Waneta, Simpson shook his head and smiled.

Waneta cried again as she described how she was tricked into confessing by Trooper Bubba Bleck, whom she called Bobby, and investigators Sue Mulvey and Bob Courtright. She said she thought they were interested in SIDS research. After she explained how each child died, she said, Mulvey told her they had concrete medical proof that Waneta had smothered the children.

"I says, 'Bobby ... do you believe this?' and he throws his hands in the air and says, 'Who am I?' And I says, 'Well, I didn't, couldn't have done anything like that.' I says, 'Who could do anything that horrible?' "

Afterward, she said, Mulvey kept suggesting in detail how Waneta had smothered the children.

"She just kept at me for I don't know how long, and then I finally said, 'Yeah, I guess I did. If you said I did.' "

"Why did you say that?" Urbanski asked.

"Because I couldn't stand the pressure. I just wanted her to leave me alone so I could go home."

Waneta repeated what she'd said in the dress rehearsal about the stenographic statement: She testified that she had no recollection of it. Bob Simpson's cross-examination wasn't so easily dismissed.

Waneta had dreaded Simpson's questions, but Annette Gorski, Miller's longtime paralegal, had given her a tip: Avoid eye contact. Waneta picked out a point in the back of the courtroom to focus on during cross-examination, and she only took her eyes off that spot to throw Tim an occasional wink.

For Simpson, the cross-examination was a chance to strip away the facade he thought Waneta had presented throughout the trial. If Waneta liked talking about her poor health, Simpson would oblige her. He asked about the doctors she'd seen, the medications she'd taken, her operations, her suicidal depression after her children died. He pressed Waneta about one doctor who had been unable to find the illness she claimed to have had and had sent her away.

"Do you recall a Dr. Mahoney who decided he didn't want to treat you anymore because you complained about an illness that he couldn't find?" Simpson asked. "He couldn't find it and he terminated you?"

"He didn't terminate me," Waneta said.

"He did not find anything to support your claimed illness, did he?"

"I don't know.'"

Simpson thought Waneta's inability to recall the stenographic statement would ring hollow with the jury. For the prosecutor, the transcribed interview was the next best thing to a videotaped confession. It showed her describing each child's death the same way Mulvey had taken it down in the signed statement. Simpson pointed out where Waneta had even corrected Courtright and Mulvey during the second interview. But when Simpson asked how she could have given such consistent accounts if she was in a daze, Waneta stuck to her denial.

"I just was gone," she said. "I don't remember any of it."

It wasn't until after lunch that Simpson noticed Waneta had been avoiding eye contact. He took this as a good sign. It meant either he was getting under her skin, or she had something to hide. He decided it was a good time to bring up a sore point—the failed adoption of Scottie.

SIMPSON: Have you reviewed the adoption records with respect to Scottie prior to coming to court today?

HOYT: No.

SIMPSON: Have your attorneys discussed the contents of those adoption records with you?

HOYT: No.

SIMPSON: If I told you that Scottie was placed in your home on November 15, 1971, would you dispute that?

HOYT: I don't know, because I don't remember the time.

SIMPSON: If I told you that your psychiatrist told you to remove, to get the child out of your house on November 25, 1971, would you dispute that?

HOYT: I don't know.

SIMPSON: If I told you that you told your psychiatrist that you were going to do harm to this child, would you dispute that?

HOYT: I don't know.

SIMPSON: Did you tell your psychiatrist or the mental health worker to get the child out of your house before you wrang [*sic*] its neck?

HOYT: I don't know.

SIMPSON: Is it possible that you did?

HOYT: No.

SIMPSON: Did you call Alberta Weisz, the Tioga County Department of Social Services worker, on a weekend and tell her to get that child out of your house before you did it harm?

HOYT: No.

SIMPSON: You deny that?

HOYT: I don't deny calling her.

SIMPSON: You deny saying that?

HOYT: I deny—I didn't say that, no.

SIMPSON: What did you say?

HOYT: I called her and I told her that we weren't ready to handle the child yet. It was too soon after Noah dying.

SIMPSON: Didn't you tell her that you might harm the child?

HOYT: No, I didn't.

SIMPSON: Did you tell Dr. Jafri that you had evil thoughts, and that you were going to wring the child's neck?

HOYT: No.

SIMPSON: So if the mental health records show otherwise you would dispute that, is that correct?

HOYT: I don't remember saying anything like that.

SIMPSON: Is it possible that you said it?

HOYT: I don't know.

Urbanski objected, saying the adoption should be off-limits because the jury could prejudge Waneta on a statement about another child. The case had to be decided on what had happened to the five Hoyt children, he argued. But Sgueglia allowed the questions to stand. Urbanski's passing reference to the adoption on direct examination had opened the door for Simpson to bring out the caseworker's damaging reports on Waneta.

Fitzpatrick watched Waneta closely from the fifth row of the gallery. His back had been bothering him, and he felt himself stiffening up on the rigid courtroom bench. He didn't dare shift to a more comfortable position because he thought the wooden seat might creak.

"I was afraid Miller would jump up and say, 'Judge,

could you tell Mr. Fitzpatrick to be quiet?' " he later said.

Waneta knew he was there, anyway. She asked Urbanski later why Fitzpatrick was allowed to sit in on the trial; she was worried he might be intimidating the jury.

Simpson ended his cross-examination with an attempt to expose what he believed was Waneta's real motive for killing her children. He didn't expect any revelations, but he wanted the satisfaction of seeing her reaction. He snapped off the questions indignantly:

SIMPSON: Isn't it a fact that you love attention, Mrs. Hoyt?

HOYT: No.

SIMPSON: Don't you love attention? You have to be the center of attention at all times?

HOYT: No.

SIMPSON: Isn't it a fact that you couldn't stand to have these children around crying because you were no longer the center of your husband's universe?

HOYT: They didn't cry all the time.

SIMPSON: You said in your statement that they cried all the time, and that's why you killed them.

HOYT: I didn't kill them.

SIMPSON: You did tell the police that, didn't you?

HOYT: That's what they suggested I did.

SIMPSON: Don't you enjoy the attention you've gotten in connection with this trial, Mrs. Hoyt?

HOYT: No, sir!

SIMPSON: You haven't enjoyed it at all?

HOYT: No, sir.

SIMPSON: You're under intense pressure being here today?

HOYT: Yes, sir.

SIMPSON: You wish you were someplace else?

HOYT: Yes, sir.

SIMPSON: You're nervous?

HOYT: Yes.
SIMPSON: Well, you're handling it very well.

Waneta never showed any signs of cracking under Simpson's cross-examination. She appeared to be calm, her answers matter-of-fact. In the final exchange, she became defiant. But she had remembered only half of Miller's advice: She denied, but she forgot to cry. Simpson had given the jury a glimpse of the willfulness that lay beneath Waneta's frail exterior.

As the jury left the courtroom for a break, Waneta staggered back to the defense table, breathing heavily. She knew she had not done well. Tim and other relatives rushed over and helped her to the back of the courtroom.

Urbanski and Miller had scheduled five more witnesses to follow Waneta, so the jurors wouldn't have her testimony fresh in their minds when they began deliberations. The rest of their defense would have two goals: bolster Waneta's claim that she was tricked into confessing and build sympathy for her. Miller began the final push with Tim Hoyt.

Chapter Twenty-four

Tim Hoyt remained an enigma to the people who had investigated his children's deaths. He was obviously a loyal husband. He'd stuck by Waneta for thirty-one years, through illnesses real and imagined, through suicide threats, and a failed adoption. But members of the Hoyt task force were baffled by Tim's devotion to Waneta in the face of the evidence that she'd smothered their five children. Did he really believe she was innocent, or did he love her so much he could forgive her for anything, including the murders of his kids? Had he locked up his doubts the way he and Waneta closed off the second floor of their house when they couldn't afford to heat it? When Tim followed Waneta to the witness stand, he defined their relationship in simple terms: "I love her, she loves me. I take care of her, she takes care of me."

Testifying in Waneta's defense seemed just one more way for Tim to take care of his wife. His plaid sports coat hung open as he slouched in the witness chair, exposing a slight potbelly clad in a clashing striped shirt. He wore his sideburns long, in the fashion popular in the 1970s. Bob Miller's questions took Tim back to the day of Waneta's arrest. Tim described his encounter with the state police investigators who picked him up at Cornell, took his statement at the barracks outside Ithaca, then drove him to see Waneta in Owego.

At the defense table, Waneta seemed to drift in and out of a trance. When she wasn't wiping her eyes, they were locked in a faraway gaze. She used the hand that Tim ordinarily clutched to cover her mouth during most of his testimony.

Miller asked Tim what he did after learning that the police had a statement from Waneta saying she'd killed the five children.

"I confronted her with the situation, because she was crying," Tim said. "And she said to me, 'I did not do this thing. They told me that I killed my children. I did not do this.' "

"What happened? How did you come to affix your signature to that document?"

"I was—excuse me—mad as hell. I was terribly upset, and when I was asked to sign it, I said, 'I sign in protest, damn it!' " Tim shouted the answer, pounding his fist on an imaginary table. "But I didn't write 'damn it' or 'in protest' on it. I just made that statement."

Bill Fitzpatrick listened in disgust. He had been at the state police barracks the day Waneta confessed, and he had heard her convince Tim that it was true, she had killed their children. If it were up to Fitzpatrick, Tim Hoyt would be indicted for perjury.

But like every other step in the prosecution, the decision on how to deal with Tim Hoyt belonged to District Attorney Bob Simpson. He was more interested in making a case against Waneta than against her husband. Simpson's cross-examination was firm but without rancor, and he soon drew out the key point he wanted to make: Tim was at work every time his children had breathing problems, and by the time he got home, they were dead.

Simpson tried to undermine Waneta's credibility by questioning Tim about the third page of his wife's signed confession. Tim had co-signed the page after Investigator Sue Mulvey took down Waneta's addendum, but he told Simpson, "I don't recall any of that."

The DA let the matter go, confident that the jury

wouldn't believe Tim's memory lapse any more than Waneta's lack of recall on the stenographic statement.

The testimony of Jay Hoyt seemed to offer nothing except the fact that his mother was distraught when he saw her at the state police barracks and that she was still upset when he saw her at the Tioga County Jail a few hours later. But Waneta's lawyers knew the unspoken value of Jay's appearance: He was living proof of his mother's love.

Assistant District Attorney Peggy Drake kept Jay on the stand for one minute. She and Simpson had agreed before the trial that they would only hurt themselves by grilling Jay. If there was anybody other than the five dead children who deserved sympathy, Simpson thought, it was Jay. Drake had one point to make in her four-question cross-examination: The state police had taken care to bring the teenager to see his mother at the barracks.

With his testimony complete, Jay was free to remain in the courtroom. He embraced his parents at the defense table, then took a seat in the gallery.

Monday also brought the testimony of two other witnesses with sympathy for Waneta—Natalie Hilliard, her best friend, and the Rev. Donald Washburn, former pastor of the United Methodist Church in Newark Valley.

Hilliard recalled the day she looked out the front window of her home and saw Waneta carrying Jimmy's body. Hilliard ran out to meet Waneta, and they took Jimmy to the Hilliards' house. The boy had no blood on his face, Hilliard said. But under cross-examination, she also said Jimmy was a healthy boy.

Washburn had been assigned to the church in Newark Valley a month before Noah died. Parishioners had pointed out Tim and Waneta as a couple with special needs, he said. He also testified about Waneta collapsing at Noah's funeral. "I saw a lady carrying a very heavy load," he said.

The next day psychologist Charles Ewing took the stand.

Ewing represented the defense's last hope of blunting the impact of Waneta's confession. The forensic psychologist and law professor had testified in more than four hundred cases, for either the prosecution or the defense. Prosecutors in New York City had called on him to examine subway gunman Bernhard Goetz.

When Ray Urbanski called him to the stand, Ewing, a slight figure with an outgoing personality, stopped to shake hands with Judge Vincent Sgueglia. He started his testimony with a list of the problems he'd seen in Waneta in their ten interviews. She was weak, depressed, worrisome, unassertive, submissive, excessively sensitive, fearful, and introverted, he said.

Ewing testified that he diagnosed three personality disorders: Waneta suffered from major depression, was overly dependent on her husband, and was afraid of social interaction. Waneta's multiple disorders made her extremely vulnerable to manipulation by authority figures, he said.

Ewing said he believed Waneta would easily cave in to suggestions from the police. In his opinion Waneta could not have freely confessed to the state police, and therefore the statements they had were not reliable.

Under the rules of evidence, Urbanski wasn't allowed to ask Ewing whether he believed Waneta was telling the truth. Yet, regardless of his ultimate conclusion, Ewing had served the defense's needs.

Then Simpson committed what the defense lawyers thought was his only mistake in the trial.

"What she told the state police could have been true?" Simpson asked Ewing on cross-examination.

"It could have been true?" Ewing repeated.

"Yes."

"I don't think so."

"I didn't ask you that. What she told the state police could have been true?"

"In my opinion? No, it couldn't have been true."

Simpson's question had opened the door for Ewing to offer the conclusion that Urbanski couldn't ask for. The jury had heard from an expert witness that Waneta's confession was false. Minutes later, Simpson widened the breach.

"Now, tell me what you are saying that the police did wrong," he said.

"I'm not saying they did anything wrong," Ewing said. "I'm not here to judge the police. If you want me to, I'll give you my opinion."

"No, I don't want your opinion. Now, you've already rendered—"

Urbanski interrupted: "That's exactly what his question asked for, Your Honor."

Sgueglia agreed, and Ewing got to expand on his analysis of how the state police had manipulated Waneta.

"The police in this case used somebody who was known to Mrs. Hoyt, who Mrs. Hoyt trusted, Mrs. Hoyt thought of as a friend, to deceive her, to guile her into consenting to participate in what she thought was going to be a research interview, an interview that would help other people regarding sudden infant death syndrome," Ewing said. "Then the police brought in a woman who was not portrayed to her as a police officer—"

"Aha!" Simpson shouted as he spun around to face Ewing. The prosecutor had found a discrepancy between what Waneta had told Ewing and what she'd told the jury. She had testified that Sue Mulvey was introduced to her as a police investigator.

It was a minor recovery for Simpson. Ewing had painted a picture of Waneta as a woman easily manipulated. The psychologist said he'd never seen a wife so dependent on her husband and that she had probably demonstrated it right in the courtroom.

"Oh, I've seen it all right," Simpson said. "You can bet your money on that."

What Simpson didn't know was that another psychologist hired by the defense had come to different conclusions about Waneta Hoyt.

Two months before the trial, Ray Urbanski had taken a flight to London, England, to arrange for Waneta to be examined by Gisli Gudjonsson, one of the world's leading authorities on the psychology of police interviews. Gudjonsson, a former police investigator in Iceland and now a psychology professor at the University of London, had developed a test to measure an individual's susceptibility to suggestions during police interrogations. The Gudjonsson Suggestibility Scale was widely known among psychologists who studied police interviews. Gudjonsson was best known, perhaps, for his involvement in the case of four Irishmen who were convicted in 1975 of carrying out fatal bombings for the IRA in Guildford, England. Gudjonsson's review of the police interrogations helped the "Guildford Four" win their freedom after fourteen years in prison. The case inspired the 1993 movie *In the Name of the Father.*

Gudjonsson arrived in Tioga County three weeks before the start of Waneta's trial. He spent a week reading documents in the case, talking to Waneta about her children's deaths and the state police interview, and administering his suggestibility test.

The test typically involved Gudjonsson's reading aloud a fictitious account of a robbery. After a fifty-minute delay, Gudjonsson would ask his subject twenty questions about the robbery, fifteen of them subtly misleading. Then he would tell the subject that he or she had made several errors, even if none had been made, and ask the questions again. By noting changes between the first and second set of answers, Gudjonsson could measure the extent to which the subject gave in to the misleading questions. The test score indicated how easily the person could be swayed by suggestions from police.

Gudjonsson spent three days interviewing and testing Waneta in the dining room of Miller's mansion in Waverly. Waneta seemed to like the psychologist, whom she called "Dr. Goody-John." The day after the last interview, Gudjonsson assembled his findings. The results were devastating for Waneta's credibility. Her score on the suggestibility test not only fell into the category of true confessors, but Gudjonsson found her to be manipulative.

The psychologist never told Waneta the results of the test. He broke the news to Urbanski during a car ride. A long silence followed.

"I get the impression you're disappointed," Gudjonsson said.

Urbanski was. With the trial just two weeks away, Urbanski and Miller had to drop their plans to use the famous psychologist as a witness. They went with Ewing instead, and Urbanski was glad they did. By capitalizing on the opening that Simpson gave him on cross-examination, Ewing had delivered a bonus to the defense. Urbanski thought the jurors would see Ewing's testimony as decisive.

"They can't believe that confession," Urbanski told Miller.

Some of Waneta's supporters thought the same. Tim's sister, Janet Kuenzli, gave Ewing a thumbs-up sign from the gallery when the lawyers had their backs turned during a sidebar conference.

Simpson had one chance the next morning to counter the effect of Ewing's testimony. On Wednesday, April 16, the last day of testimony, the prosecutor called Dr. David Barry as a rebuttal witness. Although Barry, contradicting Ewing, said Waneta didn't suffer from any personality disorders, the defense turned the psychiatrist's testimony to its advantage.

On cross-examination, Miller presented a hypothetical situation that described the circumstances of Waneta's confession. He asked Barry whether it was significant that a person being questioned thought she had been invited to an interview for a research project.

"If that's the way it happened, I'd say that there was some significance," Barry said. "Your hypothetical describes a situation in which Mrs. Hoyt was clearly anticipating quite a different course for the discussion than the one it eventually took."

Barry had essentially agreed with Ewing: If police had told Waneta they wanted to talk with her for SIDS research, then she had been manipulated. The defense lawyers felt they'd scored a coup.

But the thrill was short-lived. In the middle of Barry's testimony, a court attendant handed Urbanski a note with a cryptic message: "Must object. Otherwise, statute of limitations waived."

Urbanski knew immediately what the words meant. He looked at Miller, raised his eyebrows, and left the courtroom.

The message had come from the New York State Defenders Association in Albany. Urbanski had asked the organization to double-check whether Waneta would walk away from the trial free if she was convicted of manslaughter instead of murder. Urbanski and Miller believed that Waneta couldn't be punished for manslaughter because the time limit for prosecution on that crime had expired five years after Noah died.

But the public defenders association said Waneta's lawyers were wrong. If Waneta asked to have the jury consider the lesser charge, the five-year statute of limitations was waived, and she could face prison if convicted. The only way Waneta could avoid punishment for a manslaughter conviction was if the judge submitted the charge to the jury over the defendant's objections, and Sgueglia wasn't going to do that.

Urbanski went to the law library on the first floor of the courthouse to look up the cases that the public defenders' association cited as precedents. After Barry, the trial's last witness, had testified, Urbanski pulled Miller aside and explained what had happened.

Waneta's lawyers had never told her about the original manslaughter option. Now that they knew the fallback plan didn't guarantee Waneta's freedom, Miller and Urbanski had to confront their client with a tougher choice.

The lawyers saw outright acquittal as a long shot. The question that remained was how much time Waneta would spend in prison. The lawyers believed that, given a choice between murder and manslaughter, the jury would convict Waneta of the less serious charge, and she would face as little as two years in prison.

Without the manslaughter charge, Miller and Urbanski thought the jury would not let her walk and would probably convict her of murder. A murder conviction could put Waneta in prison for life.

The decision was Waneta's.

At the lunch break, Miller went into Sgueglia's chambers and asked him to adjourn the trial to give Waneta time to think. Sgueglia granted the request, but his response wasn't quite what Miller had in mind.

"You've got an hour and fifteen minutes to discuss it," the judge said.

Chapter Twenty-five

District Attorney Bob Simpson was as surprised as anyone by the bulletin that Waneta Hoyt's lawyers received from the public defenders association. Like Bob Miller and Ray Urbanski, Simpson had labored under the misconception that Waneta would go free if the jury convicted her of manslaughter instead of murder. The prosecutor had been prepared to argue that a guilty verdict on the less serious charge would still show that the Hoyt children did not die natural deaths—even if their mother did go unpunished. Suddenly he no longer had to worry about a hollow victory. But he wanted to confirm his new understanding.

As soon as Judge Vincent Sgueglia ordered the seventy-five-minute lunch break, Simpson and Assistant District Attorney Peggy Drake started searching law books for the cases Urbanski had mentioned, but not by name. Unable to find the court cases, Simpson went to find Waneta's lawyers.

"What the hell? Show me," Simpson said as he walked into the defense lawyers' conference room at the courthouse. In a gesture typical of the courtesy that prevailed before the Hoyt trial, Miller and Urbanski gave their opponent the cases.

The rulings, neither of which ever reached New York state's highest appeals court, barred defendants from using the statute of limitations to escape punishment for a charge they'd asked a jury to consider. They couldn't have it both ways, and in this case, neither could Waneta.

Although a manslaughter conviction wouldn't guarantee freedom for Waneta, Simpson knew she still might ask to have the charge presented to the jury. Rather than gamble that the jury would find she hadn't done anything wrong, Waneta could hedge her bets and provide an option for jurors who thought she was guilty of something less serious than murder. The prosecution had a more direct course: Whatever Waneta decided, Simpson wanted her convicted of murder. But with the testimony of Charles Ewing and Dr. David Barry fresh in the jurors' minds, Simpson knew he had some convincing to do.

Miller and Urbanski had their own convincing to do. They sat Tim and Waneta down at the start of the lunch break to explain where the case stood. The lawyers discussed how they'd been counting on the statute of limitations to set Waneta free if she was convicted of manslaughter. But that strategy had collapsed, they said, and they showed Waneta the court cases. Miller then went over Waneta's options.

Miller was convinced that the jury would acquit Waneta of the five counts of intentional murder. Even the statements Waneta gave the state police didn't support the conclusion that she'd deliberately smothered her children. The other five murder charges—the so-called depraved-murder counts—were more difficult to dismiss. Those counts accused Waneta of acting with such recklessness in trying to stop her children from crying that she disregarded the obvious risk that they would die.

Miller told Waneta he thought the jurors would have trouble acquitting her of reckless murder, if that was the only choice left. But if given the option, the jury might settle for manslaughter, which also implied recklessness, rather than intent. The difference between manslaughter and reckless murder was a question of degree: It would be up to the jurors to decide how depraved Waneta's actions were. Considering Waneta's sympathetic appearance during the trial, Miller believed the jury would settle for the lowest possible charge.

On the other hand, if the jurors believed the prosecution hadn't presented enough evidence to support any murder count, Waneta wouldn't want to give them another charge to consider. If murder was their only option, and even one juror believed she was innocent, the result would be a mistrial rather than conviction.

Miller didn't hold out much hope of a hung jury, however. He expected the jurors to deliver a unanimous verdict, one way or the other. He encouraged Waneta to let the jurors consider manslaughter charges.

"They're going to want to compromise," he told Waneta. "They're going to want to go down to something."

"If they don't have anything to go down to, it's only one way or the other," she said. "Do you think they'll acquit me?"

"I have no idea. But I wouldn't want to make that gamble."

"But I didn't do anything."

"OK, Waneta. That's not what we're talking about here," Miller said. "The jury is going to convict you of something."

"They certainly can't convict her of murder," Tim said. "The proof was so terrible."

Each option involved predictable consequences for Waneta. Each murder conviction would carry a minimum of fifteen years in prison and a maximum of life. Each manslaughter count could bring as few as two and as many as fifteen years in prison. An acquittal, of course, promised not only freedom but vindication.

It was time for Waneta to weigh the odds.

Waneta and Tim went outside to make the decision. The day had begun with thunder and lightning and rain, but the sky was starting to clear and the temperature was approaching 67 degrees. The Hoyts walked toward the Civil War memorial at the southern end of the courthouse lawn. They stopped beneath the obelisk and faced each other, while spectators watched from a distance.

Tim seemed to do most of the talking, gesturing with his hands, as if trying to make a point. Waneta appeared to be crying. Later, Tim would say they'd reached a mutual agreement.

When they returned to the courthouse, Tim gave Miller and Urbanski the decision: "We're going for broke. All or nothing."

"Well, you'll be doing that against our advice," Miller said. "Because I advise you to take the lesser-included offenses. Because I think that's what the jury's going to convict you of."

But Waneta was adamant, and Tim saw no point in doing things halfway.

"What's the difference if it's two years or twenty-five years, one year or twenty-five years?" Tim asked. "It doesn't make any difference. She won't live anyway."

Just before one-thirty p.m. the Hoyts and their lawyers met the prosecutors in Judge Sgueglia's chambers to announce the decision. Miller asked to have the conversation put on the record. Normally in such a situation, a defendant's lawyer does all the talking, even in chambers. But Miller insisted that Waneta speak for herself.

"Do you understand this, Mrs. Hoyt?" Sgueglia asked. "Do you understand that if you're convicted of manslaughter you're subject to a much lesser sentence?"

"Yes, I understand it," she said.

"With that in mind, do you still only want a murder charge?"

"I only want the murder charge."

Bob Miller had about ten minutes to rethink his summation for the trial. Summations had always been his strength. The final argument allowed him to show passion for his client and indignation against the government. Miller knew how to sway a jury. He'd planned to argue that Waneta should be found innocent of all the charges, but that if she was guilty of anything, it was manslaughter. He had a good record of getting jurors to bite on lower charges. Twice he had robbed Simpson of murder convictions that way. But Waneta's decision forced Miller to try for something he'd accomplished in three of his previous twelve murder trials: a complete acquittal.

His eye still red and painful, Miller stood at the lectern and addressed the jury. He attacked the way the state police had obtained Waneta's confession, focusing on Trooper Bubba Bleck's role as a trusted figure. Miller repeated Waneta's claim that the investigators told her they wanted to interview her for a SIDS research project.

"The taking of her into their company was done by deceit and it was done in a manner that was professionally geared to gain her confidence," Miller said.

Investigator Sue Mulvey listened to Miller's summation from the balcony. It was her first appearance in the courtroom since her testimony two weeks earlier. She smirked and shook her head as Miller criticized the job she'd done.

Miller moved on to Charles Ewing and Dr. David Barry, the two witnesses that Waneta's lawyers felt had helped their case the most.

"Dr. Barry is a very interesting witness, and it's ironic that he turns out to be the last witness in the entire trial," Miller said.

Barry had essentially agreed with Ewing, Miller said: If Waneta had thought she was being interviewed for a SIDS project, then once the interview became accusatory, the state police should have advised her of her constitutional rights again.

Miller made a second attempt to exploit Simpson's mistake in cross-examining Ewing, reminding the jurors that the psychologist had testified that Waneta did not speak the truth in her confession.

The public defender spoke for sixty-four minutes, leaning over the lectern most of the time and only occasionally venturing in front of the jury box. He told the jurors that the bedrock of the prosecution's case, the medical opinions of Drs. Janice Ophoven and Michael Baden, had been undermined by the testimony of Dr. Dorothy Kelly. Multiple SIDS deaths did occur in families, he said, and Kelly had seen it happen.

The name of Waneta's other key medical expert was noticeably absent from Miller's summation. In the end, the testimony of Dr. Alfred Steinschneider proved useless to the woman whose children helped launch his career as a SIDS researcher.

As he started to wrap up his summation, Miller came to the sticking point that Waneta's decision had created. He had to try to convince the jury she was completely innocent, despite her vivid description of smothering her children. Miller fell back on the trial lawyer's maxim: If the facts support your case, but not the law, stick to the facts; if the law supports your case, but not the facts, stick to the law; but if neither the facts nor the law supports your case, try to confuse the jury. Miller decided to try a little diversion, hoping the jury was ignorant of criminal law.

"I submit to you that by any reading of this, these statements, or the transcribed statement, that the elements of murder in the second degree are not present, even in their version of what she said," Miller said.

Then the payoff: "She may be guilty of something, but not that."

The statement puzzled the prosecution. How could a

defense lawyer say his client might be guilty of anything in a case like this? But Miller was hoping the jurors would think that if they found Waneta innocent of murder, she could be tried later on other charges. He was counting on the likelihood the jurors didn't know that prosecutors can't try a defendant again after an acquittal.

With that out of the way, Miller worked himself up to a big finish.

"Whenever society begins to fall apart, or when a totalitarian system starts to take over, the first thing that happens is that they start to adjust the court system," he said. "You are the only people between the incredible power of the government and the common person who is charged with a crime."

Simpson represented the power of the government. For a year, he had quietly worked in the shadow of Bill Fitzpatrick. He never made an appearance on *Eye to Eye with Connie Chung*. He wasn't profiled in big-city newspapers. In most national stories about the Hoyt case, Simpson's name wasn't even mentioned. That's how he preferred it. Simpson just wanted to do his job, with time to play a little hockey on the side. He saw the prosecution of Waneta Hoyt as just another part of the job. He hadn't asked for the high-profile case, but he'd taken it. He'd made the decision to confront Waneta, to charge her with murder, to bring her to trial. He'd picked the jury and marshaled the evidence, and now he planned to finish the job.

With a yellow legal pad on the lectern to guide him, Simpson took the jury through the deaths of the Hoyt children by recounting how many days each child had lived. He pointed out that Molly had been in the hospital for fifty-four of the seventy-nine days she lived. Noah lived eighty-one days, all but three of them in the hospital. Simpson ticked off the dates when Molly and Noah were sent home, and the times they had to be resuscitated, always by Waneta. Tim was never there to witness any of his kids suffering a breathing problem.

Simpson paced before the jury, occasionally halting his unconscious swagger to make a point. Unlike Miller, Simpson referred to Steinschneider, contrasting his testimony with what the jurors heard from former nurses at Upstate Medical Center, who had seen nothing wrong with Molly and Noah.

"We brought three nurses down from Syracuse, and we did that for a reason," he said. "We did it, obviously, so that you would have a chance to listen to people who have no ax to grind in this case, who have no reason to fabricate, who have no reason to make up a story, who don't have a research project that they conducted in connection with it, who have no reason to justify a prior finding. Just four honest, hardworking women to testify what kind of children these were."

Simpson was so confident in the testimony of his medical experts that he implied that it was all the jury needed to convict Waneta of murder.

"Forget about the confession," he said. "There is something wrong here. You can take some of these things away, and you wouldn't be suspicious. If the children had these life-threatening problems in the hospital, we wouldn't be here today. If there were other people in the neighborhood who had seen these problems, we wouldn't be here today. If we had some sickness we could see for these children, if we had some hospital record that showed them as other than normal, healthy children, we wouldn't be here today. But the coincidences mount and mount and mount in this case, so we don't have coincidences anymore."

Simpson then brought the jurors to the confession. He read large portions of Waneta's signed statement and excerpts from the transcript of the second interview. He ridiculed Waneta's claim that she had been in such a state of shock that she blocked out the interview taken down by the stenographer.

"Nobody who's a zombie, as she described herself, who's in the mental state she's in when that second statement was taken, could ever, ever recall those things," Simpson said. "It's absolutely, humanly not possible."

Simpson's flat voice became impassioned while Waneta sat across the courtroom weeping. The DA inhaled deeply, as if preparing to breathe life into her victims.

"These kids didn't ask to be brought into this world," he said. "Mrs. Hoyt made a conscious decision to have five children. When she made that decision, she had an obligation to protect these children. She had an obligation to keep them safe. She had an obligation to listen to their crying. She had an obligation to put up with all the things that parents have to put up with.

"Five young people aren't here today because of her. Today they would have ranged in age, I think, from twenty-four to thirty-one, if they were still alive. They would have had families. They would do all the things that you and I have enjoyed doing during the course of our lives. They don't get that opportunity. And they don't get that opportunity because their mother couldn't stand their crying. That's not a good enough reason. Kids cry."

Simpson drew on Ophoven's description of a suffocating infant. It takes two minutes of smothering to render a child unconscious, he said, another two minutes to kill. He reminded the jurors how two-and-a-half-year-old Jimmy Hoyt flailed his arms and legs as Waneta pressed the bath towel into his face. That was clear evidence that Waneta's intent was nothing short of death for her baby, Simpson said.

Then Simpson held up the picture of Jimmy dressed in his cowboy shirt. "We didn't introduce a lot of pictures in this trial, but we did introduce one," he said. His voice cracked.

Waneta's crying intensified. "Why is he doing this?" she asked, repeating the question she'd asked when Simpson introduced the picture as evidence.

"This is a boy, Jimmy, who struggled for his life, and two and a half minutes of agony that boy had to undergo before he died at two and a half years of age," Simpson said. "And this woman should pay for that because she intended to kill him, and that's all she ever intended to do. Whatever her motive, whatever was bothering her, that could have only been her intent, to kill that youngster."

Simpson had picked up on Miller's "power of government" phrase. He'd heard defense lawyers use it in summations before. This time, he was prepared to turn it against Waneta Hoyt.

"The incredible power of the government is nothing compared to the incredible power Mrs. Hoyt had over five children. Now, Mrs. Hoyt has a defense. She has defense lawyers. She has to have us prove she has done something wrong. Well, Eric, Julie, Jimmy, Molly, Noah—they didn't have that. They didn't have anybody to defend them. You talk about power—the power of the pillow, the power of the towel, the power of the shoulder. That's incredible power. And she killed her kids and she should be convicted of murder."

By the time Simpson finished, Tim and Waneta had their heads pressed together. Waneta was sobbing, and Tim was telling her, as he had throughout the trial, that everything would be all right.

The prosecutor's summation affected Urbanski and Miller, too. They said it was not only the best closing argument they'd ever seen Simpson make, but the best they'd ever seen by a prosecutor. They'd never seen Simpson that emotional, that prepared, that convincing.

"I damn near cried," Urbanski said.

As the jurors headed out of the courtroom, a few of

them wiped away tears. They would return the next morning, and for the first time they would talk to each other about what they'd seen and heard over the past four weeks, and they would decide what to do about it.

Chapter Twenty-six

Waneta Hoyt's jurors sat silently around a T-shaped table Thursday morning, April 20, and stared at each other. For four weeks, Judge Vincent Sgueglia had warned the six men and six women not to talk about the murder trial that had consumed most of their waking hours. He had told them not to discuss the case with anyone; not among themselves, not with their spouses. He had ordered them not to read about the trial in the newspapers, or listen to accounts on TV or radio.

But in the last hour, Sgueglia had given the jurors a new set of instructions. He read aloud the ten murder charges against Waneta Hoyt—one count of intentional murder and one count of depraved murder for the death of each of her five children. The judge explained the elements of the two crimes, the difference between intent and recklessness, and he instructed the jurors on the meaning of reasonable doubt. He told them to take the law as he had explained it, apply it to the evidence they'd heard in court, and decide whether Waneta Hoyt was guilty of each of the charges. Then he sent them off to deliberate in the jury room, which was tucked into one of the towers that anchored the corners of the Tioga County Courthouse. Once the door was closed, the jurors took a moment to catch their breath.

"OK," one of them said, "now we can talk."

The jurors started out a little insecure, a little uncertain about how to deal with everything that had hap-

pened in court. They'd sat through the lawyers'
opening and closing statements. In between, they'd listened to the testimony of thirty-three witnesses—nine
of them doctors. Some of what they heard had moved
them to tears. They'd also seen witnesses become emotional, most noticeably Senior Investigator Bob Courtright, nurse's aide Gail Pfeiffer, and Waneta Hoyt. But
Sgueglia had cautioned them about that, too. The jurors should not let sympathy for either side affect their
decision, he said.

Shawn Conway, the thirty-six-year-old jury foreman,
asked if anybody in the room had any doubt that
Waneta was guilty. More than half the jurors raised
their hands. One who didn't was William Morgan, the
seventy-one-year-old retired IBM worker who had
started out as an alternate juror. The defense had seen
his shift to the final jury as a good omen; Waneta's
psychic, Phil Jordan, thought he was sympathetic. But
Morgan had made up his mind early that Waneta was
guilty.

Those with doubts shared a common concern—
Waneta's confession. Some were bothered by the way
the state police had obtained her statements. The group
believed the medical evidence alone wasn't strong
enough to convict her, so they decided to tear into the
confession and get back to the corroboration later. Less
than an hour after they started deliberating, the jurors
asked to have the testimony of Trooper Bubba Bleck
and Investigator Sue Mulvey read back in court. The
court reporter started digging out the testimony while
the jurors lunched on sandwiches and continued to
talk.

Lynne Rocha, Juror No. 5, was one of four jurors
troubled by the state police interviews. Rocha, a fifty-
one-year-old waitress and mother of four, suspected
the police might have tricked Waneta into confessing
by telling her she'd simply be taking part in a SIDS research project. Rocha didn't like the idea that Bleck,

someone Waneta knew, was brought along to make her feel safe. Other jurors wondered whether the police had put the words of the confession in Waneta's mouth. They questioned why the police didn't video-tape the confession through the one-way mirror.

But the jurors disagreed with psychologist Charles Ewing's opinion that Waneta had not been truthful when she made the statements. Ewing might have had more influence on the jury if he had stopped after saying he believed the police had manipulated Waneta. The jurors thought he crossed the line from detached expert to advocate when he offered his opinion on the validity of her statements.

"He was just reaching too far," Rocha said.

The blunder the defense thought District Attorney Bob Simpson made in his cross-examination of Ewing turned out not to be a mistake after all.

Waneta's testimony didn't carry much weight either. The jurors thought her inability to recall the steno-graphic statement defied common sense. They thought Waneta sounded disingenuous when she told the court how shocked she was by the investigators' suspicions. And her emotions didn't ring true when she talked about her children's deaths. The only time Waneta's tears seemed real to the jury was when she cried about her mother's death.

Sgueglia brought the jurors back into the courtroom after lunch, and the court reporter read Bleck's and Mulvey's testimony to them. Rocha listened hard and caught something she had missed when Bleck was on the witness stand, describing how Waneta had agreed to accompany them to the state police barracks.

"Mrs. Hoyt said that would be fine," Bleck had testified. "But she was a little nervous. She grabbed my hand and she said, as long as I could go with them."

Four words clinched it for Rocha: "She grabbed my hand." Now it was clear. At the moment the state police asked Waneta to accompany them to the Owego barracks to talk about her children's deaths, she had reached out to a trusted figure for support. Rocha didn't believe Waneta would have grabbed Bleck's hand if she thought she was going to the barracks to talk about a research project.

"I don't think she was a touchy-feely person," said Rocha. "She knew something was up, even if it was in the back of her head. She knew that something wasn't quite what they were saying, otherwise she wouldn't have grabbed his hand."

After watching Waneta Hoyt in court for four weeks and listening to her testify for three hours, Rocha felt she knew the defendant. By constantly holding her husband's hand in court, Waneta had offered a glimpse of the desperation behind her gesture toward Bleck.

Just before three p.m., the jurors asked to have Waneta's two statements sent into the jury room. Courtright's emotion-choked reading lingered over the printed pages.

"This was hard for him, too," Rocha said. "It was evidence that he really did believe she did it, and deserved to be on trial."

The jurors passed the statements around the table, reading silently until one or another of them raised a point for discussion. Waneta's description of smothering Jimmy with a towel made them pause. The jurors noticed he'd died just three weeks after his younger sister, Julie. Some of the jurors who were convinced of Waneta's guilt wondered aloud why Tim Hoyt hadn't seen the obvious. Even now, Tim didn't seem to believe that his wife had killed their children. Rocha thought she understood why.

"He just can't say it did happen, no matter what the evidence, because he lived with her," she said. "He couldn't live with knowing he was that blind."

The jurors read the statements periodically over three or four hours. Rocha made her argument about the significance of Waneta's grabbing Bleck's hand.

The other jurors agreed that the state police had legally obtained the statements and that Waneta was telling the truth when she described smothering her kids.

With the confession behind them, the jurors moved on to the corroboration. They needed to decide whether the prosecution had offered enough medical evidence to back up Waneta's confession. They asked to see the children's death certificates and the findings of the original autopsies of Jimmy, Molly, and Noah.

At eight-thirty p.m., Sgueglia called the jurors into court to ask if they thought they would finish that night.

"I don't think we're that close to a verdict," Morgan said. The jurors had been talking for nearly nine hours and had barely touched on the medical evidence.

Sgueglia ordered the jurors sequestered. They were put up at the Treadway Inn, where they were barred from watching television or reading newspapers. The Hoyt case had returned to the place where Drs. Janice Ophoven and Michael Baden had convinced Simpson that he was looking at homicides. One year later, under the same roof, a dozen people were turning over the same evidence in their minds.

For Waneta Hoyt, the weight of the deliberations had eased as the day wore on. Her eyes started tearing during Sgueglia's instructions to the jury. "I didn't do that," she whispered to Tim each time Sgueglia read a charge. By the time Sgueglia was done shortly after eleven a.m., Waneta was sobbing.

After the jury went out, Tim and Waneta joined family and friends in a glass-walled room that opened onto one of the courtroom balconies. They passed some of the time holding hands around a table and reading from a Bible. Waneta's supporters had a prayer for the jurors: "Grant them the wisdom of making the right decision."

Waneta's outlook brightened the longer the jury stayed out. She wandered downstairs and strolled through the courtroom, her hands clasped casually behind her back. During the evening, while the jurors were dissecting her confession, Waneta made small talk with a sheriff's deputy.

"Hey, John, do you have a rope?" she asked Deputy John Colella. He looked at her with a puzzled expression.

"You know," she said, "a rope, to skip rope." Waneta smiled at her joke.

Simpson and Courtright passed the time in an office near the courtroom, with Assistant District Attorney Peggy Drake and Bill Fitzpatrick, who refused to let a bout with the flu keep him away from the final episode of the case that he had pursued for nine years. The cops and prosecutors poked fun at each other to cut the tension.

"You and Waneta go to the same hairstylist?" Simpson asked Courtright, who never let a strand of his white mane get out of place.

Bob Miller chain-smoked Winstons as he waited with Annette Gorski, his paralegal, in the defense lawyers' conference room. Ray Urbanski, the other half of Waneta's defense team, had reluctantly abandoned Miller to travel to an out-of-state wedding. He made stops along the way to check in with Miller. As Thursday afternoon turned into Thursday night, and the jury continued deliberating, Urbanski's optimism grew.

Sgueglia held court with candy bars. After dismissing the jury for the night, Sgueglia retrieved a bag of miniature Snickers bars from his chambers and tossed them into the gallery from his elevated bench. Fitzpatrick smiled as the reporters and spectators around him reached for the candy.

"Hey, what about them?" someone called, and Sgueglia turned his aim to what had become the Hoyts' side of the courtroom. Waneta smiled as the candy sailed over the defense table and into the hands of her relatives. One Hoyt wasn't amused: Jay stomped out of the courtroom.

Sgueglia realized that his playful gesture, which he'd intended for reporters, had gone too far. He hadn't seen Jay sitting in the front row. He'd even forgotten that Waneta was still in the courtroom. The next morning he apologized to them both.

By Friday morning, the jury had settled into two camps. Nine jurors believed Waneta was responsible for her children's deaths; three weren't convinced she was guilty, including Lynne Rocha, who had concerns about the medical corroboration. But there was no sharp division in the group. The jurors simply picked up where they'd left off with the medical evidence.

Dr. Alfred Steinschneider's testimony didn't impress any of them. He'd come across as self-serving. Some believed he had an interest in covering up his mistakes and was apparently hoping that Waneta would be acquitted so he wouldn't look bad.

The jurors found the testimony of the nurses from Upstate Medical Center more persuasive. It showed that Molly and Noah Hoyt were healthy, not suffering from the abnormalities Steinschneider had described in his paper.

Dr. Dorothy Kelly had raised doubts in some jurors' minds about whether the Hoyt children were completely healthy before they died. She had pointed out notes in the medical records about the children vomiting and said that the vomiting suggested they might have suffered from a disorder of the central nervous system. Kelly's opinion was canceled by the rebuttal testimony of Dr. John Brooks, who said it's perfectly normal for infants to vomit.

Ophoven's testimony proved decisive. Aside from the confession, the jurors saw no stronger evidence pointing to murder than Ophoven's insistence that five children in one family could not die as Waneta said they had.

"That woman would have staked her life on it," said Rocha.

For Rocha, the horror of what happened in the Hoyt family had hit home when Simpson handed Ophoven each child's birth certificate and death certificate. The DA's slow refrain underscored the point: "Eric's birth certificate, Eric's death certificate. Julie's birth certificate, Julie's death certificate . . ."

"It made them come really alive for me," Rocha said. "One after the other, alive and then dead, alive and then dead."

The insights that Ophoven brought to the case as a pediatric forensic pathologist won over Rocha and the two other wavering jurors. The twelve jurors believed, beyond a reasonable doubt, that Waneta Hoyt was guilty of murder. But they still weren't sure which crime she'd committed. They had to choose between intentional murder and reckless murder. The decision would have no practical effect; both crimes carried the same penalty. But the final verdict would say a lot about what the jurors thought of Waneta Hoyt.

For Waneta's sake, the jurors didn't want to draw out the deliberations. But they also wanted to make sure they had understood Sgueglia's instructions on the law. At eleven a.m., the jury sent the judge a note asking him to recite the definitions of the two murder charges again.

Bob Miller saw the implications: If the jurors were seeking clarification on the two murder statutes, they weren't thinking about an acquittal. Miller tried to prepare Waneta and Tim and their supporters.

"It doesn't look very good," Miller said. "That kind of question is not the kind of question that we would want them to ask."

Earlier that morning, Waneta had called a friend to say she couldn't be found guilty. "I didn't do it," she said. "God can't let this happen to me." Now she cried.

Miller had resigned himself to the inevitable. He encountered Simpson in the hallway.

"You know, your buddy's in there," Simpson said, motioning to the office where the prosecution team was waiting out the deliberations. Miller knew who it was that Simpson meant. The public defender marched into the office and introduced himself to his antagonist.

"Mr. Fitzpatrick, I'm Bob Miller. I just wanted to tell you, you've got one hell of an imagination. You had a good hunch. At least you made us earn our salaries for the last year around here."

The two men shook hands.

"You did a hell of a job," Fitzpatrick said. The fact that the jury had been out for so many hours spoke for the quality of Waneta's defense, he told Miller.

After Sgueglia repeated his instructions on the law, the jurors returned to their room and tried to sort out which crime Waneta had committed when she smothered her children. She had told the police she only meant to stop the children from crying. Jail deputies heard her say the same thing right after her arrest. Waneta had said nothing to show she intended to murder her children.

"Well, wait a minute," Rocha said. She thought of Jimmy, the only Hoyt child old enough to resist his mother. Didn't Waneta show intent when she smothered him? Rocha asked the other jurors to recall Ophoven's testimony:

"She said it takes two minutes to kill a child."

Rocha didn't think her point was getting across, but she had an idea. Rocha had carried a small couch pillow to court each day to ease the strain of sitting for hours in the jury box. She had taken the pillow into the jury room. Now she walked over to Conway, the foreman, and held the pillow up so it just touched his face.

"Start timing me," she said.

The jurors fell silent as the seconds ticked by.

"See?" she asked. "Do you see what I mean? She's

thinking now. She's holding this baby down while this baby is struggling, trying to get out. This child is wiggling. This is more than just holding a baby to your chest and maybe not even thinking you're killing the baby, or putting a pillow over a baby's head and walking out of the room. This was much more than that."

The terror of the demonstration got to Rocha after a minute—half the time Ophoven said it took to render a baby unconscious. Rocha had made her point. She removed the pillow from Conway's face and returned to her seat.

Another juror suggested that Waneta decided to kill Jimmy because the boy had seen his mother murder Julie three weeks earlier. But that argument, along with Rocha's demonstration, failed. Other jurors pointed out that in Waneta's confession, she said she only wanted to stop Jimmy's crying. Rocha gave in. All the children, the jury decided, died because their mother acted recklessly, not intentionally.

Conway asked for a vote shortly before noon. It was the first formal vote since the jurors had started deliberations more than twenty-four hours earlier. The vote was unanimous, as the law required. Rocha burst into tears, followed by half a dozen other jurors. One of them, Melvin Schrader, a forty-four-year-old quality assurance worker at Loral Federal Systems Inc., had been one of the jurors who'd needed convincing, along with Rocha. He walked over, put his arm around her, and said, "It's OK. It's OK."

The jurors took a few minutes to compose themselves. Rocha sent out a note asking to have one more item sent to the jury room: a box of tissues. She then wrote a note to Sgueglia, asking him to let the jurors leave the courtroom first, with an escort who would take them to their cars. They were too upset to talk to reporters.

At twelve-fifteen P.M., Conway wrote the jury's last note to the judge: "We have reached a verdict."

Deputies quietly passed the word to the lawyers so that the principals in the case could get seated before everybody else rushed into court. Tim and Waneta returned to the defense table with Miller and Annette Gorski.

"Do you think we're going to be OK?" Waneta asked the paralegal. Gorski nodded. She knew better, but she'd grown too close to Waneta in the last year to force the defendant to face the harsher reality.

"Is it OK if Jay sits there?" Waneta asked Miller, indicating the chair beside her. Her lawyer said it was no problem. Waneta would face her fate as she sat between her two men. Miller reached across to Jay, took his hand, and gave him a piece of advice.

"You need to be strong for your mother," the lawyer whispered.

Once the news of the impending verdict spread through the courthouse, reporters, photographers, and spectators swarmed back to the courtroom. Sgueglia told the crowd the jurors didn't want anyone to approach them after the verdict. As of that moment, he said, everyone would remain seated until the jurors had delivered their verdict and left the courtroom.

"I also want to caution everyone here that there is to be no outbreaks—in either event," he said. "I obviously don't know what the verdict is. But I ask you please, to the best of your ability, control your emotions."

Tim and Waneta clasped hands. Jay sat erect, his hair matted by the auto-racing cap he'd just removed. Miller and Gorski sat with their eyes closed and their hands folded in front of their faces, as if in prayer. Simpson and Drake sat stone-faced, their hands folded on the table in front of them.

After a nod from the judge, a court attendant knocked three times on the jury room door, then opened it. All six women were in tears when they took their seats in the jury box. Conway rose with the ten-page verdict sheet trembling in his hands.

"In this case of the people versus Waneta Hoyt, indictment number 94-41, what's your verdict concerning the first count of the indictment, murder in the second degree?" the court clerk asked. It was the intentional-murder charge for Eric's death.

"Not guilty," Conway said.

The words seemed to jolt Jay Hoyt to life. His eyes opened wide, he took a quick breath, smiled, and turned to his mother. He looked for recognition in her face that it was over, that they'd won. But Waneta knew. She looked her son in the eye, as if to say, "Wait. There's more."

The clerk asked Conway for the verdict on the second count, reckless murder.

"Guilty."

Jay winced, lowered his head and cried. Waneta simply shook her head. The head-shaking intensified as Conway read the remaining verdicts. They were the same for all the Hoyt children: Waneta was not guilty of intentional murder, but she was guilty of such depraved indifference to human life that she recklessly caused her children's deaths when she smothered their cries.

"Why are they doing this to me?" she asked. "I didn't kill my babies. I just tried to get help for them."

She cried lightly at first, then sobbed so hard her chest shook. Tim cradled his wife in one arm and reached out to comfort Jay with his other hand. He didn't cry. Later, Tim told his brothers he regretted not shedding tears for Waneta, but he felt from the beginning he had to remain strong for his family.

"I'm the guy she's leaning on," Tim would say. "I've got to keep my composure and I've got to go home to my son and tell him that everything's OK and to keep the faith. There's a lot of times I'd just like to break down and cry, but I can't do it."

Tears flowed in the gallery behind Waneta. Her niece, Penny Hoyt, collapsed into the lap of Tim's sister Ann Schultheis.

As the clerk finished polling the jurors to confirm each verdict, Sgueglia saw how painful the decision had been for them.

"Many of you are crying," the judge said. "That's an indication of how difficult—" His voice cracked, his eyes brimmed with tears, and more jurors started weeping. The judge managed to get out a few words of praise for their hard work.

"There's no expression that I can make to you of the thanks this court feels for what you've done. So I'm just going to say, thank you." As the jurors gathered their belongings, the rest of the courtroom seemed in a state of suspended animation—except for Senior Investigator Bob Courtright.

The Lama had ignored Sgueglia's order and left the courtroom balcony as soon as he heard the first guilty verdict. That was all he needed to know. He put in a call to the state police barracks outside Binghamton, where Sue Mulvey worked. She was out investigating another case, and Courtright asked the troopers to send her a radio message about the verdict.

Courtright took grim satisfaction from the outcome. He had started with Fitzpatrick's hunch, no documents, no witnesses, no weapons, and five young victims, and he had solved a serial murder case that had been hidden for three decades. The meticulous investigation by the Hoyt task force left a blueprint for police officers confronting similar cases. But Courtright saw no reason to celebrate.

"You've got five dead kids," he said. "You've got Jay, whose life is in bad shape because of this. You got the husband; his life is turned upside-down. You got a forty-eight-year-old-woman in jail, prison for the rest of her life. Kind of depressing when you think about it."

At the first guilty verdict, Bob Simpson discreetly reached over and squeezed Peggy Drake's upper arm. It was his way of saying "thanks" to the assistant prosecutor who had helped him do his job.

For Bob Miller, the verdict carried a bitter twist. By acquitting Waneta of intentional murder and convicting her of reckless murder, the jurors had headed in the direction he and Urbanski had thought they would. A manslaughter conviction would have looked good to this jury, Miller thought; or maybe criminally negligent homicide, an even less serious crime. He was right. Three of the jurors said afterward they probably would have convicted Waneta of a lesser charge. The jurors had talked about how living with the knowledge of what she had done to her children seemed to have turned Waneta into a woman who looked old beyond her years.

With the jurors gone, the Tioga County Courthouse became the scene of countless little dramas. Sgueglia called Deputy John Gregrow, Waneta's cousin, to the bench. The judge wanted Waneta removed from the courtroom immediately so that her family wouldn't crowd around and make it difficult for deputies to take her away. At the deputies' command, Waneta and Tim rose to go to the judge's chambers. Waneta called for Jay to follow them.

In chambers, the deputies put Waneta in handcuffs. "Why are they doing this to me?" she screamed. "I didn't kill my babies!" The deputies brought Waneta outside for the short walk across the street to the Tioga County Jail. Jay, still red-eyed from crying, charged at one of the television photographers waiting to capture the "perp walk."

"Jay, don't, please!" Waneta called. "Jay, come on. I love you, son. Don't do that. Walk with me, please."

Jay obeyed. He walked protectively in front of his mother, the same way he'd led the phalanx of Hoyt men that escorted Waneta to court the first day of her trial.

Reporters cornered the lawyers in and around the courthouse. Bob Miller faced a clutch of reporters near the courthouse steps. It was a difficult case, he said, an American tragedy.

On the sidewalk outside his office, Simpson said he hoped the verdict would open the door for the prosecution of similar cases.

"It's a landmark case. Anybody in any jurisdiction in this country who has multiple deaths, unexplained deaths at this time, can take a look at them and they've probably got a homicide in there somewhere. I'm very happy with Bill Fitzpatrick for bringing this to light. It's because of him, and him alone, that justice has been done."

Fitzpatrick, still battling the flu, had sat impassively in the gallery and let the verdict sink in. He watched the outpouring of tears around the courtroom, and he thought about the five children who were murdered because they cried.

A few minutes later, he said, "I hope some of the tears that were shed today were shed for Molly and Noah, Julie, James, and Eric, not just Waneta Hoyt."

Epilogue

Three weeks after the trial, Waneta Hoyt turned forty-nine. She spent the day at the Tioga County jail, the first of many birthdays she could expect to spend behind bars. Judge Vincent Sgueglia would decide just how many on June 23, when he was scheduled to sentence .her.

State law gave Sgueglia little leeway for compassion; he was required to sentence Waneta to prison. He had two issues to decide: first, how much time she should serve for each of the five murders; then, whether she should serve the terms all at once—concurrent sentences—or one after the other—consecutive sentences.

He could sentence Waneta to a term ranging from fifteen years to life to a maximum of twenty-five years to life for each conviction. If he gave her the minimum and made the sentences concurrent, Waneta would be eligible for parole in 2010, when she would be sixty-three. Concurrent sentences of twenty-five years to life would keep Waneta in prison until she was seventy-four. Consecutive sentences would ensure that she died there.

Keenly aware that her fate rested in Sgueglia's hands, Waneta wrote a rambling four-page letter to the judge on May 5.

"I don't know why you [as a judge] as respected as you are, allowed this whole case to happen. I had no more of an idea what was happening to me than the man in the moon," she said. "We had bad representation from the beginning. A lawyer not well, no money. Is that why I was railroaded?"

Waneta pleaded with Sgueglia to meet with her. She promised to tell him the whole truth. The judge passed the letter on to her lawyers. Responding to Waneta directly would have been an ethical violation for Sgueglia: if he allowed her to bypass her attorneys, she might inadvertently jeopardize her rights.

On June 1, Waneta wrote to the judge a second time, rearguing her case in six tightly scrawled pages. She complained again about her representation by Bob Miller and Ray Urbanski and begged the judge not to send her to prison. She asked Sgueglia to hear her out in person and again got no response.

Three weeks before she was to be sentenced, Waneta wrote a third letter to Sgueglia. This time the judge had to respond: She wanted to fire Miller and Urbanski.

"I regret to say that these two gentlemen misrepresented me in my trial," Waneta wrote. She said Miller was a good man, but he had been in such agony from his eye ailment that he could not concentrate on her trial. More witnesses could have spoken up in her defense, but they had not been called to testify, she said.

Sgueglia took up the matter on the morning Waneta was to be sentenced. Although he said he could find nothing wrong with the job that Miller and Urbanski had done, he allowed Waneta to retain a new lawyer. He delayed sentencing for ten weeks to give the new lawyer time to review the case, file motions to set aside the conviction, and start Waneta's appeal to a higher court. He also told Waneta and Tim that since they had given up the services of the public defender, they would have to pay the new lawyer themselves.

The Hoyts had picked William Sullivan, Jr., a former prosecutor from Ithaca who had gained a reputation as a hard-nosed defense lawyer. He had made headlines representing a woman who was convicted as an accomplice in the slaying of a family of four near Ithaca in 1989. The woman's son, who had been a suspect in the murders, had been shot to death when the state police raided his home. The woman was freed from prison after the state police admitted she had been framed with fabricated fingerprints. The case exposed an evidence-tampering scandal that sent five state police investigators to prison and resulted in the dismissal of another.

With that experience, Sullivan began looking at the state police investigation of Waneta. He targeted Senior Investigator Bob Courtright, who abruptly announced his retirement in August.

Once again Tim threw himself into Waneta's defense. He performed legwork for Sullivan and tried to figure out how to pay the legal fees.

Tim had found a job at a sawmill in the valley that paid him about $140 a week, but otherwise the Hoyts' financial picture remained bleak. The family was a year behind on their rent, and Tim was driving a 1979 Ford Thunderbird that had been given to him with 200,000 miles on it. Waneta had stopped receiving Social Security disability checks when she was convicted, and her daily collect phone calls from jail ran the family's monthly phone bill up to $70.

"I've got only one thing in mind: I want my wife the hell out of jail 'cause she didn't do anything," Tim said.

He started a fund drive with the help of the Reverend James Willard and the First Congregational Church of Berkshire. They put up posters around the county and in a handful of states to raise money. The poster, which showed a picture of a young Waneta with a full head of thick black hair, contained a dismaying thought for any parent who had lost more than one child.

"The full consequences of this conviction are yet to be realized," the poster said. "It will act as a springboard to the 'righteous prosecution' of any woman who ever suffered more than one unexplained child death."

But after its first three months, the Hoyt Legal Defense Fund totaled less than $1,000. Waneta was not getting the support she had hoped for from her friends and neighbors and from SIDS groups.

It wasn't for lack of trying. Even as she was writing to Sgueglia, she was pleading her case in letters she sent to national television talk shows and network news programs. Although the jail's longstanding ban on cameras prevented Waneta from giving televised interviews, she managed to get the word out about her case. She conducted mini-news conferences during visiting hours at the jail, holding court with reporters from local TV stations and newspapers from regional newspapers, and the *New York Times*. Waneta attacked the state police, prosecutors, the media, her lawyers, and SIDS groups. She said she wanted the world to see who she really was.

"I'm not the cold, vulgar person that people say I am," she said during one session with reporters. Tim, as usual, held her hand as she spoke. "We've been together for thirty-one years. If anything happened, he certainly would know, wouldn't he?"

When she couldn't get attention from reporters, she turned to the other women prisoners.

"The first month she was in here, all she ever said was that she was innocent. I started to believe her, thinking she was just a victim of Tioga County's district attorney," said Tammy Karpinski, another prisoner.

But Karpinski and the other women on the cell block started to see another side to Waneta. They noticed how Waneta sat on her bed and kept a wary eye on the other prisoners. She accused new arrivals of being FBI agents sent in to trap her, Karpinski said.

"She thinks everybody is talking about her and plotting against her. If she's not the center of attention she starts holding her heart, saying she's having a heart attack," Karpinski said.

One day Waneta clutched her chest and collapsed. She was taken in an ambulance to the hospital but returned to her cell later that day. Tim complained that she wasn't getting all of her medication for high blood pressure. She made two other brief trips to the hospital after collapsing.

"The scariest night with her was when she started pulling her own hair and screaming that the TV was too loud," Karpinski said. "It's like she just snapped! In her confession she said she killed her kids 'cause they wouldn't stop crying and that she couldn't stand the noise. Just like the TV, and it scared us all. I no longer think she's innocent."

Waneta also was wearing thin on some of her family. George Hoyt didn't like the way Waneta had treated his daughter Penny, the teenager who had helped research articles on SIDS in preparation for the trial and who had fainted when she heard the guilty verdict. Penny later visited her aunt in jail and became upset when Waneta made her feel guilty for not doing enough to help, George said. He told his daughter not to visit Waneta again.

Waneta also lashed out at Dr. Alfred Steinschneider. She said she did not know until after her arrest how far Steinschneider had risen since their contact in 1971 at Upstate Medical Center. Nor did she know that Molly and Noah had been part of the famous paper in *Pediatrics* that launched Steinschneider's career as one of the nation's top SIDS researchers. Since the trial she had grown to resent his success.

"He's gotten rich and famous because of it. And look at me," Waneta complained.

At the American SIDS Institute in Atlanta, Steinschneider tried to put Waneta and the trial behind him. As far as he was concerned, the trial had added nothing to the understanding of SIDS. The jury had decided a legal issue, not a medical issue, he said. Even if Waneta had smothered her children, he argued, the breathing abnormalities he had found might eventually have caused their deaths.

The legal judgment on Waneta Hoyt left no room for interpretation: Her crimes were sins of commission; her motive, the jury had decided, was depraved indifference to whether her children lived or died. When Waneta walked into Sgueglia's courtroom for sentencing on the morning of September 11, she seemed to sense that the penalty would be equally harsh. She clutched the Bible that she had kept in her purse throughout the trial. Tim took his place beside her at the defense table.

Before Sgueglia could pass sentence, he had to dispense with the motions for a new trial that had been filed by Waneta's new lawyer. After attacking her former attorneys, Sullivan proceeded to attack Bob Courtright's credibility as the lead investigator. Courtright had said that he was leaving the state police because he simply thought it was time to go. He was approaching his fifty-fifth birthday, which would make him eligible for retirement. But Sullivan said Courtright had quit in August after admitting to internal affairs investigators that he had threatened to kill a man in an off-duty dispute.

District Attorney Bob Simpson sat stone-faced as Sullivan ticked off the accusations. But when it came time for him to respond, Simpson could barely contain his anger. His fists were clenched and he scowled as he spoke.

"In defense of an investigator who I don't think needs much defense, these allegations are disgraceful," Simpson said. "It's a disgrace to a good investigator, and there's not one item of evidence that is anything but hearsay. Mr. Sullivan's conduct in court today, with the television cameras here, is inexcusable."

Sullivan's unsubstantiated allegations had nothing to do with the Hoyt investigation, Simpson said. But Sullivan argued that because Courtright's credibility was now in question, Waneta deserved a new trial. Sgueglia denied that request and others Sullivan made in a desperate attempt to have Waneta set free.

"She will die in jail," Sullivan said. "And probably the prosecutors will stand up and cheer at that point."

Simpson countered by saying doctors had examined Waneta and found no illnesses.

The district attorney handed off the job of recommending a punishment for Waneta to his assistant, Peggy Drake. The presence of Drake, seven months pregnant with her second child, introduced a maternal image that stood in sharp contrast to Waneta's crimes.

"Eric, Julie, James, Molly, and Noah would've been young adults today had they survived, had they been permitted by their mother to survive," Drake told the judge. "What they would've done with their lives, what they would've contributed to society, we don't know. We don't know because their mother took their lives. Their mother should've protected them, their mother should've cared for them, their mother should've nurtured them . . . Instead, she took their lives because they were crying, and she could not stand their crying."

Drake asked Sgueglia to put Waneta away for good. She asked for the maximum—five consecutive sentences of twenty-five years to life.

When Waneta finally got her chance to talk to Sgueglia, she rose to her feet, hugging her Bible. The judge said he could not hear her and asked her to come closer.

"I don't mean no disrespect to no one," Waneta began, her voice beginning to break. "But I'm an innocent woman. I tried very hard to save my children. I did the best I could . . . Why this story has come out like this, I don't know. I loved all my kids, and I'll love them till the day I die. All I can say is, God forgive all of those who have done this to me. Justice will come before God."

Sgueglia showed no trace of the emotion that had overcome him when the jury announced its verdict. He looked at Waneta with his sad eyes and spoke in even tones.

"There is no amount of sentence that could bring those children back to life," he said. "There is nothing in our powers to do anything about it."

Sgueglia gave Waneta five minimum sentences of fifteen years to life. But he told her she would have to serve one sentence after the other: fifteen years for Eric, fifteen for James, fifteen for Julie, fifteen for Molly, and fifteen for Noah, a minimum of seventy-five years before she could be considered for parole.

In effect, it was a life sentence.

Waneta was destined for New York state's maximum-security prison for women, Bedford Hills Correctional Facility, about thirty miles north of New York City. There she would join Marybeth Tinning, who had another thirteen years to serve before she was eligible for parole.

Sgueglia told Waneta he had only one more thing to say. He asked her to consider her surviving son.

The judge saw Jay as Waneta's last victim. His unflagging loyalty to the only mother he had ever known had left him vulnerable to her manipulation, Sgueglia thought, and she was smothering him with a lie. Jay, seated directly behind his mother, turned red. His eyes welled with tears, and he buried his face in his hands.

The judge, his hands folded before him on the bench, leaned forward, looked into Waneta's eyes, and said:

"Whatever you tell anybody in this life—whatever you tell your husband, whatever you tell your lawyer, whatever you tell me, whatever you tell your God—you owe it to that boy to tell him the truth."

For Bill Fitzpatrick, the truth was self-evident: Waneta Hoyt had committed the most despicable crimes imaginable. But in a letter to the editor published in the Syracuse *Post-Standard*, Fitzpatrick also blamed Dr. Steinschneider and his apnea theory of SIDS.

"The self-serving arrogance of Steinschneider and his supporters in blindly maintaining allegiance to his thoroughly discredited theory is appalling. Wouldn't it be refreshing just once to hear him say, 'I made a mistake, and it is tragic that Molly and Noah are dead'?"

Fitzpatrick had grown alarmed about how readily foul play could be overlooked in cases of sudden infant death. In another one of the twists of fate that had guided his career, a brief appearance by Fitzpatrick in a television story about the Hoyt investigation had led to the discovery of an even older case of multiple infanticide.

A month before Waneta's trial, Fitzpatrick talked about the case on an NBC-TV news show. One of the people who saw the show was Leonard Hare, a twenty-eight-year-old service station-equipment repairman who lived in Weedsport, thirty miles west of Syracuse. The Hoyt children's deaths struck an eerie chord with Hare.

Hare had grown up in a troubled family. He and an older sister were placed in foster care when their parents' marriage broke up. They eventually lived with their father. When Hare was ten, an aunt told him that he had three brothers whom he'd never met. Two brothers were born before Hare and had died mysteriously when they were children in the 1960s. A younger brother had been put up for adoption as a baby.

When Hare got older, he started gathering evidence that showed that the two children who died had been abused by their mother, who later remarried. The first child, Thomas, had apparently choked to death on his own vomit in 1964. He was seven months old. The second child, William, was nearly three years old when he died in 1967. The cause of death was listed as crib death. But Hare knew from having children of his own that toddlers didn't succumb to SIDS. He called Fitzpatrick the day after seeing the TV report about the Hoyt case.

Fitzpatrick and Onondaga County medical examiner Dr. Sigmund Menchel arranged to have the bodies of the two boys exhumed from their graves near Syracuse. After reviewing the original autopsies and conducting his own examinations, Menchel concluded that the two deaths were homicides. The cause of Thomas's death was obvious: His skull was fractured.

Just six days before the Hoyt trial started, police investigators interviewed Hare's mother, Dorothy Mae King. The forty-eight-year-old grandmother admitted battering Thomas and choking William to death. She said she killed the children because she couldn't stand their crying. She was charged with murdering both boys, and Fitzpatrick said he would prosecute the case personally.

The fallout didn't stop there. Dr. Menchel, who had been appointed less than a year earlier, uncovered the suspicious death of an infant from a neighboring county that had been overlooked by the medical examiner's office years ago. The police investigation of that case was reopened. In August 1995, Menchel announced that he would review all of the deaths of children under age thirteen that the medical examiner's office had handled during the past thirty years.

The head of a local SIDS support group worried that Menchel's review would unnecessarily torment innocent parents who had grieved for years over the deaths of their babies.

"I think it's going to be disastrous," said Nessa Vercillo-DeGirolamo, coordinator of the Syracuse-area chapter of the SIDS Alliance. "It's necessary in one percent of the cases, and the other ninety-nine percent, it's a witch hunt."

The backlash showed that emotions still ran deep whenever the specter of murder overshadowed the discussion of sudden infant death. Today SIDs claims the lives of roughly six thousand babies each year in the United States. It remains the leading cause of death of children between one and twelve months of age. Try as they might, SIDS advocacy groups have been unable to erase the suspicion that SIDS conceals a disturbing number of infanticides. The suspicion endures because the very definition of SIDS—a sudden infant death unexpected by medical history and which remains unexplained after a thorough *postmortem* examination—does not rule out the possibility of homicidal smothering.

Nobody knows for sure just how many deaths attributed to SIDS are actually homicides. Some experts, such as Dr. Stuart Asch, the psychiatrist who questioned Steinschneider's 1972 study in an exchange of letters, believe as many as fifteen percent of all SIDS babies die as a result of being smothered by their mothers. Others, such as forensic pathologists Drs. Dominick and Vincent Di Maio, the father and son who concluded that Steinschneider's research described a case of serial infanticide, believe the percentage of smotherings classified as SIDS is far lower.

Recent studies estimate that anywhere from two to ten percent of SIDS deaths are actually homicides. That represents from 120 to 600 undetected homicides each year. These undetected infanticides are not just a concern for law enforcement officials. They lie at the heart of one of the most crucial issues in SIDS research: the question of whether SIDS runs in families.

A generation of research has ruled out a genetic link for SIDS. Statistical studies have shown consistently that the likelihood of SIDS recurring in a family is less than one percent. But some researchers see this as a significant rate of recurrence, and many doctors believe that subsequent siblings of SIDS victims have an increased risk of succumbing to the syndrome. This is why Dr. Steinschneider and others urge parents who have lost a child to SIDS to put their later babies on apnea monitors.

But as the cases of Stephen Van Der Sluys, Marybeth Tinning, and Waneta Hoyt show, some cases of recurring SIDS are actually homicides. And recurring SIDS may hide a proportionally larger share of homicides than the basic syndrome. That's because the definition of recurring SIDS—the sudden unexplained deaths of two or more infants in the same family—also fits the profile of Munchausen syndrome by proxy.

One of the hallmarks of Munchausen syndrome by proxy is that it is recurrent by nature. A Munchausen mother will not stop abusing her child until she is caught or the child dies. And if she is not caught after the first death, the mother may continue killing until she runs out of children.

SIDS and Munchausen syndrome by proxy converge in another troubling way. The well-documented habit Munchausen mothers have of repeatedly smothering their children to induce apnea spells fits neatly into the apnea theory of SIDS. In a cruel twist, these near-miss episodes reinforce the belief that doctors can identify babies at high risk of succumbing to SIDS and perhaps save them. But as the deaths of Molly and Noah Hoyt showed, an apnea monitor offers no protection against a murderous mother.

The overlapping patterns of Munchausen syndrome by proxy and multiple SIDS suggest that the rate of recurring SIDS might plunge to insignificance if all of the homicides could be excluded. But the question of whether SIDS runs in families will be difficult to answer until law enforcement and medicine figure out a way to draw the line between SIDS and infanticide. In the meantime, parents who have lost a child to SIDS will continue to agonize about the risks their subsequent children face.

Tragically, several measures that would help detect homicides masquerading as SIDS have been largely ignored. Many medical examiners agree that every sudden unexpected infant death should be subject to a complete death-scene investigation in addition to a forensic autopsy. Many states consider the cost of such efforts prohibitive, and only about half even require an autopsy.

Some doctors also have suggested that psychosocial assessments should be made of families in which children die. More recently some have advocated the establishment of a nationwide computer registry on sudden infant deaths.

But many doctors and SIDS parents believe such measures will inevitably lead to the persecution of innocent parents. They doubt whether forensic pathologists, police, and prosecutors have the training and tact to conduct investigations without traumatizing grieving parents or unjustly accusing those who unnecessarily blame themselves for their children's deaths. But the advocates of SIDS parents have no answer for cases like Waneta Hoyt's, in which a more aggressive investigation earlier on might have saved some of her children. And that makes children like Eric, Julie, James, Molly, and Noah Hoyt the ultimate victims of SIDS.